Praise

NEMESIS

"Mind-blowing…outrageous exci…

"A stomach-churning thriller."

"Lots of scientific detail…there's als
the tail of this pacey thriller."
—*Books* magazine

SPLINTERED ICON

"It's hard not to get sucked into Bill Napier's incredible vortex. Truly an extraordinary tale, and one that throws the perfect bridge from England to the Americas…Sir Walter Raleigh's *Da Vinci Code*. More, it's smart as hell. It reads like an exploding brush fire…what a ride! *Splintered Icon* is a really terrific novel, head and shoulders above the genre."
—Jeff Long, *New York Times*
bestselling author of *The Descent*

"Napier nimbly twists two separate tales into a thrilling novel of exploration, discovery, and, ultimately, survival. Fans of Dan Brown, take note, this is a one-sitting book."
—Jack DuBrul, *USA Today*
bestselling author of *The Medusa Stone*

"Intriguing and imaginative. An inventive piece of storytelling."
—Steve Berry, national bestselling
author of *The Amber Room*

"Deftly mixing history, science, and fiction, Napier keeps the action escalating toward a satisfying climax."
—*Publishers Weekly*

St. Martin's Paperbacks Titles by
BILL NAPIER

Revelation

The Lure

Nemesis

Splintered Icon

THE FURIES

BILL NAPIER

St. Martin's Paperbacks

This is a work of fiction. All of the characters, organizations, and events portrayed in this novel are either products of the author's imagination or are used fictitiously.

THE FURIES

Copyright © 2009 by Bill Napier.

Cover photograph © Getty Images

All rights reserved.

For information address St. Martin's Press, 175 Fifth Avenue, New York, NY 10010.

ISBN: 978-0-312-94783-5

Printed in the United States of America

St. Martin's Paperbacks edition / October 2009

St. Martin's Paperbacks are published by St. Martin's Press, 175 Fifth Avenue, New York, NY 10010.

10 9 8 7 6 5 4 3 2 1

For Sean

Table of Contents

Phoenix and Chamonix:

FRIDAY, PRESENT DAY

UFO:

FOSSIL CREEK, ARIZONA, 0430

Under a brilliant Milky Way, the figures are puny. Bent double, they might be crabs scuttling over rocks, and the *whump-whump* filling the air around them the wing beats of some giant mythical bird. But as the big Chinook soars up and away, its navigation lights off, the creek returns to a silence broken only by the gurgling river.

Dressed like astronauts, they work swiftly, using subdued flashlights to set up trestle tables, microscopes, and flasks. The heavy gloves turn this into a clumsy operation. Only then do they begin to explore the creek, and it is fifteen minutes before they find Joe Wupatki at the edge of the river. His cell phone is clutched tightly in his hand. His face is black and blistered, his eyes are staring, and his facial muscles are still contorted by his last efforts to breathe.

It was never established just what Joe Wupatki was doing in Fossil Creek at two o'clock in the morning, and it had been hard to take his flying saucer call seriously. Nevertheless he was a respected elder of the Tonto Apache reservation, and if Old Joe said he'd seen a UFO crashing in the creek, then so be it. This was the logic that sent the first patrol car out from Payson.

Within half an hour the solitary patrolman reported that

he had reached Strawberry and was about to turn west, onto the unsafe, unpaved road that plunges steeply down the Mogollon Rim to Fossil Creek. This was his last message. When he failed to respond to calls, a second patrolman was sent out. When he, too, fell silent, three more cars were dispatched from Flagstaff, a good hour to the north. These were high-clearance, four-wheel-drive vehicles—the report had come from remote, rugged hill country—and the officers, by now sensing trouble, took rifles.

Arriving at the Strawberry turnoff, one of these officers managed to croak a few garbled, choking words, but the telephonist could make no sense of them, and from then on the vehicle's radio sent only the occasional indistinct noise, like tapping or bumping, and what might have been groaning. These sounds, too, eventually stopped.

As the mysterious silence continued, the dispatcher, by now on her own in the little police station, became increasingly agitated. Her nerve finally gave out and just after four o'clock she roused her boss, who called Phoenix Air Support, who sent out a Eurocopter. It drifted up and down the Mogollon Rim road, saw nothing until, up the Rim, it scanned a little parking lot next to an all-night diner just outside Strawberry. The Nightsun illuminated a dozen corpses scattered over the tarmac, some in police uniform. At least they were presumed to be corpses since they weren't moving and were lying in various unnatural positions. The police vehicles, three of them, still had headlights on. One had smashed into the side of the diner.

A chain of dead-of-night phone calls followed, and as the bowl of night faded from black to dark blue to deep scarlet, the sun rose to reveal men and women, protective suits now pink in the Arizona dawn, swarming over the base of the pine-covered canyon. Their findings triggered a series of events that would, inside a week, lead to the brink of war.

ALPINE REDOUBT:

CHAMONIX, MIDNIGHT

"I have a gun."

The woman in the front passenger seat turns, surprised and suddenly alarmed. In the dark, she can make out a thin, pockmarked face.

"In case a little persuasion . . ."

"It won't be needed."

At least I hope not. She checks her surroundings against the GPS screen. "Nearly there."

There are lights ahead and to the left, below them; that has to be Chamonix. The monstrous peak to the right, its top in blackness, must be Mont Blanc. A string of lights marks out the route of a cable car, disappearing into cloud like an illuminated Jack's Beanstalk. "Up there."

"Up there? Are you sure?" the driver wants to know with a touch of alarm, and he wants to know in French: *La bas? Vous êtes sur?* He swings the car in front of a passing truck and the truck driver hoots angrily, but then they are off the main highway, onto a narrow, steep, winding road with a surface made of compacted snow. Already big snowflakes are streaming across the headlight beams: a skirmishing patrol. The main army is billowing down from the summit.

A mobile phone rings in the woman's pocket. She listens

for a few seconds and puts it back without replying. "Weather's closing in. If we're not at Sallanches in forty minutes, the pilot will refuse to fly."

"*Quarante minutes? Mais c'est impossible, ça.*" The driver hardly seems under control of the car, which is slithering dangerously on the hairpin bends, wheels spinning.

"Go faster."

"Hello, Lewis. It's been what, a year?"

Thin, shivering, in her midforties. Short white hair, astute eyes, sharp nose and the collar of a long red coat pulled up around her neck. Never one for humor, her face seems harsher than he remembers it.

"Hello, Jocelyn. How did you find me?"

"We seek him here, we seek him there. You're a damned elusive man, Lewis. I'll explain as we go." Snow is already beginning to blanket the car parked outside. He can just make out two dark figures within. Someone has left a trail in the deep snow. It disappears round the side of the chalet.

"Go where?"

"London." She catches his glance. "French Secret Service. Lewis, you did get the call?"

"I've done the White Queen flashing red, Jocelyn. Please get someone else."

"There is no one else."

"Didn't you hear me? I'm off the list, finished with it."

A faint sound from behind. Lewis turns. A man is standing in the hallway, smiling apologetically. He is dusted with snow and his boots are white.

Jocelyn says, "Sorry, Lewis. But you're only off the list when we say so."

The pilot slides open a side window and stares down, his eyes searching anxiously. Momentarily, a freezing blizzard gusts around the cabin. Sharp thinks about the pinnacles around and realizes with a surge of fear, *The idiot's lost!* Next to him, in the rear seats and out of the pilot's hearing, the woman's brow is clammy. "The prime minister asked for you, on my recommendation. Against stiff opposition, I may say."

Sharp stares. "Jocelyn, I'm a cook in a two-star restaurant."

"We don't want you for your pepperoni pizza."

"What then?"

"Item One. A crank letter arrived at Downing Street this morning." She is having to raise her voice against the noise of the engine. In the back-scattered light of the headlamps, Sharp can see that her face is white. The little propeller plane is bumping like a speedboat on a rough sea, and he feels his own stomach turning queasy. He has given up trying to make his seat belt work and is gripping the armrests of his seat.

"They must get these all the time."

"By the sackload, they tell me. Item Two. Twelve hours ago there was a bioweapons attack on an Indian reservation in Arizona." She pulls a laptop out of her black briefcase.

Sharp watches the movie, the men in protective suits, the FBI, the reservation and state police crawling over the site, which is scattered with thousands of metal shards. Halfway through he says, "I recognize him."

"Merrifield, the undersecretary of defense."

"Okay, I give up. How do an Arizona explosion and a crank letter connect?"

"The Arizona attack isn't yet public knowledge. But whoever wrote the letter knows all about it." She rummages in a briefcase.

"Jocelyn, I don't want to hear this." He feels his brow wet, from fear and nausea.

"I know. Take a look anyway." She clicks on an overhead light; in the light, the MI6 officer looks as if she could vomit at any moment.

The folder is marked TOP SECRET and carries the MI6 logo—a brain within a green C topped by a crown. Sharp turns the pages. The aerial photographs draw his attention. There are the familiar features that he'd hoped never to see again: fallen trees snapped off at the roots and radiating out from a powerful blast, their inner surfaces blackened. But there's something not quite right about them, things don't quite fit: The pattern isn't quite circular, and where is the bomb crater? Jocelyn says, "The bomb spread pulmonary anthrax spores . . ."

"What?"

". . . about five kilometers downwind. It exploded on an Apache reservation and only about forty people died. But if this had gone off in Manhattan or London . . . Oh God . . . excuse me." She puts a paper bag to her mouth and Sharp tries not to look as she spews into it, making a lot of noise and gasping miserably in between bouts of throwing up. Then she makes her way unsteadily to the front of the aircraft, taps the pilot's shoulder, and waves the spew bag at him. The wipers are clicking briskly on the cockpit windscreen to no effect: The aircraft's headlights are just illuminating a wall of snow. The pilot slides the window open, and Jocelyn's bag disappears into the night.

"Sorry about that," Jocelyn says, looking weak and relieved. To Sharp's perplexity she pulls out a makeup bag and does a perfect lipstick job in the bouncing aircraft.

"Jocelyn, I've retired, I'm out of it, I'm not going back to it. *Comprendo?*"

"Uh-huh. Keep reading."

Sharp turns more pages. He comes to a photograph showing an Indian reservation cop cradling a big hunk of metal in her hands. It is contorted from the pressure of the explosion, and the edges are jagged, and it is engraved. The engraving is about six inches across, distorted but easily recognizable. It shows an eagle, its head in profile and its feathered wings spread horizontally. The talons of this eagle hold a disk as big as the bird itself, and filling this disk is the ancient Sanskrit emblem of love and well-being. A swastika.

"A bomb with a swastika?"

"An anthrax bomb, Lewis. An anthrax bomb with a swastika. Which turns up in Arizona sixty years after the end of the war."

"I'm sorry but that's unbelievable."

Jocelyn continues: "It gets worse. I'm calling it a bomb,

but it looks as if the device was disk-shaped and it actually flew. The local cops are calling it a flying saucer."

A flying saucer. *A Nazi flying saucer.* Something stirs at the back of Sharp's mind. He looks out of the window again but there is still nothing to be seen; only the red sweep of the aircraft's underlight reflecting back from dense streaming cloud. "Okay, the Nazis played with anthrax in the Third Reich but they never used it. And Nazi flying saucers are just comic book fantasy."

"Nevertheless there it is. We need your esoteric knowledge, Lewis. Nobody knows more about the Nazi secret weapon programs than you." She adds: "Except maybe Alec Duncan at King's College. He's the stiff opposition, by the way. He thinks you're a crank, a rank amateur, a dilettante, whatever."

"And you recommended this amateur two-star cook over a professor of modern history at Cambridge?"

"Come on, Lewis, we both know he's an over-the-hill pen pusher. Look how he got it wrong on the Nazi atom bomb. You know more than he does on the Hitler weapons. And you were a first-rate NBC officer, which Duncan never was." The plane suddenly takes a steep banking turn and dives. Papers float to the ceiling. For a moment Sharp thinks they are upside down; he looks out the window and glimpses ice and rock hurtling past; but then they level out.

"Sorry about that!" the pilot shouts back. He's trying for a devil-may-care tone, but the edginess in his voice comes through.

Sharp flicks through more pictures, trying to make out the details in the badly shaking aircraft. "For a weapon like this I'd look to China or North Korea, or maybe something from the old Soviet Biopreparat program. There are a lot of unemployed bioweapons scientists over there with hungry families."

"A plausible if scary thought, Lewis. But what about the swastika?"

"Can we get some sense of realism into this? How could a Nazi weapon get to Arizona? How come it suddenly appears on the scene sixty years after the war's end? And why explode it on an Indian reservation? Maybe it's a home-grown effort by local lunatics, the swastika put there to throw you off the scent."

"These are questions we want you to answer. The same terms as last time. A straight one hundred thousand pounds into the Aruba account. You access it through the same passport as before. Which you still have?"

"In a safe. But it's not worth it. Look what happened the last time." He peers out at the blackness. He can use the money—he needs it! But it really isn't worth it. He's finished with the pressure . . . "Where do you come into it, Jocelyn?"

"I own you for the duration." She smiles but not too much in case Sharp thinks she is joking. "And a few others—you'll meet them shortly. I report to C, who informs the MOD, the prime minister, and the London Resilience Forum. Cobra's been activated and will meet twice daily until this thing is solved. As I said, not everybody's happy about having you on the team. There were—there are—questions about your suitability."

"About my suitability."

"Well, you have—how can I put it—dropped out. From a highflier with a promising career to a part-time cook in one spectacular plunge."

"Six have a dossier on me? Is that what it says?"

"You're the main man, Lewis."

"Let me off at Geneva and I'll find my own way back. By the way, has this guy flown a plane before?"

Jocelyn bites her lip, as if she is keeping frustration in check. "How are you making out as a cook?"

"I just help out in Franco's when there's an overload. I blew everything—severance pay and the last Aruba lump—on the chalet. I give lectures to students and historical societies in the winter. In the summer I write military histories."

"Is there any money in that?" She laces the question with cynicism.

"It's grim," Sharp admits. "I'm hoping the books will begin to pay the mortgage. Stuffed shirts like Duncan have been giving me sniffy reviews, but Joe Public seems to like my style and I'm acquiring a following. Look, Jocelyn, I'm making a new life for myself and I love everything I do." He waves the top-secret report. "I need this like a hole in the head."

"You sound like a man with a plan, Lewis. I suppose the long hair and the designer stubble are part of it? Well, I'm sorry to haul you away from the hippie lifestyle, but . . ."

". . . but your country needs you. Wave a flag, bang a drum, tootle a flute, and the yokels come running. Thanks, but I've done that. Not anymore."

"As it happens, your country does need you," she snaps. "We think another device like this one may be used against London a week today and in case you've lost track this is Saturday morning and we don't even know where to start looking and in case you didn't hear that I'll say it again we have seven days to save London and we don't know where to start and unfortunately I'm stuck with Lewis Pepperoni Sharp and I need you like a drowning man needs air. I don't like it, I don't want it, but there you are."

It takes Sharp several seconds, while Jocelyn watches his internal turmoil. "And you think this because some psycho wrote a letter?"

Tight-lipped, she hands over another sheet of paper in the bumping aircraft.

London

SATURDAY

THREE LITTLE MAIDS:

DOWNING STREET, 0730

Three little maids from school are we,
Meg, and Alec, and Tiffanee.

And boy, do we have something for you!

PINPOINT PUPILS   eye pain oh what pain.

DROOLING

slow heart rate
asphyxia
runny nose
incontinence, and how!
nausea

  COMING YOUR WAY SOON in a flying saucer

And convulsions and paralysis, both at once,
and rapid breathing and respiratory failure,
both at once. Two impossible things before breakfast.
Hubble bubble toil and trouble, roaring drunk and seeing
double.

THE PLAGUE OF THEBES HA HA HA.

*So every good tree bringeth forth fruit, but the trees alas
are down . . .
And Strawberry is not a fruit.*

> *Tickety boo
> We're coming for you
> And by the way
> Sep 1 is the day*

VALE LONDINIUM

"What do our forensic psychologists say?" The prime minister looks across the table at a thin, serious blond woman. He is a small, thin man, smaller than she had imagined from his television images. He is sitting directly across from her, tie loose and jacket draped over the back of his chair.

The Home Office psychologist returns the look over the top of her half-moon spectacles. "There's very little to go on, Prime Minister. For example, for all we know the writer could be suffering from paranoid schizophrenia, but you might not pick that up in a short communication."

"If we could have it in simple language."

"The letter is bizarre, and we did look into whether this reveals some sort of thought disorder like derailment or incoherence, which could suggest delusional beliefs of some sort. I mean, how does a runny nose come from a flying saucer, or *the Plague of Thebes* follow from *two impossible things before breakfast*? Are we dealing with tangentiality here? But there are no other indicators such as semantic paraphasia, perseveration . . ."

"Is he a nutter, Dr. Melrose?" the prime minister interrupts.

The psychologist winces. "We think the bizarreness is calculated. If there's psychosis in the letter, we don't see it. The writer is tightly controlled and focused."

"A hoaxer?"

"Impossible to say. But we think whoever wrote this has some serious intent."

"Thank you, Doctor." The prime minister pauses. Then: "If you would leave us now." The forensic psychologist blinks nervously, taps papers on the polished oak table, and strides out.

"We can't even contemplate evacuating London because of a crank letter." The home secretary is using a tone of voice that doesn't allow argument.

The PM waves the letter in frustration. "But suppose this is a genuine threat and we do nothing about it? The public would hang us from the lampposts."

"All you have is a piece of paper."

The intelligence chief clears his throat. He is a bulky man with thick, hairy hands and a coarse-featured face that makes him look like a wrestler. "Revealing an insider's knowledge of a deadly weapon and making a threat—specific in time and space—against us."

The home secretary sighs. "Even if we evacuated London, they'd just wait until the city was back to normal and then fire off their wretched device. We can't abandon London—and if we did they'd just turn their attention to Birmingham or someplace."

The chief of intelligence says, "I've set up a small task force, some of our best people from Five, Six, and GCHQ. There's no place for turf wars in this situation." C likes the phrase *task force,* and uses it often. It has a gung-ho, action-man sound to it; much better than *committee,* even if it means the same. He'd even toyed with *war party* at some stage in the past, but decided that would be too colorful for the gray suits of Whitehall. "They need to tell us what this crazy letter means, if anything, and tell us quickly."

The home secretary sniffs skeptically. "It's a piece of insane nonsense, obviously."

C ignores him. "And as you know we're trying to get hold of this Lewis Sharp on the off chance that the swastika implies some connection with the Nazis."

"My God, Gordon, how can a man of your caliber take

such an idea seriously?" The home secretary shakes his head. "It's not as if you people have nothing else to do. What is it, thirty known groups actively planning atrocities against us?"

"It does seem a long shot," the intelligence chief says mildly. "And we are stretched to breaking point. Tell me, Home Secretary. Do you want to gamble the population of London on your opinion?"

The prime minister cuts into the sudden antagonism. "I go with Gordon, we can't put a chip like that on a roulette table. What are we doing about the Americans?"

"We're liaising with their FBI through a young woman by the name of Ambra Volpe. She'll be on the next Los Angeles flight. And I'm due in Legoland five minutes ago. I'm briefing a few senior civil servants, police and army officers, et cetera."

"I'll join you," says the home secretary.

C nods. "The shuttle's downstairs. We'll take it over." By *over* he means *under,* referring to the secret tunnel under the Thames joining Whitehall and the MI6 building.

The prime minister says, "Gordon, if there's anything in this, we only have until Friday. I don't want you to feel constrained by legal niceties. Just make sure that whatever you do is deniable."

C nods again. "I understand completely, Prime Minister." *Anything messy can be handled by the SAS,* he tells himself.

The home secretary says, "I'll issue Certificates of Immunity in the Public Interest if anything gets out."

The prime minister stays alone in the first-floor study after the others have left. He reads the strange letter carefully again, checking points one by one against the MI6 chief's notes.

Three little maids from school are we . . .

MI6 BUILDING

VAUXHALL CROSS, 0830

Somewhere around Geneva, the snow transforms itself into gusty rain. A Learjet is waiting and takes them smoothly across France and the Channel; they arrive at RAF Northolt an hour later in a bleak but dry dawn. A black Jaguar is waiting on the runway, purring quietly. A man and woman, both late twenties, are standing next to it. Jocelyn does the introductions.

"This is Craig Downey from GCHQ. He does cryptography."

A round-faced, cheerful man takes Sharp's hand. "And I have a classics background. The weirdness in that letter."

The woman: slim, olive-skinned, dark eyes, shoulder-length black hair. Sharp knows she can't possibly be Five or Six. The brown leather trousers, Prada boots, white blouse, and suede bolero don't fit the "drab anonymity" dress code of the intelligence services.

She introduces herself. "I'm Ambra Volpe, from Six." Her voice has a slight Italian inflection. "I'm off to LA now but I thought I'd say hello first."

"Jocelyn owns you, too?"

"Yes, she's my slave master." She gives her boss a cheeky smile but Jocelyn stays forbiddingly dour. "Is there anything in that swastika or is it just a decoy by some local militia? What do I tell FBI and Homeland?"

A quick, focused mind. No social chitchat—friendly but straight to the point. Sharp likes that. He says, "Tell them I don't know. It could go either way."

There are documents and Sharp, next to Downey in the rear of the Jaguar, starts to fill them in as Ambra Volpe takes it quickly around the back of the Lear, past a big AWAC and along a wet, narrow airfield road. She pays no attention to speed limits on the trip into town, and they arrive at Vauxhall Cross just after half past eight in the morning. She takes the car to the rear of the MI6 building and into the underground car park, gives Sharp a farewell wave, and steps into another car, a company one to judge by the dismal paintwork.

Despite himself, Sharp can't suppress a flutter of excitement as they enter the secret building. It is his second visit, and memories flood back. Through the big swing doors into the spacious, space-age reception area. Sharp hands over his mobile phone and watches the security man put it in a pigeonhole in exchange for a tag. A woman next to him is getting rid of a laptop and a mobile phone. He hands over a passport and the completed documentation and to his surprise the guard immediately gives him a pass, complete with his photograph. "All right, sir, in you go." Then Sharp remembers—they'd photographed him last time, when his hair was army-short and he'd had a shave. The woman is being escorted to a photo booth.

And at last he has swiped himself through the revolving sealed capsule and he is in, into the otherworld. Jocelyn, waiting on the other side, glances at her watch and leads them swiftly to a lift.

"How much do you remember about this place?"

"Not much. It was pretty rushed last time, too."

"It's Category A security," she explains. "I have to escort you everywhere, including the loo. It has target status HIS, HTA, and HPT, where *H* is 'hostile' or 'high' and *A* is 'attack' and you can guess the rest. Half of it's underground.

The windows look green because the glass is nearly ten centimeters thick. We have triple glazing and wire mesh everywhere, and computer suites and technical areas that you won't see and whose floor areas are secret."

Downey says, "But if you want to be really naughty, and should you happen to be passing the planning office of Lambeth Council . . ." He grins wickedly. Jocelyn frowns her disapproval.

Emerging a few floors up, Jocelyn taps her watch. Sharp and Downey break into a trot while Jocelyn waves them on. Sharp is disappointed to find that the interior of this most secret of buildings seems quite ordinary, comprising a warren of corridors marked by doors with mysterious acronyms. Here and there they pass open-plan offices, which he finds hard to reconcile with MI6's legendary ethos of secrecy. Downey seems to know the way and scurries quickly on, glancing at his watch, while Sharp chases after him, feeling like Alice following the White Rabbit.

"What do we know about this Lewis Sharp fellow?" The minister speaks over his shoulder. He is looking down at the neat garden hidden from the public, the row of steps, the line of trees, the river beyond. After three days of heavy rain, the Thames is dark brown and flowing swiftly.

Next to him, the head of MI6 sips at an oversweet coffee. "Army brat. Father and grandfather before him were career soldiers. His father made full colonel. Young Sharp made major—NBC officer—at thirty, remarkably young. Worked with Five briefly on the dirty bomb scare a couple of years ago."

The hesitation is so slight that the home secretary wonders if he imagined it. "But?"

C retrieves a manila folder from the big oval table and returns to the triple-glazed window. It has a label with a string of numbers and, crayoned on it in red, SHARP, LEWIS C. The photograph shows a well-built man in his thirties, with short, sandy hair and a round, alert face. The eyes are intensely blue, and there is a hint of humor, if not mischief, around his mouth. C reads from a sheet headed with the *Semper Occultis* logo. "Threw it all in shortly thereafter, and disappeared. Dropped out, basically."

"Any reason?"

"None given here."

"There's more?" The minister is still picking up vibrations.

"He's made a study of the Nazi secret weapons program. Even wrote a book about it. He impressed my people during the dirty bomb incident. If there's anything in this Nazi connection, he might just have the esoteric knowledge we need."

"When you say dropped out . . ."

"If I may interject, Minister?" The man sidling up to them is holding a cup of tea and a saucer. He is tall, sixtyish, dark-skinned as if he has spent some years abroad, and has a hairstyle like a monk's tonsure.

C says, "Home Secretary, may I introduce Professor Alec Duncan?"

The home secretary says, "Forgive me, but where do you come into this?"

"Alec Duncan is a Cambridge historian."

"I have a background in the history of biowarfare. I worked with Sharp briefly on the Nazi secret weapons program."

"Ah." The home secretary puts an *at last we're getting somewhere* tone into his voice.

"I can give you a little background on him. To say he worked with me is a bit of an exaggeration. He came to King's College for a few months, trying to research the secret weapons program of the Third Reich under my tutelage. I'm afraid he didn't get very far."

"My people tell me he's a first-class NBC officer."

Duncan's lips twitch into something like a smile. "Was, Minister. He now earns his living as a part-time cook, somewhere in the French Alps."

"A cook, somewhere in the French Alps," the home secretary repeats tonelessly.

"His historical research was a bit outlandish. He had a

tendency to give too much weight to unreliable stories from old men from the period. He started out on a PhD all fired up and enthusiastic, but frankly he wasn't up to it. I wouldn't take anything he says about Nazi secret weapons too seriously. And . . ." The professor hesitates.

"Well?"

"To put it bluntly, he's a crank."

The minister turns to the chief of intelligence. "And you're putting this cook, this washed-up ex-army-officer, this crank, this failed PhD on the team."

"Interesting to hear that," C says to Duncan. "My information is that he knows as much about the Hitler secret weapons program as anyone, including you."

The lips twitch again. "I'm afraid you've been misinformed."

The home secretary asks, "What's your view on the Nazi link?"

The professor gives a wise smile. "The Nazi flying saucer business is a playground for lunatics. There's no documentation. As I said, all we have are unreliable claims by a few old men. And the idea of machines like that spraying anthrax around is just off the wall."

The minister assimilates this, and then turns to the chief of intelligence. "I'd feel more comfortable with the fate of London in a pair of safe hands."

"My sentiments exactly. But in my line of business people who don't go beyond the facts rarely get as far as them. After all, what do we lose by letting this Sharp loose on the problem? If there happens to be anything in it . . ."

"He'll mislead the team," Duncan says. "Or he will if you listen to him."

There is an awkward silence. A couple of Special Branch heavies, just within hearing range, are making a good job of pretending not to listen. The minister says, "Well, where the hell is he?"

At that moment Sharp and Downey stride puffing into the room.

ISLAMIC TERROR SYNDICATE

"First, I welcome the home secretary to our deliberations. What I want to do here is determine whether we can get any insights into this Fossil Creek incident from the British end."

"Islamic Terror Syndicate," the home secretary declares. "It has to be al-Qaeda."

"No," says the chief of intelligence. He nods at the Middle East desk officer, a woman in her midtwenties with black, wavy hair, wearing jeans and a drab gray sweater.

She nods back. "We can't connect ITS with the Arizona device."

"Come on. JTAC tells me that two hundred Britons have received training . . ."

"Perhaps if you will allow Judith to report," C suggests mildly.

The home secretary gives a brusque nod, and the girl from the Middle East desk starts to read: . . . *Shirwan al-Hilali sighted in Kuwait International Airport three weeks ago . . . our Saudi intelligence contacts report an unusual movement of funds into . . . the Voice of Jihad have issued a statement . . . the Omanis have detained . . .*

One by one the team work their way through the overseas reports. Europe, the Middle East, Africa, the Americas, and the Far East all say much the same thing—in the shifting, murky web of international terror organizations, there is nothing to connect a crashed UFO in Arizona. At least, nothing visible.

"Very well." The home secretary sounds unconvinced. "That leaves the enemy within."

The MI5 man reports. He throws up a PowerPoint diagram looking literally like a huge, murky web. It is spattered with red dots. He talks in a rapid monotone about phone and Internet traffic analysis, social network traces, field operations groups, graph theory, and Granovetter algorithms, to an accompaniment of hand-waving, blinking red dots, and flashing yellow threads like a fairground advertisement. The upshot, he tells the increasingly glazed eyes facing him, is that Five can find no sign of any "special operation" in the pipeline that might connect with the Arizona device.

The home secretary says, "What about this so-called Nazi connection? The swastika engraved on the side of this thing. I understand there's some disagreement among our experts."

The professor licks his lips and adopts a knowing smile. "There's only one expert here. I'm sure Lewis would agree with me, wouldn't you, Lewis? And I think I can rule out any idea about a Nazi weapon. It's just too far-fetched."

"Spell that out, please," the home secretary says.

Duncan gives a quick glance at Sharp, sitting across the table from him. "The notion that the Nazis developed some sort of aerial device for spraying anthrax around is just preposterous. The only witnesses either lack credibility or only have secondhand stories to tell. If there was such a weapon, why wasn't it used during the war? Why does it suddenly turn up sixty years later? Hitler had a horror of poison gas. Even a superficial study will show that the Nazis never got into bioweapons."

"Sharp?"

"A superficial study would give that impression. But I've gone into this rather less superficially than Professor Duncan—you would agree, Alec? Dig deeper and you find that the Nazis did in fact have a chemical and biological weapons program. And it makes no sense to develop the chemicals without developing some means of delivery. In practice that means dispersal from the air. Okay, we don't know what they did in that line, but a lot went on in wartime Bavaria that we don't know about even today."

Duncan gives Sharp a scimitar smile. "I'm sorry to be blunt again, but Nazi flying saucers spraying anthrax are for people who read comic books, not for serious historians."

Sharp catches a couple of the Special Branch men grinning slyly at each other. *What am I doing here? I'm finished with this stuff, making a new life for myself. Was I brought to London to listen to this idiot spouting rubbish? This rip-off artist, this giant egoist whose only interest is in showing people how important he is?* But even as these questions go through his head, he knows the answers. *I know what I'm doing here. I can't bury myself in libraries researching my next book while this threat is hanging over London and Duncan is left to screw them up.*

Duncan is still holding court. Sharp drags himself back to the present.

". . . nothing in navy CinC records or U-boat loading lists . . . main item is this. How could such a weapon have been transported across the Atlantic? By ship? By aircraft? The Luftwaffe didn't have the range, and no such journeys by the German navy could have gone undiscovered; nor are there any records of such. And the device is far too large to have gone into a submarine; U-boat hatches were scarcely wide enough to allow their torpedoes in. Transport of such a device from Germany to the States would have been impossible in wartime conditions."

The home secretary looks across at Sharp.

"I agree."

The home secretary's eyebrows go up. "You concede Professor Duncan's point?"

"I do."

"But . . . ?"

"But Professor Duncan has overlooked one thing." Sharp pauses, aware of astute eyes assessing him. Duncan is smiling and shaking his head. "Local hillbillies might be able to produce a few teaspoons of anthrax. The Arizona device carried a ton of the stuff. Whoever built it had the backing of large-scale industrial muscle."

The home secretary turns grimly to C, who is watching the exchange dispassionately, his big hands clasped behind his neck. "A fucking ton of anthrax. I'm having lunch with the PM in forty minutes. What do I tell him? That the Arizona device was a one-off? That the letter is a hoax? That we allow people to flood London for their Saturday shopping?"

The head of MI6 spreads his hands in an Italian-like gesture. "What can I say, Minister? I don't know."

"For Christ's sake, Gordon, we know *something*. *Someone* sent that letter. Someone who knew about the anthrax-spreading machine."

PAUL'S WALK:

SAFE HOUSE

"No way will we crack this by Saturday." Jocelyn is at the wheel of an old Saab.

"You'd better be wrong about that." Sharp is still mentally in transition between the Mont Blanc massif and central London, still mentally fighting Duncan.

"Lewis, are you serious? You really think this is a genuine Nazi weapon rather than homespun militia?"

Sharp, in the backseat, says, "Forget a local terrorist group, it's beyond them. There's a degree of sophistication about that device."

Downey, in the passenger seat next to Jocelyn, turns around to Sharp. "Don't underestimate the banjo players. They may be homespun but you can be sure there's a lot of sophistication in among the moonshine. And you can get recipes for anthrax on the Web. All you need is a dead cat."

"A helluva lot of dead cats."

"Everybody's nervous these days," Downey says, apropos of nothing. The Gherkin is on their left, peering over rooftops from time to time. They pass the College of Arms, all dark red bricks and tall, gilt-topped wrought-iron fencing.

A traffic light turns red, and Jocelyn stops with a curse. "Alec Duncan's briefing the PM, he'll join us shortly. We were all mightily entertained seeing the pair of you at each other's throats. What is it between the professor and you?"

"It doesn't matter."

"He says you're incompetent, a crank."

"Jocelyn, you're being naughty."

"Well?" Jocelyn's fingers are strumming impatiently on the steering wheel.

"The man's a parasite. For my first war book I put some work into aspects of the Nazi nuclear weapons program, such as it was. I found a wartime sketch of a primitive atomic weapon in a German library archive. It was unsigned but I managed to chase up the source. It was exciting stuff—it put a whole new perspective on the German atom bomb project— and I discussed it with Duncan. God, I was naive. The next thing I knew there was a paper on the subject with his name on it. He's spent the last two years putting himself forward as the big cheese on the topic. He's Batman, I'm Robin. That's his message."

"Didn't you complain?"

"Who to? His pals on the Senate? He's the big professor and I'm nobody."

"He says you dropped out of a PhD program."

"I opted out, when I saw what he was like."

"And that's when you cleared off, took up a life of glorious irresponsibility. And here you are, dragged back into the thick of it, poor thing. First the army says you'll never get past major . . ."

"I got fed up with the pack mentality . . ."

". . . then you get ripped off at the outset of an academic career."

"Are you any good as a cook?" Downey asks. Jocelyn winces, but Sharp laughs.

The light turns green, and Jocelyn takes off smartly. "What gives with these Third Reich secret weapon stories? Was it all propaganda and false rumors?"

"No, there was a huge secret weapons program. A lot of it was crazy stuff that only existed in Himmler's head, but there were also real weapons. There was a plan for a thousand-ton tank called the Mouse, with guns bigger than a battleship's. They had ideas for vertical-takeoff-and-landing aircraft, and transatlantic bombers, and fourteen-g jets. They were going to build a people's fighter in the thousands—a manned doodlebug—with a suicide pilot. They put sixteen-year-old boys into plywood jets that broke up in flight."

"But you're saying not all the wonder weapons were rubbish." Now she is doing a loop and turning back on the opposite carriageway. "Not all fantasies in Himmler's head."

"The V1 and V2 were real enough. Eisenhower had to divert an army to capture the launch sites. There were plans for a transatlantic rocket. But there was so much secrecy that even today we're not sure we've uncovered everything. If the Nazis had held out another six months, some of these weapons would have come online."

"By which time the Allies had the atom bomb. *Quelle horreur.*"

"The Nazi flying saucers? What about them?" Downey asks.

"The stories are unsubstantiated rubbish. A whole mythos has grown up about anti-gravity machines, underground labs in Antarctica, crap like that." Mentally, Sharp is beginning to think of Downey as the Doughnut—the alliteration with the doughnut-shaped GCHQ building has clicked. "We know of at least two circular-wing aircraft, but they got nowhere. The AS-6 was twenty feet across, propeller-driven with a 240-horsepower engine. But it slewed from side to side on the runway and flew like a porpoise. They gave up on it."

Downey says, "What are you saying, Lewis? That Duncan was right all along? A flying saucer carrying anthrax spores is nonsense?"

"There were designs for at least fifteen others, but if there were prototypes the Nazis destroyed them at the end of the Third Reich, to keep them out of Allied hands. There are no records; nothing. Duncan's right on that. But there is one thing."

Jocelyn is turning left into a narrow lane. She trickles the car down a steeply descending ramp ending at a corrugated steel shutter. "You were saying. One thing." She pushes a card in a slot, and the shutter rumbles up noisily.

Sharp says, "Okay, the Nazi bioweapons program was the biggest secret of the war. But we do know something about it, thanks to the Russians. After the war they found documents hidden down a mine in Silesia. They also found twelve thousand tons of nerve gas and anthrax."

Downey gives a nervous giggle as Jocelyn takes them into the underground car park. "Lewis, for a scary moment there I thought you said twelve thousand tons."

The Doughnut looks around. "My God, this is grim."

"Hey, this is a cool pad," Sharp says, following him in.

The bleakness of the brick walls is broken up by a few art nouveau pictures and a 1970s Hammer movie poster, all Dracula and fangs and nubile wenches in distress. Everything looks new, executive pad, sterile.

Jocelyn says, "It's a safe house borrowed from Special Branch. You eat, sleep, and breathe here until you've cracked the problem. Hanslope Park fixed up communications early this morning. Right, we don't have a minute to waste. Let's get started."

"You spotted the sarin clue?" Downey asks.

"Sarin? Where?"

Downey runs his fingers down Jocelyn's photocopy.

```
Slow heart rate
Asphyxia
Runny nose
Incontinence, and how!
Nausea
```

"And these are the symptoms of sarin poisoning. Whoever wrote that knew what they were talking about."

Sharp settles into a white leather armchair. "That's another big hole in the hillbilly theory. I believe it's beyond the resources of a terrorist group to make even one bioweapon. Two different weapons, one anthrax and one sarin—now, that's impossible. Talking of which, *Two impossible things before breakfast* is a quote from Alice in Wonderland. The Red King always believed in two impossible things before breakfast. Right, Craig? Not many Arizona hillbillies know that."

"It was the White Queen and six impossible things. An Arizona hillbilly could get it wrong."

Sharp asks, "What gives with this Plague of Thebes?"

"This guy Oedipus bumps off his father and marries his mother, and then turns up in Thebes. The gods are cheesed off by these antics and they send a plague on the people of Thebes as a punishment. Around 400 BC Sophocles writes a play about it called *Oedipus Rex* and he bases it on a real plague of the time, okay? We know what that real plague was, because it was written up by Thucydides, who happened to live through it."

"Thucydides?" Jocelyn says.

"A Greek historian. And Sophocles modeled the Plague of Thebes of his story on the real Plague of Athens, and that plague was bubonic. The letter writer's toying with us. He's telling us there's another bomb and it's going to spread bubonic plague."

Sharp says, "That can't be right. Bubonic plague is spread by *Yersinia pestis,* which comes from fleas. Unless the Huns found a way to keep infected fleas alive for sixty years . . ."

Downey shakes his head in irritation. "I was about to say. The writer's a Bible basher—*by their fruits ye shall know them* et cetera. So look at the Bible. God punished the pharaoh with the ten plagues of Egypt, but only one of the ten plagues is an actual disease. It's the fifth plague, which the modern medics have identified from the symptoms. You take that line, the writer's telling us that his Good-Bye London machine is *anthrax,* just like the Fossil Creek one."

Jocelyn says, "Thebes is a decoy? Is that what you're saying?"

"Don't you believe it," Downey says. "That letter's chock-ablock with clues—not a word is wasted. The writer's teasing us with Thebes. He's telling us something."

There is a brief silence. Then Jocelyn says, "Look, do I have to remind you people that if we don't beat this before Saturday we could end up with the whole of central London taken out? Can you even *visualize* it? Who gathers the bodies up? Where do we bury them? It mustn't come to that."

Jocelyn is still pale from the bumpy flight, Sharp thinks. He says, "There's another possibility. In 1950, when they made the decision to develop a hydrogen bomb, Oppenheimer wasn't too happy."

"Oppenheimer?"

"You know—J. Robert Oppenheimer, who developed the atom bomb."

"You said atom bomb." The Doughnut sits upright. "That's not nice."

Sharp continues: "Oppenheimer was at a Washington party where they were celebrating President Truman's decision to go ahead with the hydrogen bomb. A reporter sees Oppenheimer standing alone, with a long face, and asks him the problem. Oppenheimer says, 'This is the Plague of Thebes.'"

Downey shakes his head. "Don't say atom bomb, Lewis."

Sharp says, "People who think al-Qaeda can grab a handful of plutonium and turn it into an atom bomb have no idea of the complexity of the task."

Downey says, "I'm glad you said that, considering it's their sacred duty to try."

"A nuke acquired from some nuclear power, now, that's another matter."

There is a nervous silence. Then Downey, looking over the letter, says, "Something odd here. *Three little maids from school are we.* But there's no Meg or Alec or Tiffanee in *The Mikado.*"

The front door opens and Duncan, fresh from briefing the PM, strides into the room. He gives Sharp a what-are-you-doing-here look and Sharp thinks, *Christ come to cleanse the Temple.* Jocelyn jumps straight into it. "Professor Duncan, we have very little time to crack this thing. I need your assessment of Sharp's thesis. Could the Nazis really have developed a bioweapon? Talk to me."

He sits on a couch, holding a DVD. "There's nothing new about biowarfare, Ms. Towers, it's been around for thousands of years. The Romans threw gone-off meat into wells to poison the enemy's drinking water. In the fourteenth century the Tatars catapulted the bodies of plague victims over the walls of a Black Sea city they were besieging. People escaped in sailing ships and carried the plague all over Europe. It knocked off nearly half the population. Three-quarters of Norwegians died. Look."

He moves over to a computer and inserts the DVD. The movie shows something like an incoming tide, moving across a map of Europe south to north, starting up from Sicily, spreading up Italy, fanning out across the Alps, and flowing all the way to Norway. "It crossed Europe in the space of a couple of years. So that particular biowarfare got out of hand."

Jocelyn agrees. "I'd have said."

"There have been four great ages of plague. Really pandemics or superplagues, sometimes made up of wave after wave of ordinary plague."

"Ordinary plagues," Sharp repeats in a dull voice. *What makes a plague ordinary?*

Duncan throws up a list on the screen:

THE PLAGUE OF ATHENS 430 BC
This started in Ethiopia and traveled through Egypt, making its way around the eastern Mediterranean in 430 BC. From the first symptoms to death was days or hours. You bled from everywhere. Your internal organs dissolved.

THE PLAGUE OF JUSTINIAN AD 540
The Plague of Justinian started in Egypt in AD 540, just after a mysterious worldwide cooling of the earth. At its peak it killed ten thousand people a day in Constantinople. It kept coming back in waves over the next fifty years.

THE BLACK DEATH 14TH–17TH CENTURIES
The Black Death started the third great age of
plagues. The waves came back for three hundred
years. Again, your organs dissolved. The pain could
drive you mad.

UNNAMED, 20TH CENTURY, DORMANT
And the fourth age started in the late 19th century,
although it's been quiet up to now. A new strain
evolved in China and took some ocean cruises around
the world. This pandemic started bubonic, evolved
into the pneumonic version. It's washed over Asia a
few times. It's still lurking dormant—don't get bitten
by a prairie dog.

Jocelyn shakes her head impatiently. "Professor, we need
to know whether any of these could be delivered in a weapon.
Explain bubonic, briefly if you please."

The Plague of Thebes, modeled on the Athens one. "It's
spread through bacteria called *Yersinia pestis,* which enter
the bloodstream through flea bites. A few vocal deniers say it
was a virus like Ebola but they're wrong: The bacteria find
their way to the lymph nodes, where they multiply at great
speed. I have another movie."

The movie shows little rod-shaped bugs multiplying at
great speed. "The nodes swell into black lumps called bu-
boes, which by all accounts are excruciatingly painful."

Jocelyn says, "We must have antidotes."

"One Friday night in Las Vegas a few years back, federal
agents released a few gallons of simulated plague slurry on
the streets, to see how it spread around town. I can tell you
that if the stuff had been real, people would've gone down
much faster than the emergency services could have reacted.
Like a wildfire, totally out of control. Antidotes couldn't
cope. But it's a lousy weapon. Your own side gets it."

"There are people out there who don't care," Sharp says.

"Transmission is by fleas?" Jocelyn asks.

"Yes."

Jocelyn is tapping the coffee table nervously with a pen. "So much for the Plague of Thebes and similar clues. Unless Lewis wants to tell us that the Nazis found some way to store infected fleas for sixty years."

"Sarin, then?" Sharp asks.

Duncan makes a big play of shaking his head. "Useless. It decays quickly. A few weeks or months after its creation, it has become almost harmless, at least as a nerve gas. Sixty-year-old sarin is thoroughly dead."

"And we can forget about your Oppenheimer speculation, Sharp." Jocelyn is tapping again. "Even I know that the Nazis got nowhere with an atom bomb. In summary, the reference to plague is nonsense, the reference to sarin is nonsense, Lewis's speculation about an atomic device is nonsense. It now seems to me the letter itself is a piece of clever nonsense. The sense I get from this meeting is that the letter was designed to confuse us, to make us dissipate our resources in pursuit of red herrings. The swastika engraving probably likewise. Whoever had the device has been giving us the runaround and we've been falling for it." She looks over at Sharp thoughtfully. "What do you say, Lewis? Time for you to go home?"

"I wish." Sharp crosses to the big window, frustrated and afraid. A glass-roofed clipper is taking off from the pier across the river, aiming for a gap in the Millennium Bridge. A slight movement attracts him to the pathway below. A well-built young man with a shaven head, leather jerkin, and earphones. Looking up, his back to the river. Their eyes meet for a brief second. The man turns away, strolls off. The incident makes Sharp feel uneasy, but he can't think why. And he can just hear the sounds of a party from an upriver flat, the occasional gust of laughter on the limit of hearing. The deep *thump-thump* of the bass sounds like backing for "Three Little Maids from School Are We." A party, on Saturday morning?

Don't be so bloody paranoid. At this rate you'll be getting messages from aliens through the wall sockets.

One of the terminals has a direct link to the FBI team. Letters, being pieced together from the shattered casing of the UFO. Sharp lists them on a sheet of paper, sits down and stares:

```
RK E  OH T  PHO  IS
```

Jocelyn finds scissors in a kitchen drawer, separates out the letters, and Sharp starts to shuffle them in different combinations, getting nowhere. Downey glances over Sharp's shoulder. "By the way, *IS* might be *SI* upside down and *OH* might be *HO*. *PHO* isn't a common letter combination in German, which argues against your Nazi theory. It could well be a bit of *Phoenix,* like they've signed themselves *THE PHOENIX MILITIA* or something. That would more or less prove the hillbilly theory. *RK* is a slightly unusual combination, there won't be too many words with *RK* in English, like *MARKSMEN* or *WORKERS.* I'll see what I can do when I'm back."

Downey suddenly heads for the door.

"Where the hell are you off to?"

"Covent Garden, Jocelyn. I want to get a music score for *The Mikado,* and a video of *Breakfast at Tiffany's,* and I want to see how the movie connects with Meg Ryan and Alec Baldwin who didn't come until years later."

"Look, stop faffing about," Jocelyn snaps. "We've no time for nonsense."

Downey turns at the door. "Don't be so dorky, I'm not one of Lewis's squaddies. That letter has hidden meanings, and *Meg, Alec,* and *Tiffanee* are in there for a reason." He disappears.

Jocelyn and Duncan also head for the door. She turns to Sharp. "If you believe the letter, London gets it on Saturday. I want hard results over breakfast tomorrow. It would be nice to avoid a million dead."

Sharp waves her good-bye. The theatrical exit, he thinks, wasn't necessary. They have all the drama they can handle.

Los Angeles

SATURDAY

AMBRA VOLPE

A slight change in engine note on the 747, and Ambra Volpe is awake. She puts her seat upright, fastens her belt, and adjusts her watch and mind to Sunday afternoon. The big aircraft starts to bump, and streaks of cloud drift past the window.

The reflection that looks back from her compact mirror has a wide, slightly sensual mouth, shoulder-length black hair, and olive complexion. She has made the most of her dark skin with a simple gold necklace and hoop earrings. She might be Italian, which is hardly surprising as her parents are second-generation Italians, her father a retired gardener with the city council. The old ones live in the Meadows, a Nottingham district known for its drugs, guns, and bargain-basement house prices. The "Meadows taxi"—a steady stream of police cars between the district and the St. Anne's HQ—runs past the front window of her parents' mid-terraced council flat. She hasn't seen them in a year, misses them. She looks down at Los Angeles, sprawling endlessly below like some megalopolis out of a science-fiction movie, wisps of cloud below her seeming to rise up and and drift past more rapidly as the big aircraft approaches the ground. The long journey, first across the Atlantic and then across the States, has left her weary. But she still has that tingling excitement.

Not the gut-fierce fright of the Pakistan job, where things had gone terribly wrong, but still . . .

Ambra's future was decreed by her mother at an early age: Leave school at sixteen, run Uncle Dino's café, and bring in money as quickly as possible. Don't get pregnant, not until you've married a nice Catholic boy, then give your parents lots of grandchildren. But by age twelve Ambra was already aware of a world beyond the Meadows; by fourteen she was sick of the Saturday-night gang warfare and the drunks urinating on their doorstep. Into puberty, Mama began to introduce, by subtle means, a string of nice Catholic boys, all of them cloned from a farm in Dullsville. At her sixteenth birthday party, faced with yet another dim-wit introduced by her beaming mother, something clicked inside Ambra. There had to be something better than this! She knew she'd reached a point in her life where she faced a choice: go down, or go up. She chose to go up. Three years at a "posh" school, with noisy financial support from Uncle Dino, yielded a string of casual boyfriends and top-grade A-levels. Another three gave her a First in modern languages, a mountain of student debt, a six-month placement in Kiev, and a glorious, short-lived affair with a Ukrainian businessman.

For a joke—or was it a dare?—she sent her CV to PO Box 1301, the MI6 recruiting address, after a celebratory night out with some university friends. To her surprise an application form arrived a couple of days later, and then a phone call inviting her to an address in Carlton House Terrace, which turned out to be something like a small cottage, the devil to find. Hoops of interviews followed, along with prolonged, discreet questioning of her bewildered family. Ambra decided that the joke had gone far enough. She disappeared into China, intending to teach English, but instead ended up modeling. The job paid more but she soon felt that it should have come with a health warning: Modeling can rot your brain. Back in the UK after three months, she again moved in with Mum and Dad in her old room. But by now the gap between them had grown as wide as the Atlantic, and she felt their cramped little world closing in on her once more. And then, out of the blue, there was another telephone call . . .

The clunk of landing gear snaps Ambra out of her daydream, back into the real world. She runs light lipstick over her mouth and returns the disapproving glance from the old woman next to her with a wide smile.

On the ground, she waits impatiently at the carousel for her overnight bag, sweaty and tired but anxious to get going on the assignment. A tall, black-haired man in his thirties at the far end of the customs hall; well built but with the beginnings of a paunch. Watchful, in the way of policemen everywhere. That, and the Armani suit and the flat-top hair. She collects her bag and walks straight up to him. "Mr. Caddon, I presume?"

Caddon leads her briskly away from the long customs queues to a side door, doesn't offer to take her bag. His tone says that he is in no mood for pleasantries. "I'm taking you straight to Wilshire Boulevard. We'll brief you there. Frankly I'm not quite clear how you can help us, Ms. Volpe. Consensus here is that this is an in-house job."

"And I'm the token Brit?" Caddon doesn't reply, and Ambra adds, "What about the letter to the prime minister?"

"It's screwball stuff, Ms. Volpe, you know that."

"But the screwball knows all about your UFO, Mr. Caddon."

Biologically, Ambra thinks, she is somewhere around two in the morning, but her mind is in such a feverish state that she knows she wouldn't be able to sleep anyway. Her head and nose are stuffy, a nuisance she puts down to the sudden, unaccustomed change in temperature and humidity. And she has a briefing to assimilate. Caddon leads the way through busy corridors to his office, where a third man is waiting.

"Ambra, meet the brains of the outfit, Tony Spada. Tony, this is Mizz Ambra Volpe, the liaison officer from British intelligence."

Spada and Ambra shake hands. Caddon's partner is a small, slightly hunched, and wrinkled man with, like Ambra, Italian features. She risks a personal remark, immediately regrets it as over-familiar. "You look like Inspector Columbo, Mr. Spada."

Spada grins. "Hey, I have two eyes and no cigar."

The pleasantries over, Caddon plunges straight into it. "A couple of dozen eyewitnesses saw a spinning disk weaving in the sky like a Frisbee about two o'clock in the morning. The geniuses downstairs triangulated and gave us a trajectory." The map on the screen shows a wavy yellow line starting in hill country east of Superstition Mountain and moving almost north toward Fossil Creek.

"How are Homeland Security keeping it out of the public domain?"

Caddon waves at a press release on his desk. "They've put out some crap about a military exercise, closed off the reservation, squawked out cell phones, and so on. A local TV network has picked up on the crashed UFO, but who believes stories like that?"

"But Mr. Caddon, there are delivery vans, school buses . . ."

". . . and ninety corpses with families beginning to wonder why their folks haven't come home, not to mention a highway closed down. The bubble will burst tonight. It's bound to."

"Why are they keeping it quiet?"

"Maybe the device was being delivered somewhere and there are bad guys waiting for it who don't know it's gone pear-shaped. Look, we can't have more than an hour or two of silence left, but it might give us an edge."

"The London letter says you don't have an edge."

Spada says, "Here we are with a major terrorist act on American soil and what are we doing about it? Trying to hush it up."

"What about the apex of the flight path?"

"Coming to it, Ms. Volpe. Aforesaid triangulation led us to search the area around Apache Junction, Apache Trail—an old raiding route—Goldfield ghost town, et cetera. We finally homed in on this."

Now the map has gone and a camera is panning slowly across a desiccated, cactus-covered foreground. It stops at a low, blackened structure of girders over a disused shaft. "This is near a one-horse town called Globe, which is surrounded with old copper mines. We think the device was stored down this one, hauled up, and fired."

"Your evidence?"

"Fresh scrapings up the shaft side. And this." The camera is panning some more. "A block and tackle from a pickup truck, with a hundred yards of chain. And here are the people who hauled it up."

An indoor scene, a mortuary. Four bodies, two of them young men, the other two looking like sausages someone had forgotten about on a barbecue. "The recognizable guys are Mexicans, probably illegal immigrants. The blowtorched ones are Caucasians, not yet identified. The Mexicans were shot in the back, running, with a single handgun, a nine-millimeter Luger, 115-grain bullets, lead hollow-point. Our guess is they were hired to lift the bomb out of the shaft, and then killed."

"And the cremated pair?"

"They were standing up, a few yards from the device. Somehow they ended up under its exhaust flame." A few gruesome close-ups follow. "We're trying to reconstruct their faces, but as you can imagine we're not hopeful about getting anything useful. There was nothing to identify the bodies, no wallets or the like, but we have the teeth."

Now the movie is showing a car, its paintwork scorched and blistered. "A white Pontiac," Caddon confirms. "A Hertz car rented at LA airport in a fictitious name. The man on desk duty at the time remembers nothing about the customer."

"You say it flew. What was the means of propulsion?"

"Hold on. There." The movie shows the beginnings of an assembled jigsaw, laid out on the floor of an aircraft hangar.

Ambra thinks she recognizes something. "Are these venturi tubes?"

"Venturi tubes? How do you know about venturi tubes?" Caddon asks, surprised. "The Girl Scouts teach you?"

"I had business in an arms bazaar some time ago." She doesn't expand on that.

Caddon looks at her with something like respect. "Four venturi tubes," he confirms. "Preliminary X-ray fluorescence says it's high-tensile steel, very strong. Armaments quality. They're doing a detailed analysis now, and we should have the results tomorrow. But there are no combustion chambers. The device was powered by some sort of solid fuel. We're still analyzing the black residue on the tubes."

"Simple assembly, then," Ambra says. "A glorified skyrocket. Could amateurs have built this? Schoolboys even?"

"They'd have to be damned smart, Ms. Volpe. Now, here's something interesting." The camera is panning over scraps of metal, most of the markings illegible; underneath they are labeled:

RK E PHO OH W T IS

"That's all we have so far but they're still coming in. We can't make sense of them. And we have this"—the Third Reich symbol appears on the screen—"and now here we're three miles downwind from the crash site."

A row of wooden buildings. Authentic Indian pottery stacked on a veranda, a shop window displaying silver jewelry, brightly patterned rugs, and a little varnished rocking horse. A man lying curled up on the veranda, apparently asleep. "The spores drifted through this cluster of houses on Highway 87." The camera pans slowly over an empty road and pauses at a car park, where a couple of pickup trucks and half a dozen motorbikes are gleaming in the morning sun. Two men are lying facedown. An elderly woman is sitting with her back to a

Chrysler, white-haired and openmouthed, staring unblinkingly into the sun. An old man is hanging half out of the car. "Now we're going inside the diner."

Into Katie's Diner—THE BEST ITALIAN COOKING IN ARIZONA. An American flag pinned to the wall, and under it, in red crayon: THESE COLORS DON'T RUN. Another crayoned notice: THIS ESTABLISHMENT HAS THE APPROVAL OF THE FRIDAY NITE CAR CLUB. Left through the double door and into the diner itself. Ambra feels herself tensing up in anticipation.

Sixties vinyl glued to the walls; Elvis leaning against a pink Chevrolet, all wings and chrome, the photo curling away from the wall.

And an overweight man in leather gear with shoulder-length gray hair, his head resting against the table. The camera zooms in: red eyes from a Dracula movie, black tongue, grotesquely swollen and sticking out of his mouth. Blood from ears, eyes, and nose making little congealed rivulets and merging into a pool, gluing his hair to the table. Flies crawling, drinking greedily, their proboscises dipped in the sticky liquid.

"The mechanism of death? I was told anthrax."

"The bacterial spores thereof. They're silent, invisible, and odorless."

"I thought it needed a high dosage to be fatal."

"Yeah. You have to breathe in about ten thousand of them. They produce a toxin in the bloodstream. Mortality's about ninety percent."

Spada says, "It starts off like flu. Symptoms usually don't appear for about twenty-four hours, and it kills you a few days later. But these people died within minutes, Ambra, it's got us bamboozled. I can call you Ambra? Ms. Volpe seems formal but maybe you Brits like it that way?"

"Ambra will do fine. You were saying."

"I was saying it's got us bamboozled. Maybe the spores had some genetic mutation."

"What else do you have?" Ambra feels her stuffed-up sinuses gradually developing into a full-blown headache.

"Nothing."

"Mr. Caddon, we need a solution by Saturday. Are you telling me you have nothing?"

Caddon manages a sour grin. "Like you said, Ambra, you Brits have something. A screwball letter saying *Arrividerci, London*."

VIRGIL RABBIT AND THE DENTIST:

FBI BUILDING, 1830

"Nothing."

Pepperoni pizza, Ambra notices, is the dish of choice in the FBI war room. Outside, it is hot and sticky, and the air conditioner at the window isn't really coping. A couple of electric fans are circulating stale air and pizza scent around in an endless, pointless flow. She is sitting next to Tony Spada.

The man who has just delivered this one-word report is an unshaven FBI agent from Phoenix. He has shoulder-length, unkempt hair spilling down over an olive-green rain jacket, and he looks as if he has come straight from a redneck survivalist camp. To judge by his bleary eyes and slurred speech, he hasn't slept for a couple of days, a fact that draws no sympathy whatever from the equally exhausted team listening to him. He flicks through a few sheets of paper, facing his audience crammed into the stuffy little office.

"That's it?" Caddon asks. "Nothing?"

The Phoenix agent shrugs. "We have an old idiot, guy who calls himself Virtual Reality . . ."

"Are you serious?"

"His original name was Virgil Rabbit."

"If my name was Virgil Rabbit, I'd change it, too," Spada declares. "But not to Virtual Reality."

The man from Phoenix continues: "He's a preacher, or

was. Ministered to a small community in the Catalina foothills. Spent five years in Phoenix FCI for digging up cadavers and mutilating them. First he buries them wearing his preacher's hat, then after a few weeks he digs them up wearing his grave robber's hat."

"Whatever turns you on," Caddon says. "What reason did this Virtual Rabbit give for his behavior?"

"Virtual Reality or Virgil Rabbit, not Virtual Rabbit. He gave none. He got out last fall, by the way, now living in uptown Phoenix."

One of the older men on the team gives the Phoenix man a puzzled look. "So how does this Virgil Reality connect with anthrax?"

"Take a look at this." Mr. Phoenix bites into a slice of pizza and presses a button on a remote control. A handful of photographs come up on screen, showing first a white-haired, skeletally thin man in face-on and profile. He has the vacant, enthusiastic eyes of the deranged. Then a succession of photographs of a hut, its interior so squalid that Ambra can almost smell it. The Phoenix man supplies a running commentary: "The state police raided his property with a little help from Fort Detrick personnel in bioprotection suits. Found a handful of anthrax spores on site." The photograph shows a test tube, half filled with what looks like milk, clamped on a stand. A succession of stills takes them down steps to a heavily locked door. On the other side of the door, four corpses are laid out on camp beds. They are partially decomposed, desiccated, half-grinning with lips pulled back from their teeth, and their chests and stomachs are opened up—"standard Y-cut"—Ambra stares, horrified, while her pizza wonders whether to go down or up. She glances surreptitiously around; the FBI agents are happily continuing to munch theirs. And then, mercifully, the slide show is throwing up a sequence of crudely typed sheets. "They found this in the guy's cabin. A do-it-yourself manual on extracting anthrax bacilli from cadavers. He typed it up himself."

"Did he now?" Caddon says thoughtfully.

Mr. Phoenix shakes his head regretfully. "I only just got the Fort Detrick report on the spores. The ones this guy was growing are different from the ones collected in Fossil Creek. Didn't know you got more than one kind of anthrax spore."

"What are you saying?"

"He's just a harmless lunatic."

Ambra wonders about the FBI definition of *harmless*. "What about your militias?"

Mr. Phoenix gives the British visitor a tolerant smile. "We take them seriously, which is why we've had most of them under surveillance for quite a while. Some real hate merchants in there, but mostly they're just grown-up boys acting out their make-believe, sinking a few beers and having a good time on weekends."

Spada reassures her. "They're mostly just glorified Boy Scouts."

"With guns," Ambra says. There is an awkward silence, and she adds, "*Somebody* pulled that device up the shaft."

"The pickup truck was stolen from a builder's yard in Coolidge, Arizona, four days ago. No CCTV cameras, no nothing."

"Anything else?"

"Nothing. We're checking the dental records of the burned-out guys."

Caddon sighs, and the Phoenix man adds, "Neal, be sensible here. Our banjo-playing militias could only produce test-tube quantities of anthrax. The crashed UFO had a ton of the stuff. That's industrial scale. The militia trail is dead before it starts."

"What's the alternative? A Nazi flying saucer?"

Mr. Phoenix sighs. "Okay, that's even worse. That's comic book stuff."

Caddon says, "So." He crosses to the whiteboard and writes:

Virgil Rabbit → local screwball → makes anthrax
by the teaspoon

Real WWII Nazis → UFO with a ton of anthrax
turns up in Arizona? → nuts!

No known connection between the above

The Phoenix agent says, "So where do hillbillies get their
hands on a ton of anthrax? Where does anyone get their hands
on that?"

Spada says, "Maybe they have a secret factory." There is
an outburst of derisory laughter.

Ambra was there a year ago, on the trail of potential
suicide bombers who had entered the UK via the Channel
Tunnel and then just disappeared. There is that horrible,
disturbing moment when you suddenly realize that the trail
has dried up . . .

THE YELLOW BOXSTER:

FBI BUILDING, 2000

"Douse the lights, Tony boy." Caddon presses a button on the video recorder. Spada obliges, then moves over to sit next to Ambra in the small, darkened office. He may have no cigar but, close up, he smells of cigar smoke; it irresistibly strengthens the resemblance to Inspector Columbo in Ambra's mind. The rest of the team have cleared off and Ambra is being given the last of her briefing. She is dizzy with exhaustion, and the threatened headache has finally arrived and planted itself solidly on top of her skull.

The movie shows the inside of a shop. Gift baskets, racks of sweaters, cowboy hats piled high, glass cases showing jewelry, scenes of the Old West around the walls. "This is from the store across the road from Katie's Diner. It's the parking lot at the diner I want you to look at."

An elderly couple in the shop appear, moving erratically from item to item. At the counter, someone wraps up a sweater and takes their money, all in jerky movements like an old movie. "There. The car pulling in."

"A white Pontiac," says Spada unnecessarily.

Two men are stepping out of the Pontiac. Frustratingly, the camera is angled so that only their legs are visible. Over the next few minutes, their legs appear and disappear from view. Caddon says, "They're waiting for someone. And here he comes." A bright yellow Porsche turns in and stops. Another pair of legs. The three pairs of legs stand together and then disappear in the direction of the diner in funny, jerky walks.

"I'll speed it on a bit, they were in the diner for about an hour." Caddon presses a button on a remote control. "Here."

"Are those the same legs?"

"Uh-huh, and they're going into the same cars." The Pontiac and the yellow sports car take off in opposite directions.

"I couldn't make out the plates," says Spada.

"Signal Processing could. The Pontiac is our phony LA rental."

Ambra feels a surge of excitement. Within the last hour, one of the corpses at the UFO launch site has been recognized as the man who had hired the Pontiac. He's a dentist. He spends his weekends with a white supremacist outfit called the Phoenix Storks. They shoot up a few beer cans with Schwarzenegger armaments at weekends, then it's home in time to put the kids to bed and watch TV. Harmless fantasists, they'd told her. *Maybe the chase is on again? Maybe.* "And the flash car?"

"A Porsche Boxster, with a California plate ending in *07*. Now we ask ourselves, how many canary-yellow Porsche Boxsters are there in California with license plates ending in *07*? Answer, seven." Caddon counts with his fingers. "A restaurant owner, a grocery chain owner, an interior decorator, an eye surgeon, two rich widows, and a Hollywood musician."

"No drug dealers?"

"The top pushers go for Maseratis and Ferraris hereabouts, Ms. Volpe. But yeah, they're all high-society California respectability. No closet Nazis, no al-Qaeda connections, no nothing. However, one of them paid for the meal in Katie's Diner with a credit card."

"The musician?"

"Hey, Ambra, how did you get that?"

"Telepathy. And the name on your folder. I've seen it somewhere."

"His name is Alekos Demos." Caddon skims down the papers he has brought with him. "A freeborn American, with no criminal track record, not even a traffic violation. Model citizen. So naturally we don't hold any data on him."

"Naturally," says Spada, settling back for the spiel.

Caddon reads some more. "He's aged fifty-two, 180 pounds, five feet four inches, with mild heart trouble." Caddon starts to pace up and down, as if he is lecturing. "An only child of Greek parents who arrived from Greece in 1947. Seems they had a rough time under the occupation, most of their family was butchered. Studied accounting in England for a couple of years, thereby avoiding 'Nam. Returned to Berkeley, dropped out of a master's, played the clubs with a pop group called the Stoats, started composing music around then. Now big in the movie business. Owns homes in Spain and Morocco but his main residence is in Burbank. Hangs around gay bars in LA. At the moment he's in his La Jolla pad with one of his boys and I don't mean a son. No known political affiliations. And here he is in all his glory."

The screen throws up a picture taken at some party. Demos is grinning hugely at some young man. The musician is heavily wrinkled, with shoulder-length bleached hair and a hooked nose that makes him look like a lecherous Indian chief. Stubby fingers hold an over-large cigar.

"We'll take him first thing tomorrow, Tony. Just remember this is a respectable citizen, and the meeting at Strawberry may be totally innocent or related to his sexual proclivities, which comes to the same thing."

"In other words be tactful," Spada says.

"Or he'll have your nuts. He and the governor are old pals."

Ambra asks, "What about me? Do I go shopping or what?"

Caddon pulls a jacket from the back of a chair. "That's up to you, Ms. Volpe. Frankly, I can't find a use for you."

Spring Offensive:
THE CONVENT, APRIL 1943

DELIVERANCE:

BERLIN

How to explain? How to tell them what it was like? The young ones are sitting across from me, all rapt attention, like children waiting for a bedtime story. Between us there is a chasm, a gulf of time that no words can bridge. It wasn't the events, it was the atmosphere, the spirit of the times. We were all drunk with it. It was a living nightmare, yes. But it was also a time of heroism and sacrifice. We had a sense of being part of something huge, a conflict in which monsters roamed the earth and the rules of civilization were thrown aside, and whose outcome would set the direction of humanity for centuries . . . but how to explain all this? I hardly know where to start, I tell them. The girl says, Anywhere at all. She has dark brown, intelligent eyes. Curious eyes; they say they are journalists. Maybe. Outside, the Siberian winter is closing in. But my living room is a cocoon of warmth. Why don't I start with my first day in Berlin, after I was pulled off the Eastern Front? That would be good, she tells me. Berlin was my favorite city, I say.

"Krafft. Major Krafft. I am to present myself to Standartenführer Brück." An overweight, uniformed woman glanced at my papers, lifted a telephone, and pointed to a broad flight of stairs without a word.

The Waffen-SS colonel was watery-eyed, wiry, and wrinkled, with close-cropped hair and an exaggerated military manner. He was short of a right arm, which no doubt explained both the desk job and the sour expression. I clicked my heels and stood to attention.

"Sturmbannführer von Krafft, I expected you yesterday."

"I had a problem getting out, sir."

Brück looked up and down my uniform. "You might have tidied yourself up."

"I'm sorry, sir. I was bundled on a truck, then straight on to a supply plane, and here I am. I haven't slept for some days."

Brück wrinkled his nose. "And you smell."

The office reeked of cigarette smoke. *I must be bad if he can smell me through this.* "It's been some weeks since I changed clothes."

"You probably think that's an excuse. Sit down." The colonel flicked through some sheets of paper with a single, nicotine-stained hand. "Cadet school graduate, given the dagger automatically. Time was when it was granted only to the men of the highest order. Now all you have to do is pass an exam. Still, you've acquired an interesting little display of Christmas decorations. Close Combat, Wound Badge in silver, Iron Cross, Infantry Assault . . ."

"The usual, sir." It wasn't false modesty; I'd seen too much real courage go unrewarded to be impressed with my own tinsel.

"*Ja, ja,* the usual." He looked up. "Where were you wounded? In the back?"

I couldn't believe I'd heard that. "In the thigh. A few centimeters to the right and I'd be a soprano."

The colonel chose not to smile. "And how is it with II Rangers?"

"You know conditions in the East, I'm sure. We've lost a third of our original strength. But we're still the crack corps."

Brück nodded. "Papa Hausser's exploits around Karkhov are a candle in the dark. You've blunted a major Ivan offensive by all accounts. However, it's not all sweetness and light." He leaned back in his chair and looked at me speculatively. "We've had a couple of bad reports about you."

"Bad reports?"

The colonel paused, no doubt to keep me on edge. "Insubordination. Two incidents, no less."

"I only remember one."

"And refusal to obey an order."

"I wasn't about to shoot a boy because he kept pigeons."

"You reptile, Krafft. The pigeons could have been used to carry messages."

"Not after I'd shot them."

"I would have had you executed on the spot." The colonel tossed the paper onto the desk and tried out a hard stare.

I made no response, and he tried again. "And it seems you lack enthusiasm. Not military enthusiasm—you didn't get those baubles for nothing. But it seems, I quote, 'Sturmbannführer Krafft is not a convinced standard bearer of the National Socialist ideology.'" Another accusing look.

And still no response. He was coming to a boil, but after the front I was past caring about anything. He snapped, "I'm also informed that on entering this building five minutes ago, you used your Wehrmacht rather than Waffen-SS rank."

The fat bitch at the desk.

"This is contrary to the Reichsführer's explicit orders. Do you have some problem that we should know about?"

"I don't know what you're talking about, sir."

The colonel pretended to read some more. "Still, your behavior on the front is exemplary, and the men you command think highly of you. We can't afford to lose men like you. Unfortunately we may be about to do just that. You're being offered a chance to leave the Waffen-SS."

"What?"

Brück slid a sheet of paper toward me. "A certificate of honorable discharge. Unsigned as yet." He looked at me curiously.

"Sir?"

"They tell me that most of your company were killed."

"We were unlucky. We ran into a strong Ivan patrol. We had to shoot our way out."

"Leaving some men behind . . ."

". . . I had absolutely no choice . . ."

"No matter. They're presumably now either dead or prisoners, which comes to the same thing. Reichsführer Himmler is of the opinion that you're more use to the war effort as a live civilian in Bavaria than a dead soldier on the Russian front."

"Himmler? Bavaria?" My head was whirling.

"I don't know what's going on here, either, but any soldier on the front would give his right arm to be in your place." He grinned ghoulishly. "You're being offered work that by its nature must be voluntary. The aforesaid work, I quote, may change the course of the war. This work, I quote again, is not without risk. You will retain your rank . . ."

"I'll be able to keep my dagger?"

"You will. But the rank will be an honorary one. In effect you'll be a civilian, whatever our Reichsheini likes to think about these honorary ranks he scatters around."

"Sir, why me? Can't you tell me more? What sort of secret work?"

"It's so secret, apparently, that you can't even be told what it is. Apparently you have some particular qualifications."

"I'm just an engineer with a science background."

"Shut up. Don't tell me any more. By the way, this extraordinary offer remains confidential under pain of death. The request for your services comes from Reichsheini himself. See, his signature."

I looked over the Reich-headed paper. The date was two days ago; they'd pulled me off the front immediately. "But it is a request, not an order."

"That is correct. You are being asked to volunteer. If you decline, you will be returned to the Eastern Front immediately. It's your decision. Go away and think about it. Just don't take all day. Mind you, I'm here until God knows when."

Dear Little Bruv . . .

I read my crumpled letter for the third time that day, slid it into a pocket, and took another sip of real coffee. I watched a couple of girls, lips bright red and faces white, arms linked and chattering. They passed by among the crowd drifting along the Ku-damm, paying me no attention. Real coffee, real girls. And Berlin, my favorite city.

I must have been mad. A letter like that would have had me put up against a wall. Not that it mattered when I thought I was a goner anyway, but now—I'd burn it as soon as I got the chance.

My hand was trembling and making little waves on the coffee as I lifted the cup. I wondered if it was just exhaustion or slight shell shock. Three days of noise. Three days without sleep. Three days of being hammered in that fucking town. The din! And little fat Willie being sliced in two, and Kurt getting it squarely in the chest, and . . .

This is a dream. I'll wake up and find myself back in Bo-godukhov with Willie's guts wrapped around me and the Ivans flaming the cellar. I took a deep breath to calm down, looked for reassurance in the Berlin crowds, the familiar buildings, and the smells of coffee and pastry.

What to do? Go back to Hell? I stretched out a hand, observed its trembling dispassionately, as if it weren't a part of me. An elderly couple at the table next to me gave me an alarmed look, as if they'd found themselves next to a lunatic. *Go back?*

The one-armed colonel, of course, had it sized up perfectly. Most soldiers would give anything to be taken off the front, maybe even an arm. As for a posting in Bavaria! Visions of Alpine meadows and cowbells and snow-covered peaks filled my head.

No question, duty lay where Himmler wanted me to go. But I knew that if I took it, it wouldn't be duty. It would be an escape from the front. Bavaria was the coward's way out, and I knew it, and the sour colonel knew it. Which was why he'd been goading me.

Ten to three! I wanted to sit here forever, but I'd delayed as long as I dared. I brushed pastry crumbs from my uniform and made my way quickly to the waiting car. As I approached, the corporal threw down his cigarette, ground it under his polished leather boots, and jumped smartly into the driver's seat. The man fired the car into life and took off smoothly, heading for the ministry building.

"Herr Colonel, I accept the assignment."

Brück slid over a form without a word. The air was thick with hostility. "I took you for a fighting man, Krafft." His tone was harsh.

"If I'm more useful in Bavaria, so be it." I scribbled my signature. *Done!*

"Stop shaking. Get yourself some civilian clothes with this." He tossed an envelope at me, almost contemptuously. "Tonight you have a room in the Brandenburger Hof, no less—someone thinks you're worth it."

"Fantastic. I can have a bath."

The colonel looked as if he had something to say about my familiar attitude, but of course I was now a civilian. "There's a rail warrant in there. The trains are more or less keeping to timetable at the moment. Make your way to Munich first thing tomorrow and change trains for Mittelwald, which is a one-stop village in the Bavarian Alps, apparently. Be there within twenty-four hours. This evening's yours. Find yourself a couple of whores. From what I've heard of the Russian women . . . Now get out of here, you lucky bastard."

I emerged into the sunshine, into civilized Berlin, still half thinking I was in a dream. *Whores, hell. What I need is sleep.*

NIGHT TRAIN:

BERLIN TO MITTELWALD

I awoke early and after breakfast found my way on to a Munich train. Not even the cold morning air shifted my feeling that I was inside a dream, that I'd waken to find Willie's guts wrapped around me and the Ivans flaming the cellar. And in a crowded compartment I promptly fell asleep again.

When next I woke up, the blackout blinds were down and the train was jolting to a halt. Doors were banging and the compartment had almost emptied. I was shivering with cold; hours of exposure to the sulfurous smoke had irritated my throat and was nipping my eyes; I could feel my lungs in outline.

"Munich! Munich!" The woman had a thick Bavarian accent, and her throat was hoarse from shouting. I made my way to the waiting room. The benches were full of huddled humanity, but coke was glowing bright red in an open fireplace. Inexplicably, crates of cabbage were piled high in a corner, creating a smell that merged revoltingly with the sulfur and sweat.

Forty minutes later, as I boarded the train for Vienna, it was almost dark and the platform was crowded with soldiers, itinerant workers, farmers and their wives; snow was threatening. A whistle blew, the train moved out in clouds of steam, and I stood in the crowded corridor for an hour, shivering in the freezing air. A group of noisy delinquents in uniform were sharing a packet of Josma, oblivious to the Reich's strictures on cigarettes. Didn't they know our scientists had found a connection with lung cancer? I spent the journey breathing in more smoke.

"Mittelwald! Mittelwald!"

The station was tiny and deserted, and I thought maybe I'd been sent to the end of the world. There was a dusting of snow, and a half-moon showed that I was at the center of a circle of snow-covered peaks. There wasn't a ticket collector or any other soul to be seen. An acetylene lamp spluttering on a wall created a little circle of white light in the gloom; snow-flakes were drifting lightly down past it. The air! It was pure and fresh and exquisite, and I cleared my lungs with a few deep, icy breaths. From the dark, someone blew a whistle, and the train moved off; next stop Vienna. I hitched my kit bag onto my shoulder, wondering what would happen next.

A man emerged from the dark. He was in a naval duffel coat, the hood thrown up and his face almost invisible. He could have been a medieval monk. His voice was deep and gravelly, with a heavy smoker's hoarseness. "Sturmbannfüh-rer Krafft? Do you know the coldest place in the universe? It's not the North Pole. It's Mittelwald railway platform in the winter. And I've been standing on it for two hours, waiting for you."

"You're lucky. I nearly didn't get out at all." I heard a sudden noise behind me and turned, alarmed, my heart hammering briefly in my chest. Urban fighting did that. But it was only a girl, early twenties, carrying a rucksack almost as big as herself.

"Dr. Daniela Bauer?" the monk asked. She nodded wearily.

"I'm Max," I said, "Max Krafft." I was too exhausted even to click my heels.

"Daniela." Terrific smile, even in the half dark. I hadn't been this close to a girl in two years.

The monk turned without a word. There was still nobody

to collect tickets. He took the wheel of an over-large car while the woman called Daniela bundled into the back, propping her bag on the seat and sitting close up against me. I felt close to fainting.

The big engine purred into life. We drove through a small village, dark in the blackout but with snow reflecting moonlight off the steep roofs. It might have been a ghost town.

The road climbed quickly and we soon found ourselves slithering around steep bends, the clutch snatching between gear changes. From time to time I glimpsed roofs dwindling far below me. The big car was over-hot, and the smell of stale tobacco came drifting back from the driver. I was too exhausted to speak, and the young woman next to me seemed to be in the same state. Finally I got it out, in slurred words: "Where are we heading?"

The driver was taking it slowly around a hairpin bend. "A convent."

"I'm not a nun."

"But you'll be taking a vow of silence, my friend."

THE POOR CLARES:

MIDNIGHT

So, Maximilian von Krafft, here you are! Two days ago you were a resident of Hell. Tonight you are three thousand kilometers away, in the peace and safety of the Bavarian Alps, and sliding between the sheets of a nun's bed.

What sort of nun? A dried-up old prune? Or was she young and hot-bodied, seething with repressions? Despite my exhaustion, I grinned at the delicious thought.

The car had taken us up into some other reality, a planet of ice giants and snow and waterfalls and misty fingers probing down gullies. I was too exhausted to stay awake and too nervous to sleep. Next to me, the girl was silent. The car was stuffy, the air a mixture of hot oil, tobacco, and perfume. And then in the distance something artificial was emerging, something squat and massive.

"The Poor Clares." That crunching gravel voice.

"It really is a convent?"

"Was. We've cleared out the Christian *scheisse*." The road turned into a broad asphalt courtyard. We stepped out. A few trucks and cars were just visible in outline, moonlight reflecting off chrome and glass here and there. The air was icy. A soldier, rifle over shoulder, emerged from the dark. He waved a torch over the driver's pass. I was momentarily dazzled by torchlight in my face, but then we were waved through the archway.

The driver led us, in near pitch black, along a pillared cloister. The courtyard had a light covering of snow and what looked like a big fountain in a corner. There was a broad flight of stairs, and then a long, narrow corridor and the smell of polished wood. The driver threw his hood back but his face was still unrecognizable in the near dark. He opened a heavy wooden door, which creaked. "Krafft, your room for the duration of the war. Watch your head. Make sure you pull the blackout curtain every night or I'll have your balls. Dr. Bauer, come with me."

I hit my shin on a low table, cursed, and groped my way toward an arched window, just visible. Some more blind groping led to a light switch, and I blinked in the harsh glare as I surveyed my new home.

A nun's cell. The room was sparse but, at maybe four meters by five, bigger than I would have expected; and it had a high curved ceiling. Sparse but with everything I needed: a single bed, a chair at a small oak desk, shelving for books, and a cupboard that revealed some empty shelves. There was a little crucifix with Jesus over the desk and a picture of the Führer on the opposite wall; so they hadn't cleared out all the Christian *scheisse*. Two messiahs confronting each other.

I was too exhausted to think. I stripped to my underwear and slipped between icy sheets, fantasizing briefly about the previous occupant. I listened. No deafening guns. No roaring aircraft or rattling tanks, and nobody bawling orders. Nobody dying, or trying to stuff their bowels back into their bellies. No screaming wounded. I wondered about my company, whether Ivan had finally cut them off, how many were still alive. That nagging feeling of guilt wouldn't go away. *Why should I be having it so good?*

I drifted into sleep, next door to Heaven, but with the feeling that somewhere down the line the Devil would be presenting his bill.

* * *

A heavy knock on the door. *"Raus! Raus!"* Footsteps, and then the door of the cell next to me was being hammered, and so on all along the corridor. In moments there was the sound of voices, male and female.

I rolled out of bed, tingling with curiosity. I pulled back the blackout curtain and was faced with a turquoise lake reflecting, mirror-like, snow-covered Alps against a blue sky. A high mountain glacier covered half the face of the tallest peak. There was sloping rocky ground for a few kilometers around, and a scattering of outbuildings, and here and there patches of green. Little spirals of smoke were rising from the chimneys of a few chalets in the middle distance.

Surprisingly, there was a full-length mirror on the back of the door. Such an aid to vanity couldn't have been for the nuns; I surmised that someone had put it in place after the nuns cleared out. Uncertain what I was about to face, I pulled my service uniform, cleaned and pressed at the Brandenburger Hof, out of the kit bag. My SS rank was now honorary, but I still had that entitlement. My leather boots were still streaked with Russian mud but I felt a curious reluctance to polish it off. The officer in the mirror looked approvingly at the result: black panzer combat jacket and trousers, aluminum piping around collar, oak leaves insignia, Iron Cross Second Class round my neck. I finished it off with the cap, with the eagle and cockade. The skip was lightly frayed at the edges. Then I stepped out into a long wooden corridor. Doors left and right led, I suspected, to the cells of the erstwhile nuns. At the end was a broad spiral staircase, the steps smooth with the passages of centuries, and I went down this, following the sound of conversation.

A man in his thirties was standing at the bottom of the stairs, arms akimbo. He was dressed in civilian clothes, lederhosen, gray shirt, and a hand-knit yellow pullover. The roundness of his chubby face was enhanced by round spectacles. His hair was short, reddish, and close-cropped. He snapped, "Why do we believe in Germany and the Führer?"

I clicked my heels. "Because we believe in God, we believe in Germany which He created in His world, and in the Führer, Adolf Hitler, whom He has sent us."

"Whom must we primarily serve?"

"Our people and the Führer, Adolf Hitler."

"Why do you obey?"

"From inner conviction, from belief in Germany, in the Führer, in the Movement, and in the SS, and from loyalty."

"Your boots are filthy."

"Karkhov mud."

"A badge of honor, then. No doubt you'll keep them dirty as long as possible."

"Absolutely."

"Yes, they told me you'd turned up at last, Krafft. My name is Hess, Kurt Hess, but you will address me as Standartenführer or Director. Come to my office, please."

"You're a strange mixture, Krafft. I can't quite make you out." Hess was making a show of flicking through papers. I thought it was the same dossier the one-armed colonel had looked through in the Berlin HQ.

"I don't seem strange to me."

"Good stock. Your family were financial supporters of the Führer in the early days. Your family tree is pure Aryan at least as far back as 1750." Hess looked up quickly and sprang a surprise. "Are you proud of the fact?"

"It's not something I think much about."

"Catholic, I see. Does that cause you any problems? Any conflict with your membership in the Order?"

"Not at all. It's sometimes necessary to do hard things in war."

"You're entitled to use the *von* prefix, but you don't. Why not?"

"I do use it from time to time, mainly to impress waiters."

"Yes, a facetious answer that is entirely in keeping with the report I have in front of me. I think you'll find, Krafft, that I'm not particularly tolerant when it comes to insubordination of any sort. Am I making myself clear?"

"Your lucidity is faultless."

Hess gave me a long, cold stare. I knew the technique: Domination is asserted through the eyeballs. From my first day in the SS, I'd developed a counter-technique, which was to visualize tiny people climbing down the officer's forehead, using wrinkles as handholds; or dancing on his head; or opening doors in his head and waving. For bawling officers, a roaring parrot on the shoulder was useful. The technique had been amazingly helpful: while other recruits of my age had grown pale, crumpled, or hyperventilated in the face of the bullying tirades, my problem had been keeping a straight face. And now I was staring at Hess's forehead, fascinated by the little woman who'd opened a window, thrown out a bucket of water, and was now giving me a friendly wave.

Hess flushed. "You're down here as a mountaineer. Where have you climbed?"

"Here and there. Mostly in the Swiss Alps, but I was with Steiner's Kanchenjunga expedition."

"Well, don't get any bright ideas about indulging your hobby hereabouts. You'll have no time for it."

I stayed silent.

Hess tried another hard stare. " 'There are too many men in the SS who are neither sincere nor idealistic.' Those are the words of the Reichsführer himself. Do they apply to you, Krafft?"

"I like to think, Director, that I'm both sincere and idealistic. But my SS rank is now honorary, remember? Ehrenführer. In effect I'm a civilian again. And I still haven't been told a damned thing. Why exactly am I here?"

"Let's start as we mean to go on, Krafft. Civilian or not, honorary rank or not, I would ask you to remember who you're speaking to, namely the director of this project. It would be better if you used a more respectful tone." He leaned back in his chair. "You're here to win the war for the Reich."

THE FENRIS WOLF

"Do you ride, Krafft?" There was a subtle insult in the question, asked of a member of an old Schwabian family; the sneer was thinly disguised.

I gave him the effortless smile of a man amused by the antics of a social inferior overstepping himself, a smile designed to infuriate. "Now and then, Herr Director."

Hess flushed again. We strode together out of the central courtyard. Through the archway, sentries snapping to attention. The air was cold and clear, with only a few clouds enveloping the highest peaks. A path took us around to the back of the convent, and I was surprised to see, about fifty meters from the main building, what appeared to be stables. I could smell leather and horses even from this distance; memories flooded back.

Nuns on horses! "Did the nuns ride?" I asked, surprised.

"Of course not, you fool. I converted their woodshed."

"The Habsburgs used to hunt for chamois in this area," I said. I didn't know why I said that, and I didn't know how I knew. An old, stooped man emerged from the stables and tried to snap to attention. His breath was steaming in the cold air, and he was blue at the lips.

"Krafft, meet my one luxury. Myers, this is Sturmbannführer von Krafft." Myers smiled respectfully and half bowed. "Myers was with von der Marwitz's cavalry corps at Kaelen bridge in Belgium in 1914, which is why he's short of a foot. Saddle up Gog and Magog, please."

I hadn't been on a horse for years. It was wonderful to feel a saddle again, hear the creak of leather, and feel the wind in my hair. Magog, I soon discovered, was willful and high-spirited. Herr Colonel took Gog off at a brisk gallop. I let him take the lead; Magog was keeping up easily. About halfway around the big lake, I gave her full rein, bending forward like a jockey, and pulled past my new director. After a mile, I slowed to a trot and Hess caught up, red-faced and puffing. The ground was beginning to fall away below us; it was marked by huge gray boulders sticking up through the snow.

"It's as well you stopped. There's a precipice just a little ahead." We wheeled our horses back toward the convent. "Krafft, I want you to find how pathogens survive an explosion."

"Is that why I was pulled back from the front? To find out how bugs survive an explosion?"

"That's a key part of the jigsaw."

"I don't know a damned thing about pathogens. I'm an engineer. And anyway, what use is that to anyone?"

"And having found that, I want you to devise a means of spreading them over a very wide area." Hess patted Gog's head. The path back was broad, and we trotted side by side. Wisps of mist were rising from the lake on our left. "What we intend to do here is win the war for Germany and the Führer."

"Win the war from a convent?"

"What I'm about to tell you is so secret that not even the Weapons Research Office is aware of it. In Spandau they have a factory that contains fermentation vats. But they're not fermenting beer. No, not beer. Plague bacilli and anthrax spores. In huge amounts. And they have developed an amazing new poison gas. We are sure the Allies have nothing like it."

"Huge amounts? And what is this gas?"

Hess ignored the interruption. "What we need is an efficient means of dispersing these deadly things over a wide area. Maybe at altitude, say from bursting artillery shells. You have a unique combination of talents for the job. You're an artilleryman, you're an engineer, and before that you worked in the physical sciences at Leipzig."

"You want to find some way to blast deadly germs or poison gas quickly over a wide area, at altitude?"

"That's the idea. Reichsmarschall Goering has a keen personal interest in this project, and I have to report its progress personally to him. You may even have the honor of meeting the Reichsmarschall at some stage. I am to develop a weapon that will wreak havoc on the enemy, both in the battlefield and on his civilian population. If we could stop Ivan in his tracks . . ."

"Who's the girl?"

"Ha! I thought she might interest you. Her name is Daniela Bauer. She comes from a good family. Her father is General Bauer, a Wehrmacht man with a desk job in Berlin. Old Prussian nobility, you know the type." Again that hint of a sneer.

"Does she do bugs?"

"No, she does mathematics. Real applied mathematics, not the Jewish abstract rubbish. We'll need her to find out how the germs or the chemicals spread in various circumstances, what the extent of the lethal dosage would be, and so on. She and you are key players here."

"Dynamite explodes at four kilometers a second. Going from rest to that speed over the diameter of a bursting shell would rip anything to bits, even a microorganism. How do you know a wonder weapon like that is even possible?"

Myer was waiting in the distance. For the first time I saw the precipitous, winding road that I'd been driven up the previous evening. But there was also a quick way down: a cable car station in the courtyard. The cable car itself was out of sight, and the cable was vibrating tautly; someone was going down or coming up.

"Some more things we should get clear at the outset, Krafft. I directed the Kaiser-Wilhelm Institute on the leadership principle, and I intend to do the same here. I do not accept the doctrine of free discussion with superiors, and you will not question my judgment. If I say this weapon is possible, that is all you need to know. Is that understood?"

Nasty little despot. Never seen action at the front. Socially inferior, knows it. I said, "Of course."

Hess paused, searching for intonations in my voice. We were three-quarters of the way around the lake, and the convent was ahead of us. I said, "What happened to the nuns?"

"What?"

"Where did the nuns go?"

Hess looked bewildered. "What does that have to do with anything?"

I stroked Magog's neck. "Just curious."

"You will carry out a feasibility study in the shortest possible time. You will have everything you need, technical staff, apparatus, the lot. It goes without saying that this is one of the closest secrets of the war." Hess adopted a confidential tone. "Even the Führer does not necessarily know about this."

"What?"

"He has an aversion to poisonous gas."

"The Führer doesn't strike me as the type who would care much about enemy soldiers, Standartenführer."

"Of course he doesn't," Hess snapped, "and then neither should you. But the wind blows from west to east, Krafft. If we used poison gas against the British and Americans, it could give them the excuse they need to send gas across the Channel or even onto the Western Front if they ever got a toehold in Europe. The Slavs, of course, are another matter. What we need is a weapon of such overwhelming power that it leads to a quick victory, whomever we use it against. This is to be Hermann Goering's birthday present for the Führer. He himself has told me that this is the most secret project of the war. Between ourselves"—Hess lowered his voice, although there wasn't another human being in sight—"I hear that the Reichsmarschall is not in favor with the Führer. The gift would do Goering no harm. Think about how you will do this, Krafft. And think quickly."

We left Myers to unsaddle Gog and Magog. As we approached the archway, just outside the hearing of the sentries, Hess asked, "You don't have moral qualms about this, Krafft? About using bacteria and gas?"

"Why should I? A weapon is a weapon."

Hess nodded his satisfaction. "That's what I expected to hear. Pity for enemies of the state is unworthy of a Waffen-SS man. And the state defines right and wrong."

"Of course. Right being what serves the interests of the state."

"Correct. We're going to unleash the Fenris Wolf, Krafft, and it's going to devour the enemy from London to Los Angeles. I need a hundred percent effort from you on this." Hess's eyes had an enthusiastic glow.

"You'll get it if you feed me. I last ate twenty-four hours ago."

"My heart bleeds for you. A pampered soul, are we? The spoiled child of a rich family, a connoisseur of fine food and wine?"

"Absolutely. I recommend scabby Kharkov horsemeat, casseroled with turnip."

Hess made a grisly face. "You'll find that wartime austerity stops outside the convent door."

BOSCH

The first trucks of a long convoy pulled in to the forecourt just as we reached the convent. I watched fascinated as desks, benches, baths, electric generators, kettles, a huge variety of pots—some of them big enough to cook food for a brigade—were unloaded by a dozen soldiers to the gruff commands of an army sergeant and two corporals. Noise echoed off the high gray walls.

A Wehrmacht major was approaching smartly. Hess was still breathless. "I have things to do, Krafft. Find Bosch and Webber. Bosch is our procurement officer. Anything you need, speak to him. Webber is your personal assistant." He turned abruptly away.

The convent was a massive square building, maybe a hundred meters on each side, with a green, onion-shaped steeple at the northwest corner. The forecourt was to the south, at the edge of a sheer cliff that curved sharply to the west of the convent, making it unapproachable from south or west and giving the impression that it was built more for defense than the contemplative life. The cable car station was at the far end of the forecourt, the cable itself passing over the road below. A stone wall separating forecourt from cliff looked modern, and for that matter I didn't think the nuns would run to an asphalt forecourt. I turned my attention to the entrance. This was an ornate, heavy oak door flanked by stained glass; gentle shepherd with crook holding a lamb on one side, fierce-looking character with a long white beard glaring down from the clouds on the other. I went inside.

Through the door, the bustle died and I found myself in an atrium with low doors leading off. There was a small, heavily grilled window; maybe the only communication the nuns had with the outside world. Through a door at random, and I found myself in a long high-ceilinged hall, with overhead beams and tall windows throwing strips of colored light on the floor. I walked along it, passing the tombs of Simon the Child, Eduardo de Clari, some bishops.

I looked at the shafts of sunlight and thought I was on the south side of the building, with the cliff on the other side of the wall. A low, heavy door at the end of this hall led to another hall. Rooms led off and there were flights of stairs, some going up, some going down. A door was held open with a fire extinguisher. Inside was a long refectory. There were benches along three of the walls, with a central clearing area for the servers. Beyond it was a door leading, presumably, to the kitchen. There was a little group of people clustered at one of the benches, drinking coffee—real coffee, from the smell. I had the feeling that I'd get to know these people very well. I passed by unnoticed.

On to the east wing. Here there was a small library, what looked like a community room, and a couple of classrooms. I wondered if maybe the nuns had supported themselves by teaching. I wandered into the library and had a quick look at the shelves. It was filled with theological books that meant nothing to me. More Christian *scheisse* they'd forgotten to clear out.

The doors of the north wing were marked with little brass plaques. There were several parlors, something called a bishop's procuratory, a surgery and dispensary, and, surprisingly, a couple of carpentry workshops.

Around to the west wing, completing the circuit. I came across the steps I'd climbed the previous night, and the corridor with the cells leading off. I counted a dozen cells. There was another flight of steps, up to a second floor. I went up these. Another couple of workrooms and what looked like a novitiates' dormitory, a couple of dozen single beds side by side, sheets and pillows gone, only the mattresses remaining. I guessed the upper floors of the other wings would be much the same.

I looked out of a narrow window and saw the forecourt below me, now completely congested. Trucks were reversing, corporals and sergeants bawling and gesticulating. Another convoy of trucks was winding up the road while trucks from the first, having unloaded their cargoes, were descending. It reminded me of an army of ants. But the second convoy toiling up the hill was different: soldiers, a full Wehrmacht company! We had serious protection.

The circuit completed, I now trotted briskly down the stairs, back to the central courtyard, which now looked like an Eastern bazaar. I found that the grumbling, sweating soldiers gave way quickly to me. Of course; the uniform. Not the Allgemeine–SS but still black. I made my way out of the building and began to explore the environs. Standing on its own, about a hundred meters from both convent and stables, was what might have been a laundry. I made my way to it.

Close up, the laundry turned out to be made of brick and so was presumably a modern addition to the convent. The interior was dark. Metal pillars supported iron beams. There were high narrow windows and numerous ventilation chimneys. The building was about twenty meters long by ten wide, and there were about thirty men and women huddled together, along with a handful of dirty-faced children. They were poorly dressed in a mixture of Slavic dresses and cheap suits. There were no beds and there was no heating. Straw bales, clearly from the stables, were scattered around and provided the only furniture. There was a pervasive smell of urine. There was a rustle as everyone stood up and caps were removed.

I had a dozen words of Polish, picked up in fraught circumstances. I tried a few of them out on a thin, nervous woman standing on a straw bale. "Are you Polish? Russian?"

"I am a Pole, sir. From Cracow."

"What are you doing here?"

The reply was an incomprehensible mutter. I looked around the gray faces. The air was thick with the smell of sweat and fear, even coming through that of the urine. My uniform again. I left without a word.

Promise of Terror:

THE CONVENT, 1943

PISTOLS AT A COLD DAWN

I stuck the Karkhov boots in the back of a cupboard, folded away my SS uniform, and changed into a sports jacket and trousers bought in prewar London, in Jermyn Street, on a holiday with Papa and Bruv. The jacket was tweed and cut in a style that was unmistakably English, not the Bavarian *Tracht* that was the favorite of patriotic Nazis. I tried the outrageous yellow tie with elephants, but didn't have the nerve for it, and I took it off and kept my shirt open-necked. The outfit had been with me from Poland, stuffed in a duffel bag, and it was badly creased. It had crossed Russia with me almost to the Urals, returned to Berlin, and come with me down to this mysterious place. I'd worn it twice in three years. The civilian in the long mirror looked at me; he marveled at the transformation of the external man, and wondered about the inner one. Could I get back to the way things were? Or was brutalization for life? I didn't know. But I was determined to let my hair grow, get rid of the bullet head.

It occurred to me that I hadn't eaten for almost a day. I wandered along the corridors in the direction of the refectory. Wandered! I smiled at the memory of my training sergeant. *What are you, Krafft, a girlie? Don't mince, march!*

The refectory had a lingering smell of bratwurst sausage,

and the sound of clattering dishes was coming from the direction of the kitchen. Two women, a man, and what looked like a schoolboy, all in civilian clothes, were still there at one of the tables. The older man was thirtyish, nearly bald with round spectacles and a small, round face. He reminded me of my old music teacher. He stood up and extended his hand. "Max Krafft? I'm Bartholomew Bosch, a name that is easily remembered. This is your first day here, I gather."

"That's right." *I've seen you somewhere.*

"I'd like to introduce the ladies first, Edith Zimmerman and Daniela Bauer."

"I'm a chemist," said Edith Zimmerman. She had a slightly pointed nose, a small, prim mouth, and short, almost boyish black hair.

"I'm a mathematician, for my sins. And we've met." Daniela Bauer smiled. It was a mischievous smile, broad-mouthed and exposing perfect teeth. I didn't know what to make of it.

"And this is Willi Webber. Your factotum."

The schoolboy blushed, half stood, sat down, stood up, and sat down again.

A middle-aged, stooped woman, thin as a rake, approached and stood deferentially next to me, just over my shoulder.

"They don't know much German," Edith said. "There's bratwurst and dumplings, or you can have steak. I think there's trout on the menu."

"I'll have the steak." The thin woman understood, half bowed, and headed for the kitchen. I said, "Presumably I'm dreaming."

Edith Zimmerman swirled sugar at the bottom of her coffee cup. "The staff here are Slavs and Poles. They're here to serve us. We're not expected to fraternize with them in any way."

"Have you seen where they sleep?" Daniela said. "They'll freeze to death in that laundry."

"So far as I can see there will be just six or seven of us." Edith spoke in a precise, clipped voice, like a spinstery schoolteacher. "We're all overhead, on the first floor. There's a second floor above that, which will belong to the technicians when they arrive. The kitchen staff sleep in the laundry and the guards, when they arrive, will have a novitiates' dormitory. We're protected by a full brigade, would you believe?"

"They're arriving now. What's the chain of command? What exactly is expected of us, and what's the time scale?"

Bosch said, "I think we're someone's bright idea."

"Goering's?" I wondered.

"This has the hallmark of Heinrich Himmler." Crazy science. Everyone knew what Daniela meant but nobody was about to spell it out. Not until we knew one another a lot better.

"I think it's up to us to do whatever we're going to do in the biochemical line," Edith said. "So long as we produce a superweapon that will finish the war."

"Is that all?" Webber was risking a flippant remark. Edith gave him an icy stare, and his cheeks flushed a deep crimson.

I said, "Willi, I want to talk to you about that. Do you care if we skip lunch?"

"No, no, not at all."

Bosch said, "Get the kitchen to bring you sandwiches. So far as I can see we'll be living like Eastern potentates here for the duration."

"You're our procurements officer, right? What was your army rank?"

"Major. In civilian life I was a professor of literature at Leipzig."

"A very young professor. That's where I've seen you. I was a student there. You outrank me on all counts, Professor."

"But now I fetch things for you."

"I'd like some airguns and plasticine, please."

The air pistols and rifles arrived at dawn the next day, and I had to admire the little professor's entrepreneurial skills. Presumably some Munich sports shop had been opened up for the occasion. The plasticine arrived at lunchtime, delivered by a motorcycle courier. Now all I needed was a place to fire them.

I scouted the convent once more. I remembered the stone steps; they led down to a warren of cellars barred by several heavy locked doors. It was damp, dismal, and cold. I'd had enough of damp, dismal, and cold. I took wooden spiral stairs up to the minaret and walked around the little parapet, disturbing pigeons. There was ice in the air, and the mountains were now hidden by heavy cloud, a reminder that Alpine weather could be treacherous. At ground level, chatter was coming from the library. A life-like statue stood in a dark corner. As my eyes adapted I almost jumped. It was wearing the uniform of an SS major. I gave him a smart salute and got an icy stare in return. *The hell with you.*

The kitchen. It was brightly lit, warm, and had lots of space. Half a dozen Slavs of both sexes were scrubbing and clearing. I chased them out. They seemed exhausted and glad to go.

I collected an armful of air pistols, rifles, and slabs of brightly colored plasticine from the refectory and carried them through to a kitchen bench. I summoned Willi Webber from the library. Now I pummeled a slab of pink plasticine, turning it into a slab about three centimeters on a side and two deep. It stuck easily on the whitewashed wall. I was ready to win the war.

I started with the lowest-power air pistol, resting my elbows on a table and pointing the gun at the little slab of plasticine. The pellet smacked into it with a satisfying *plop*. Willi Webber stuck a matchstick into the tunnel so created. "Six millimeters, Herr Krafft," he said, making the very first penciled entry in a hard-backed notebook.

"What's the pellet speed, do you think?"

"I've no idea, Herr Krafft."

"If you call me Herr Krafft again I'll shoot you. The name is Max. Would you say a hundred meters a second?"

"Shoot the gun horizontally, Herr Krafft. See how far the pellets fall over a fixed distance and work out the speed from that."

"Good idea. If I aim between your eyes and hit you in the balls, it's a slow mover."

Willi risked a grin. It was a big step for him.

By three o'clock that morning, with a variety of air pistols and rifles, and by freezing plasticine to various degrees of hardness, we were able to draw up a simple table. Cold plasticine was best; the pellets neither bounced back out nor penetrated too deeply, giving them too leisurely a stop. Four degrees Celsius, it turned out, was about right. For that temperature, drooping with tiredness, we were able to summarize the night's work:

Pellet Velocity (meters/ second)	Stopping Distance in Plasticine (mm)	Shots Fired	Deceleration (meters/sec/ sec)
100.0	5.2	17	96,150
250.0	13.3	12	2,350,000
310.0	19.0	9	2,530,000

Now all we needed were some bugs to put in the cavities of the pellets, and some way to count the proportion that survived being slammed into the cold plasticine. For that, I would have to collaborate with Edith Zimmerman, a maiden as icy as the plasticine we'd been handling.

The pellet speeds were far too low. They were slamming into the plasticine at a few hundred meters a second, whereas the blast from dynamite would hit bacteria at four thousand meters a second. And what was it that would kill the bugs, anyway? Not velocity, but maybe the acceleration? So far we had attained twenty-five thousand g, enough to turn a human being into fine mince, but what would it to do a microorganism? Or maybe the killing factor was the rate of change of acceleration, like the jerk you got when a car smashed into a wall? It was all unexplored territory! Still, we'd made a start.

And there was the thrill of doing something new, of going where nobody else had been, an addictive drug you won't understand if you haven't sampled it.

At the end of my first working day in the convent, with a glorious pink-and-yellow dawn breaking over the pinnacles, I decided to give my nun a name: Sister Lucy. I slid between Sister Lucy's sheets and wished her good night with a feeling of contentment. In my mind, she was beginning to resemble the enigmatic Daniela Bauer.

I drifted off, listening to the wonderful silence of the mountains. Maybe I was going to win the greatest conflict in history with a few air pistols, maybe not. Either way, it was a lot better than the Eastern Front.

WARTIME CHOCOLATE

"Sheep's blood. Horse's blood. Also some fungi with obscure names—I'll write them down for you. And chocolate. And that's it."

Bosch skimmed over his scribbled notes. "Blood and fungus I can get you, Edith, but I may have to justify the chocolate. Belgian or what?"

"Ground-up cocoa beans, you idiot." She decided to laugh, to show that she had recognized a joke.

More scribbling. "What do you want with this stuff?"

Edith, Daniela, Bosch, and I were in the north wing parlor. Hess had been true to his word—wartime austerity stopped outside the convent. Comfortable leather armchairs were scattered around. There were art deco lamps on antique tables; paintings with a Slavic look about them lined the walls, and there were even a few "degenerate" paintings from twentieth-century artists. The floor was covered by rugs from India and Persia, some of them with burn marks as if they had lain in front of domestic fires. Either the nuns had lived a life of remarkable opulence, or it had all been plundered from the occupied territories by the Fat One. Or maybe by Rosenberg, the party philosopher and Goering's rival in pillage.

Sheets of smoke hovered over us, the product of an early-morning cigarette dangling elegantly between Edith's fingers and drooping ash. She explained, "I mix them with various compounds to create nutrients for different bacteria. We end up with stuff that looks like jelly. These jellies get spread thinly in petri dishes on a tray. The tray is kept sterile and warm. The bugs, being cozy and well fed, multiply to the point where we can see them under a microscope. If a lot have survived, the colony will grow quickly. If there are just a few, we'll see little colored spots, tiny colonies that will take time to grow and merge into a single big colony on the dish. Is that clear?"

"It will no doubt become so, in time," said Bosch, adding real sugar to his coffee. "Have you decided on a laboratory?"

"I'll take the carpentry workshops upstairs."

"Very well. I'll have them cleared out and your benches set up there." Bosch checked the list. "You said two incubation chambers and four microscopes."

"Especially the new fluorescence microscope developed by Dr. Auguste Hirt at Strasbourg. It's state-of-the-art."

"Thy will be done."

"And I'll need at least three lab assistants. People who know how to light a Bunsen burner, basically."

Bosch frowned. "That could be a problem. National Socialist ideology doesn't allow a woman to give orders to men."

"I have a brilliant solution, Professor. Make them women."

"What about you, Max?" Bosch attached a fresh sheet of paper to his clipboard.

I said, "Say we bake clay until it's sterile. I take a little of it, soak it with a measured droplet of water infested by bugs or spores, and stuff it into the back of an air pellet. If we know how many bugs there are in a cubic millimeter, then we know how many we're shooting out of the gun. Then the pellet hits plasticine and the jolt kills some of the bugs— maybe all of them, maybe none. Edith finds out how many have survived the ride."

Edith took in a lungful of smoke and blew it down her nose. "I scoop the clay from the back of Max's slug and put it in a petri dish. I use the number and size of the colonies that grow to work out the survival rate."

I said, "I then increase the speed of the shots and plot their survival rate against force of impact. It's basic data needed for whatever weapon we create."

"Sounds plausible," said Bosch doubtfully. He scribbled some more. "But what I meant was, do you have a shopping list?"

"A few lathes, welding equipment and a couple of welders, a strong compression pump, some high-pressure steel pipes whose spec I still have to work on, and half a dozen cylinders of compressed hydrogen. And a sphere the size of a beach ball made of armament steel four centimeters thick. To be going on with."

"I don't want you to feel constrained by the fact that there's a war on and you can hardly requisition a paper clip. No, don't feel inhibited at all, Max. But couldn't you stick to air pistols?"

"They lack muzzle velocity, my dear Professor Bosch, as do rifles. I want to fire Edith's bugs out of a gas gun at four kilometers a second and smash them into a steel plate. Anyway, I still think her chocolate is your biggest challenge."

"Where do you want this set up?"

"In the laundry."

Edith adopted a *you can't be serious* expression, and Bosch pursed his lips. "You can't be serious, Max. That's where the Poles and Slavs live."

"I'll be conducting experiments at extreme pressures, far higher than anyone else has gone. If anything goes wrong, it would be nice to leave the convent standing. The slave labor can go into the novitiates' dormitory in the north wing. It's unused."

"I'll have to speak to Hess." Bosch sounded doubtful.

"Do that. I'll design the gun over the next few days and give you precise specifications. I'll need Daniela's mathematics."

Bosch looked at Daniela, who had been following the

conversation with languid interest. She said, "A big black-board and lots of chalk. And I like this room. Just get rid of the portraits—all these people staring at me while I work. I don't suppose you can get me a piano?"

Bosch stood up. "Not a problem. When would you people like your apparatus?"

Edith flicked ash onto an expensive rug. "How soon do you want us to win the war?"

"Out of the question."

"Look, I need an outbuilding." I was facing Hess and an-other man over a huge desk in the bishop's procuratory, which had apparently been commandeered as Hess's office. "You've told me you don't want to draw attention to this place with external construction work. Fine. But I can't carry out this high-pressure stuff inside the convent, it's far too dangerous. The laundry's the only logical possibility."

"Krafft, we're talking about Slavs here. Slavs and Poles. We can't forget the atrocities they committed against us."

"Herr Director, I've just come from Hausser's Waffen-SS . . ."

"Enough. Such people are expected to sleep in barns, sta-bles, huts, outbuildings. And you want them in dormitories? Can you possibly be serious? Maybe you'd like to tuck them in at night?"

"I'm not talking about their welfare. I appreciate they're allowed to exist only insofar as they are useful to us and that they should be grateful they aren't digging their own graves in Poland and Russia. But I need the laundry for dangerous experimental work."

The statue I had seen earlier was standing next to Hess. He was tall, blond, and thin-faced, in his late twenties. He would have been handsome except that his light blue eyes were too close together in his head, and his nose was a little too pointed. He reminded me of a greyhound. His voice was soft, almost sibilant. "You must understand that the labor force does not come within your jurisdiction, Herr Krafft.

Security is my responsibility, and that includes the workers from the occupied territories."

"I understand that, Sturmbannführer Oberlin."

Hess said, "Good. No more discussion. We'll build you a steel chamber in the chapel. Put your high-pressure stuff in there. Bosch will see to it."

I had one last shot but I knew it wouldn't work. "These people will freeze to death out there come the winter. Surely they're more useful to us alive."

Oberlin looked at me thoughtfully through narrowed eyes. Hess was looking puzzled. "But that's not a problem, Krafft. We'll just requisition more."

THE FIRING ROOM

I had to hand it to Bosch. The man seemed to rustle up equipment out of thin air. Within days a small team of welders appeared and began to put together steel plates, to make a firing room in the form of a small steel cabinet at the far end of the chapel. A small flask of anthrax spores from Spandau turned up a week later, on the same day that an army truck disgorged a baby grand—a Blüthner, what else? The steel sphere and tubes I asked for took a little longer, but considering that they'd had to be ordered and built in one of the Krupps armament factories in the Ruhr, their delivery within three weeks of demand was amazing. Willi Webber and I had a gas gun built and operational within a month.

Now a routine began. We started cautiously, using gas pressures not much more than those inside a volcano. The anthrax stayed firmly in its flask, and instead we targeted a harmless soil bacterium supplied by Edith. As our confidence grew, we began to tweak up pressures. It took about three hours to set up a shot, and we managed five or six shots a day. And each day, we tweaked the pressure up a little more than the day before, and felt a little more edgy than the day before.

There seemed to be about a dozen security staff and the

same number of workshop people. Edith acquired half a dozen lab technicians and machinists. By Hess's instructions, the scientists ate at a separate table in the refectory. In the event, our hours were so erratic that we often did not meet as a group at mealtime for days, and it was quite common for one or other of us to eat alone, an island of solitude in a sea of chatter.

A curious custom evolved, unplanned. At eleven o'clock each morning we would drift into the former classroom, which had now been converted into Daniela's office. A blackboard took up almost an entire wall, coffee seemed to be permanently ready on a little stove, and a dozen armchairs, tables, and desks were scattered around haphazardly. It was an eclectic collection, and I wondered where they'd been confiscated from. Daniela didn't seem to have a fixed desk, flitting between them from day to day. And over coffee, we would talk about our progress.

Always in a group. Somehow, I never seemed to find myself alone with Daniela: There was always someone around, whether a couple of dozen people in the refectory or three or four scientists in her office. Once I passed her in a cloister. Snow was drifting down onto the quadrangle and she had a suit collar turned up against the cold. She smiled at me, that damned Mona Lisa thing I couldn't decipher. "Heil Hitler, Max."

Hello, Daniela. Why don't you and I get away for a weekend in Vienna? You could introduce me to this famous Meissel and Schadn restaurant.

I'd love that, Max. What a wonderful idea.

Let's take in a concert, Mozart or Mahler. Or visit the fairground. Or what about the pictures? By the way do you ski? Do you have a boyfriend?

"Heil Hitler, Daniela." We passed by, my fantasies dissolving and my stomach in knots.

I sensed trouble from the way Hess strode in. The outer door let in a brief flood of light as the director entered the darkened chapel. Bosch, Willi, and I were in the firing room; I was seated at a bank of dials and switches. A cable stretched across the floor like a thick black snake and disappeared into a hole in a wall. Hess spotted it just in time.

"I want to see for myself. Just ignore me," said Hess with uncharacteristic modesty.

A metal flask was sitting on its own on the communion table, under a spotlight. It seemed somehow to be the focus of the room. "What's that? A poisoned chalice?"

"Actually, yes," Bosch said. "It holds anthrax spores, which is why it has its very own spotlight. Knock it over and you die."

"Horribly," I added for fun. "Didn't you read ZUTRITT VERBOTEN? We're about to fire the gun."

"So what's the game?"

"It's like I said. We're almost ready to fire."

Hess strode over to the steel chamber and peered through a small rectangle of bulletproof glass. "What am I seeing?"

I joined him at an adjacent rectangle. "That weight on the end of a wire . . ."

"It reminds me of a pendulum from a grandfather clock."

"It is. Just before firing we'll enter the firing chamber, pull it back at forty-five degrees to the vertical, and switch on an electromagnet to hold it there. Then we'll clear out. We'll throw a switch from here and the pendulum will swing and hit the firing pin—that brass thing at the end of the horizontal tube."

"Which looks remarkably like a shotgun barrel." The barrel led into a steel sphere half a meter across.

"Yes, Herr Director, it is, with a standard twenty-millimeter cartridge. Inside the shotgun tube there's a nylon piston with a very tight fit, gas-tight. When the gun fires, it drives the piston into the sphere, which is made of Krupps armament steel, very high tensile strength."

"So, you fire a shotgun into this sphere of high-pressure gas."

"Right. Very high-pressure gas."

"It's pumped up now?"

"Yes. And I don't trust entirely the firing chamber, Kurt. You wouldn't want to be here if the gas gun blows."

"Thank you for that reassurance, Krafft. So what happens when you fire the shotgun?"

"Look at the other tube, the one coming out of the far end of the sphere. It has a hard vacuum inside it, and between the vacuum and the high-pressure gas in the sphere lies a metal disk, close to bursting. When we fire the gun, it tips the balance and the disk breaks. The gas in the sphere throws the projectile at a huge acceleration along the second tube into the target chamber, that big cylinder at the end."

"Why does it need to be a meter long?"

"It holds high-speed cameras and other instruments to measure the speed of the projectile. That's why the chapel is nearly dark. We need to protect the photographic plates."

"What sort of projectiles?"

"Hollow steel marbles holding the bugs. Any tough sphere will do. We've even used a ruby."

"How fast can the marbles move?"

"We're pushing half a kilometer a second. A dynamite shock wave travels at four. We need to get to that speed before we can start on the spore survival rates."

"You need to octuple your projectile speed?"

"Yes."

"How will you do that?"

"We could build a bigger gun."

"But?"

"It would take time, and probably create a fresh set of problems."

The door opened and Edith slithered in, wearing a white lab coat and gloves. "Does nobody read notices around here?" I asked.

Hess started on a cigar. "You were saying?"

Webber had joined us from a dark corner of the chapel. "Instead, we're trying to increase the pressure of the compressed gas, and also making the bursting disk thicker and stronger. Either way, by the time the compressed gas bursts through, it's going faster. We get closer to simulating an explosion."

"But it also gets more dangerous because we're approaching the bursting strength of steel. We're dealing with massive pressures, Kurt."

Hess said, "You engineers. You're always full of caution. You have a built-in margin of error, right?"

"If we exceed it . . . ," I started.

The director shook his head impatiently. "How long will it take you to get the figures we need? To get up to four kilometers a second?"

"We're firing six shots a day, tweaking the pressure up each time. We should get to three kilometers a second in the next three months, four a second in the next four. If the gun doesn't explode."

"Four months? Four months?" Hess raised his voice. "In four months Ivan could be pissing on the tulips in the Tiergarten."

Edith said, "That's just for the anthrax spores, isn't that so, Max?"

"Right."

"If we're going to do sarin, to see how the chemical survives a four-kilometers-a-second shock wave, you'll have to start the experiments all over again, this time with sarin. Right?"

"Maybe, maybe not."

Webber said, "Sarin will be harder to handle, sir. It frightens me."

Hess said, angrily, "You people are talking about eight months to get the answers we need. Maybe a year."

"Looks like it."

"Before we even build the weapon?"

"We need the basic data before we know what to build."

Hess took a lungful of cigar smoke. "Indeed. And you will supply it within six weeks. Not eight months, Krafft. Six weeks."

I made a cardinal mistake: I laughed. "Don't be stupid. It

can't be done. We're nearly at the limit now. If we jump straight to the highest pressures . . ."

"Six weeks. And you're at the limit with your insubordination. If you call me stupid again, I'll have you put up against a wall and shot." Hess turned sharply away. Edith flashed me a malicious smile and followed Herr Director out the door.

BOMBER!

Slot the disks. Pump the hydrogen. Set the pendulum. Fire! Give the agar plates, or the smashed fragments of pellet, to Edith to incubate the bugs and count the colonies. Then slot the disks. Pump the hydrogen. Set the pendulum. Fire! Count the colonies.

Slot. Pump. Set. Fire! Count.

In the morning Edith comes in, hardly recognizable under lab coat, gloves, face mask, and hair net, carrying sterile agar plates. At the end of the day—or night—she comes to collect. Daniela comes at random intervals to collect numbers. Let her do the slide rule stuff: mean, standard deviation, regression, least squares fit. All of it elementary, far below her talents. She'll come into her own later.

Now slot in a stronger disk. Pump more hydrogen. Watch the pressure gauge, licking lips. Set the pendulum. Fire! Count. We pass the safety margin, our dials routinely go into the red; God knows what that's doing to the steel sphere.

Break for Christmas? Nobody on the front is breaking for Christmas. The Russian tide is coming in, a steady, inexorable flow toward the Fatherland. Nobody says so, but the triumphalism of the early days has gradually been replaced by a sense of impending catastrophe. In the convent we have a growing suspicion that we may be the only people standing between the Tiergarten tulips and the Magyar hordes.

I love Daniela's visits, anticipate them eagerly. They are a break from slot, pump, set, fire . . . Sometimes she collects the data and leaves without a word, sometimes she says something romantic like "We need another fifty percent pellet speed." Always she has a smile. Always the need to crank up the pressure. It's never enough. When she leaves, there is a faint trace of perfume in the chapel. Sometimes I imagine I also sense a bodily smell, something female, primitive, maybe even animal.

Don't get obsessed, Max.

She's taken to playing the baby grand at nights, sometimes for ten minutes, sometimes for an hour. The music lightens the dark creepy halls, defies the silent tombs, drifts along the cloisters. Sometimes it's Mozart, sometimes it's a beer hall ditty, sometimes it's a few snatches of theme tune from a film. Often too faint to be heard, depending on the wind. Sometime she sings. But on a still night, it's as if she's playing at my open window. Then I hear her footsteps light on the corridor outside as she heads for her room, and I drift off to sleep.

The crash hammered its way into my head, shaking my bed like a jelly. I leaped up, heart pounding. A rain of plaster flakes was falling from the ceiling, and my books had been shaken off the shelves. I grabbed a dressing gown and rushed to the door, barefoot.

The bomb had gone straight through the ceiling and floor at the end of the corridor, making jagged holes about two meters across. Already black smoke was pouring up from below and spreading along the ceiling. It was an acrid, choking, rubbery smell.

Doors were being flung open. Hess appeared at his door in underpants and hairy legs, hair tousled and mouth open in astonishment. He started to cough violently. Daniela emerged from the room next to him, apparently wearing nothing more than a fur coat. She caught my eye; she seemed to be trying to convey something with her expression, but I didn't know what. Other scientists were streaming into the corridor, and I turned back to my room and pulled on clothes frantically.

And now I saw that my window had been blown out of its frame. The shock wave must have bounced around the courtyard. Shards of glass were embedded in the books. It was still dark, and the tips of the highest peaks were catching pink light from rising sun. Back into the corridor, where the smoke was already black. The sound of retching came from all around. Trying not to breathe, I sprinted along to the stairs, colliding with cold, half-naked bodies.

The enemy had recently broken the Gustav line in Italy, putting the whole of southern Germany in reach of their bombers. They'd already plastered Munich. But a bomb didn't make sense. A bomb would have destroyed the convent. Unless it hadn't exploded. With a dry mouth I realized that the explosion must have come upward from the firing room.

Willi! He often worked late.

"Is it safe?" Hess grabbed me by the sleeve. His eyes were wide with fear, and he was speaking through a handkerchief held over his mouth and nose. "What about the spores?"

We were clustered at the far end of the courtyard along with a couple of dozen bewildered soldiers, some in uniform, some shivering in underclothes. Black smoke was still billowing out of a hole in the side of the chapel and one in the roof, which had lost half its slates. There was a stench of burning rubber, and splinters of door and window and roof slates were scattered across the courtyard.

"We were targeting harmless soil bacteria. The spores are in a cellar."

Relief transformed Hess's face. He became Herr Director immediately. "Your gas gun? How could it have gone off by itself?"

"It couldn't explode by itself. Someone was working with it."

Hess gaped for a second, and then shouted, "Has anyone seen Webber?"

Daniela said, "Oh God." She had managed to dress but was still wearing the fur coat.

I thought, if Willi was in the chamber when the gun exploded, he would now be seventy kilos of mince smeared over the chapel walls. Orange and yellow flames were almost hidden by the black, billowing smoke.

Oberlin had somehow managed to emerge from the chaos in full SS uniform. I wondered if he slept in it. He started to shout orders in a clipped, nasal tone. Half a dozen soldiers scurried away, and we watched uselessly as the men ran back from the direction of the stables, gasping with exertion and dragging a hose, which they struggled to connect to a water main in the courtyard.

"What's burning?" Bosch asked anxiously. "Is there anything dangerous?"

"Just rubber," I said. "That and a couple of chairs were the only flammable things in the chapel. So long as the fire doesn't spread." I was lying. If the anthrax flask had blown open, we were already dead.

The fire was out within ten minutes. A few meters of thick insulating rubber had generated an amazing volume of smoke. The hole in the side of the chapel was man-sized. Hess and I ran in through it, holding our breaths. My eyes were stinging but I could make out that the steel chamber had buckled outward from the internal explosion. A hole in the ceiling overhead showed where the steel roof had split open. I glimpsed gray sky overhead through the rising plume of smoke. But in the semi-dark I couldn't see much more, and in any case could only linger for a few seconds; eyes streaming, we ran back out coughing. Hess ran over to the fountain and started to vomit.

"Is Willi there?"

"I don't know, Daniela. We didn't get inside the chamber."

"This is your fault, Krafft." Hess was wiping his face with a sodden handkerchief. He stared at me malevolently through red, streaming eyes. "You built an unsafe gun. What happens to the project now? Everything we've done here is for nothing. What happens to the war now?"

"Herr Director." Oberlin's voice had a warning tone, and he was nodding toward the soldiers. Security.

"Well, get them out of here!" Hess shouted angrily. "Clear the courtyard."

"What went wrong, Max?" Edith was shivering in the cold morning air, a dressing gown pulled around her shoulders.

Bosch's tone was a mixture of fear and accusation. "Ask our director here. He's been pushing Max and Willi to take shortcuts, isn't that right, Kurt? You've been trying to get them on to high bullet speeds in one jump?"

"Since when did I have to justify myself to you, Bosch? But I do have to justify myself to Hermann Goering. What am I going to tell him? That we can't help the war effort? That the Reich is finished? Is that a message you would like to deliver?"

"Poor Willi," said Daniela.

"What was the state of play with your experiments?" Edith asked.

"Sometimes we got a hundred percent spore survival, sometimes fifty percent in identical conditions. I don't understand that, not yet. When you pushed the speed up, the survival rate dropped. But this was all at very low energies, not enough to simulate dispersal from an explosion. I can't make a secure extrapolation, not yet."

"We still don't have the basic data?"

"That's it, Edith."

"He'll have to be scraped off the walls." Something like dread was beginning to tinge Bosch's voice; his face was gray.

"Did he have a family?"

"How long will it take you to build another gas gun?" Hess asked, ignoring Daniela's question.

"You know the first one took four months. Maybe I could do it again in two."

"Two months before we get another gun? Do you know what that means? How many Germans will die in two months because of your incompetence? What extra territory will we have to claw back from Ivan? In two months the war could slide into an irreversible situation."

"I'll see what I can do."

"Listen to the genius. He'll see what he can do." Hess was both shouting and shivering, whether from cold or anger wasn't clear. "What am I going to tell the Reichsmarschall? That you'll see what you can do?"

It took two soldiers with crowbars to prise open the steel door of the firing room. Willi's greatcoat was stuck against a wall, and in the dull light it took me a few seconds to see that Willi was the glue. Both the soldiers ran out, and I heard vomiting. I insisted they come back in with flashlights.

The pressure dial was smashed, but its reading at the moment of explosion could just be made out. It had gone far into the red. Shards of metal were recognizable as remnants of the high-pressure sphere, which had clearly exploded. The hydrogen cylinders had been blown off their mountings but were otherwise almost untouched.

I now checked the gauges on the cylinders, but I already knew the answer. One gauge had been blown off, but the other two registered empty. Someone had emptied the lot into the sphere, a cylinder at a time. I found the anthrax flask in a corner, under rubble. It was still intact. Momentarily, I felt my knees go weak.

The stench of the lingering smoke was getting to me and I had to take a few minutes in the courtyard. My head was whirling. Back inside the steel box, I started to kick aside metal fragments with the toe of my boot. I found what I was looking for after some minutes: the gun barrel, still more or less intact. I squinted along it, holding it against the morning light now coming in. Two disks, buckled and jammed some centimeters into the barrel. Two disks, one of them rammed well up the barrel, out of sight. When Willi inserted the second disk and fired the gun, the pressure went far beyond anything the steel sphere could stand.

Either Willi had committed suicide in spectacular fashion, or it was sabotage.

Los Angeles

SUNDAY

THE HOLLYWOOD MUSICIAN:

LA JOLLA

A man from the Wright-Patterson Air Force Base turns up with thick spectacles and frizzy hair, declares himself to be Dr. Hardcastle, and shows a computer simulation. We still don't know the flight characteristics, he explains, and so we're relying heavily on the eyewitness reports. He tells the FBI team that to disperse anthrax over a wide area just by spinning the spores out, you'd need a helluva spin, but on the other hand, maybe the UFO—except that it isn't a UFO anymore, it's an Identified Flying Object, making it an IFO—did have a helluva spin. He hints at heavy pressure from the White House and a rush job.

Then he shows a movie. This gives some preliminary simulations for a Manhattan hit. They watch the little saucer drifting like a Frisbee above the skyscrapers, spirals of white stuff coming out like water from a lawn sprinkler before spreading into invisibility. The death toll could be as little as forty thousand or as much as a million, depending on the time of day, wind, and weather—little arrows show a system of whirls and eddies around the skyscrapers—and the unknown rate of spin. It has to be assumed that the bad guys know all this stuff and have their own scenarios worked out. True, Arizona hillbillies probably don't know aerodynamics from Milk Duds, but the guys who built the machine surely did, and they might have left notes or an instruction manual.

Are you telling us that home-grown terrorists couldn't have built this machine? Caddon wants to know. Badly.

This device is the product of a highly sophisticated team of scientists and engineers backed up by industrial muscle. Whether moonshine-drinking survivalists could attain those standards is your department, guys. By the way, Wright-Patterson hasn't considered sites for mass burial, or the financial knock-on and suchlike, doesn't consider stuff like that as part of their remit. Hardcastle hints at an imminent White House briefing and takes his leave, trailing aftershave and dismay.

Caddon and Spada leave, too, heading for La Jolla and an interview with the governor's friend. It is both the slenderest of leads and all they've got. They maintain a thoughtful silence all the way down Interstate 5. Hardcastle's throwaway phrase, *mass burial,* travels in the car with them.

"I love this Spanish Revival stuff."

"It's Hollywood Spanish, boss. Fake to the core."

"Ten-million-dollar fakes, Tony." They are winding up a long, quiet road. Here and there, through screening poplars, they glimpse red pantiled roofs, sprinklers on lawns, pools with springboards.

"Number 1100, here we are." Spada trickles the car through open gates and takes it up a long winding driveway. A metal plaque, discreetly stuck in the lawn, informs them that INTRUDERS FACE ARMED RESPONSE.

"Mr. Demos? FBI." Caddon shows his badge.

The Hollywood musician is wearing shorts, sandals, sunglasses, and a hairy chest. American-born or not, there is a Mediterranean inflection in his deep voice. "I deny everything."

Caddon remembers that this is the governor's friend and smiles. "We'd like to ask you some questions, sir."

"What about?" He isn't inviting them in, Caddon notices.

"May we come in?"

"I don't think so."

"If you prefer, we can go downtown. We'd rather keep things informal, though. Easier for everyone."

Demos grunts and gestures them in with his head.

He leads them into a room, air-conditioned cool, with a simple rustic charm that Caddon mentally prices at a quarter of a million. Rough adobe walls converge gently toward a high beamed ceiling. Everything is new. No history reveals itself, not an item or a memento to hint at a past that was anything other than wealthy. Demos has just sprung from the earth, rich.

The musician indicates chairs, hand-tooled leather. Through the French windows Caddon glimpses a blond, suntanned man splashing in the pool. He is young and muscular and has dragons tattooed on his biceps. The Pacific lies below them, in the middle distance.

"You were in Strawberry yesterday lunchtime, sir."

"Was I? Never heard of the place." Demos's eyes are inscrutable behind the sunglasses.

"If you blink, you miss it. You had a meal at Katie's Diner."

"If you say so."

"Your credit card says so. You had spaghetti bolognese, a glass of Chianti, a coffee."

"That sounds kind of intrusive."

"What were you doing in Strawberry?"

"I'm a musician, Agent Caddon. I compose theme tunes for movies."

"Sorry. I don't see the connection."

"Atmosphere."

"Atmosphere, right."

Demos adopts an air of patient explanation. "In the movie I'm doing, these guys bury a body in the mountains and years later it's found by some backpacker. And when they find a letter in the remains, it opens up a can of worms. I need to get that sense of wilderness, a sort of edgy primitiveness, into the music, and to do that I need to surround myself with that ambience. Do you understand what I'm saying?"

"I'll take your word for it, Mr. Demos. Creative thinking

isn't my thing. Did you have lunch with two men in Katie's Diner?"

"Do I need a lawyer for that?"

"Who were they?"

"I've no idea. 'Having lunch' makes it sound business-like, but it wasn't like that at all. It was just a casual conversation with a couple of guys I met by chance. Is that what this is about?"

"It is, Mr. Demos. Can you describe these men?"

"Bet you got them on CCTV somewhere."

"We'd rather get the descriptions from you."

"Hell, I can hardly remember them. One guy was about my age and height, brown leather jacket, dark-skinned, Southern California accent. Wrinkled face, like mine, come to think of it. The other guy was about forty, five feet ten, thin, pale-faced, didn't say much, smoked a lot. I doubt if I'd even recognize him if he walked in the door."

"What did you talk about?"

"Nothing much."

"Please try to remember."

"The hiking trails, the clean air compared with LA, stuff like that."

"Did they tell you anything of their business?"

"Not a thing."

"Do you know where they had come from? Where they were going?"

"How would I know? I told you, they said nothing."

"And you don't know these men?"

"You must be having difficulty with your hearing. I keep telling you: never seen them before, never seen them since."

Caddon stands up, and Spada follows. "Well, that's it. It was just something we had to check out."

The mouth below Demos's sunglasses forms a lopsided grin. "Am I allowed to know what these people were up to?"

Caddon grins back. "They're owing on a parking ticket."

Spada unwraps chewing gum with his forearms on the steering wheel. "These guys were waiting for him."

Caddon looks wistfully out at the ten-million-dollar fakes. "Edgy primitiveness. I wish I could do edgy primitiveness to music."

"And he's never heard of Strawberry but he just happens to know the area all around it. You agree, boss? He's lying through his teeth?"

They reach El Paseo Grande and turn right, heading north, back toward LA and the real world. The Pacific sparkles to their left, but its horizon is lost in a brown haze. Caddon says, "Tony, he's lying through his teeth."

"Right, boss."

"Why? What's in it for him? Do the preacher, the fried dentist, and the musician connect? And how does a rich Hollywood musician connect to a freaking anthrax bomb?"

"Don't know, boss. But if you believe the limeys, we'd better find out before Saturday."

Alekos Demos, with a worried frown, watches the FBI men disappear down the hill.

He walks back to the French windows toward the pool. Dragon biceps—what's his name, Romer or Romeo, something like that?—has helped himself to gin and tonic from the cart and is lounging back on a deck chair. He looks up languidly at the approaching musician, takes a sip. Something faintly over-familiar, insolent even, about the body language.

Sad little nonentity, thinks he has a hold over me. I've seen off a dozen guys like you. "Put the booze down, I need you fit to drive. Get dressed, get down the road, and make a call from a public phone in town. I'll give you the number."

"Hey, what am I, your lackey?"

"So long as you're using my pool and drinking my gin, yes. Now move."

Fifteen minutes later, the young man is putting coins in a pay phone and punching numbers. The voice that answers is English, cultured, female. "Mr. Goldstein's office."

"I've been asked to give you a message. I don't understand it."

"Oh, and who asked you? Who might you be?"

"He told me to say this is one of his nancy-boys." *The humiliating bastard.*

A cool, "I see. And the message?"

"He needs to speak to the tin can right away. That's what he said. He says invite the tin can and his friends to the party. Like I say, I don't know what he means."

"You wouldn't. Tell him I'll arrange it. Good-bye."

SEARCH WARRANT:

DOWNTOWN LA, MIDAFTERNOON

"His Honor will see you now."

About frigging time, Your Honor. For two hours Caddon has fumed in the small anteroom to courtroom 341 of the Royal Federal Building, East Temple, downtown LA, unable even to smoke a cigarette. *Laws and Torts,* he's decided by the third or fourth reading, is the most boring magazine ever produced in the history of the universe.

"Remember. Stick to the factual stuff. Let me do the talking on the legalities. We're way out on a limb here." For the tenth time. Caddon grunts. The FBI lawyer is small, female, and Chinese in origin.

Judge Woodman has vertical gray hair and a wrinkled face. His complexion is purplish, which might be due to heart, booze, or sun. He is leaning back, staring quizzically at the FBI agent over half-moon spectacles. Caddon glimpses bright yellow suspenders under the judge's robe and thinks all he needs is overalls, a clay pipe, and a plow. The judge waves a hand at plastic chairs, and Caddon and Ms. Wang spread themselves around the big office. A deli sandwich on the judge's desk lies on top of its plastic casing. It is beginning to curl at the edges, but it reminds Caddon that he is hungry. He has a brief whimsy about asking the judge for the sandwich and being locked up for contempt.

"Okay," says the judge. He has an accent like a midwestern rancher. "Been through your affidavit. Don't like it. Don't like it one little bit. In fact it smells."

Caddon's heart sinks. "Your Honor, this is our first and only lead in the matter. Alekos Demos is a musician who writes scores for movies. He's well known in the business. Lives alone, part of the LA gay scene."

The judge waves sheets of paper. Caddon recognizes them as the affidavit. "I guess I'm missing something. What's the nature of the lead?"

"What it says. A few hours before the bomb exploded, the guys who hired the Pontiac had a boozy lunch with this musician."

There is a silence. Then: "Forgive me, Agent Caddon, but my question was, What is the nature of your lead?"

"That's it."

The judge puffs out his cheeks. "I'll try again. What's the evidence that the lunch was connected with the bomb? Maybe it had to do with his sexual activities."

"Sir, it wasn't a casual meeting. These people were waiting for an hour for Demos to arrive."

"I guess I'm stupid." Judge Woodman scratches his head, trying to look stupid. "Do you want a search warrant because the guy was late for a meeting, or because he's gay, or because he's a musician? Or maybe because he's Greek?"

Ms. Wang says, "Give us a chance here, Your Honor. Because he's connected with two men who pulled an anthrax bomb out of a mine shaft. There could be a lot of lives riding on this, sir."

"I sympathize, but Ms. Wang, you know damned well I can't lawfully issue a warrant without a legal basis. You can't just get a warrant to do anything you like. Now, what I'm asking you for the fourth and I hope the last time, is this: What do you claim is the allowable circumstance for a legal search?"

"Your Honor, the legal basis is obvious. Probable cause that a crime has been committed and that another one—a major atrocity—is about to be committed against American citizens."

The judge takes off his spectacles and wipes them with a handkerchief.

Caddon's frustration boils over. "Look, I know this guy's a pal of the governor . . ."

Ms. Wang shoots Caddon a look of pure invective. Woodman says, gently, "Stop right there, Agent Caddon." He turns to the FBI lawyer. "Justify your probable cause."

"Demos met two of the terrorists a few hours before the bomb went off. His claim that it was a casual meeting was unconvincing. His demeanor when questioned about it was suspicious. He claimed he'd never heard of Strawberry but then changed his story when the agents told him they knew otherwise." This last is an elastic interpretation of Demos's testimony, but she hopes it might slip through.

"The demeanor of the musician," Woodman repeats thoughtfully. "Shifty-eyed, was he?"

Come on, Judge. Ms. Wang says, "Your Honor, case law is clear on this matter. The central issue has to be probable cause. As you know it's not defined in the Fourth Amendment. It's a judicial invention, no more. *Dumbra* versus *United States*, 268 US 435, 1925: The term *probable cause* means less than evidence that would justify condemnation. It doesn't have to be strong enough to prove guilt in a criminal trial."

"You've come anticipating the problem, Ms. Wang, I'm impressed." Woodman taps at a laptop, grunts, and then shambles heavily over to the bookcase. He takes a heavy volume back, flops it down on his desk, and flicks through the pages. "On the other hand, since we're quoting cases, *Byars* versus *United States*, 273 US 28, 1927. Mere assertion isn't enough. The fact that Agent Caddon here declares that Demos is shifty-eyed . . ."

"Come on, sir, *United States* versus *Ventresca*, 1965. Warrants are favored in law and should not be frustrated by the hypercritical interpretations of legal technicians."

"Being shifty-eyed is good enough, then?"

"And there was the meeting." Frustration is creeping into the FBI lawyer's voice.

"You want me to intrude on the rights of everyone these

guys ever spoke to? What would you do with the warrant, anyway?" The judge scans the pages again. "It says here you're trying to pursue this inquiry with discretion, before the bomb incident becomes public knowledge."

Caddon says, "Which could happen at any moment. We'd search the house in his absence. In and out like ghosts. He'd never know we'd been in."

"You must be desperate. You know damned well there are rules. Before a law enforcement officer can break and enter the premises, he has to give notice."

The FBI officer recrosses her legs. "You could issue a no-knock warrant, Your Honor. It can be authorized if there's probable cause to believe that evidence may be quickly destroyed."

"You're pushing your luck, Ms. Wang. That applies to narcotics cases."

"You could and should extend it to the present situation. I believe it's vital, for the protection of Americans, that the FBI has access to this man's home. The Patriot Act allows federal agents, with the permission of the courts, to obtain business records where terrorism affecting national security is concerned. And this is a terrorism case down to its toenails."

Caddon says, before the judge has a chance to open his mouth, "And we want to look at his business records."

"I seem to have missed that bit in the affidavit."

We're losing it. Caddon knew it wasn't going to work, but he said it anyway: "Actually, Your Honor, you're right. We are desperate. Maybe there's another bomb, we just don't know. But we need to find out before it gets used, next time maybe against a conurbation instead of an Indian reservation."

Damn.

Woodman gives Caddon a stony stare. "I guess, ah, Native Americans don't count."

Wang says, "My colleague didn't mean that. It's been a long wait out there."

"Don't lose your cool, Agent Wang, I know exactly what he meant."

Wang says, "It's not as if we're asking to torture him, Judge."

"I know, I know. It's just a little thing, this Alekos Demos won't even know you've been in his house. We're all jittery. Every few weeks we get a security alert. Hell, I have a daughter in New York and a son and grandson in Chicago, do you think I don't want you to get this other bomb? If it exists, and that's a matter we haven't touched on."

"Your Honor . . ."

Woodman raises his hand, cutting off Caddon. "Sometimes I wonder if all these alerts are intended to control us in some way."

"This isn't a political matter, Your Honor."

"But you know damned well where the barricade starts, Ms. Wang. Isn't it tempting, with what's riding on this, to give way on the little thing? In and out like ghosts and he'll never know? But it's a slippery slope, Ms. Wang. The moment you concede on that, you no longer have a limit beyond which you can't go. You end up with Watergate." Woodman bows his head, unconsciously slips a hand under his robe, and pings his suspenders a few times. Then he says, "In my opinion what you're requesting amounts to an unacceptable violation of this citizen's constitutional rights. The request for a search warrant is denied."

"Your Honor . . ."

The judge at last picks up the sandwich and takes a massive bite. With his mouth full he says, "And that's final."

"The governor's friend, right?" Caddon, next to Spada at the wheel, is visibly angry.

"What are you saying, boss?"

"You know what I'm saying."

"You think Judge Woodman was got at?" Spada's tone is incredulous.

"It makes no sense, rejecting a warrant like that. Woodman was got at."

"Boss, the governor can't bend the Justice Department, not even for a pal. It could finish his career."

"If it got out. Take a risk like that, the stakes have to be sky-high."

Spada takes a nervous look in the mirror, slows the vehicle to a trickle. The Dodge truck behind them slows, then accelerates and pulls past swiftly. "It worries me, what you're saying. As if the governor might somehow be in on the UFO and the judge might be bent. That's insane."

"Yeah. I can't believe I said it." Caddon looks out reflectively at the broad city streets. Then: "I want surveillance on the musician, 24/7."

THE MOVIE CRITIC:

BEVERLY HILLS HOTEL, EVENING

"Screw the Constitution," Caddon finally says. "The hell with citizens' rights."

"Exactly my opinion, boss. Judicial oversight is horse manure."

"Can I quote you people?" Ambra asks.

It is now twenty minutes to six, and Ambra Volpe, having snatched a few glorious hours of sleep in the Radisson Wilshire Plaza, has been in the FBI building for almost two hours with Caddon, Spada, and half a dozen other agents. In midafternoon Demos emerged from his La Jolla pad, headed north on the freeway to LA, and ensconced himself in the L'Ermitage Hotel on Burton Way. However, since he has now been questioned by the FBI, he has in effect been alerted, and the team thinks he's unlikely to contact anyone on nefarious business, either in the hotel or in any public place, assuming he's into that sort of thing.

But there's a worrying gap in the hoped-for 24/7 surveillance, a place where, for a few vital hours, not even the FBI can penetrate. The logic connecting Demos to the crashed Arizona UFO is slender to vanishing point in the first place, but they have nothing else and Hardcastle's *mass burial* remains a potent, unspoken phrase driving them to desperation.

Spada's team have found that there is a movie premiere in Burbank that very evening. Demos composed the score for *The Andromeda Dossier* and is a guest. In fact the movie is due to start in an hour and twenty minutes. This party is being held, eccentrically, in a garden center well out of town, in an area called Ramirez Canyon. Their problem is that entry to the aforesaid party is by invitation only, and since a number of major stars are in the movie, security is tight. The center is ringed with an electronically sensitive fence and night-vision cameras. It's a place where 24/7 fails, where Demos knows that he can talk freely with anyone inside. Caddon needs to get someone inside the party like a drowning man needs air. The question of planting someone in the party is involving the FBI agents in ever more inventive scenarios, some of which would do credit to a movie script, and none of which survives scrutiny.

The exchange between Caddon and Spada doesn't reflect any subversive or revolutionary beliefs on their part so much as desperation, compounded by Judge Woodman's suspicious rejection of a reasonable search warrant application and the fact that the movie is due to start in an hour and twenty minutes. Most of all, however, the radical comments reflect the fact that the federal officers have finally seen how to get someone into the party; but to do so, they are going to have to take someone else out. In fact, they are going to have to poison him. And they are feeling bad about that.

Joshua Bernstein is fiftyish, wrinkled, with thinning, curly hair and a permanent, carefully cultivated sour expression. He started his journalistic career covering births and deaths for a small Orange County newspaper and, discovering a talent for wit and sarcasm, found himself drawn first into sports coverage, then politics, and finally into the business of theater and movie criticism. It was in this arena that he found his natural home. A single bad review, delivered with the classic Bernstein wit and sneer, could keep audiences out like a steel barrier, crash a new production, cost a million or two, and damage careers. And the more feared he was, the more he was lionized by those at his mercy.

And so it is that Bernstein finds himself in the Polo Lounge of the Beverly Hills Hotel, rounding off a dinner of lobster pie with zabaglione and sambuca; while Caddon, three tables away, stares reflectively into a glass of bourbon, and Spada, dressed as a waiter, slips a card into the lock of Bernstein's second-floor room.

No warrant applications to corrupt judges, not this time.

Around ten o'clock, Bernstein finishes his fifth sambuca; why not, Universal is picking up the tab. A black girl of stunning beauty, wearing a red cocktail dress, on her own at a nearby table, gives him a coy smile. He replies with a look that says *Wrong sex, darling.* He stands up unsteadily, wonders about a couple of bourbons at the Sunset Lounge, but decides he'd had enough live piano music to last him the rest of the year. Instead he makes his way erratically to his room. He wonders vaguely about using the hotel pool, and even in a fantasy moment thinks about the jogging paths, but it has been a long day. Easier just to watch some crap on TV and then crash out.

In the bathroom he runs water and turns on the controls for the whirlpool tub; in a minute it is foaming like a witch's cauldron. He slips his clothes off and only then sees the silver tray, the champagne bottle, and the crystal goblet on the big oval table, next to a basket of flowers.

FROM THE PRODUCTION TEAM OF *THE ANDROMEDA DOSSIER.* Bernstein tosses the card aside and works on the bottle; the cork pops and hits the ceiling. He sniggers, stumbles toward the oversized walk-in closet, and comes out with a packet of cigars. He switches on the bathroom TV and settles into the hot Jacuzzi, alternating between swigging from the champagne bottle and puffing the Don Tomás.

At first, he thinks it might be the sudden hot water and the cigar, maybe with a little too much alcohol. Then, as he feels his brow begin to sweat, he wonders about the lobster pie. And finally, as nausea and giddiness suddenly take a grip and he struggles out of the whirling water, an unworthy thought enters the noble Bernstein's head: He can't sue for hot water, cigar smoke, or alcohol, but they might pay him to shut up about iffy lobster.

Fifteen minutes later, exhausted and evacuated, he crawls toward the nearest of the three telephones, leaving a trail of vomit and slime. He almost reaches it, gasping and pulling himself up to the desk, when another surge of bloody diarrhea pours down his legs onto the Turkish rug. His stomach seems to be in flames. He manages to lift the receiver, looks at the instructions through blurred eyes, mucus dribbling from his mouth, and then jabs a number. His voice comes out as a croak. "Help."

"Sir?"

"You and your lobster pie." And another painful spasm grips his stomach, and bloody diarrhea pours down his legs again, and he vomits noisily into the mouthpiece, and he thinks maybe he is about to die.

Russian Tide:

THE CONVENT, 1944

VAN DE GRAFF GENERATOR:

MAY 1944

You have to see it from the director's point of view, I tell them. We were struggling for the Fatherland, racing desperately against the incoming Russian tide. What was Hess to tell Goering? Sorry, Fat Hermann, I've just lost you the Second World War. The Reich is about to go down and you're going down with it. Our wonder weapon was sabotaged, you see. What would Fat Hermann say to that? *I quite understand, Hess, think nothing of it*? They're pretty tired, the young ones, and they seem tense about something, but they manage to smile. Hess wasn't smiling in those days. Hess only smiled when he had you by the balls and he was squeezing.

"You have something to tell me, Krafft." Hess's tone was a blend of murder and despair. *I wouldn't want to be in your shoes, Kurt, when you have to face Goering.* And sabotage or not, he had mentally transferred the blame for the explosion onto me.

Four hundred years of Christian holiness surrounded us, seeping out of the gray pillars. The Virgin Mary was recessed into a wall. Some clown had made her a headscarf from a swastika flag, tied in a knot under her chin. Hess and I were walking slowly in step through the chapel. Daylight streaming through the stained-glass windows made multi-colored strips on the flagstones, and the click of our heels echoed from the hard dolomite limestone around us.

"I can do it. We can recover from this."

Hess stopped in midstride. "What are you talking about?"

I rubbed my arms. It wasn't much warmer in here than outside. "The high-pressure gun was always dangerous."

"It was sabotage, Krafft, not mechanical failure. Sabotage of a device for which you carried responsibility."

We resumed our slow walk, the hostility between us almost tangible. "I awoke in the early hours with an idea. It just hit me. Dr. Hess, we don't need high-pressure guns or steel chambers. We can get straight into the hypervelocity regime with a completely different approach. And we can do it soon."

Hess, the drowning man, snatched at the lifeline. "You owe me this. What is this great idea, Krafft?"

"We go for a Van de Graff accelerator."

"You'd better explain that."

Now we were at the Crusader's tomb, Eduardo de Clari. The man was on his back, arms folded across his chest, sword at his side, an expression of piety on his bearded, white-marble face. I wondered about him: Why the piety? A high slaughter-count of Muslims? If we win the war, will we have St. Adolf in a hundred years?

"Krafft?"

"Sorry."

"How?"

"You tip a little thimbleful of fine, electrically charged dust into an evacuated tube. There's a set of metal rings surrounding the tube. You put a huge pulse of electricity into the rings, creating a massive magnetic field. The dust is accelerated along the tube. Daniela's done the calculations, and we think you could get fantastic speeds out of this with a high-enough voltage. Maybe three or four kilometers a second inside a tube just a meter long."

"Time scale?" Hess snapped. Herr Director was taking over again.

"These accelerators already exist. I believe there's one in Leiden University. But we'd need to modify it. If we work like maniacs I could have one up and running inside six weeks."

"I want you to do it in three."

NATZWEILER

THE VOSGES

My heart gave a little jump as I walked into the refectory. Daniela was there, alone, with her back to me. The rest of the refectory was filled with workshop staff and technicians and noise and chatter. The place had an odor of bratwurst and cabbage and coffee. I sat down across from her.

"Hello, Max." She gave me a wan smile. No Heil Hitler this time. She was hollow-eyed and looked exhausted.

"Hello. Have you ordered?" We were having to raise our voices over the babble and the clatter of cutlery and plates.

"Just coffee."

"I think we're almost there with the survival rates."

The Van de Graff accelerator had turned up at the convent within a couple of days. Accompanying it were its entire operating staff from Leiden University, half a dozen men ranging from a senior professor to a sixteen-year-old technician; a surgical team tending a patient. I shared their humiliation when they were assigned to the laundry. Colleagues and equals, sharing straw bales with kitchen staff and chambermaids—forced labor from Poland and Russia! I shared their embarrassment when they turned up in the chapel under guard, unkempt, smelling and shivering with cold. They were sullen and uncooperative and I couldn't blame them. But there was a war on and I needed the accelerator to work. It wouldn't. It would not perform, it was just one big problem. The accelerator hissed and buzzed. The air crackled and stank with ozone. Long spidery arcs of electricity kept spreading into the far corners of the chapel, to the ill-disguised glee of the Dutchmen and the alarm of the guards.

Oberlin found the solution on the third day. A hanging. He marched into the chapel with four guards and hauled out the young technician. The beams in the entrance hall of the convent were high, and it took several throws before the SS sergeant got the rope over it. Daniela had disappeared and reappeared minutes later, breathless and distraught, with Hess in tow. The Dutch professor told the director in anguished tones that the technician was vital to the operation of the machine. Hess didn't believe him. The argument raged back and forth while the boy sobbed, his arms held by two of Oberlin's men and his life in the balance. Hess finally ordered him hanged, ignoring the professor's frantic pleas. The boy kicked as the sergeant hauled on the rope. The Dutchmen watched this demonstration of German authority with expressions that told me we had better not lose the war. Daniela took the director aside, spoke to him quietly and urgently. Whatever she said, Hess nodded curtly, waved the now unconscious boy down, and strode off. After that, work had proceeded at miraculous speed, the machine covering in days what Willi Webber and I had taken months to achieve. Within three weeks— two of them waiting in frustration while the agar plates incubated—we had all the raw experimental data we needed for anthrax spores.

The next step was the dreaded sarin. For this another scientist had been co-opted, an Otto Klein from an IG Farben works, code-named Hochwerk, somewhere near the Polish Protectorate. He was a burly, bearded Nazi absolutely devoid of humor. He came with half a dozen white protective suits, which we had to wear in the presence of the scary chemical. A shower room had to be improvised in the chapel, which involved heavy drilling through the massive stone walls. It took nearly a day just to clear the dust. But he worked efficiently, and in another week we had what we needed for sarin, too, and nobody had died.

Now we just had to analyze the data and develop a weapon to end the war.

"That's terrific, Max, and so quick! So, should we get started on the analysis?"

"I'll bring the figures along to your office after breakfast."

"I've a much better idea. Why don't we get some sandwiches and coffee, have Myers saddle up horses, and do our work in the meadow? It's a lovely morning and we can have a picnic. Just the two of us."

For a second, I thought I was hearing things. I stood up, trying to look nonchalant while wanting to dance on the table. "Good idea. You order some breakfast stuff and I'll collect the data."

No question, a high-speed crash was bad for bugs. Daniela sat on a log, slim ankles poking under her long skirt, a light breeze ruffling her hair. I read out numbers while she calculated and plotted points on a graph.

The vital thing, it turned out, was the shock the bugs experienced when they came to a halt, the momentary slam of driving into a steel plate at huge speed. She calculated the peak shock pressure for each slam of the accelerator. At a third of a kilometer per second, about one in ten thousand bacteria survived the impact. At 1.3 km/second, the number was nearer one in a hundred thousand. At an incredible 5 km/sec, the highest speed we got from the Leiden machine, the tremendous slam yielded a survival rate down to one in ten million, depending on the bug. Daniela used a slide rule and plotted everything out on a logarithmic scale, and everything

Impact Speed (meters/ second)	Shock Pressure 2-Sigma (gigapascals)	Shots Fired	Surviving Fraction (Rhod. eryth.)	Scatter
100.0	0.052	17	96%*	±4.1
250.0	0.13	12	93%*	±4.3
310.0	0.16	9	90%*	±4.0
350	3.0	1	1.5×10^{-4}	
1,300	12.0	1	7.6×10^{-5}	
5,400	78.0	1	1.8×10^{-6}	

*From Plasticine Age. All else Van de Graff. *Bacillus subtilis* spores used for 5.4 km/s shot.

fit beautifully onto a straight line. Our airgun pellet trials, with bugs moving at snail speed and getting soft parachute landings on plasticine, belonged to the Stone Age.

The spores were tougher. But still, at five kilometers a second, about the travel speed of a shock through high explosive, only one in ten thousand spores survived.

"Meaning that if we explode an artillery shell loaded with anthrax spores, we kill nearly all of them." Daniela looked at me meditatively. "That doesn't sound like a convincing weapon, does it?"

Something like relief in her voice? No, impossible. "Never underestimate a good engineer. But yes, we have a problem."

"The sarin's destroyed more easily than the spores."

"I suppose that's because the spores have evolved to protect themselves when the environment gets tough. They just curl up and wait for better times. They'll live more or less forever unless they're blown to bits." *Is there something between you and Hess, Daniela? I've seen the way he looks at you and the way you look back. Can you possibly be interested in that worm?* "We've reached a key point. I suppose the next thing is to find some way around this, and find out what the lethal dosages are for these horrors."

Daniela stood up and brushed crumbs from her skirt. "We should be getting back. Report to the others."

This close, the urge to grab her and kiss her was almost beyond my power to resist. I blurted out, "What is it between you and Hess? I'm sorry, I shouldn't have asked. None of my business."

She kissed me lightly on the lips, a hand on my chest. She must have felt my heart hammering. "Dear Max. I know you like me a lot. But keep your distance from me, darling. There are things about me you don't know and I can't tell."

The Dutchmen disappeared a couple of days later, along with the Van de Graff accelerator. Bosch mentioned that he'd seen them going down the hill as they had come up it, in the back of a truck, under escort from SS men. They can't be returned to the university, knowing what they now know, I said. Where will they be taken?

Not our problem, Bosch said.

I agreed. Not our problem. Neither is Sister Lucy.

Bosch gave me a puzzled look but something told him not to pursue the matter.

A plume of ocher dust shot into the air and the deep *whump!* of the explosion reached us seconds later. The dust began to drift downwind, and the noise echoed back from a score of mountains before settling down into a decaying, rolling thunder.

"What are you playing with? Anthrax spores?" Hess wanted to know as we jumped into the little Kugelwagen.

"Rhodococcus erythropolis," I said. "Among other soil bacteria. All quite harmless, you needn't worry about turning blue or foaming at the mouth. *Schnell.* I need to get there quickly, while the microorganisms are still alive."

"What are you doing with them?" Hess adopted a snappy tone to show that he didn't approve of my lack of deference, my man-to-man attitude. I had it nicely calculated: not quite insubordinate, but neither showing the respectful tone Hess felt he was due.

I slammed into gear and accelerated away even before Herr Director had pulled the truck door shut. "This is a final check, Kurt. Lab results against a field trial. If the figures match, we're ready for the next stage." The truck hurtled at an angle down a steep meadowy slope, the grass slippery with rain, toward a track skirting a gorge. Hess gripped the dashboard with white hands.

"Hey, easy!" Hess called out in alarm as the truck hammered into a pothole near the edge of the road. I caught him glimpsing down at a fast, tumbling Alpine stream about fifty meters below us.

Edith was already scrambling into the bomb crater, followed by a couple of khaki-clad soldiers. As the truck slowed, Hess said, "Krafft, how would you like a weekend in Strasbourg?"

"Strasbourg? In the Vosges? I'd love that. I might get some climbing in. And it'll get me out of this nuthouse. I assume there's a catch."

"Don't be so cynical, you're too young."

"It's the Russian front. It puts years on you."

"It's your own fault for letting it get to you. You have to retain your vision. 'The trick is to do hard things and yet remain a decent fellow.' Heinrich Himmler, Reichsführer-SS."

I switched off the engine. "I know what you're getting at. 'We all have our feet in the gutter, but some of us are looking at the stars.' "

"That's the spirit." Hess stuck his jaw out, Mussolini-style. We jumped out and marched toward the smoking crater. The grass around it was flattened outward from the blast.

"Oscar Wilde, English homosexual."

"You're not as smart as you think, Krafft. I happen to know he was Irish. Well, hurry up and còllect your soil. We're booked into the Swissotel in Strasbourg and we have a flight laid on. Just Edith, you, and me."

"I haven't climbed for years."

"I have a big treat for you, and it's not going up and down

mountains." Hess gave an unpleasant grin that left me with a vague sense of unease.

The entrance gate was a high wooden scaffolding, over which was a simple notice: NATZWEILER-STRUTHOF. A double ring of low, barbed-wire fences stretched around a few acres of sloping ground. Outside the fences were a grass meadow, then trees, and beyond that, in the distance, hills poking through a morning mist. Gray-painted wooden watchtowers were spaced at intervals just outside the fence. Inside were closely packed rows of broad, squat buildings, green-roofed. Hundreds of prisoners of both sexes stood or sat huddled in groups, in blue-and-white-striped tunics, breaths steaming in the freezing air. I began to feel my skin creep without being sure why. I spotted, in an open area that I assumed was for roll calls, a wooden gallows. *Scheisse.*

"The place is quiet just now," the SS officer said, offering chairs with a wave of the hand. A stove was burning warmly in the hut. He looked as if he was fresh from university, smartly dressed, but the shine on his boots was marred by smears of something. "Most of the inmates are used by DEST . . ."

"DEST?" Hess asked, warming his hands at the stove.

"The SS Materials Company," the officer explained. "We have a granite quarry nearby. It makes sense to get something useful out of the flotsam they send to us. They'll be back late tonight." He smiled knowingly. "Those who make it through the day, that is. But we have no problems with labor supply. They just keep coming."

"What sort of people do you have here?"

"Several hundred NN prisoners." He smiled again. "There I go, more acronyms. *Nacht und Nebel.*"

"Night and Fog. You mean . . ."

"Enemies of the state. People who just disappear, taken by the Gestapo in the night."

"Naturally families and friends wonder where they have gone."

"And naturally they never find out. The midnight knock,

all part of the rich tapestry of control. Well, lady and gentlemen, for you the mystery of Night and Fog is solved. This is where the disappeared end up."

The officer stood up and walked over to the window. Frost had melted on the glass, and he wiped the condensation away with a handkerchief. "We also have quite a few partisans, Norwegians, French, Belgians, and Dutch. Four English saboteurs awaiting special treatment, all female, and we have a steady supply of Gypsies."

Hess turned his head to the window. "It's a beautiful setting."

"And isolated. Tucked away in the mountains. That's one of its great attractions. Nobody knows about this place, even less about what goes on here. Obviously the prisoners can't send any correspondence."

"And yet you're only forty minutes from Strasbourg."

"The university's medical faculty finds it convenient. Our laboratory attracts a steady stream of researchers. Professor Hirt travels to someplace in Poland and brings back prisoners with interesting skeletal structures for the university. I'm told they have one of the finest collections in Europe."

"He brings them in alive?" I asked.

The SS man blinked in surprise. "Naturally. We deflesh the skeletons here. The university has a fine anatomical display of skulls. And Professor von Haagen does excellent work here on wound infection, mustard gas symptoms, typhus, smallpox, diphtheria, and cholera. Rest assured we have the necessary facilities to meet your requirements. Are you all right?"

The question was directed at me. "Just a little light-headed. It's been a long trip."

"You needn't have any qualms about using the prisoners for your own purposes, you know. They all come into the category of lives not worth living, or already condemned."

Hess stood up. "We should get busy. There's a tight deadline on our project. And poor Max looks as if he needs some fresh air."

"Of course. I've asked our camp doctor, Werner Rohde, to show you the laboratory and the gas chamber. You have full

use of them for the next two days. The chamber is just outside the wire. It's small but useful for fast turnaround. Beyond
that—well, there is pressure from other groups, you know."
He laughed lightly.

"Two days will suffice. Thank you very much."

"Glad to help. I'll get a few of my men and you can just
take a stroll around the camp. Select as you go, that's what
they're here for. How many do you need?"

The question was directed at Hess, who said, "We'll need
calibration curves for a wide range of body weights. Also we
want to know the time taken to die as a function of dosage."
He turned to me: "Krafft? How many?"

How many prisoners? I felt my face going pale. I stood
up. "I need some air. I'm not very good on winding roads." I
was conscious of Hess, Edith, and the SS officer's eyes following me to the door. Edith was full of matronly disapproval, Hess was tight-lipped and angry. The SS man seemed
puzzled.

I stood in the mud and breathed in the air. It was cold and
clear but carried a smell of something—something unpleasant. I couldn't identify it.

How did I get into this?

The others emerged from the hut. The SS officer was
pulling on gloves. He and Hess marched off chattering in
the direction of a low, whitewashed building with a long
metal chimney projecting horizontally from a wall before
turning skyward. Hess threw me a glance that didn't bode
well for my future. Edith joined me, offering a wartime cigarette. I shook my head.

"You're shivering," she said, cupping her hands around a
match. She nodded toward the gallows, about a hundred meters away. "It looks like there's less shit round about there."

"I don't suppose it's a popular meeting place. It's not exactly the Tiergarten." We walked slowly toward the gallows.

And how am I going to get out of it?

Edith took in a lungful of smoke, breathed it out through
her nostrils. "You're not giving a good impression, Max. How
did you imagine we were going to find the lethal dosage?"

"Never gave it a thought."

"You're a liar. You must have guessed."

"I'm just an engineer. If you'd asked me, I'd have said animals."

"All this condemned human material, assembled here for experimentation, and you want to use animals? I've never heard anything so stupid! Some things just have to be done, that's all. We've just got to win this war. Do you want the Bolsheviks in your precious Tiergarten? We're fighting for the survival of the Reich. No, we're fighting for the Aryan race itself. Our work can save us."

I nodded in the direction of a huddled group. "There are children here."

Edith puffed sharply at her cigarette. "Oh, snap out of it, for Christ's sake. Medical research with these types is perfectly legal. It's been authorized by Himmler himself. You're going to help us choose suitable subjects whether you like it or not. It's your plain duty. Now, what are your requirements?"

"I won't do it."

"God in Heaven. Don't say that to Hess. He'd put you inside here, it's just the sort of bizarre joke that would appeal to him."

"The possibility has occurred to me."

"If you thought of it, and I thought of it, even an idiot like Hess will think of it. What's the matter with you? Look, Max, you're one of the brightest people I know but you're also one of the most stupid. Have you thought about the consequences if you refuse?"

"For the war effort?"

"For Max Krafft."

I frowned, but stayed silent. We'd reached the gallows, which was suddenly acquiring a very personal significance.

"Hess doesn't like you, Max, all he needs is an excuse. Look, I can't tell you not to have a conscience about this. But I can ask whether you're going to put your personal feelings above your duty to your country."

I closed my eyes, breathed in the stench. Edith waited until

I'd opened them again. "I don't like it, either, but someone has to do it. Are you going to stand back feeling all righteous and superior while the rest of us do your dirty work for you? Hey you! Come here! Over here! And you!"

Reluctantly, a Gypsy boy of about fourteen shambled toward us, followed by a large, heavily built man. The boy's face was filthy, and insects were crawling around his hair. He was skinny and trembling. The man removed his blue-and-white cap deferentially. "They must feed you well, with a belly like that," said Edith. "How long have you been here?"

"Two days, madame." The accent was foreign, perhaps Dutch.

Edith turned to me. "There, I've got you a couple already. Two people at the extreme ends of the mass spectrum. Tell you what, I'll select them, you won't even have to choose them. All you have to do is weigh them, measure the dosage they get, and see how long they last. Put crosses on a piece of paper, that's all that's being asked of you."

I said, "What's your name, little one?"

Edith, sharply: "Don't speak to them that way."

"Bleeker, sir." The boy had understood German; his voice was weak and shaky.

"And you? What do you do?"

"Kloppman, sir. I'm a baker from Leiden." The man's eyes were brimming with dread.

"Clear off, the pair of you."

Edith dropped the stub of her cigarette, looked as if she was going to grind it into the frozen ground, then changed her mind. "Even easier for you, Max. Just fetch the vials from the back of the car and bring them over to the laboratory. That will keep you nice and detached from the process, won't it? Your conscience can run to that? Just fetch the vials. In exchange, we'll keep your skull out of Dr. Hirt's fine collection."

The three-point rule. Three points of contact, three limbs holding on. Toes wedged in; left fist, red and raw, jammed in a crack. Right hand exploring.

I ease myself along the limestone face. Sleet is falling and the cold is marrow-deep, penetrating, ferocious. I welcome it, love the pain. The cliff face curves. The tree line is now below me and I look down at the jagged limestone slabs three hundred meters below. On my own; no ropes; light fading; rock beginning to overhang: I think maybe I've lost my mind.

Chimney now visible. Easing into it, spread-eagled, groping at the limit. Cheek against hard icy wet slippery rock. Taking big gulps of breath—exertion, fear, rage, whatever. Insanity. The grass and rock on the traverse behind me will now be ice-coated: can't go back. But now I see that the chimney flares upward, a wedge ascent won't work: can't go up, either. Stuck, well and truly stuck.

Now I spot a crack on the far wall of the chimney, finger-thick. Would have to break the three-point rule, leap across the gap like a monkey.

Three hundred meters below, my grave, waiting. Cloud drifts over it. Solid cloud, made from big hunks of cotton wool, it'll catch me if I fall, I'll float gently down.

Fuck the three-point rule. Fuck the Reich. Fuck the Führer and his gang of midgets.

I tense up, take a deep breath, and leap for the crack.

THE SUPERMEN:

CONVENT WINE CELLAR

"The origin of the Aryan race lies in outer space. We entered the atmosphere as tiny shoots encased in ice. Our leaders are descended from the Vikings, and our homeland was a huge empty territory of mountains and forests. We conquered that wilderness, we were huge and strong and fierce, and we intermarried with no other race. *Blut und Boden*. That is our cosmic inheritance."

"Blood and soil, right. Raise you a Médoc." My speech was slurred and my mouth felt numb. I was freezing, even in the greatcoat with its collar pulled up. I corkscrewed the bottle open and slid it across the oak table. It cleared a path through a century of dust.

Otto Klein, the man from IG Farben, was too busy pontificating to notice the cold. "Your problem, Max, is that you have no feel for history. No understanding of the forces that have molded us. You know of Hoerbiger's Cosmic Ice?"

"Two pairs, you win. I've heard of it—some rubbish." The cellar smelled old and musty and was lined with racks of wine. The far end was lost in gloom apart from a crucifix on the wall, its silver reflecting light from a few candles on the table. Half a dozen wine bottles stood open between us. It was well after midnight, and the candles were beginning to gutter. We were trying to get drunk as quickly as possible.

Oberlin's men had discovered the secret cellar only that morning. A low, heavy oak door, its key long missing, had given away to a few blows with a sledgehammer. The origin of the wine cellar was a mystery. Edith guessed the wine was to provide hospitality to visiting bishops and the like.

Klein sniffed at it, then poured a quarter of the bottle into a cup and gulped back a mouthful. He belched, wiped his lips with his sleeve, and said, "Wonderful. One of the grand crus. It takes forever to develop but when it's ready!"

"You were saying. Ice."

"The Greek epic tales did not originate under soft Mediterranean skies, but in the cold Baltic. They were brought south by our ancestors and handed down through the generations. The heroic tales they tell are theirs. We came from ice, we grew powerful in ice."

"I get you. Troy was really in Norway."

"And it has taken an Austrian, Hans Hoerbiger, an engineer like you, to put the Jewish scientists in place just as the Führer has cleansed the nation of the Jewish infection."

"Your call."

"Once upon a time a star exploded. The water from this star condensed into blocks of ice in interstellar space. A ring of this ice formed our solar system, with many planets, only a few of which still exist. Our earth had several moons."

"At the risk of sounding stupid, where did these moons go, Otto?"

"One by one they spiraled down to earth, disintegrating as they fell. The last such falling moon is remembered by our early ancestors. They recorded them in myth whose meaning has all but vanished. Note how the Greeks, and before them the Babylonians, describe gods battling it out in the sky, hurling weapons to earth that flatten forests, set the land on fire, and create giant tidal waves. Note how the Midgard serpent straddles the sky, burning up everything below it, destroying whole kingdoms. These are tales of real events, Krafft, handed down through the ages until the reality is forgotten and today we think they are just fairy tales."

"They're not?"

"One day our moon, too, will spiral down to the earth, breaking into pieces and plunging us into another ice age, like the one from which our ancestors emerged."

"I'm sure you're right. And it's your call."

But Klein had the face of a drunken evangelist; there was no stopping him. "As the ice age passed, our race became soft. We gradually lost our roots, we dwindled into modernity. It has taken a genius like Adolf Hitler to gather up once again all the peoples of Germania and return us to the path of strength, communion with nature, and racial purity."

"I said your call."

Klein waved cigar smoke away from his eyes and leaned back. His jacket was unbuttoned, and there was a red wine stain on his shirt. He fanned out his cards and looked speculatively over them at me.

"I know things about you, Krafft."

"I suspect Oberlin has asked you to spy on me. Any defeatist talk, lack of enthusiasm for the war, or similar tendencies."

"Landed family, old money. Connected with the duchess of Sachsen-Anhalt and the Hanfstaengls, all of you financial supporters of our Führer in the early days. You have plenty of society friends . . ."

"Spoken with a sneer, my dear Otto. You sound like our director."

". . . but you're not a club man. Entitled to use the *von* prefix but for some reason you choose not to do so. Catholic; no Jews in your ancestry at least as far back as the Thirty Years' War. Nominally a party member but in fact you're disappointingly apolitical. Too good for us, are you?"

"Two pairs again. So what are you going to report?"

"A failure to embrace the National Socialist cause with enthusiasm. A dangerous individualism. A tendency toward insubordination. But basically a good German and an invaluable member of the team."

"I'm grateful."

"You're not drinking. Did you know, Max, that the ancestors of our race lived on a great northern island, Atlantis? Also known as Thule? Even you know that Atlantis sank below the waves in a great cataclysm. After it sank, there was a diaspora of the survivors. We spread to northern Europe and the Middle East." The man's face was flushed, and his eyes were shining.

I half filled an enamel mug and took a sip. It could probably have done with another couple of years. *Where are the nuns?* That question again; Catholic saint struggling with SS sinner. "Your deal," I reminded Klein.

He gulped back the wine as if he were at some *Bierfest.* Some dribbled unnoticed down from the corner of his mouth. He shuffled the deck clumsily, cigar in hand, dealt the cards, and held his close to his face, concentrating. "Ancient Germany preserved that Atlantean civilization. They kept our race strong and pure through a program of eugenics. They preserved the strong and rejected the weak."

"Rejected the weak? What does that mean in plain language?"

Klein adopted a *one must be hard* expression over the top of his cards. "*Lebensunwertes,* life unworthy of life. Conditions were too harsh to support the unsupportable. Read *Germania,* by Tacitus—in the Latin, of course, unless you're illiterate. There you will learn something else: We were free from all taint of racial intermarriage. Tacitus notes that we were a distinct, unmixed race, unlike any others. That is how we lived then and how we will live again."

"Painting ourselves with woad?"

"Mankind is a rabble led by an elite. We need supermen and super-races. Do you think life has evolved by cooperation? No, it has progressed by the struggle to survive, by the strong eradicating the weak, the intelligent eradicating the stupid, the superior eradicating the inferior. Without this process we would never have emerged from a prehuman state at all. We would indeed still be painting ourselves with woad, Max. That is why our Aryan race must conquer the inferior ones. That is why we must remain strong and uncontaminated. We owe the strength and purity we have now to our ancient pagan culture, kept alive by the Armenschaft. Just one card?"

"This gets more bizarre by the minute. The who?"

"A secret order. The knowledge of our Atlantean civilization was encoded and given to the Rabbis in the form of the Kabbalah."

"The Rabbis, I see."

"Did you know that Jesus was an Aryan? Raise you the last bottle."

"*Mein Gott,* Otto, how much of this drivel do you believe?"

"All of it. The Jews would not have killed one of their own. And medieval Europe, with its Knights Templar and its monasteries"—Klein waved the wine bottle around—"preserved the ancient, Aryan way of life."

"So when did the rot set in?"

"Your tone is noted, but luckily for you I am drinking Château Margaux. Had it been some cheap Languedoc . . ." Klein made a throat-cutting gesture. "The rot, as you call it, set in with the spread of modern liberal ideas. Nietzsche, Gobineau, Haeckel, all foresaw the dangers of racial contamination with inferiors such as Indians and Negroes, reminded us of the superiority of the Germanic peoples. Look at your skull."

"Sorry?"

"It's Nordic. As are those of Daniela, Edith, and Hess. What our scientists call dolichocephalic. You are all plainly Aryan and plainly superior human beings. Bosch I'm not so sure about. His skull is more rounded, more *Homo alpinus.* I suspect his bloodline has Jewish contamination somewhere up the line. The Jews and the Slavs, they are brachycephalic"— Klein slurred the word—"short and broad. These are the *untermenschen,* the inferior races who threaten to dilute our Germanic genius." Wreaths of cigar smoke were scattering the candlelight and half hiding the Farben chemist's face.

"I was facing these Slavs on the battlefield not long ago. The word *inferior* didn't spring to mind."

Klein paused to refresh his dried throat straight from the bottle. "But through it all, despite the corrupting liberalism of the Habsburg Empire, despite the rise of Bolshevism, our old ways were secretly preserved. The Armenschaft evolved into several lodges, and by the early twentieth century the chief among these was the Thule Society. I have heard rumors"—he tapped the side of his nose knowingly—"that they created the German Workers Party to attract a mass membership. It was the Führer who took this party and molded it into the German National Socialist Movement. And it was the Führer who has taken our defeated and betrayed country from the North Cape to Africa, from Calais to the Caucasus. We are privileged to be present at the delivery of . . . Ach!" I'd laid out a flush, but my stomach was beginning to revolt, and I declined the offered wine.

A couple of candles had died, and the others were under way. The dying light, thrown upward on his face and the smoke, was giving Klein a demonic look. It reminded me of some image of Faust I'd seen—where, where? In the Berlin Opera House? No, it was an old Fritz Lang movie starring Max Schreck, and it wasn't Faust, it was Nosferatu. "So you see, Max, there is an unbroken line of descent from our Atlantis heritage to our National Socialist Movement. The Führer, and Reichsführer-SS Himmler, are reestablishing our ancient values, purifying our Germanic race, restoring it to its true place at the pinnacle of evolution."

I threw my cards down. "This is what the Macaronis call a fiasco. I've had enough. I'm off to bed."

"What's the matter, Max? You look nervous." Another candle died, and Klein stood up unsteadily. He staggered, knocked his chair over, and gave a high-pitched laugh. "You're not scared of the dark, are you?"

"Not the dark, Otto. The Dark Age. The one we're creating."

THE FLYING CIRCUS:

DANIELA'S STUDY

I endured a sweaty, sleepless night, embroiled in damp sheets, the long wakeful periods interspersed by brief, frightening dreams. A bloodstained meat hook kept recurring, and an Alsatian, and a terrified boy—a weird hybrid between Bleeker and a blond-haired Hitler Youth. The images were so lurid that I wondered if I'd inhaled a tiny quantity of the nerve gas. At one point I awoke choking, panicking, and gasping for breath. I groped for my watch and the light switch—it was three in the morning. Daniela was still playing, chords of Chopin just audible through the open window. But at last, with the sky growing light through a chink in the blackout curtain, exhaustion drove me to sleep.

Half an hour later an army orderly knocked stiffly on my door. A red-faced young subaltern, buttons shiny on his tunic; I'd seen him in the canteen. "Standartenführer Dr. Hess requests that you have breakfast promptly this morning. He has something to announce in Dr. Bauer's office at eight o'clock." I listened to the soldier receding down the corridor, *march-march, knock-knock,* the message being repeated word for word in a loud, strident voice; the embodiment of Prussian military virtue: no brain necessary, just a well-trained spinal cord.

Hess made his theatrical entrance at three minutes past

eight. I'd brought in a cup of black coffee and put it with shaky hands on a table. I was nursing a monstrous headache—was it the wine, or a whiff of nerve gas?—and my throat was raw from the night's choking. Klein had the complexion of a man hovering between life and death. He caught my eye and managed a bleak smile.

The director marched importantly into the room and dumped sheets of paper on the desk in front of the blackboard. "Heil Hitler! I have the lethal dosage for tabun 146, and it's wonderful." His eyes were shining. Bosch rubbed a hand tensely over his mouth. "Shut the door, Dr. Zimmermann. Let's keep this among the six of us."

Edith closed the door, and Hess continued. "A raindrop. That's all it takes, a raindrop. A one-millimeter sphere of our nerve agent. Put a single drop on your skin, and you die."

Bosch blinked. "Unbelievable. How did you find that out?"

I snapped, "Don't ask stupid questions." I was suddenly gripped by an insane desire to kill all of them.

Hess turned a chair backward and straddled it; they did this in American movies. "Ignore Max, our heroic SS man has a weak stomach. And it goes by body weight. The calibration is a hundredth of a milligram for each kilogram of body weight—can you believe that?" He held up a piece of graph paper showing about a dozen crosses scattered about a thick straight line, ran a nicotine-stained finger along the line.

The bottom cross, that would be little Bleeker. The top one would be the baker. Had Hess needed all the crosses for the straight line? Couldn't he have skimped on one or two? Maybe sacrificed a decimal place in exchange for three lives? The nightmares flickered at the back of my mind, threatening my sanity. I sensed something just on the edge of my vision, caught Daniela giving me the briefest glance, her dark eyes full of expression. But meaning what? Disapproval? A warning, *Keep yourself under control*? But why should she warn me? Confused, I looked away quickly.

Hess, straddling the chair backward, was in his element. "What we have to do now is match scenarios of destruction of military interest to a practical weapon. Krafft, you're the munitions man. Here you are, summoned to the Eagle's Nest. You are bringing the Führer a beautiful birthday present, a big weapon to gladden his heart. What would you like to bring him?"

"I have a big weapon?" There was an outburst of ribald laughter from the men. Edith put a hand over her mouth.

Hess flushed. "This is not a subject for stupid humor. I can tell you this. We can tap into the industrial might of the Reich. If we wish, we can ask for hundreds of tons to be created."

I felt myself going pale. "Did I hear you say hundreds of tons?" *Does this idiot want to wipe out the human race?*

Daniela was smiling. "We could turn London into a giant cemetery."

"Only if we can deliver it." Hess was still red-faced in the morning sun streaming through the big windows. He scowled. "Think of something, a present for the Führer."

"Smuggle a big one into Trafalgar Square and set it off."

I'd intended it as an absurdity. But to my horror, Hess was nodding his approval. "Now, that's what I call thinking big. Let's get a handle on this. Daniela, use your mathematics. What would it take to destroy a city? Even London? Show us the theoretical possibilities. Then we can back off and look at the real-world prospects."

I watched her all the way to the blackboard, the slim waist, the slight, unconscious sway of her hips; it was enough to drive a monk mad. I watched her as she paced up and down for a minute, unconsciously tapping her teeth with a piece of chalk. Then she glanced up and said, "If we could carpet an area ten kilometers long by five wide with our magic gas, we'd take out the Churchill gang, the English War Office, the whole British government. We'd decapitate England."

Hess stood up. This was the kind of talk he was wanting to hear, and anyway, straddling the chair backward was beginning to strain his thighs. He stood at the other end of the blackboard from Daniela. Encouragement flowed out of him telepathically. "An act that, if threatened against other English cities, would finish the war in the west. And then we could turn it against the Bolsheviks in the east. Result, victory!"

Klein was shaking his skull-like head. "If only."

Hess turned to Daniela. "How would you do it?"

Daniela narrowed her eyes thoughtfully, and seemed to be talking half to herself. "Rain, Kurt. A drizzle so light that just a single raindrop hits each Londoner. We'd have to get liquid sarin high up and disperse it as a fine mist. Let it drift with the wind and settle down over the city like a blanket." She began to scribble on the blackboard. "Say we have a mild breeze, maybe ten meters a second. What's the falling speed of a tiny raindrop, say a tenth of a millimeter across?"

"How would I know something like that?" Hess asked.

Edith said, "I'd guess a millimeter a second."

Daniela said, "It's a question of balancing forces. The weight of the drop is balanced by the resistance of the air it's falling through." She turned to the blackboard, scribbled equations.

"Don't give me abstract mathematics. What are you, a white Jew? Give me real numbers," Hess demanded. "Krafft, what's the density of air?"

"At sea level? A thousand times down on sarin."

Bosch said, "So it's down to the size of the droplets?"

Daniela completed her scribbling. "Yes. If your lethal raindrop is a tenth of a millimeter in radius, it'll fall at four-tenths of a millimeter per second. You weren't far off, Edith."

Hess asked, "Say our raindrop is falling at four-tenths of a millimeter per second and being blown along in the wind at ten meters a second. How high do we have to start it, say we want to blanket ten kilometers?"

I said, "Ten meters up."

"Rubbish, Krafft. You have to start it higher than the rooftops. At least a hundred meters up." I nodded, irritated by the fact that the humorless Nazi was right.

Daniela scribbled some more. "A blanket ten kilometers long, five wide, and say a hundred meters deep has a volume of—"

"Five cubic kilometers," Edith interrupted.

"Right again," Daniela said. "Now think of a barrel of air.

Say a good English citizen in a breeze is exposed to a hundred barrels of air in ten seconds."

"In ten seconds the raindrop falls so much." Edith held a finger horizontally.

"Exactly. We just need one drop of sarin in those hundred cubic meters, which means, for blanketing London to a depth of a hundred meters"—scribble scribble, the chalk giving a nerve-jarring squeak—"five hundred million drops. We need to blanket London in a fine mist, invisibly fine." In this male-dominated company, the women seemed to be running the discussion.

Hess said, "I told you the lethal dose is half a milligram for an average human. That's the weight of your raindrop, half a milligram."

"So that works out at"—scribble scribble again—"half a ton. If this stuff has the same density as water, we could put that in a sphere—"

Edith was clapping her hands. "A meter across. We can wipe out London with a bomb a meter across! Oh joy, oh Jerusalem!"

"What a present!" Hess's eyes were shining. "But could we do it? Could we make something to match Daniela's figures?"

Bosch was pacing up and down at the back of the room like a restless lion. "Dispersal. That's the big issue. How to disperse that amount of material over a city. What's the actual mechanism of death?"

Hess was still on a high. "You should have seen it. At sublethal doses the victim got a runny nose, headache, hallucinations, and ended up foaming at the mouth, like a rabid dog. A bit higher and they had problems breathing, then they would go into these spectacular convulsions. Soon they would lose consciousness and die. But the super-lethal doses, they were amazing. The prisoners went into huge convulsions within seconds. They choked to death, whether from the stuff foaming out of their mouths or from loss of control of breathing I don't know and I don't care."

I said, "There was a reduction in something called cholinesterase. It seems this stuff controls muscles, and the nerve gas destroys it. Meaning your brain can't control your body. You just can't function and you can't stop shaking." *I'm one of you. Create that impression.*

Christ, I am *one of you.*

Daniela had been calculating some more on the board. Now she turned to me. "Max, you're our deliveryman. What do you think of a one-ton bomb? Could you explode it at height, let the wind carry the aerosol over London?"

Bosch said, "You would just get a thin stream. It would be useless."

"We're forgetting something. Willi Webber and I found that the shock from high explosive destroys nearly everything, bacteria, spores, sarin."

Klein was pacing up and down. "You know this for a fact?"

"I've just spent months proving it."

Bosch's tone was challenging. "You're the clever engineer, Max. Think of something that will disperse without destroying, like carrying the bugs along on a plume, or spraying them. What about something like an American crop duster, crisscrossing London?"

Hess laughed. "Carrying a ton? We'd need lots of them, a regular flying circus, weaving around the barrage balloons as they sprayed. I can't go to Hermann Goering with that."

Edith was pacing up and down, too, her hands on top of her head. "Anyway, you'd need extremely fine nozzles, and I don't know if these even exist. Even if they do, they'd take forever to disperse the lethal dosage."

Hess said, "The English won't allow our Luftwaffe to fly up and down as if they were spraying a field, and that's that. No further discussion of that notion."

Klein looked across at me. "The Führer has been bombarding London with vengeance rockets. They must carry a ton of warhead. What about it, Max? Could we disperse anthrax from the warheads a kilometer up?"

Daniela said, "These things must come in at two or three kilometers a second. Anything you did in that line would just give local dispersion, not citywide."

"Come up with something." Hess gave a ghoulish grin.

"And don't forget anthrax, the spores thereof. I'm hoping that Daniela will tell us we could kill a million Londoners with it. I want the stench from the corpses to reach France."

"What's the lethal dosage?" Edith wanted to know.

"It's high," Hess admitted. "Ten thousand spores."

"They have to be breathed in?" Daniela asked.

"They have to be breathed in. They're about five microns across, just the right size for getting stuck in your lungs. Any smaller and you'd breathe them back out, much bigger and they'd get trapped in your throat, where they're less effective."

"Okay, we can work on that. Say we take in half a liter of air every time we breathe, and say we take a breath every five seconds. If we can create a mist that will hang in the air for, say, five minutes, then our Londoners are breathing in"—she counted on her fingers—"thirty liters of London air."

"That comes out at a lethal dose of three spores per cubic centimeter," Bosch said. "Completely invisible! Wonderful, wonderful. Multiply that by five cubic kilometers to get the number of spores . . ."

Bosch was writing on paper, racing Daniela on her blackboard. He looked up and said, "Seven and a half tons," just as she was writing the number on the board.

"Useless." Bosch crumpled his paper. "Where do we get that amount of spores?"

"No, not useless." Hess was shaking his head. "We could get that amount. I've been speaking to people in Spandau. They can produce huge amounts from liquid cultures. You should have seen their vat, just like a huge beer fermentation vat. They'll make twenty of them if we want. If anthrax is desiccated and kept out of sunlight, it will last for centuries. It's a natural for a weapon. And I don't believe your seven and a half tons. All we need to do is create an anthrax mist that lingers for an hour over London. If we can do that, we do the job. Think of it! An invisible miasma spreading over London, like a medieval plague."

"What are the symptoms?" That question again. This time Daniela was asking. I thought there was a trace of unsteadiness in her voice, but dismissed it as imagination. *God, I need to sleep.*

"It takes a day or two to get a hold. It begins like flu, but the fever just keeps rising. Soon you can hardly breathe. Then you go into shock, then a coma. Mortality is eighty percent, better even than smallpox."

"Sounds like a dream," Bosch said. "I agree with you, Kurt, we should pursue the anthrax option also."

"How do we get the fine mist? The invisible miasma? That's the brick wall. How to disperse our magic potions without destroying them? High explosives are out. Crop dusters are out. What's left? I want you people to tell me." Hess sat down and put his feet up on a desk, steepling his hands and narrowing his eyes. I suddenly realized that the man, having no ideas of his own, was fishing in the intellectual pond around him. And if we gave him any ideas, he would no doubt collect the credit when he transmitted them to Goering.

The director, having done his deep-thinker pose, stood up and marched toward the door. He turned. "You will give me the design for a working weapon. You will do so within five days." He waited until the howls of protest had died down. "This has been a wonderful morning." He clicked his heels and gave the fascist salute. "Heil Hitler!"

"Heil Hitler," I chanted with the others. *Arschloch.*

Los Angeles

SUNDAY

INVITATION TO A MOVIE PREMIERE:

SUNDAY EVENING

First contact, the critical point of an infiltration. Sometimes scary, always nerve racking. Ambra takes a deep breath while Caddon nods his encouragement. She says, "Hello? My name is Linda Black. Joshua Bernstein's assistant."

"That's Mr. Bernstein of the *Chicago Tribune*?" A faint rustle of paper, and then, "He's on our guest list for this evening."

"He is. Unfortunately Mr. Bernstein's been taken ill, quite suddenly. He has a touch of gastroenteritis and he's not going to make it to the premiere."

"I'm very sorry to hear that." A hesitation, then: "Does this mean the *Tribune* won't be able to do a review?"

"Joshua's keen to do it if he possibly can. He wondered if I might come along to the premiere as a stand-in. I know it's not very satisfactory, but if you could arrange for a reel to be sent to the Cinema Room here for a private screening, he thought he might be well enough to view it tomorrow and catch the Wednesday edition."

"That would be terrific, Ms. Black. I'll get a ticket to you right away. Where are you staying?"

"We're at the Pink Palace." Alias the Beverly Hills Hotel; Ambra uses the popular nickname. "Incidentally, do you have a guest list?"

"Yes of course. Why?"

"I'd like to do a little homework on people involved in the movie."

A tiny hesitation. "It's a bit irregular."

Spada has an expression like a man facing Doomsday. Ambra gives a blasé wave.

"You know Joshua. He likes to get a little chitchat by way of background. Obviously he'd prefer to do the chatting himself, but it's the best we can do at short notice."

"Any interviewing of the stars would have to be arranged through our publicity department."

"I won't be interviewing anyone, not formally. Just getting background for Joshua's review. You know, like the overall budget for the production."

"Two hundred and forty million, give or take. Let me get back to you."

Ambra puts the phone down. "I hate lying."

Spada says, "But you do it so well."

"Ms. Black? I've cleared the matter of the guest list with Mr. Goldstein, on condition that anything said by the stars this evening is off the record. Give me your e-mail address and I'll shoot it through."

"Fax it to me at the Palace."

"Sorry, but I need to send it directly through to Joshua's office rather than an open line to a hotel. I couldn't possibly fax it. Security, you understand."

This is one smart cookie. "But that's no use to me. I'm right here on the boulevard."

"I don't know what to do about that. Surely you can log in from the Palace?"

On the extension line, Spada is making grotesque faces, mouthing something. Ambra shrugs angrily. He does it again and this time she recognizes the words: *Don't bloody lose it!* She scribbles: *Bernstein's e-mail address, Chicago Tribune. NOW!*

Spada starts to bash frantically at a laptop keyboard.

"Of course, what am I thinking? That'll be fine."

A long pause, and then: "The address?"

Spada is on his feet, stabbing his fingers towards the laptop's screen like a sorcerer and doing something like a war dance.

Ambra says, "You know, I can never remember my own e-mail address."

"The address?" Bristling with suspicion.

Spada is scribbling. He cracks his shin on a low table, screams silently and thrusts a piece of paper in front of Ambra. She reads the e-mail address calmly into the telephone.

"What damned use is that?"

Spada is holding a wet towel to his shin, groaning quietly. Hairy legs, like a gorilla's.

Ambra continues, "It'll just be sent encrypted."

Caddon is tapping into a cell phone. "I assume that's an example of British humor. I'll get on it now."

THE RAMIREZ CANYON GARDEN CENTER

"They've hired thugs," Caddon complains, putting down the car phone. "Snap Security, they think they're licensed to kill. Half of them have been down for violence."

"So what?" Ambra replies. "It's a big star affair. They want to keep gate-crashers out."

"Something's going on in there." Ambra is in an ankle-length turquoise dress with a crossover shoestring strap at the back, the V stretching to the bottom of her spine. Well-toned, tanned legs peek out coyly from a slit at the front. The effect is finished with a sweep of beads and stones from her left shoulder down to the bottom right. Her hair is twisted up at the top, ending in a spike with a little feather stuck in the back. "You look like a movie star."

"I feel like a poodle."

"I couldn't even plant a waiter. The catering firm's owned by O'Reilly's cousin. Big family concern."

"Family as in Mafia?"

"I wish. At least we'd know who we're dealing with."

"For heaven's sake, Neal, it's just a party."

"It's a twenty-two-acre perimeter. Stick with the crowd, don't get maneuvered into a dark corner."

"I'll be good."

"What did they issue you with?"

"I'm not into guns," says Ambra.

"Jeez."

"I don't come from a gun society."

"Well listen to our pious tea-drinking limey."

Spada, driving the stretch limo, slows. The headlights pick up a stream, and the car makes bow waves as it crosses.

"Are you sure this is the right road?" Caddon asks. After the movie, Spada had slipped the car unobtrusively onto the end of a convoy of limos and Lincolns heading away from the cinema. But the headlights of the car he's been following have disappeared and they've lost the convoy somewhere in the gulleys north of LA.

"Trust me, boss. Hey, I think that's Barbra Streisand's old place."

"Stuff Barbra Streisand's old place, where's the frigging party?"

"Stay cool, man." Lights appear scattered over a foothill a couple of miles ahead. "Hey!"

Caddon exhales. "By the way, Ambra, that's a thousand bucks' worth of jewelry, and that's just the rental."

"I'll try not to lose the necklace in the soup."

"Likewise, spill tomato juice on that nice little Versace number and I'll invoice your MI6."

"Versace? Can't be. Nobody even measured me up, Neal."

"Tony does it by eye and yes it's Versace, it's a Keira Knightley throwaway, and it's also twenty thousand bucks out of my budget. Final check. Distress code word?"

"Orange Glow. Do we need the melodrama?"

"And you don't do guns," Caddon confirms. "You're a freaking pacifist or something."

"Just a snubbie, a hammerless J-frame Smith and Wesson. It's blue with a flower on the handle. Quite pretty." She gives Caddon a simple-country-girl smile.

"And that transmitter has a maximum range of two hundred yards. Keep within that distance of the parking lot."

Spada squeezes the big limousine around a sharp bend

and heads up an unpaved winding track toward a blaze of light on the hillside. A Louis XIV flunkie opens the door. A squat, bald-headed man with a Hitler mustache and a tuxedo examines the invitation card and attempts a smile. "Ms. Black, welcome, enjoy the evening."

Spada trickles the limo over to a dark corner of the parking lot, as far as possible from the Rollers, the Continentals, and the smoking chauffeurs. In the near dark, the FBI men retrieve metal boxes and monitors from the trunk and quickly assemble equipment in the passenger compartment. The monitor screen glares bright blue in the rear of the car. Caddon curses, pulls shades down, puts on a headset. Spada picks up an image intensifier and begins to scan the lot, reading license numbers into a microphone. And forty minutes' drive to the south, at a workstation in the Bureau, another two agents collate these one by one with the owners of the cars, and check the owners one by one against the guest list.

Away from Caddon's anxious cosseting, Ambra finds that she is breathing heavily, checks herself. But she can't stop her heart pounding in her chest.

The August night air is sticky. Cicadas are shrilling in the dark. Now the next barrier, the big one: mine host, welcoming guests at the gates of the Ramirez Canyon Garden Center. "Linda Black? Pat O'Reilly. Don't believe we've met." Ambra feels her carpal bones being squeezed by a big, hairy hand. Astute eyes, set in a small, round face, assess her. "I understand Mr. Bernstein couldn't make it." The voice comes from midchest.

Yes, we poisoned him.

Ambra smiles. "He has a spot of tummy trouble. I'm a poor substitute, I know." *But it lets me in to spy on your guests.* "Joshua can still do the review from the Palace if I leave early. I'll give him the chat from here and we'll make tomorrow's *Tribune.*" *I hate lying, but I do it so well.*

"Sure, sure."

Something in the voice? Or the way he's looking at me?

The producer's trophy wife, all Botox and liposuction, holds out a limp hand. "Enjoy the evening, Ms. Black."

She walks under a balloon-draped archway with THE ANDROMEDA DOSSIER glowing in big blue neon letters. *You're through. And don't be so bloody paranoid.*

Trying to hide her relief, Ambra hitches the strap of her cocktail bag onto her shoulder. Chatter from a hundred voices is coming out of a marquee. Another Louis XIV flunkie, maybe a student on a vacation job, approaches with a tray. She lifts a grapefruit juice.

The big star is holding court, five feet four inches in platform heels and a velvet tuxedo. No sign of the leading lady. And a quick scan of the marquee reveals no sign of Demos.

Back out into the warm air, honeysuckle competing with the Dior perfume. Over in the Chinese Garden a jazz quartet, all scarlet jackets and bowler hats, is playing "Speak Softly Love" from *The Godfather*. It seems appropriate. Over to the right, close to the fence, she sees a six-seater Bell helicopter.

"Hi there."

Thirtyish, athletic, short blond hair, expensive smile. Vaguely familiar, possibly some minor actor she is supposed to recognize. "You on your own?"

Get rid of him.

"Uh-huh."

"Nice party, huh?"

"Only just got here. How do I get rid of you?"

He laughs. "Hey, you're English. Seen the Japanese garden?"

"No, I haven't seen the Japanese garden."

"I'll take you to it. By the way, the name's Joe Scarlatti. That's a nice dress." Running his eyes up and down her body.

"Yes, I'm good at it."

"Huh?"

"Lots of experience."

"Sorry? I don't get your drift."

"Dressing up." Ambra pauses, then gives a delighted, deep-throated laugh. "Hey, you've made my evening! You really think I'm a woman!"

The muscleman's eyes are beginning to glaze over. "You don't mean . . . ?"

"I do this all the time. Don't you like boys? I thought they all like boys in this business. Now, where are those Japanese gardens you're taking me to?"

The muscleman suddenly roars with laughter. "Okay, mister or mizz, I won't bother you no more." He's still laughing as he disappears into the dark.

The Japanese garden. Little groups in conversation. A scaly dragon, four claws, five long talons to a claw. Mouth open, showing big teeth and a long tongue. She taps its body experimentally: fiberglass. Geisha girls, also fiberglass, throwing long shadows from the lanterns. Keep moving, don't stop.

Demos, where are you?

The movie is turning out to be a disaster. Not *The Andromeda Dossier,* although Caddon is beginning to wish it all the ills in the world, but the one being produced by the Englishwoman and transmitted to the TV monitor in the back of the limo. The screen shows close-ups of wineglasses, cardboard plates with cute little holders for the aforesaid glasses, microscopic sausage rolls. In between the canapé close-ups the camera whirls dizzyingly and Caddon catches a succession of inanely grinning, surgically improved faces, useless overpaid showbiz dross that lives in fake Spanish Revival homes and would be better employed digging ditches or being flogged to death on a naval brig.

Away from the marquee lights, the camera isn't picking up properly and faces appear a ghastly, ghost-like white. And now the woman is heading farther up the party, almost out of range, and the visual transmission is beginning to fail altogether.

Spada, meantime, is grunting into a telephone receiver, scribbling notes.

"Sound's beginning to go," Caddon says in frustration. "She's at the limit."

"What's going on?" Something on the TV monitor.

Caddon stares, too, trying to make out the shapes. "Looks

like four people, no, five. Heading up the hill. What's the stupid woman doing?"

"Looks like she's going after them, boss."

"Loved your music, Mr. Demos. Made the movie, in my opinion." This from a big-budget producer.

"Thanks."

"Especially that scene where the dam starts to crack. The score was even scarier than the *Psycho* shower. It's going to be iconic."

Demos manages a modest smile and wonders what the guy's after.

Normally he'd bask in the praise—and why not, he deserves it—but something else is filling his mind. The Tin Can, has he made it? Goldstein's secretary said he was flying in from Montego Bay. He looks around, anxious for once to get away from the adulatory crowd around him.

"How do you compose music, Mr. Demos?" This from a minor actor in the movie. "I mean, does it just jump into your head?"

Demos says, "Sometimes, yeah, from nowhere, sometimes I even wake up in the night with a theme, driving me nuts. Other times I go for weeks or months and get nothing and I begin to think, *Hell, I'm past it.* It helps to visit the settings."

"That could be difficult for a *Star Trek* movie," someone says, and the little crowd laughs.

Demos drifts away. To his relief he has spotted an old man, not fifty yards from him, at the other end of the marquee: the Tin Can. He's with a young Japanese man in a tuxedo. Good, good. Are the others here? They've had to come from Europe, Japan, North Korea. But they're needed here, now.

The Tin Can and his Japanese companion spot him. Now they drift casually toward the exit. Demos wends his way, also casually, through the fantasy women, the actors on the make, the babble.

Outside, the pair are heading up the slope toward the rear

of the garden center, away from the party, the Tin Can using his walking stick. For a frail eighty-year-old he can move. Here and there others are detaching themselves from groups, drifting into the dark. Demos follows. The air smells of dry vegetation, reminds him that it's the wildfire season. He catches up; he can hardly make out their faces in the shadows. They follow the Tin Can without conversation. Near the top of the garden center, far from the party, the Can waves his walking stick at a long, Victorian-style greenhouse, all wrought-iron pillars and trees in silhouette. They turn into it.

The Tin Can presses a button on his throat. The voice that comes out is toneless and metallic. "What happened?"

Demos says, "How do I know?"

"You were responsible for recovering the weapon."

"I wasn't there. That was the arrangement. We agreed to keep a layer between us and the device. Maybe it was in a bad state after all this time."

"Why hasn't the incident reached the media? It must have left corpses for miles downwind." This from a young woman, also dressed like an actress at a movie premiere, speaking good English with a German accent.

Demos says, "How would I know?"

"You don't know much."

"It'll break at any moment, it's bound to."

The Can says, "What's the word from the governor's office?"

A man, educated Boston accent, says, "The FBI have identified the bodies at the mine shaft."

The Hollywood musician's face is sweaty. "We're unraveling. Maybe we should abandon the project."

The actress says, "With what's at stake? Don't be stupid."

The Boston man says, "We're in too deep to pull out now. Your useful idiots can't be traced back to us. That's right, isn't it? They can't be traced back to us?"

"I had a visit from two FBI agents yesterday." Demos's voice has a slight tremble.

"What?" There is a sudden collective stillness.

"They have me on CCTV speaking to two of the patriotic militia just hours before the accident."

"You fool. Where?"

"In some restaurant. I told the FBI it was a casual encounter."

"And did they believe you?"

"I don't know."

The actress says, "You have stupidity coming out of your ears."

The Boston man says, "That and the wreckage are terrific leads for the FBI. Maybe you're under surveillance, Demos. Maybe we all are."

"No. This is a safe area."

"Vladimir, this gets worse by the minute." A small, squat Japanese man facing the Tin Can has loosened his bow tie, and, like Demos, his face is coated with sweat.

The metallic voice says, "We cannot abandon the project. We will never get another opportunity like this. So. We proceed as planned. We will use one of the other weapons. I have teams retrieving them now." He turns to the Boston man. "You did compose a decoy letter?"

"Anonymous hand delivery to the British embassy in Washington. Real stuff in it, as you said, to make them focus on it. But buried deep enough they'll never work out the message by Friday."

"Real stuff in it?" The German woman's voice is filled with alarm. "What are you saying?"

"Enough to suck them in."

"Are you mad? Giving them real information?"

"Not mad, lady, clever. Without it the letter had no credibility. With it, they'll squander their resources chasing wild geese. It contains no hint of our real purpose. And one of the Phoenix militia has his prints all over it."

The Tin Can says, "Excellent. That will sow real confusion. The North Korean woman contacts our satellite man tomorrow. If she delivers the codes, the Pentagon will find itself blind for a crucial fifteen minutes."

The Japanese man says, "I don't trust the bitch. She has an agenda."

"We all have our agendas," the actress says. "I prefer to call them dreams."

The Tin Can says, "We must never meet again like this. And I will tolerate no more mistakes. Just a few more days. Meantime, we keep our eyes open and watch our backs."

For a startled moment Demos imagines he sees a figure inside the greenhouse, crouching among the bushes. A trick of the shadows—he shakes the illusion off. The Tin Can is right. Don't panic.

In the back of the stretch limo, Caddon is close to panic. Ambra's microphone is out of range, and it seems to be close to a fountain, or some sort of water flow. But Caddon is hearing enough snatches of conversation to make him aware that he is listening in on some very serious people; that whatever they're up to, it's big and bad and imminent; that the English intelligence woman must be real close to them; and that she must thereby be exposing herself to a gigantic risk.

As the conversation unfolds he can hardly believe his ears, keeps squeezing his headset up against them. It's beginning to sound like some fantastic convocation of terrorist groups, one from Germany, one from Japan, maybe one from America. And someone coming in from North Korea? Next to him, Spada, an earpiece jammed to his ear, is openmouthed with amazement, and forgetting to breathe.

No Demos, but faces harder to recognize in the shadows, away from the big marquee and the barbecue chimerae.

Single white female, Dior perfume attracting the male of the species like insects to pheromone. Someone says hi there; Ambra passes on.

Nothing here. Should have spotted him by now. Keep circulating.

Demos? Maybe, maybe. He has company, about a hundred meters away. Three of them, heading for the dark shadows. No, four. Five, one a female. They're into the shadows, away from the party. She loses sight of them. *Damn!*

A vine-covered barn. Conservatory attached, about the size of a tropical house, lit up with strings of multicolored lights and looking like an ocean liner in the dark.

Ambra winds her way swiftly along a curving path through cacti, then across lawn studded with obelisks and spheres, toward the barn. Orion, club raised, poking his head over the black silhouette of the Ramirez Mountains, Los Angeles glowing orange to her right.

Orange Glow, the distress call. Transmitter in her hair, little microphone picking up everything. Reassuring. But the range is only two hundred meters; must be on the limit.

The barn is lit up, but empty. Plows, scythes, barrels, bales of hay decorate the interior. Through to the conservatory. A blaze of color: lemon trees, banana trees, date palms; African violets scenting the air; but no humans.

Lost them. Ambra becomes aware that her jaw is clenched tightly. *Calm down, this is a safe environment. Not like the Pakistan job.*

Out again. Where the hell?

Voices. Subdued. From a big greenhouse farther up, almost at the perimeter.

Subdued but angry. Tinged with fear? Some instinct makes Ambra approach cautiously, on a wide circle, making sure she is not silhouetted. She stops near the open greenhouse door, risks a glance. Bushes and trees. Human silhouettes at the other end, about fifty meters away. She takes a chance. She crouches down, slips quickly inside, and approaches through the bushes, murdering the Versace number, now rolled up around her thighs. The damp soil close to her nose threatens to make her sneeze. The voice is in English, although the accent is foreign. But instead of a reply, there is a metallic, tinny buzz. It seems to have a syntax, but it isn't human. She daren't approach any closer, hears the blood pounding in her ears. Water is spraying somewhere, ruining the acoustics. Baffled and frustrated, she can neither make out the words nor recognize the individuals.

There's a final exchange, and another long, tinny rasping, a voice and yet not a voice, like Darth Vader. She feels goose pimples on her arms. Then the figures are marching away. Ambra retrieves shoes and handbag, scrabbling desperately in the dark, and runs out. The men are visible in outline, spreading out, occluding the party lights down the hill. She follows them down past the conservatory. And now they have reached the fringes of the party; it's okay to approach more closely. They have split up. She sees Demos chatting with a young actor, the man with the metal voice heading for the drinks. He is limping, carries a walking stick.

Ambra ignores Demos and his new friend, follows the man with the stick. He reaches an unoccupied trestle table, picks up drinks and canapés. He has his back to her. She wanders, puts down her glass, puts little cocktail sausages onto a plate. She's within a meter of the man before she looks up, casually.

And sees a face she will never forget.

The right-hand side is a mass of red and white scar tissue, rippled like water. He has no eyebrows, and his right eye is devoid of eyelashes. His right hand, holding a glass of champagne, is scarred. Their eyes meet.

Ambra, embarrassed at staring, says, "Have you seen the Japanese garden?"

The man presses a finger against his throat, and the voice that comes out is like a tin can speaking. "And you are?"

"Linda Black. How do you do?"

"Ah yes, Linda Black."

The man touches his throat again and a metallic whisper passes into the ear of his neighbor, who glances coldly at Ambra and strides off.

The Tin Can says: "And how is Joshua? I understand he was taken ill rather suddenly." *Something in his tone of voice—or is it just the artificiality of it?* It occurs to Ambra that the eye without the lashes doesn't blink. It just stares.

"Yes, an upset stomach. I'm sure he'll recover quickly."

"I know he will."

She becomes aware of the third man, pretending to pick food, drifting around behind her, ever so casually.

O'Reilly, flanked by two men in tuxes, corvettes escorting a battleship. One is barrel-chested, the other absurdly thin. They remind Ambra irresistibly of Laurel and Hardy, but there is nothing humorous about their turned-down mouths and glassy eyes. A short, dumpy woman of about forty is struggling to keep up with them. She is looking at Ambra through thick spectacles with something like malice. And the bonhomie has gone from O'Reilly's face.

Ambra, wired up to the eyeballs, wonders if somebody has spotted the fact; noticed the camera, the lens on her Versace dress looking like a big opal set in diamonds, the fiber-optic cable embedded in the strap, the transmitter tucked inside her twisted-up hair, the aerial with the feather attached.

O'Reilly gives her the answer. "Enjoying the party, I hope? Ms. Linda Black, Joshua's assistant, may I introduce Ms. Linda Black, Joshua's assistant?"

MIKI

UNION STATION, SUNDAY MORNING

"Why are you visiting the United States?"

The passport has been created by world-class craftsmen; likewise the visa obtained, so it said, from the American embassy in Tokyo. The real Etsuko Nakamura will not arrive until tomorrow, by which time the counterfeit one, now calmly facing the immigration officer, will have vanished into the bowels of America. *Nothing can possibly be wrong.* The young immigration man's searching stare has to be part of the technique. "For cultural reasons."

"Is that business or pleasure?"

"Business. I am a singer. I will be rehearsing with the Haydn Symphony Orchestra. That will also be a pleasure."

The young immigration man slowly scans her visa and then stares at a computer screen. Her calmness begins to waver; she feels her heart thumping in her chest.

Then: "Enjoy your stay, Miss Nakamura."

She now merges with the arrivals throng, drifting with the flow so as not to attract attention. There's no point in trying to avoid the CCTV cameras; she will now be on half a dozen videotapes. Outside the airport—nearly there!—she joins a taxi queue in an agony of impatience, desperate to lose herself in the vast city she was looking down on minutes earlier.

She is beginning to tremble, a delayed reaction. A taxi, come on, come on!

She gives up on the taxi queue and takes the airport shuttle into town, keeping to herself. Fortunately nobody around her seems inclined to talk. She gazes out at the high canyons, the mind-boggling volume of traffic, the shop windows laden with luxuries—unbelievable luxuries. She enters Union Station, as instructed. More prodigious wealth! Shops, restaurants, and offices inside a railway station! And a confusing array of platforms and monitor screens. In the ladies' room she disappears into a cubicle, takes off her coat, skirt, and shoes, puts on jeans, sneakers, and a nondescript windbreaker from her red carry bag, and stuffs the red bag and its contents into a dull gray one. She waits three minutes, calming down, listening to the comings and goings. A couple of women are gossiping while washing their hands; they seem to go on forever. But at last they disappear. Miki takes a deep breath and emerges from the cubicle. She checks herself quickly in the mirror, turning up her collar and putting on dark glasses.

Another deep breath and she is out.

For the first time since arriving, she feels secure. She is now invisible; she cannot be connected with the woman who arrived at the airport a short while ago. She takes a Yellow Cab to an address in Chinatown, the stress of the entry draining out of her like a fluid. The taxi driver says, "Just arrived in LA?"; she grunts and he takes the hint.

She has been told the motel is run-down, but what makes it beautiful is that it has no CCTV camera at the front desk. In her room she looks at the heavy patterned curtains, the comfortable bed, the television, the do-it-yourself coffee tray, the shower and toilet connected to the room. If this is run-down . . .

She experiments with the shower, then strips herself naked, looks at her trim body approvingly in a full-length mirror, and then stands under a stream of warm water for a glorious fifteen minutes. Then she dries herself and lies out on the bed, emptying her mind of everything, relaxing her muscles from toe to head, preparing herself mentally.

Telephone ringing. She awakens with a jerk. The digital clock on the television set tells her she has been asleep for almost an hour. The voice is male, deep, Midwest Republican, all Christian Right and family values. "Miss Nakamura? George McCall here."

"George, it's been a year."

"I look forward to hearing you sing again. Could we have dinner tonight? Shall we meet, say seven o'clock at the Natural History Museum?"

"I look forward to that, and to seeing you again."

The coded exchange complete, with no duress words, Miki puts down the receiver and smiles. Things are moving along like clockwork, tick tick tick. She has succeeded in the most difficult phase, entering the country undetected, and the team has made contact. Everything and everyone is in place. And from now on, things are going to happen fast. She looks again at the digital clock. She'll watch American television for an hour, to see what brand of opium keeps this huddled mass stupefied.

She settles back on the bed, relieved and contented.

London

SUNDAY–MONDAY

LONDON EYE

There is a short corridor with bedrooms leading off. After a couple of hours of juggling letters, Sharp looks in on Downey. The GCHQ man's bed is empty, hasn't been slept in. Sharp goes back to the crazy letter and tries again to make sense out of it, unsure whether the whole thing is a colossal waste of time. He is beginning to develop a headache himself. When the phone rings, he is surprised to see that two more hours have passed. Downey.

"Lewis, I'm being followed."

"Where are you?"

"The Millennium Wheel, the Big Eye Thing, whatever the Christ they call it. There are three of them. A man and woman together, and a man on his own, skinhead type about thirty, leather bomber jacket, dark glasses."

"How do you know they're following you?"

"I saw the couple when I was passing St. Paul's Cathedral. The man came on at Newgate, coming from the Old Bailey. I spotted them again at the Covent Garden when I was looking for the music score. Lewis, I need someone to pull me in."

"Craig, are you in a crowd now?"

"Yes, I'm in a queue for the Big Eye. The couple have joined the queue. I don't see the skinhead. Pull me in, Lewis, please."

"Look, calm down. Are you sure they're following you?"

"A hundred percent. How come I see them in the street, then at Covent Garden, then at the Big Wheel?"

"These are all tourist spots. It's not such a big coincidence. Craig, you're imagining things."

"The safe house isn't safe, Lewis. They must know about it, it's the only way they could have picked up on me."

"That's impossible."

"I need help."

"I'll phone Jocelyn now, she'll get a car around. There'll be somebody there in minutes. Just hang on, stick with crowds."

"Something I don't get. I heard them talking—they're Americans."

"There you go, then, just innocent tourists."

"For God's sake, get that car here. Pull me in."

"There was no sign of him. Our officers scoured the embankment on both sides. They went all through the Tate Modern, looked at the ferries and saw everyone who came off the London Eye. He obviously panicked and ran off somewhere."

"The safe house isn't safe."

"That's ridiculous." Jocelyn shakes her head emphatically.

"I don't want a visit from bad guys." Jocelyn raises her eyeballs scornfully, but Sharp persists. "Why take a chance? We could clear off. Find someplace else."

"Look, Lewis, Craig's a cryptographer. All he does is work at a desk all day. He has this overactive imagination, coupled with no field experience and the nerves of a frightened kitten."

"He must have a powerful imagination," Sharp says. "The man was terrified."

She glances across the river at the Tate. "Maybe the stress has gotten to him. Maybe he's gone off his trolley."

"Jocelyn, you can never be absolutely sure about anything. But the Americans he saw in Covent Garden turned up at the London Eye."

Jocelyn manages to look and sound like a scolding schoolmistress. "Pure coincidence. Both of them are bog standard tourist spots. There's a problem with all this pursuit non-sense. This is a highly secure operation. No way could it have been compromised. The safe house really is just that. Safe."

"Is it, Jocelyn?"

Jocelyn puts a hand to her head in a show of exasperation. "This is plain stupid. Special Branch can't just come up with safe houses at the drop of a hat. And we've gone to a lot of trouble to set up secure communications here with the FBI and Six."

"What about a couple of armed policemen?" Sharp suggests.

She groans. "It's not practical, Lewis. You and Craig have to do your work here in total secrecy. You can't do that in a plod-infested flat."

"I'm a soldier, I can handle a pistol. Give me one," Sharp says. "Purely as a precaution."

"I'll speak to the commissioner. He'll say no."

"Jocelyn, look what's at stake. We can't take risks."

"The biggest risk we're running, Lewis, is that we don't get to the bottom of this before Saturday. No more distractions, please. Get on with your analysis and give me something I can present to the chief tomorrow morning. Something more substantial than the fantasies of our excitable young man from GCHQ."

"If that's what they are. Fantasies."

"It would be nice if Craig turned up." She glances at the kitchen clock.

VLAD THE IMPALER

"Vlad the Impaler."

Sharp, in green boxer shorts and gripping an early-morning mug of coffee, sits down heavily on a chair and peers intently at the terminal screen. Ambra's garden center movie is showing, faces flitting across the terminal, disembodied arms holding glasses or plates, clusters of people, obelisks and spheres and dragons and Geisha girls and thugs. Quite a few males are looking straight at the camera, which is not surprising considering its location at the apex of Ambra's cleavage. Sharp has triggered the Web cam and is conversing with Caddon in Los Angeles on a second screen.

"Say again?"

"The disfigured guy. I've seen him." Sharp taps his forehead. "It's not a face you forget."

"A name, Lewis. We need a name. This guy doesn't appear on the guest list, and I'd like to know why not. Who is he?"

Sharp stares at the lidless eye and the scarred cheek. There's a draft of cold air, and the door clicks behind him. Jocelyn. She sits next to Sharp. He tells Caddon, "If you keep bugging me, I won't remember."

"Try association of ideas. What do you know about him?"

"He's rich and Russian." Then: "Gotcha. A NATO conference in Sweden three years ago. He's a microbiologist. Some jokers were calling him Vlad the Inhaler because of his noisy breath."

There is a long silence. Then Caddon is saying, thoughtfully, "What in the name of Jesus is a microbiologist doing at a Hollywood movie premiere?"

"He's a *rich* microbiologist. As I recall he owns Baryon Biosystems."

"Hey, that's the outfit that owns the Bell helicopter."

"Got it. Vladimir Petrov."

There is a *click-click* of rapid typing over the connection. Jocelyn does the same but Caddon gets there first. "Yeah. We've been stretching our resources checking on everyone with an anthrax connection and he's on our interview list. Baryon Biosystems bought an uninhabited Caribbean island north of Cuba some years ago and put a pharmaceutical factory on it. For security, it says here."

Jocelyn is still tapping at her keyboard. "Breakthrough, Neal, breakthrough. The militia connection is suddenly hot."

"Red hot." Caddon can't keep the excitement out of his voice. "Like you said, Lewis, that was the trouble with the militia theory. Our six-fingered banjo players could only produce test-tube quantities of anthrax. To get the ton of anthrax in the Arizona UFO, you would need giant fermentation vats. No way could they build and hide that in backpacker country. But Baryon Biosystems could do it, on this Cuban island. We have no jurisdiction there. Anything could be going on. It's the missing link."

Jocelyn says, "I have a *Time* magazine interview with him. It seems he flies scientists and technicians out from Florida for six-month tours of duty on the island. The work's classified. The story is the workers are fabulously well paid."

"What's his history?" Caddon asks.

"He acquired a big slice of Gulf in the seventies. It was a hostile takeover and as soon as he got it, the oil crisis hit and prices went crazy. That's when some journalist called him Vlad the Impaler. It seemed to stick, pardon the pun. He sold his oil in the nineties but kept the chemical holdings. Along came 9/11 and the military were interested in biochemistry in a big way. Twenty billion dollars big, and he got a decent slice. His timing is supernatural."

"Tell us about the scars."

Jocelyn reads some more. "A toxic blaze in one of his labs. He dragged a technician out but got burned himself. It nearly cost him his life, and the technician died anyway. He lost his voice box and half his lungs. He presses his throat to speak."

Ambra Volpe appears on a third terminal. She is still wearing her movie premiere dress and the expensive earrings and necklace, but she has let down her hair. "I can confirm that. Petrov and I spoke briefly."

"Greetings again, Miss Volpe."

"Felicitations once more, Mr. Sharp. I think Petrov, Demos, and two others used the party opportunistically as a safe haven from FBI surveillance. From what I could hear, it was a panic meeting triggered by the Fossil Creek explosion."

"And the other two? What about them?" Jocelyn asks. Her voice is harsh but Sharp thinks that might be a raw throat from the cold London drizzle.

Ambra says, "I don't know. They spotted me and I was lucky to get thrown out as a gatecrashing reporter. One German woman, maybe late twenties, and one Japanese guy about the same age. I couldn't make out their faces and the light levels were too low for the camera. Metal Voice, German, and Jap left the party in a helicopter."

"And they weren't on the guest list," Caddon says. "The studio said they came in as guests of Demos, doesn't know who they were."

"So where did they go?"

"No idea. The helicopter touched down in Griffith Park before it carried on to a Baryon Biosystems pharmaceutical works. This Vladimir Petrov is all we have."

Jocelyn says, "I have something here about him."

"We're all ears," Caddon says.

"He's a great military hero. Joined the partisans at age fourteen during the war, acquired the Bravery Medal in 1941, the Medal for the Defense of Stalingrad in 1944, the Medal for the Capture of Berlin . . ."

Caddon says, ". . . I get the picture . . ."

". . . thrown into a gulag, escaped in the fifties, and . . ."

". . . What? Escaped from a gulag?"

". . . arrived in the States in 1955, made this big killing in oil. Single, now eighty. If you believe this dossier he has a seething hatred of everything communist. It goes back to the death of his young wife in the gulag."

"Amen for a breakthrough," Caddon declares. "Petrov's a rich biochemist. He's into bioweapons with a factory on a Caribbean island we know nothing about. Ambra sees him in in intense conversation with Demos, and Demos was in contact with two guys who hauled the anthrax device up from an old mine shaft. And we know these guys were right-wing Arizona militia."

"What about the Nazi connection, Neal?" Sharp says.

"Swastika-engraving Minutemen, what else? Petrov's useful idiots, a layer between him and whatever he's up to. We can forget the Third Reich, Lewis."

Sharp says, "Why would a man like Petrov threaten London? It makes no sense."

"Come on, Lewis, keep a sense of realism. The Third Reich connection's dead."

"I disagree. Look, there are probably people in Germany still alive who were involved in creating that device. We should be looking for them, surviving German biochemists, finding out what they did in the war."

"It's a question of allocating resources. I'm sorry, Lewis, but it has to come well down the list. The way I see it, three terrorist groups—German, Japanese, and American—have come together and cooked up something massive for this Saturday. And there's a North Korean involvement of some sort. This scares me. It's bigger than anything we've seen and so far we haven't a clue. We just can't afford eccentric diversions."

Sharp says, "Neal, we can't afford a mistake. Would you

at least look into German biochemists who came over to the States postwar?"

"One of my bright young things is drawing up a list of interesting biochemists anyway. If she happens to see anything . . ." Caddon's tone says that it's a sop.

"You're off target. You still haven't met my point about Petrov. It makes no sense for someone like that to target London."

Caddon says, "The crazy letter is a decoy, designed to confuse. London may not be part of the equation. Petrov has a house in London, in Holland Park." He adds slyly, "Maybe Holland Park has answers."

Jocelyn says, "What are you suggesting, Neal? A search warrant . . ."

"No search warrants. We can't afford to frighten this guy off."

"Mr. Caddon! I hope you're not suggesting illegal entry."

Silence.

"British intelligence doesn't do burglary." Jocelyn's tone is so scandalized that for a moment Sharp almost believes her. And in the excitement of the chase, he almost forgets that Downey has been missing for twelve hours.

BURGLARY:

HOLLAND PARK

The great military hero, Sharp thinks. *Stop shivering.*

The man next to him in the huge porch senses Sharp's fear. He whispers, "It gets worse every time. Remember to keep the gloves on. DNA and stuff."

Across the road, a glimmer of gray dawn is beginning to break over Holland Park.

Mr. Nuts appears at the front door. He speaks quietly, in a Cockney accent. "Okay. I've taped over the sensors. In and out fast, right?"

There is enough street light flooding through the porch to make out the interior. The burglar leads the way along a broad, deep-carpeted corridor and turns left. The study is huge, and lined with contemporary paintings by Jon Braley, Lucy Orchard, Nick Schlee. A massive teak desk takes up the center, and a spiral stair leads up to a gallery. Mr. Nuts has slid a bookcase sideways, revealing a cream-colored safe lodged in the wall.

Sharp says, "He mustn't know the safe's been cracked."

Mr. Nuts is closing shutters and pulling heavy velvet curtains. Then he switches on a desk lamp. "Come on, come on, move it."

Mr. Bolts looks at the safe thoughtfully. Sharp momentarily wonders who dreamed up aliases of such mind-numbing stupidity, but then the burglar is saying: "TL-30, Brown—American make—E-rated. This guy's serious."

"I'm impressed," says Sharp, "whatever it means." Mr. Nuts is looking agitated, and Sharp feels his own brow dampen.

"You should be," says Mr. Bolts. "It has a cobalt plate, which means you'd burn out six drill motors and take all week trying to get through it. It has a laminated steel door eight centimeters thick. By the time you're through that with a thermal lance, the neighbors have called the fire brigade, not that it matters because you've died of smoke inhalation. Anyway there's a thermal relocker, which triggers a whole load of locks, shuts us out forever. And a jam shot on this baby would take out half the study."

"Terrific," Sharp whispers. He's had sweaty palms a couple of times in his army career, and he has them now.

Mr. Bolts manages a clammy grin. "Torches and drills are for dorks. I'm a locksmith. Judge your man: Any chance he'd leave the combination lying around?"

Sharp doesn't bother to reply.

"That's what I think. We won't waste time looking."

"And don't waste time yakking," Mr. Nuts hisses. "Get on with it."

Mr. Bolts pulls over a coffee table and takes a small jar of what looks like talcum powder from his briefcase. He dusts the electronic lock using a pastry brush and shines a small, deep-violet torch onto it at an angle. "Shit. Six numbers."

"What does that mean?"

"It means nearly forty-seven thousand combinations. At ten seconds a combination it comes to three hundred and twenty hours of trial and error, mate. If he'd settled for a four-digit number, we'd have been through it in forty-five minutes."

"So what now?"

"We do it the slo-o-w way." Mr Bolts sets up a laptop computer. Into its back, he plugs a box the size of a small book. He tapes a thin black wire from the box onto the combination lock. "Mas-Hamilton software, straight out of a Bond movie.

Interfaces with the lock at its programming port. Costs more than the contents of most safes and not really worth it unless you're into big stuff."

"How long is this going to take?"

Mr. Bolts doesn't bother to reply. Numbers begin to tumble swiftly down the laptop screen. He pulls out a Commando comic from an inside pocket and starts to read. Sharp, shivering in the unheated house, sits in Petrov's study chair.

Mr. Nuts disappears, glides back silently in five minutes. "Who is this guy, Nero? An indoor swimming pool, tellies in the bedroom ceilings, en suites bigger than my living room. And the kitchen—"

"This is just his London pad," Sharp says. "He has homes in Monaco and LA."

"Look, I said in and out quick. With my record I go down for fifteen."

Mr. Bolts says, "Patience."

In forty minutes Sharp glances through the curtains, to a disapproving hiss from Mr. Nuts. The streetlights are off, and the traffic is building up. Maybe there are cleaning ladies, probably are in a place like this.

Fifteen minutes on. Mr. Nuts is pacing up and down, breathing heavily. He says, "Time's up, guys. Let's get the hell out of here." Sharp says nothing, tries to stay calm. Maybe an early-morning postman will see closed curtains today where they were open yesterday. Maybe a neighbor.

Ten more minutes pass. Mr. Nuts's agitation is infectious. He's pacing out a rectangle. It happens to be two meters by one and a half. Sharp wonders if he should make a joke about rehearsing for the next fifteen years, but decides that might just push the nervous burglar over the edge. Mr. Bolts has given up on his supply of Commando comics and is staring at the numbers. He says, "Bingo."

The numbers have stopped tumbling. The screen is showing a six-digit numeral. He taps at the keypad, says "Yes!," pulls the safe handle down, and the heavy door swings open. It's a wonderful moment!

And an alarm screams. Pushing 150 decibels, designed to

hurt the ears, vibrate the body, and sear into the skull. Mr. Nuts wails and rushes to the door. Mr. Bolts frantically stuffs his expensive Mas-Hamilton apparatus into his briefcase and bolts out after Mr. Nuts, thrusting Sharp roughly aside. A red light from outside is strobing, penetrating the heavy curtains.

Sharp rushes to the open safe. He can't think for the screaming alarm. The bottom shelf is stuffed with banknotes, euros, dollars and sterling, share certificates, bonds, deeds to a dozen or more properties. There is an armful of A4 paper and folders. He goes frantically through the folders, tossing them onto the floor. He can hardly handle the papers for shaking. His ears are in pain.

Nothing. Statements from a dozen offshore and Swiss banks, plastic cards, subscription to *America Right*, a heap of anti-communist hate material. Bills, yachting receipts, deeds to houses in Monaco and California and Morocco and . . .

Something.

Sharp stares.

Holland Park has answers.

The noise is beginning to make Sharp feel punch-drunk. His vision is blurring. He stuffs a sheet of paper into his coat pocket and sprints out of the house. A cluster of people at the front gate. A young boy with tousled hair, father's protective arms on his shoulders, wearing an over-large tartan dressing gown, staring at Sharp with something like awe. An old man in slippers and dressing gown, walking stick raised to strike: war veteran, saw D-Day, killed ten Huns with his bare hands. Sharp yells, "I've got a shooter!" The man hesitates, falls back.

Sharp sprints the two blocks toward the spot where Mr. Nuts parked the car.

Gone.

Holland Park. Lose myself in the park. It means retracing steps. Sharp looks back. *Damn.* The war veteran is following him, full of righteous anger, wheezing and gasping. *Don't collapse, old man.* Sharp keeps running.

He stops running a block later, gasping himself, when the

patrol car, its blue light scanning the well-heeled residences like a laser in a disco, screams to a halt ahead of him. Two policemen leap out and rush at him, angry men going into a fight. Sharp hurdles a railing, rushes through a small playground. Temporarily deaf, he can't use the vital aids to survival—the sounds of pounding feet and rasping breath behind him—to judge whether they're gaining on him. Ahead of him he sees a wood, and beyond it a tall wall and another big house. If he can make it to the wood and then try for the wall . . .

London and Los Angeles

MONDAY–TUESDAY

WELLS FARGO:

FBI BUILDING, LOS ANGELES, TUESDAY MORNING

It's standing room only in the war room, about two dozen agents sharing space with surveillance equipment, computer terminals, and two coffee machines. Several FBI agents are clustered around a table, picking and choosing surveillance equipment as if they are at a bazaar. Guns are laid out on another table. Spada always gets a sly kick out of seeing female agents producing them from holsters strapped to their thighs. The new girl, a sweet, slender thing he knows only as Joanna, catches him peeping and gives him a wicked smile, which he returns shyly.

Caddon calls them to order. The London letter, blown up, is stuck on a bulletin board, critical phrases circled by a red marker pen. *Sep 1 is the day*—four days away and double-circled—puts a damper on the chat. Or maybe it's the *Pop. 7.5 million* that somebody has scribbled next to the note. Or it might be Caddon's scribble on a whiteboard:

Three little maids

Arizona was one—for sure an accidental explosion

London is two—or so they say—on Saturday

Who's three?—Timbuctoo? Paris? NY? Right here
in LA?

Who's behind this? Hun/Jap/American/North-
Korean terrorists in league?

What's behind this?

Caddon sits at the back of the room, arms clasped behind
his neck, while Tony Spada does the briefing, using a Power-
Point presentation he knocked up in the early hours.

Spada's PowerPoint shows the crashed flying saucer and its
launch site near Superstition Mountain in the Arizona boon-
docks, where it had been dragged up from some old, disused
mine shaft. It shows them pictures of the four dead men at the
site—two of them, probably Mexican illegals, shot trying to
run, the other two blowtorched under the exhaust flames of
the flying saucer. The PowerPoint incorporates a clip of the
movie of the blowtorched men outside Katie's Diner taken
about fifteen hours earlier, alive and unblowtorched, in conversation with Alecos Demos, big Hollywood musician.

I've heard of this Demos, someone says. He's a pal of the
governor. Does great movie scores. Does charity work for
Third World children.

Caddon, from the back of the room, says he doesn't care if
Demos is the Archangel Gabriel, he wants to know what this
big Hollywood musician was doing talking to two guys who
got themselves killed a few hours later launching a bioweapon.
Demos said it was a chance meeting, and Demos was lying.

Spada's PowerPoint shows another clip of movie, the one
taken with the lens between Ambra's breasts. There's a brief
close-up of Petrov's disfigured face, and chaotic snatches of
party, ground, and garden center shrubs, everything fading as
she leaves the party lights and moves into the dark. Spada tells
them that Demos was at this movie premiere party, and the
English girl saw him in intense conversation with an old Russian émigré called Vladimir Petrov and two others unidentified, a German female and a Japanese man. Petrov seems to

be the kingpin of this unholy congress and they're awaiting the arrival of a North Korean woman to trigger events.

Caddon again: Petrov's a biochemist. He's rich as hell. He owns a Caribbean island with a biochemical works that nobody can get to. Nobody knows what he does there except maybe the US government, which doesn't encourage inquiries, not even from us, and I'm beginning to think even they don't know everything. So this big Hollywood musician is seen talking to these two guys just before they launch a bioweapon, and then he's seen talking to this rich biochemist just after they launched it, and if that's a coincidence I'll retire to a cave, become a hermit, and worship Zeus.

Spada finally shows an apple core in close-up, tells them it was found not far from the scorched ground at the mine shaft. They have DNA from the apple core and the guys downstairs match it with this Virgin Rabbit lunatic in Phoenix who makes anthrax spores by the teaspoon. It would take him a hundred years to make enough to fill the flying saucer. It makes no sense. But he was there just the same.

Once everyone has the picture, tasks are assigned and there is a rapid exodus. Spada and Caddon head for the L'Ermitage, where the musician has stayed over after the premiere. He is in room 317.

Except he isn't, having checked out by the time they arrive in a fifty-miles-to-the-gallon Toyota Prius that Spada has selected from the car pool. "He's heading along Burton Way," Caddon hears over the car's intercom. "In his canary."

"His Porsche Boxster," Spada corrects him disapprovingly.

The intercom says, "He's turning onto Wilshire. He's shifting."

"Put the pedal to the metal, Tony."

Spada does so. To Caddon's astonishment the car develops a sporty rasp and accelerates like a cruise missile. Caddon tries to look nonchalant while Spada demonstrates his Italian pedigree on the crowded streets. "I had them soup it up a bit," he explains over the rasp.

Then: "Glendale Boulevard, heading north. I can't keep up."

"Should we go up North Vermont?" Spada asks, doing so. The car tilts perilously, and Caddon feels his nerve beginning to crack. "I'll get them to look at the suspension," Spada volunteers.

The intercom says, "Damn. Lost him. Congestion's hell here. Sorry, guys."

They drive along the avenue, frustrated, heading northward blindly. A stiff breeze is flapping awnings and setting papers fluttering across the streets. Then the intercom voice, filled with relief. "Got him. He's heading for Griffith Park . . . he's just gone into Zoo Drive . . . turning into the Autry museum."

"Two minutes," Spada volunteers, shooting past a meandering truck at the park's entrance. He takes a vacant slot next to a gleaming white stretch limo. Caddon, a little shaky, glances at his watch. "Two minutes twenty seconds. Time you were drawing your pension, Tony."

"Fuel injection needs tweaking up."

A well-built man wearing a lumberjack jacket and dark glasses is sitting at a round table in a plaza. He waves them over.

"The guy was shifting, I nearly lost him. He's in there." The lumberjack nods toward a small theater.

Spada says, "Is there a show on or what?"

"Nope. And you can't follow a guy into an empty theater. And this is useless." Pointing to the small device in his ear.

"So what's he doing in an empty theater?"

"Maybe he's getting more edgy primitiveness, boss," Spada suggests, unwrapping chewing gum.

"Maybe. On the other hand maybe he's waiting for someone."

MEETING MIKI

The money is all right. Of course. The woman behind the counter hardly looks at the hundred-dollar Federal Reserve bill. And although Miki knew it would be all right, she can't help a feeling of relief. It's one more barrier successfully overcome.

She emerges onto the sidewalk, burger in hand, wondering if she is conspicuous in any way. In her few hours in this country she has seen people of all types of complexion, and she is beginning to realize that being from the Far East draws no particular attention. Not even in this bastard spawn of the capitalist system, McDonald's. She is less sure of her clothes, however. Around the side of the building, she is surprised to see a line of cars, and money and food exchanging hands at a kiosk. She wonders if some people in America are so used to driving that they can no longer walk. The burger is delicious. She gobbles it hungrily, licking the unfamiliar sauce from her fingers.

She saunters along the streets, both curious and overwhelmed by the high buildings, the crowds, the huge gleaming cars, the noise—Pyongyang, at night, is a city of darkness, of empty streets, where you can hear a baby cry across the river. Here is madness. And the sidewalks are dirty with litter, something unthinkable at home. America is another planet.

She wonders where the wealth comes from, what huge slave mines are needed to finance these cars and houses, to stock the shops with these incredible luxuries, to banish the darkness with all this electric light.

The stroll is calculated, intended to check whether she is being followed. She walks a few blocks, sometimes retracing her steps, sometimes quickly glancing behind. Crossing the streets is an unfamiliar, terrifying experience. She attracts more than one angry hoot. After a few blocks she is satisfied that she is truly alone. Such freedom is, of course, the fatal weakness of this giant country, the one that will bring it down. At home, it is unthinkable for a tourist to be allowed to walk unsupervised.

She turns back, light-headed with tiredness. Getting lost would have been a disaster, but there are plenty of landmarks in Planet America. Sleep is now the important thing. In a few days this aggressive, arrogant, dirty, prodigal, undisciplined country will be taught a lesson it will never forget. On the way back she passes a department store, four stories tall and thronged with life and light. She has thousands of American dollars in her purse. The improved technology behind the new redesigned note is still being studied in the Pyongyang laboratories, but the older bills are still in circulation, and it is clear that the Americans are comfortable with them. She smiles, her tiredness suddenly lifts, and she turns into the store.

"Slick chick," the lumberjack says. Miki, smartly dressed in white sweater and slacks and carrying a leather drawstring satchel, walks into the plaza, map in hand, weaving her way through a party of bustling schoolchildren. Everything she is wearing seems new. She hesitates, looks around uncertainly, sees the Wells Fargo Theater, and makes smartly for it.

For the FBI men, the slick chick suddenly becomes the focus of close attention.

"Japanese? Chinese?" the lumberjack wonders.

"Vietnamese or Korean," Caddon says, standing up abruptly. "How did she get here?" A taxi is turning left onto the zoo road. Spada produces a camera, but the woman has gone inside.

Twenty minutes later Caddon and the lumberjack have arms around each other's shoulders in a display of camaraderie and are grinning inanely as Spada takes a series of pictures, not of his FBI colleagues but of three people along the line of sight, emerging from the theater—the Far East woman, the musician, and an old man, almost geriatric, badly disfigured and walking with a stick. Petrov!

The lumberjack walks back to the table and examines the menu, giving his ear the briefest touch. He returns Caddon's anxious look with a brief, reassuring nod. Caddon texts the pictures through to HQ with an ID request for the Far East woman. The odd trio are speaking in English, heading out of the plaza toward the parking lot. So as not to be conspicuous, the lumberjack lets them get about twenty yards ahead before he follows. He can hear everything as if they are three feet away.

You're sure there's nothing in the diary? the woman is saying in good English. *Maybe he hid it in code. A code hidden in code?*

For the tenth time, the journal gave us the locations but not the codes. There's something weird about the old man's voice. It seems more metallic than human.

Very well. How are you proceeding with the alternative route?

I'm working through the list. So far none of them has known anything. The lumberjack suddenly makes sense of a mannerism. Every time the old man speaks, he puts a hand to his throat.

Damn! Another party of schoolchildren, the third in the last hour, these kids with drawing pads and pencils, cuts across his flight path. Suddenly the directional microphone is picking up an ocean of chatter. The lumberjack tries to hustle his way through the noisy crowd. To compound the problem, the breeze, away from the shelter of the plaza, is now catching the microphone, creating an unbearable din in his ear.

But, Doctor, do you not understand, we only have three days . . .

Of course . . . confident we'll get there.

In three days? The meeting takes place in three days.

Someone on the list must have known the codes. The old man is speaking angrily, or it might be anger—it's hard to say since he doesn't raise his voice. *And I believe I now know who.*

We will take it badly if you fail.

You dare to threaten me? . . . beat Stalin's gulag . . . in the habit of failing.

Is Sophia ready?

She'll be there . . .

She's the key to all this.

I told you she'll be there . . . London . . . visa? . . . make sure you play your . . .

. . . does he say? . . . she'll trigger a war, be assured.

The lumberjack can't believe he heard that, and pushes at his earphone.

A man with a blazer and flannels—chauffeur, minder, whatever—emerges from the driver's seat of the stretch limo and helps the geriatric into the back. The limo then swallows up the Asian woman like the whale with Jonah. The musician, who has been mute throughout the exchange, growls something indistinct and heads for his canary-yellow Porsche Boxster. The lumberjack takes off after the musician, and Spada takes off after the geriatric and the female. Next to him, Caddon has the registration number of the limo into the FBI computers before it has gone a hundred yards. He fires through another photograph to HQ with the single question: *Who's the dame?* Then he hastily calls for a tail for the limousine and sets wheels turning to check who, among all the known colleagues and acquaintances of Petrov, goes by the name of Sophia.

The stretch limo drops the Korean woman off at a motel and carries on. The Korean woman's motel turns out to be surprisingly awkward for surveillance, being on the corner of a freeway with no natural stops around it. And the nearest turnoffs are about half a mile in either direction, meaning that they either have to drift up and down a big loop of busy road or stop right there in the half-empty parking lot, overlooked by her motel room. In the event, Caddon books a spare room while Spada takes the Toyota around to the side of the building, next to trash cans and garbage, but out of her line of sight while in a position to see comings and goings. They call for reinforcements, which eventually arrive in the form of a black Audi containing three agents and the English MI6 woman, Ambra Volpe.

They drink motel coffee, sitting around on the bed and a couple of hard plastic chairs, and wait.

What draws their attention to the nondescript, near-bald man who drives into the lot, none of them could have said. There has been a desultory trickle of couples, business types, the occasional family as the motel gradually fills up. Maybe it's the body language; there is something business-like about the way he steps out of his car. He stretches and looks around, as if uncertain where to go. But then the Korean woman's door clicks open. He looks around oh-so-casually, licking his lips, and walks into her room, while Caddon and Spada fume at the lack of a directional microphone.

By the time the bald one emerges twenty minutes later, carrying a small black bag, they know his name is George Novello, that he is married with no children, is a computer manager with Parallax Satellite Systems based at Valley Creek Boulevard, Exton, Pennsylvania, and that his job is maintaining a string of civilian communications satellites. They also know that he is an occasional visitor to the Pentagon as well as having security clearance to visit a couple of air force bases in New Mexico. And as the material texts into his cell phone, and Spada keeps saying *What the hell are we uncovering here, boss?*, Caddon feels his stomach tightening, and he needs to know what was said in that room like a man in a desert needs water. Novello takes off, and Spada hastily takes off after him. Minutes later Petrov's stretch limo arrives and gobbles up the Korean woman. She has luggage in hand as if she's traveling. Caddon and Ambra rush into the supercharged Toyota and follow at a safe distance with Caddon, familiar with the roads, at the wheel. They know that another FBI car is tailing the limo but can't pick it out from the stream of traffic. The limo, it soon becomes clear, is heading for the airport.

"What gives?" Caddon, puzzled, is leaning against the Toyota, having chased off the airport cops with a quick flash of his badge. Ambra has run back from the terminal building and is puffing slightly.

"They're gone."

"What?"

"Demos, Petrov, and the female. All three of them."

"There's hardly been time to check in."

"They were on the slipway when I left." Ambra looks over the roof of the terminal building. "Petrov has a private jumbo, would you believe that? And there they go."

The big 747 has a white underbelly and a steel-gray top, making it look like a giant shark. BB is painted on its tail, the logo for Baryon Biosystems. Its wheels are retracting as it heads into the sky, leaving a dark contrail. Spada glares at the receding aircraft as if it has, somehow, outwitted him. "So let's get his flight plan. The bastard's gotta land somewhere."

Ambra Volpe unstraps a leather holster from her thigh and hands it over along with the little blue gun. "I loved the flower on the butt, it was cute."

Caddon takes the weapon with surprise. "What gives, Ms. Volpe?"

"I'm going to follow that aircraft. Try to get my stuff to the terminal before I take off. Been nice meeting you, Neal."

PETROV'S LIST

Sharp cups both hands around a hot chocolate laced with brandy. His mouth is dry, he is shaking, and his heart is still thumping from the frantic sprint. The wall turned out to be a two-and-a-half-meter scramble; it would have been impossible without the army's basic training and the terror of close pursuit. There was a three-meter drop into a garden with wet, clogging earth. He'd looked up and glimpsed a struggling red face, and forearms on top of the wall, before face and forearms disappeared with an angry cry. On to a stone patio, trailing mud, with a dog barking furiously inside a big white house, all colonnades and French windows. He had sprinted along the side of the house and into a mews leading to a busy street. Then a long random walk—avoiding Underground stations and surveillance cameras—had taken him to a narrow lane leading to Oxford Street, at which point he began to feel safe and slowed down to a brisk walk.

A sheet of paper from Holland Park is spread out in front of him, the wrinkles smoothed out. And on the sheet of paper is a list of names.

Klein†
Von Steiner†
Zimmerman†

Bauer
Krafft
Hosokawa

German names, all but Hosokawa. And there are little crucifixes against three of them: Klein, von Steiner, Zimmerman.

Sharp picks up the scrambler phone, dials Jocelyn's number. "Jocelyn? Lewis here. I think we're on to something. Come over here right away."

"I can't. Not yet."

"What about Petrov's 747? Is it still on the tarmac?"

"Negative. It took off a couple of hours ago, heading for Berlin. Petrov and his gang never got off it. Ambra Volpe has just landed at Heathrow, but there are no immediate connections to Berlin and she can't follow them. Our people in Germany will pick up their trail when they land."

"With Craig missing we're a brain short. I want Ambra here, we need to pool our resources. It's urgent." Everything is urgent.

"She's in a passenger terminal. I'll give you her mobile but it's not fixed with Brahms. It's unsecured."

Sharp uses oblique language for his second call. "Wolf? This is Knife. Where are you?"

"Hello, Knife. I'm in a taxi, heading for home."

"Don't go home. Come to my house first. Did our friend give you the address?"

"She did, but I'm filthy, I'm jet-lagged, and I don't have a clean change of clothes. I'm going home to sleep."

"Come here first. There's a party and it's wild."

"Twenty minutes."

Little crucifixes. One name, Max Krafft, has been circled in pencil, and next to it is written, in Cyrillic letters: *On mojet znat*. And in the margin: *Sleza?*

Ambra Volpe has a haggard, just-crossed-the-Atlantic look. She declines an offer of coffee. Sharp swallows the last of his hot chocolate and passes over the list to Ambra. "Take a look."

She drops her holdall, takes off her jacket and lets it drop, kicks off her shoes, and flops back on a couch; it's an informal, almost familiar gesture that Sharp likes. She scans the sheet of paper. "Is this a copy? It looks like the original."

"I'd no time to copy anything. The safe was alarmed and it was a case of grab it and run."

"Ouch."

"Bad news," Sharp agrees, splayed out on an armchair. "Now Petrov will know we're on to him. He'll cover his tracks."

There is a taut silence while they assimilate the fact. Ambra waves the list in the air and Sharp scans it again. She asks, "Who are these people? How do they connect? What about the first three on the list, the ones with the crucifixes?"

Sharp asks, "How's your Russian? I can order a coffee, just about."

Ambra stretches out an elegant hand and Sharp returns the sheet. She yawns and says, "*On mojet znat* means 'he might know.'"

"He might know what?"

"Well it doesn't say, Lewis. And before you ask, *sleza* means 'teardrop.' The names being German, Lewis, adds weight to your mad theory about a Nazi weapon."

Sharp says, "Some of these names are ringing bells."

Ambra sits up abruptly. "I'm going home. Anthrax bombs or not, I need clean knickers."

THE BIBLE CODES:

UPTOWN PHOENIX

It's a sticky Tuesday afternoon and Caddon and his team are scurrying through the air above desert terrain. They have to get to Phoenix quickly.

Caddon explains the business of DNA testing in language of exaggerated simplicity to the new girl, Joanna. He does this in the eight-seater Cessna they boarded at Ontario International Airport, thirty-five miles east of downtown Los Angeles, having been transported there in a black FBI helicopter. She listens, a pupil at the feet of the master, as Caddon expounds. He explains that in the pioneering days of DNA profiling, you needed big samples of body fluid to get a match. It wasn't always reliable, and smart lawyers, more often than not, made sure that the results of testing didn't even get the length of a trial.

They were shooting fish in a barrel?

You got it. But as the technology came along, we needed less and less until now the lab people just need microscopic quantities. At the same time they've pushed the accuracy to the stage where it matches fingerprints for reliability.

The fish are shooting back? Jo says, looking impressed.

Exactly. And nowadays we can even use old and partially decayed samples. Not that there's anything old and decayed about the DNA sample we've picked up. It's a dream.

A good polymerase chain reaction, was it? Lots of short tandem repeats?

Caddon takes a long swig from a mineral water bottle and gives her a sideways look.

An apple core in the pickup truck at the Goldfield mine shaft has in fact yielded enough DNA to bring joy and sunshine into Caddon's life, and to persuade the most hardheaded skeptic that the aforesaid apple was eaten by an individual whose DNA was identical to that of one Virgil Rabbit.

"Weren't so bad in the pen. Main thing was to keep to yourself—there were some mighty peculiar people in there. Good stock of books, regular visits, one or two other perks." The preacher grins slyly as if he expects the FBI agents to chase him up on that.

For Jo the term *cathouse* is acquiring a whole new meaning. There are at least two dozen of them. The cabin stinks. It stinks of cats and unwashed human as well as other ill-defined smells. She is perched on the edge of a worn armchair that might once have been blue and looks as if it is wasting away from some terminal disease. Her clothes are covered in hundreds of little white cat hairs. She is beginning to develop an itch on her left thigh but doesn't want to draw attention to the aforesaid thigh by scratching it. A pine table is covered with books, old newspapers, cut-out magazine articles, an opened can of cat food, and three or four skinny cats, the number varying. Caddon and Spada are sitting uncomfortably on a sofa, also once blue, part of a set. Through an open door Jo can see a bedroom with an unmade bed and a dresser whose walnut veneer is beginning to peel. Sitting on the dresser is another skinny cat, its head immersed in an aluminum foil carton holding the remains of a Chinese carry-out. Next to it is a beer mug containing some green liquid that she prefers not to think about.

"This is your property, Mr. Reality?" Jo asks conversationally.

"Virtual. Call me Virtual. Hey, you're kinda young for an FBI agent. Just out of the Academy, are you?"

"That's right."

"So what was it like at Quantico?"

"Interesting. This place is yours?"

"Near the marine base, ain't it?"

"Near enough to hear their gunfire. This place is yours?"

"Sure it's mine. Gunfire, huh?" Virgil Rabbit heads for a cocktail bar and pours himself a large Grand Marnier to which he adds an equal volume of vodka.

Spada says, "Mr. Reality, you were at Goldfield a few days ago."

"Was I?"

"We've got an apple core with your DNA in it, and it says you were eating the apple next to the shaft of an old copper mine at Goldfield." This is a lie. The core was on the floor of the truck. But Caddon wants Rabbit nailed to the site of the UFO, not a pickup truck that could have been anywhere with some lawyer declaring that Rabbit was an innocent hitch-hiker.

"Maybe it's a crime to eat an apple these days. Maybe I need a lawyer. Maybe I should just clam up."

Jo notices that the hand holding the vodka is trembling slightly. It might be an age thing; the man's expression is cool enough. Caddon says, "That's up to you, sir. We'd prefer your cooperation, though. Better for everyone. Save you having to answer in front of a grand jury."

By the time Virgil Rabbit has been subpoenaed and appeared in front of a grand jury, the London saucer will have come and gone, if you were to believe the crazy letter. Jo wonders if Rabbit knows it.

"Okay, so I was at some mine shaft near Goldfield. So what?"

"Well, sir, also at the mine shaft there was this pickup truck with scorch marks and a Pontiac that looked like some-one had taken a giant blowtorch to it."

"I don't own no pickup truck and no Pontiac."

"There were also four dead people. Two of them were burned black, two of them had been shot in the back running. We're not suggesting that you were involved in any of this,"

Spada lies again. "We just want to know how the apple core got there."

Rabbit takes a big gulp of his drink. "Must've happened after I passed through."

"What were you doing there, sir?"

"Passing through. Backpacking."

"You're a backpacker, then?"

"Uh-huh. Passed through last Thursday. Don't remember no pickup truck and no Pontiac."

Two cats on the table briefly hiss and spit. Something catches Jo's eye. A newspaper cutting. She strolls casually over to the table. "The UFO they saw near Payson . . ."

Rabbit looks over his shoulder. "Kinda interesting, don't you think?"

"You go in for stuff like that, Virgil?" She can't bring herself to call him Virtual. "The paper says it was just a military exercise. Some people, every time they see lights in the sky, they think UFO."

"Or maybe every time there's a UFO, the government puts out a story about a military exercise." Rabbit gives a thin smile. "Second Thessalonians chapter two. Near the end of time we shall see the working of Satan with all power and signs and lying wonders."

"I guess we work for Satan," Caddon says.

"But there's no life out there." Jo says it to provoke.

Again that razor-thin smile. "Ain't dumb, miss. Kin tail you just want me to talk. You ever heard of the Bible code?" Jo gives an encouraging shake of the head, and Rabbit continues: "I had to do some real digging in the codes but it's all there. The UFOs come from Mars."

"Mars, right."

"There's a lot of activity on Mars now. There's about fifty thousand abductees held on the planet. There's military bases there."

"The place is a desert. You can Google it, see for yourself."

"Come on, miss, that's a cover-up. The pictures are doctored. There are even NASA employees will tell you that in private. The public just don't know what's happening on the

Red Planet. But they'll know when the End Times come." He cackles. "They'll know when Satan unleashes his forces from the planet. Won't be too long a-coming. I see this in the codes everywhere I look. Satan is the prince and the power of the air. Ephesians chapter two, verse two."

"What do you think about UFOs? They come from Mars? We'll be there in thirty years and we'll know."

"The heavens belong to God, not man. We have no right to go there. Listen to Moses speaking to the children of Israel: *If there is found among you a man or a woman who has been wicked in the sight of the Lord your God, in transgressing His covenant, who has gone and served other gods and worshipped them, either the sun or moon or any of the hosts of heaven which I have not commanded you, then you shall bring out to your gates that man or woman who has committed that wicked thing, and stone to death that man or woman with stones.* Deuteronomy seventeen, straight from the mouth of Moses. He's speaking for God and He's telling His children to kill the idolaters who . . ."

"You carry all that in your head?" Caddon asks.

"Big hunks of the Book. Read it fifty-three times."

Caddon springs it: "Are you still interested in toxins, Mr. Reality?"

"Maybe." Cautiously.

"There's something I don't understand, Virtual. How does a preacher come to be interested in toxins?"

"I ain't a preacher no more."

"I suppose the flock objected to having their loved ones dug up."

"I've repented of that particular sin and moved on."

Jo carries on strolling casually around the living room. A big tomcat arches its back and rubs itself against her leg. She looks at the titles of books in a big bookcase and can't believe some of them. Just next to the corridor leading to the bedroom is a closed door. There is a stench here, and it's not just cats. She glances back at Rabbit. He has his back to her and is paying her no attention. Spada is staring at Rabbit in a fixed, unblinking way that says he is watching her.

Rabbit is finishing his liqueur and vodka. "I'll try to explain, but it's hard if you haven't studied the Bible codes like I have. You know I'm beginning to think I want a lawyer."

"Why, there's something in the codes needs a lawyer?"

It's a wooden handle and it turns quietly. The door reveals a steep flight of steps. Rabbit's voice fades as she goes down: ". . . the face on Mars . . . the Sphinx . . . the plagues on Egypt . . ." There is another door at the bottom. "This generation is the spawn of the Devil . . ." Here the stench is terrific, and with a lurch of her stomach she recognizes it as putrefaction. ". . . the Wisdom of Solomon . . . *the bites of locusts and flies did slay, and there was not found a healing for their life* . . ." The door is unlocked, but the handle is thick with grease and something else, some dark substance.

"Hey! Keep out o' there!" Rabbit's voice is raised angrily and his face is purple.

She looks up, turns the slippery handle. "Can't hear you down here."

"You got no right to open that door."

"What's that you said? Go right ahead and open the door?"

The smell of putrefying flesh hits her like a physical blow. She finds a light switch, clicks it on, surveys the scene in the light from a dim bulb. And as she tries not to gag, she realizes why Virgil Rabbit keeps cats.

THE SPIRIT MESSENGER

"Fact One: Craig is missing. Fact Two: he told us he was being followed. The man was terrified. Use your head, Jocelyn. We've been penetrated. Someone's trying to stop us."

"Oh, use your own head, Lewis. You said yourself he was in a highly stressed condition and behaving strangely."

"This is a safe house?"

"You know damned well it is."

"I'd feel even safer with a handgun around."

"So you said. You'd end up shooting the concierge. Let's not get paranoid."

"Paranoid keeps us alive, Jocelyn. And someone wants us stopped."

"Don't be ridiculous." She hesitates, while Sharp wonders what's coming. Then: "We've lost the Petrov gang."

"Did I hear correctly? Would you repeat that, please?"

"Somewhere in the Berlin traffic. I guess our embassy people aren't too practiced . . ."

What brand of mind-boggling incompetence . . . ? "Jocelyn, I saw some botch-ups in my army days, but this . . ."

"And something else."

"Something else? How can there be more than this?"

"We have four days until Saturday, Lewis. Four days."

She slams the door on the way out.

* * *

Light, dark, light, dark, light, dark . . .

Like a lighthouse. Sharp awakens with a start. The light is flashing through the crack under his bedroom door.

Downey? No, he's still missing. Sharp is alone in the safe house.

He opens the door a crack. The computer screen is flashing on and off, making deep shadows, strobing armchairs and sofas, coffee table, Hammer movie poster, the heavy velvet curtains. But he'd switched it off! And the living room is empty. He crosses to the terminal and touches the mouse, mystified and afraid.

So you got as far as Krafft and Bauer?

Startled, he types: Who is this?

But have you found how Petrov connects to them?

I asked who you are.

And the girl called Miki? They've told you about her?

I asked who you are.

Find the common bond, Lewis. Find Krafft and Bauer before Petrov's people get to them. And find what happened at the end ot the war.

Tell me more? And say who you are.

Proceed with care. There are people who don't like what you're doing.

The screen goes dead.

Invasion:

THE CONVENT, 1944–1945

U-BOAT

You couldn't spread it around with high explosives, you couldn't spray it from aircraft, you couldn't disperse it from the *Vergeltungswaffen* that were now terrorizing London. Nevertheless, you had to make it blanket a city. The project had slipped into crisis, and only an imaginative leap would get it out. It needed a new idea.

Klein excelled as a receiver and transmitter of other people's ideas but, it soon turned out, was incapable of creating one of his own. The director was an acknowledged idiot and kept away from the discussions. It was down to Daniela, Edith, Bosch, and me, pacing the study, wandering the cloisters, riding out singly or in groups, arguing into the night, getting red-eyed and headachy and bad-tempered through lack of sleep.

Sometimes at night, after a long session, we couldn't switch off. We'd disperse, just to get away and think. One or other of us would ride out under the moon, or take a walk around the parapet. Often I wandered around the dark cloisters or the quadrangle. More than once I spotted Oberlin in the shadows, standing quietly. He could be anywhere. The man gave me the creeps. Sometimes, with moonlight throwing colored light on the stone floors, my imagination would see a ghost, and I'd wonder about Sister Lucy. Now and then Daniela played Chopin almost until dawn.

It was Bosch the literature man, the only nonscientist in the group, who came up with the idea. He did it on the fourth day of Hess's deadline. It was hand-waving and amateurish and it bristled with technical problems. I smashed through them like a panzer through a brick wall. We reported to Hess, who announced that the hand of fate was at work, that the Reich could now snatch victory from the jaws of defeat, render our women safe from the Slavic hordes, and reinstate Germania at the pinnacle of civilization for the next thousand years.

Provided, of course, that the damned thing would fit into a submarine.

"Have you people even set eyes on a U-boat hatch? Our eels are only fifty-three centimeters across and they're nightmares to load into our boats. How fat did you say your payload will be? Tell me again, I need a laugh in this job."

I looked out over row after row of U-boat hulls, and despite myself felt a momentary surge of pride. How could the war be lost with armaments like that prowling the seas? They looked like giant fish, or sharks. What terror the sight of one of these sleek, futuristic contours, rising from the deep, must cause to British merchantmen! The hulls were side by side, propped up by scaffolding over which men crawled like ants. Tall derricks dotted the landscape like creatures out of *War of the Worlds*—one of the books thrown on the bonfire in Unter den Linden, as I recalled. A big rectangle of metal was swinging on a chain, dangerously close to the window. Through a light haze, in the distance, I could make out the shattered outline of Hamburg.

"I told you, well over a meter across. Maybe two." Hess's tone was faintly disapproving: This officer's attitude was verging on the insubordinate.

"You've never been inside a boat, that's for sure. They don't come that wide."

"I would prefer a serious attitude from you, Obersteurmann Walter. You have no idea what's riding on this."

"I am serious." The provisions officer stroked his beard. "A U-boat just can't take a payload that size."

"It can. Come up with a solution in ten minutes or I'll have you shot."

"That gives me time for coffee," Walter said. "Would you like some? It's real and American."

"American coffee? Where in hell's name did you get American coffee?" I asked.

"Don't ask, your colleague really would have me shot." Walter rummaged around in some shelving under a kitchen sink and came up with three cracked mugs, a bowl of lumpy sugar, and a jam jar half filled with coffee. The sounds of the construction yard were penetrating the big, grimy window, the hiss of bright blue welding arcs interspersed with the clang of hammers on rivets. "Type VIICs," the officer called over, "with the '41 modifications. We shaved twelve tons off them by using lighter equipment, and put that into strengthening the hull. An extra half centimeter of Krupps armaments steel, which lets them go deeper."

"How deep?" Hess asked.

"What are you, an English spy? That's classified."

"But you have our clearance. *The aforementioned are to be given every . . .*"

Walter was pouring boiling water into the mugs. "Yes, yes, yes, signed and sealed by Uncle Charles himself." The typed note was in his inside pocket, straight from the Befehlshaber der Kriegsmarine, his signature—Grossadmiral Karl Donitz—scrawled across the bottom of the sheet. "The hull buckles when subjected to a quarter ton of pressure on every square centimeter. That happens at 250 meters. At which depth . . ." Walter handed over mugs. "Black. American. At which depth men die."

The crush depth. I felt a twinge of claustrophobia. Better not try to imagine it.

Hess asked, "Could you modify the hatch? Make it bigger? These look like wide foredecks to me."

The officer sipped at the aromatic liquid; he gave a deep sigh, as if he had been relieved of a pain. "It's what we in the trade call the Atlantic bow. It has the width but we'd have to remove the Schnorkel and the eighty-eight-millimeter cannon from the foredeck. Meaning the crew couldn't defend themselves in the event of air attack."

"Never mind the gun. What is this Schnorkel?"

Walter joined us at the window. "Look over there. That thick thing sticking up. It pulls air in so the submarine can stay submerged. It was a Dutch invention, but it has problems. If the valve closes suddenly at sea, the diesels keep sucking air out of the boat. After a couple of minutes the crew can't breathe, their eardrums burst, their fillings pop out, and some of them turn purple and die. It's an unpopular device."

"So removing it won't cause too much grief," I suggested. I sipped the American coffee—the aroma, the taste! Oh God.

"Meaning you have to surface for air every night. Straightforward suicide nowadays. And what about the gun? What would removing the eighty-eight do to crew morale?"

"They only need to sail the damned boat."

"And your payload would take up the whole of the forward torpedo room, depriving aforesaid crew of their bunks while you're at it. And it's not just the guns and the bunks," the officer said, warming to the theme. "These boats carry up to fourteen torpedoes, but with your cuckoo in the nest there wouldn't be space for more than the ones stored in the tubes. You'd be sending the submariners out naked."

"But it could be done?" Hess's little eyes were focused keenly on the officer.

"Sending young men into the Atlantic without weapons? Of course it can be done, if that's what you want. And why not?" Walter waved an arm expansively. "Half of them'll be dead within the year anyway."

"Be careful what you say. Defeatist talk . . ."

"Defeatist? That's not quite the way I see it."

"Oh? And how do you see it, Obersteuermann Walter?" Hess had adopted a tone of exaggerated politeness.

I knew the tone. I interrupted quickly. "We'd want to keep security tight."

"Then you don't want Blohm and Voss." The petty officer nodded in the direction of the yard. "Some of these people are forced labor. They hate us with an intensity you wouldn't believe. God knows what will happen to us if we lose the war."

"Do you need to be reminded that we will not lose the war?"

"What's your point, Obersteurmann?" I asked. The young officer seemed determined on a course of self-destruction.

"The point is that some of these workers almost certainly have contact with enemy agents. I'd advise you to use one of the smaller yards, like Flensburger Schiffau in Denmark. Security is tighter, and you could sail your boat with its magic cargo through the Kiel canal straight into the North Sea. What is this payload anyway?"

"What are you, a spy? That's classified." Hess turned to me, a happy smile making his face almost unrecognizable. "We can transport the cargo, Max. The world belongs to us. Heil Hitler."

"Heil Hitler, and death to all Bolsheviks," I said, and Walter spluttered into his American coffee.

TREASON

January 26, 1945. The Americans and the British four hundred kilometers to the west, pushing through Alsace. The Russians four hundred kilometers to the east, approaching the Austrian border. A giant pincer squeezing, the wonder weapons not yet constructed.

And a treat as rare as a yellow diamond, a night out on the town.

It was our second winter in the convent. Over the year Hess had frequently disappeared, bustling in and out importantly in a six-seater Horsch normally reserved for generals. Bosch, too, was often away on procurement exercises, after which he'd return with black-market luxuries like perfume and silk stockings for the women. Daniela showed special pleasure with every bar of Swiss chocolate the little professor smuggled in. I'd had only two trips away from the convent and its brooding mountains—Natzweiler and Hamburg. Klein, Edith, and Daniela had left the area only once. It was a bitter winter, and I'd tried yet again to have the slave labor transferred to the empty dormitories, and Oberlin had yet again refused, indeed seemed baffled by my concern.

We took the six-seater to Salzburg, Daniela at the wheel, Hess in an expansive mood, his left arm now and then stretching possessively around her shoulder. The big car had a puncture in pouring rain next to a misty lake. We were soaked through and Daniela put the car's heating on full and the inside steamed like a tropical jungle and it was mid-afternoon before Daniela was trickling the big Horsch through the narrow, Baroque streets of Mozart's birthplace.

If there was a war on, Salzburg didn't know it: The city was equidistant between the pincers. We wandered the busy town, soaking up its Italianate atmosphere. We found a restaurant, crowded, hot, and noisy, ordered bacon dumplings and drank a lot of beer. Bosch and Daniela finished off with Salzburger Nockerl, a light, sweet regional soufflé, and argued loudly over the din about the merits of Salzburg versus Viennese cooking.

By mutual consent we went to a local cinema, as if reluctant to return to the convent and the war. We spread ourselves around the smoky, crowded little bug house. I sat wedged between a couple of farmworkers, one of them smelling of manure, the other spreading his fat arms into my space. In the gloom I could just make out Hess and Daniela near the front, over to my left. Hess had his arm around her, and not for the first time I wanted to lower him into a pool of crocodiles. The newsreel showed the defense of the Oder, cheerful young heroes stemming the Russian tide to the sound of gunfire and martial music. I looked around the darkened cinema. There was a curious, almost childish thrill in knowing that *half a dozen of us in this little cinema can reverse that tide, can change history, and nobody knows but us.*

The movie showed the unlikely adventures of Baron von Munchausen in Agfacolor, another triumph of German technology. A movie about the Baron of Lies, from an industry controlled by Goebbels. In the final shot the baron blew out a candle whose smoke streamed into the word ENDE, there was a round of patriotic applause, the lights came up, and we all stood for the "Lied der Deutschen."

We were back in the convent, through thickening snow, by midnight. Bosch and Daniela had continued the culinary argument all the way, Viennese sophistication versus Salzburg regionalism. Everyone collapsed into their rooms; everyone but Daniela, who unwound at the piano. Christmas music drifted through the empty cloisters for an hour. I wondered if they could hear it in the laundry, if "Alleluia" and "Stille Nacht" helped them endure the deadly cold.

I don't know what awakened me. The music had stopped. I was thirsty, maybe it was just that. I dressed, opened the door, and sensed rather than saw a figure disappearing silently up the stairs, leading to the dormitories above.

Something about that. Something about the stealth.

I slipped my shoes off and ran silently toward the stairs. I just glimpsed a figure disappearing around the stairwell. I took the steps two at a time, breathing quietly through my mouth. Again, the figure was just disappearing as I looked. It was silent as a ghost, and moving quickly. I followed, stopping cautiously at each turn of the corridor.

A complete circuit of the cloister was possible on the second floor, as it was on the first and ground floors. On the north corridor, the figure had vanished. This was occupied by the empty dormitories. Baffled, I moved along the corridor, torn between haste and stealth.

Halfway along there was a narrow set of stairs, which I'd never explored. I went quietly down these and found myself on the first floor again. The stairs continued down. They opened into the hallway at the entrance to the convent. I wondered if the mysterious figure was sneaking out of the convent, but that didn't make sense. There were guards at the front, and in any case why not just go straight out? Why climb to the top only to go down again? Confused, I stood quietly, trying to see movements among the pillars and tombs.

A slight movement thirty meters to my left. A door, not quite closed. Not the door leading to the remainder of the wing; a small side door. I ran over, opened it quietly, found myself at a back entrance to the kitchen. I peered into the dark corners. Nobody.

Somebody. A faint, metallic clink, like a pot lid being replaced quietly. A figure that had been crouching under the table straightened up and came straight toward me. I backed out, crouching low, ran to a tomb—Edouardo de Clari—and bent down behind it.

She'd passed within two meters of me and hadn't seen me. She was breathing heavily. I couldn't make her out but I recognized the scent. I'd been sniffing Daniela's perfume all day in the car.

And then the dream shifted the way that they do, and I was in my old room on the estate, surrounded by my books. The little stuffed elephant, the hunting pictures, the sailing ship on top of the bookcase—I saw them all in amazing detail, and yet it was dark, only a little light coming in from a moon peering shyly through the window. And in my dream Sister Lucy, her voluptuous, naked body reflecting the moonlight, was sliding between the sheets, and in the instant before it faded I thought it strange that dreams that seem to last for an age can lead inexorably toward some unpredictable waking event like a telephone ringing, a bump in the night, or a woman sliding in between the sheets.

A smooth warm thigh, riding over mine. Then she was on top of me. She was light—that perfume again!—and her hair tickled my nose. She was trembling, thighs straddling me, breasts squeezing against my chest. Her cheeks were moist; she'd been crying. She began kissing me, gently at first.

"Would you like a coffee, Daniela?" She was lying, sheets up to her nose, eyes shiny in the near dark, her hair black against the pillow.

"If you can make it the real stuff."

"I'll ask one of the—no, I can't."

She gave a nervous, deep-throated laugh.

I dressed quickly, slightly embarrassed, and hurried out of the door. Ten minutes later I was back with a tray, coffee, cheese sandwiches.

"We should do this again," Daniela said.

I set the tray down on a chair. She'd been back to her room and was half dressed, wearing a cotton underskirt, stockings but no shoes, and pearl earrings. Her garters were visible through the thin underskirt.

Stockings from Bosch, perfume from Bosch. She was rummaging through papers on my desk.

"What are you doing?" I was pouring coffee.

"Looking at your lab book. You've made a schoolboy mistake here, Max. Average rate isn't the inverse of average time. Hess hates you. He really does."

"How do you know that?"

She came back and sat down on the bed. Her eyelids were red. She didn't answer.

"What have I done to him?"

"Can't you see?"

I shook my head in bewilderment.

"God, you're insensitive. Hess is a failure, and you remind him of that fact every time you open your mouth. Nobody takes him seriously. Everybody knows how he got his directorship at the Kaiser-Wilhelm Institute."

"I don't."

Daniela laughed quietly. "By wearing a brown shirt. By singing the 'Horst Wesselied' louder than anyone else. By shouting *Zeig Heil* to everyone he passed in the corridors. By racial attacks on his professor, thinly disguised as scientific criticism. And when the time came, and the non-Aryan professors were thrown out, he had made all the right friends to let him walk into the directorship. He's a third-rater and he knows it and so did the real scientists, what's left of them at the institute. But you, Max, look at you. You rub shoulders with Nobel Prize winners. You even met Einstein once, didn't you?"

"More than once."

"You treat Hess with contempt, I see it every time you speak to him. That's a dangerous mistake but you don't see it. You think he's a fool but he's not. He has this seething jealousy of you, and he's smart enough to know that you have one big weakness. You're not one of them. You lack conviction, political conviction."

"The devil with that stuff. I'm a loyal German."

"Even that, Max, even that. He's questioning it."

"What exactly is it between you and Hess?" The question came out more harshly, more jealous even, than I had intended.

She shook her head and pulled a cardigan around her shoulders as if she was cold. "It's not something I can tell you about, Max. I'm on a tightrope—don't ask why. I try to keep him at arm's length but I can't afford to antagonize him."

"What does that mean? I can't make sense of a statement like that."

She ignored my question. "Kurt told me about Natzweiler, about the way you reacted. He thought your behavior was treasonable. Edith had to talk him out of having you arrested. It's only the fact that the project is top secret and you're essential to it . . ."

"What I saw degrades everyone who takes part in it. Sugar?"

She put a finger to my lips. "No. Don't tell me any more. I get the idea. But what can you do?"

"I've seen the effects of our stuff in tiny doses. And we're going to spray cities with it."

"You're confused?"

"No. I'm at war."

"On the wrong side."

Alarm surged through my body; it was a distinct rush of adrenaline. "I didn't hear that, Daniela."

She put her coffee down, stood up to face me. "The gangsters are dragging our country down into hell, Max. They've created their own Götterdämmerung and we're all going down in flames."

"You don't jump ship just because things are going badly. You heard Goering. Our weapons are the big surprise, the things that will turn the tide and win the war for us."

"You mean win it for the Führer and Fat Hermann and the Poisonous Dwarf, and the people who run places like Natzweiler."

I felt self-conscious, ridiculous even, but also angry. "Loyalty to the state is a fundamental duty of every citizen. Always has been. No matter who runs it."

"Is this what you want for Germany?"

"What exactly are you saying?"

"We're talking about the complete moral collapse of our country. We'll be reviled for a hundred years. They're trying to exterminate whole peoples. Wake up, Max." She paused, bit her lip, and then said, "I want us to sabotage this project."

"Is that why you jumped into bed with me?" Treason talk! I was beginning to shake with anger.

She put her head in her hands, started to cry quietly.

"Not even a general's daughter can get off with that. You were joking, otherwise it would be my duty to report you. You'd hang." I rummaged in a drawer and passed her a handkerchief.

"Open your eyes, Max." She blew her nose. "Germany's been hijacked by gangsters. Do you seriously think we should be loyal to gangsters? Obey their laws?"

"How can they be gangsters? They've been recognized by other states as the legitimate government of Germany since before the war started. How can their laws be unlawful?" My heart was pounding. I was furious, not least because she was crystallizing my own half-formed thoughts . . .

"Keep your voice down." She stamped over to my desk, picked up a sheet of paper, and waved it angrily at me. It was the calibration curve. "This is all legal and authorized, on Reich-headed paper. I saw your face when Hess was showing it. Who is this cross? X equals thirty kilograms, Y equals six minutes. Who weighs thirty kilos, Max? Who weighed thirty kilos and took six minutes to die?"

"A starving child."

"So who comes first on your love list? A starving child or your precious country? Who do you save?"

"I don't know how to answer that. What are you, Satan?"

Daniela stared at me, eyes red and wet. "You bastard! How dare you even think about it! What are you, another gangster like the rest?"

"Daniela . . ."

She gave me a stinging slap on the cheek, she was out of control. "Something you should know about me, Max. I'm Jewish. Now you can hang me twice over."

OBERLIN

The high-backed chair was empty and I was startled to hear Oberlin's voice behind me. It was as if the man had been hiding behind the door. He was wearing his high-peaked cap and flicking through sheets of paper. "Do sit down, Herr Krafft."

I ignored the instruction. I walked over to a lead-lined window and looked out over the meadow. Some farmer had put cattle out to graze; I'd heard the cowbells the previous night, after Daniela had fallen asleep, drained, in my arms.

The security chief tossed papers onto the desk and began to pace up and down his long room thoughtfully, arms behind his back, as if he were alone. I wondered if this was part of the technique: make you wonder what was coming, make you feel unsettled. Then Oberlin stopped and, legs astride, said: "There's not much going on in this convent that escapes me, Herr Krafft."

"I don't doubt it. I'm sure you have informers."

"I know, for example, that you have been sharing a bed with Daniela Bauer."

"I'd have said that's none of your business, security chief or not."

"There you are very wrong, Krafft. Cigarette?"

"The Order doesn't approve of smoking, Herr Oberlin.

Your body is the property of the state and must be kept fit and well. And you don't know everything. Otherwise you would know that I'm not a cigarette man."

Oberlin smiled for about a second, walked over to his desk, and opened a drawer. He lit a cigarette and offered me a small cigar. I took it and accepted a light from the security chief's match. "A Havana cheroot. I'm impressed."

"Confiscated from some little crook in Munich. I have an old school friend in the RSHA office there." Oberlin managed an unpleasant grin. "They let the smuggler have one of his own smokes while the firing squad waited."

I sensed that Oberlin was gathering his thoughts. I puffed on the black-market cigar—oh joy!—and waited.

The security chief sat on the edge of his desk. I felt a tinge of queasiness. It might have been the cigar; the last one had been three Christmases ago—or was it four? I stayed quiet.

Oberlin flicked ash into a tray full of cigarette stubs. "You are a member of the Nazi Party. You joined just before the war."

"Actually, my mother signed me up." It was the literal truth, but I tried to make it sound like a joke.

"I know."

How could Oberlin possibly have known that? Is there anything he doesn't know? "Forgive me, Herr Oberlin, but where is this getting us?"

Oberlin ignored the question. He resumed his pacing up and down the long room, heels clicking on the polished wooden floor. "I have the authority to put anyone in this institute up against a wall. Anyone. The Order has control of all agencies of state and party. However, it grieves me to say that the Waffen-SS sometimes owes only paper allegiance to the Reichsführer. Too many of the officer clique have no political education whatever. All they think of is drink and women. Social standing is still a criterion for promotion."

"What of it?"

"Your background is the Waffen-SS, Krafft. You are a conscript, not a volunteer. I have to consider that background in judging your degree of commitment to the state."

"Does this have something to do with the sabotage attempt, Herr Oberlin? Do you suspect me?" I kept my voice level.

Oberlin blew smoke and looked at me carefully. He didn't answer.

"I'm sure your spies will confirm that I was tucked up in bed on the night of the explosion."

"Something you should know about Daniela Bauer. She is Jewish."

He knows! Bluff it out.

"Don't be ridiculous. Her father's a Waffen-SS general."

"But her mother is Helena Rosenberg, born in Vienna in 1905, the second child of Helga and Philip Rosenberg. Helga was a professional singer, Philip was a lawyer. Both Jews. Their daughter Helena Rosenberg—Daniela's mother—is listed in the birth register of Vienna's Jewish community. Helena Rosenberg moved to Frankfurt at age twenty where, I am sorry to say, she received permission from the kaiser to study medicine. She then moved to Berlin, where we believe she met Gustav Bauer. The Jewess ensnared him into marriage."

"You're making this up."

"Helena Rosenberg took on an Aryan identity just before she married."

"How could that be done?"

"She presented herself to a Kripo Identification Office as Gisela Adler, who later turned out to be an old friend from her Vienna days. She declared that she had lost all her papers in a boating accident. Gustav Bauer, at that time a colonel in the Wehrmacht, vouched for her as this Gisela Adler. She was then issued with new papers in that name, and she married in that name. Daniela's mother is a U-boat." Oberlin used the Berlin nickname for a Jew passing himself off as Aryan. "Which makes Daniela herself half Jewish."

"I think I'll have that seat."

Oberlin stood over me. "I know you're now having sexual relations with the Jewess. You will be aware that is strictly forbidden. In particular, as an SS man, even an honorary one, the penalties are severe."

"But I had no idea. Anyway, how can you be sure this is true?"

Oberlin took the cigarette from his mouth and stubbed it out. He coughed, and I felt a fine spray. "So long as Gisela Adler in Vienna was never connected with Gisela Adler in Berlin, there was no problem. But unfortunately for both of them, a connection was made. Helena Rosenberg was recognized in a Berlin street four months ago, by someone from her Viennese past, and heard using her false name. You see, Krafft, you can never be quite sure about anything."

"Has she been arrested?"

"Max," said Oberlin, "the Gestapo aren't stupid. She was followed and her background was investigated. Knowing my colleagues, it would all be done with the utmost discretion and without raising any suspicion. When it was realized that her daughter is engaged in work vital to the outcome of the war, everything was frozen. The matter went right to Hermann Goering. The decision has been made to let Daniela Bauer continue working on this project until it has been completed. We simply cannot afford to lose her."

"You've known this for four months?"

"Correct."

"What about the director? Has he been told?" I couldn't help myself. *Get a grip, Max. Don't let this reptile control you.*

A hint of a smile. "Why do you wish to know?"

"Just curious."

Oberlin was still smiling unpleasantly. "The director has made advances to Dr. Bauer. She has rejected them, but in a way that keeps him dangling. She pretends an interest in him. And in Bosch."

I'd seen both of them acting like adolescent schoolboys around her, but it was still stunning news. He blew smoke down his nostrils. "Perhaps it is the natural tendency for the Jew to insinuate into positions of influence, perhaps it is for reasons of self-preservation, against the day when her racial origins are discovered. Either way, our director is unaware of her racial background. In my business I sometimes find it convenient to keep information, shall we say, in reserve."

"Has anyone ever told you you're a weasel?"

Oberlin waved a hand dismissively. "You're not required to like me. Few people do."

"Not even your mother?"

"You must be wondering why I'm telling you this."

I stubbed out my cigar. Oberlin continued: "We never did identify the saboteur. But the Jewish roots of Daniela Bauer have made me suspicious—it's my job, you see, to be suspicious. And there is something else."

There was something in Oberlin's expression. I waited. "What's going on in that diseased brain of yours, Oberlin?"

"Once a week some of our kitchen workers are taken to Mittelwald under guard, to buy provisions. Every six weeks or so they go to Munich for the same reason. One of these staff, a Polish woman, was found to be in possession of secret papers. Unfortunately she was shot as she tried to flee, which means we have no means of finding how she acquired the papers, or whom she was intending to hand them to."

Daniela, that night in the kitchen. Leaving something in a cooking pot? Do I tell Oberlin? Does he already know? Is he testing me? I felt a tightness in my chest.

"What were they?"

Oberlin pulled over the drawer and tossed over a handful of papers, stapled together. I shifted an empty coffee cup and flicked through the pages. I looked up, bewildered.

"You recognize them?"

"Of course I do. It's my handwriting. And I drew that—" I pointed to a rough sketch.

Oberlin said, "Can you imagine the damage that could be done if the Americans found out what we're doing? How much information has already gotten out?"

"I don't understand this. Everything gets locked away in the bishop's safes at the end of the day. Every sheet of paper has to be accounted for. You know that." We each had our own safe, and our own key. "Do you think I'm a traitor? That I handed these over to one of the Poles?"

"No traitor would be so conspicuously critical of his superiors. However, there are only two keys to your safe. I have one, and you have the other."

"Which I carry on a chain around my neck, as we all do." I unbuttoned the top of my shirt to display the key, hanging on a steel chain. *I have to tell him. My country comes first.* I felt a light sweat beginning to develop on my brow.

Oberlin was watching me closely. "Who could remove the key from around your neck? Who but the woman who shares your bed?"

I stayed silent. It was horribly possible. Oberlin continued: "I have arranged for delivery of a new safe for you. From now on the safes will be guarded day and night. The conscripted labor force will be relocated to one of our work camps in the east. Replacements will arrive tomorrow. You will not fraternize with them."

"What do you want from me, Herr Oberlin?"

"I want you to continue your intimacy with the Jewess. Gain her confidence. Make her trust you completely—I doubt if she does as yet. And when she has faith in you, use her trust to find out what game she is playing. Is she, as I believe, passing information to someone else in the convent? How is she doing it? Does she have a contact outside these walls? Be discreet, and give her no hint that she is under suspicion. And whatever you find out, report it to me." The security chief attempted a friendly smile, and I felt my skin crawl. "You see, Krafft, I'm putting a considerable amount of trust in you."

SUMMONS TO BERLIN

Hess flung open Daniela's office door. "We have to be in the Reich Chancellery by noon tomorrow. We report to Goering." He was looking pompous, flustered, and scared all at once.

Bosch paled. *"Oh mein Gott!"*

I was holding a duster, at a blackboard thick with equations. "It would take at least two days to get there. What idiot asked for that?"

"Watch your tongue, Krafft. It was the Reichsmarschall himself. Speer is sending us his private train. We have to board it in Munich by noon today. I need a progress report for the Reichsmarschall now."

"It can't be done."

"Don't argue with me!" Hess shouted, in near panic. "Type up something now. And where *zum Teufel* is Daniela?"

"Max! Get a move on!" Bosch was strutting like Mussolini; I thought he'd either caught the atmosphere of hysteria or was trying to impress Hess. The impudent squirt! Two big soft-top cars were waiting, engines purring. Streaks of mud lined the wheel rims, and swastika pennants hung limply on their hoods. A few flakes of snow were drifting down, threatening more.

"Yes, yes!" I shouted in irritation, waiting at the entrance.

Daniela appeared at last, turning up the collar of her long gray coat; between collar and fur hat, little more than eyes and nose were visible. We scurried across the courtyard. She joined Hess in the front car, pecking his cheek lightly. *Altogether too intimate, Daniela.* I climbed into the following car, next to Bosch, slamming the door hard. Bosch said, "You might have dressed a bit smarter, Max. You're meeting Goering, *verdammt nochmal.*"

The cars took off swiftly down the steep winding road, pennants fluttering, a soldier saluting smartly as we passed the sentry box. Four kilometers down the hill, the road forked, left to Mittelwald, right to Munich. The cars turned right.

"This is what the war is about," Bosch declared. We were passing through a fairy-tale Alpine village. The cars swerved out to pass a group of Hitler Youths on bicycles, led by a man wearing a Tyrolean hat. "Can you imagine the Tatar-Mongol hordes let loose on this? Raping our women, murdering our children, pissing in the street? An obscenity! It must never be allowed to happen."

"I put in two years with Panzer Troop Thirty-three in Poland and Kiev. Don't talk to me about raping women and murdering children."

Bosch peered at me closely. "Sometimes I wonder about you, Max. You know what I mean?" He studied the back of the chauffeur's neck. "People are talking about you. People in a position to do you harm."

I stayed silent.

"How long have Daniela and you been intimate?"

"What sort of a damned question is that?" The army driver had glanced briefly in the rear mirror.

"Not one a gentleman should ask, I know, but these are dangerous times." Bosch paused. "All I can do is give you some advice. Drop her, Max. Drop her now, drop her absolutely. She's more dangerous than you know."

I lapsed into a sullen silence.

The station reeked of sulfur, and it was crowded with farmers and their wives, office workers, a cluster of sleek girls with bright red lipstick, a scattering of rootless itinerants. One of them, a small, gray-skinned man with fear in his face, was being questioned by railway police. And every type of uniform seemed to be in transit: green-trimmed *polizei*, black-uniformed SS men, another troop of Hitler Youths, a few disheveled, bearded U-boat men in single file like hunting dogs—here in Munich?

We arrived in Berlin three hours behind schedule, a slippage that propelled Hess into something like paranoia. He ran on to the station road and leapt around frantically, waving his arms and bringing traffic to a halt. We jumped into a black Mercedes and an ambulance—both empty apart from their drivers—and crossed the city at crazy speed to the Reichsmarschall's Air Ministry on the Willemstrasse.

"The Reichsmarschall expected you over three hours ago. He has left for Karinhall. He prefers to be out of Berlin before the Luftgangsters arrive. However, he expects you there this evening as his guests, eight o'clock sharp." The desk lieutenant glanced at Daniela's woolen scarf, my London jacket, Edith's ridiculous out-of-fashion hat. "Dress informal, fortunately. I'd advise you to leave soon. If you get caught in a raid, you won't get there at all."

The commandeered vehicles headed for Schonow, north of the city, where the Reich Minister's personal transport would collect us. The idiot driving the Mercedes managed to get lost in a maze of rubble-strewn streets. I could see Hess up front bawling hysterically at the man. Acrid smoke was drifting in, adding to the stale cigarette smell. I looked across at a three-story building, its side cleanly removed, making it look like a giant doll's house, exposing rooms on three floors, furniture in place, carpets hanging half out, a bath dangling by its plumbing like a man holding on by his fingertips. The driver finally connected with the Westhafen Canal and sped over it heading north, still at a lunatic speed, while we tried to keep up; no doubt he was urged on by Hess, no doubt he was equally desperate to clear the city before dark, away from the vampires that were surely now winging their way out of England.

It was almost dark by the time the little motorcade swept into the forest, flanked by motorcyclists, a bike with sidecar and mounted machine gun taking up the rear. Beside me, Bosch had lapsed into an awed silence.

Then the escort stopped at a tall gate bristling with Lufftwaffe: I recognized the Goering Regiment, the Reichsmarschall's private police force. Soldiers with torches waved us on. The forest air was damp and icy. A motorcyclist led us toward a huge, ugly building, a bizarre mixture of English thatched roofs and Taj Mahal without the grace.

We crunched along a gravel path past sundials, Cupids, Roman busts, and vases taller than men, just visible in outline between shrubs. Then into a warm atrium lined with amazing works of art, no doubt contraband from the great galleries of Europe—Goering had a personal looting unit. "Stay here, please," a bespectacled Lufftwaffe captain said; apart from the close-cropped hair, he had the bearing and appearance of a schoolteacher. We stood, nervous schoolboys awaiting the summons from the headmaster.

Hess sidled up to me. He spoke in a low, almost whispering tone, icy and nervous both at once. "You won't be making any stupid comments, will you, Max? You're here as a technical expert and nothing else. So *halt das Maul* on any other issue."

"I don't know what you're talking about."

"I think you do. You will make no mention of any unpleasantness you may have seen, and you will say nothing about any misgivings you may have about our work. Have I made myself clear?"

The adjutant reappeared. "This way, gentlemen." We followed him. The corridor was ridiculously long and lined with paintings, at least one of which—*Venus* by Lucas Cranach—I'd last seen in Paris, prewar. My legs were shaking. Daniela, the Jewess summoned to meet Goering, was looking pale. Then we were into a great room lined with more paintings, with bronze nudes in each corner, a wall entirely lined with some medieval tapestry, and a long table set with food, candles burning and champagne in silver ice buckets.

We had entered the black heart of the Third Reich.

SUPPER WITH THE FAT ONE

You met Hermann Goering? You actually met him? That chasm again; the girl looking at me as if I come from Mars. To her, Goering is a figure from history as remote as Jesus Christ or Genghis Khan, or something out of a storybook. What was he like? the young man asks. I'm on my second pipe and my room has a light blue haze. Old men are entitled to their vices, and my little audience doesn't seem to mind. He was popular with the soldiers, I say, he was der Dicke to them. They sense something in my voice, and I add, But he terrified the life out of us. Yes, all of us: but especially our director. A safe seventy years after that night, I can smile at the memory. What was Goering like?

Creator of the Gestapo. Head of the Luftwaffe. Deputy head of the Third Reich and designated successor to Adolf Hitler. Cocaine addict.

Art lover; war hero; conservationist; faithful husband.

The man with power of life and death over two hundred million people had cheeks lightly tinged with rouge, and I thought he might be wearing lipstick. Certainly his nails were varnished. His stubby fingers were bedecked with rings. The pupils of his eyes were dilated. He was wearing a silver-gray uniform. It shimmered slightly with every movement, and had broad gold-braided epaulets, but it didn't conceal the wodges of fat underneath. The Grand Cross of the Iron Cross was at his neck—the only such decoration in existence, since Hermann Goering had created it simply for himself. He was lounging back in an armchair close to an open fire, face beaded with perspiration.

Apart from Goering and the convent visitors, there were four men in the enormous room. Three of them were officers; the fourth was wearing a suit and was looking at the visitors through cigarette smoke with narrowed eyes. *Gestapo*.

On the armchair across from Goering, sitting uncomfortably upright, was a man in the uniform of an SA general. The other two officers were standing at the table, heaping plates with food and cheese.

Goering heaved himself out of the armchair and approached his new guests. "Hess, you finally arrived."

"We had transport problems . . ."

Goering waved a hand. "Introduce your staff, please."

"This is Dr. Daniela Bauer. She's a mathematician." Goering nodded politely but didn't offer his hand.

"Dr. Edith Zimmerman, our microbiologist. Professor Bartholomew Bosch . . ." Bosch smiled nervously.

"Yes, I remember you, Bosch. You were a first-class procurement officer. I recommended you for the team. Has he done you all right?"

"Splendidly, Your Excellency. Here we have Dr. Max von Krafft, our engineer, and this is Dr. Otto Klein, a chemist from Farben."

Goering gave a little bow. A ringed hand pointed to the officers. "General Heinrici, Standartenführer Kammler, Colonel Heber. And Herr Hohne." This latter the Gestapo man.

His Excellency now waved his hand over the buffet. "Help yourself to nibbles. We should not stand on ceremony here. I will be most interested to learn of your progress. More than interested."

My last meal in Kharkov had been horsemeat. Goering

picked up a biscuit with a slab of meat and spread some chutney on it. It was the signal to cluster around the table.

"Reindeer's tongue." Goering smiled at Daniela's puzzlement.

Daniela nibbled a piece and said, "My first taste of it. And it's very good, Reichsmarschall."

"I am glad you like it. I shot her this morning. She was a difficult target, young and agile. And quite beautiful."

What does he mean? She returned his smile and swallowed the reindeer tongue with every sign of enjoying it.

Hess was pouring champagne for himself, Edith, Klein, and Bosch. There was no communication with the army officers. The Gestapo man stood alone.

"The salmon is very fresh," Goering told me. "I fly it in from the lakes around Helsinki." And the caviar? That puzzled me: Manstein's Army Group South had lost their toehold in the Black Sea around Odessa. But to inquire would have been tactless, if not disastrous.

One of the servants approached Goering: "They're coming in from the north, Excellency. Forty minutes."

Goering announced, "Bombers are on the way in. They'll pass overhead. But we have time." He snapped his fingers.

The pastry chef, a small, bearded man, came in carrying a silver tray. On it was an elaborate white cake decorated with meringue piping swirls and pink rosettes, topped with flowers made from sugar. "I stole him from Demel's in Vienna," Goering explained. "And this is his creation, *Spanische Windtorte,* surely the high point of Aryan civilization, *Lebensart* in the Viennese style." The Reichsmarschall had two helpings washed down with half a bottle of a sweet, golden Heuriger made, he informed us, from grapes grown on the vineyards of the Burgenland. Hess, having finished the champagne, thought he'd have a go at that.

As the buffet progressed I found it impossible to relax, but next to me, Daniela was keeping up an easy flow of chat with Goering.

At last, aides, thugs with close-cropped hair dressed in

eighteenth-century Hanoverian livery, were removing the gold plates and the candlesticks, and cigarettes and cigars were being passed around. It seemed the Order's disapproval of smoking and sybaritic luxury stopped outside Karinhall. Goering adopted the air of a man settling down to business. He snapped his fingers again. The thugs scurried up with high-backed chairs bearing the Prussian crest, spread them in a semicircle around the fire as if by prior instruction, and then vanished. I reckoned we had about twenty minutes before the Lancasters. How useful that the leadership got that sort of advance warning. I'd heard that Himmler, Goebbels, and the like scarpered to surrounding villages whenever the RAF was due to appear.

Goering took a sip at the glass of wine. "Our soldiers are the best in the world. Does anyone disagree?"

Nobody was about to disagree with the Reichsmarschall; there was a murmur of assent round the fireplace. I nodded and meant it. Bosch was leaning back and smoking a cigarette that smelled of real tobacco, a beatific expression on his face. The fool.

"But they are being overwhelmed by sheer numbers and firepower. Germany is like a man in a room whose walls are closing in. Between the Bolshevik hordes on the one side and vast quantities of American weaponry on the other, we are being crushed." The Reichsmarschall's pudgy hands closed together like a man crushing a skull. "Defeatists might even say that without some new wonder weapon, the war is lost."

The words came as a shock. Goebbels's broadcasts never mentioned the possibility of defeat. Struggle yes, but not defeat. Goebbels, of course, was full of *scheisse*.

"If this happens to be true"—Goering's eyes ranged over his supper guests—"then responsibility for the future of the Third Reich, and hence of the Aryan race, rests on your shoulders."

Grandiose stuff. I caught Kammler glancing at my sports jacket. *You might have dressed a bit smarter, Max.*

Goering paused for a few seconds, letting his words sink in. Then, in a tone that carried the lightest touch of menace:

"You have been excused military service. You have been given freedom to develop your ideas without outside interference. You have been given every facility and enjoyed every comfort while your brothers and sisters have toiled and many of them have bled to death. It is now time for you to return the favor. Standartenführer Hess. What have your people done?"

Hess was sitting as if he had a rod thrust up through his alimentary canal, gripping his wineglass in a clenched fist. He had adopted a deferential tone that I'd never before heard him use. "I have directed my group into two areas of research. One is the use of poison gas of a new type, the other is the dispersal of anthrax spores."

Goering leaned forward. "This new poison gas. Explain."

"I'm referring to the new gas invented by Dr. Gerhard Schrader of IG Farben. He has called it sarin after himself and his colleagues—Schrader, Ambros, Rudriger, and Linde. It is colorless and odorless. It acts not simply through inhalation, but by penetrating the skin. The first samples were prepared not far from here, in Spandau, while our army was liberating the former Poland."

The Reichsmarschall shook his head impatiently. "I am not interested in the history. I want to know what you have done with this gas. What you have devised."

Hess took a nervous sip. "We have designed a bomb that could wipe out a city."

Goering's expression didn't change. One of the officers, Kammler, said, "It took over a thousand enemy bombers to destroy Hamburg. And you say you can do it with a single bomb?"

"My colleague knows the technical details." Hess gave me a frightened look.

What a coward! I stood up, took a single sheet of paper from my inside pocket, unfolded it, and carried it across to the Reichsmarschall. It was a sketch of the weapon I'd drawn up that morning. To call it a report was to stretch the language to breaking point.

"What is this?" Goering asked. "A spinning top?"

"It is, Excellency. A spinning top that flies."

"And that can destroy a city?"

"Correct. We know that a cubic meter of the sarin gas, properly dispersed, could destroy all human life in, say, central London or Washington. The problem is dispersal. If we used high explosive to disperse the compound, we would simply destroy it. The same problem applies to anthrax spores—they're just killed close to an explosion. That was our big problem. To disperse without destroying."

"And your spinning top solves this problem?" The faces across from me were intense, hard, grim; their personal survival and that of the Reich were inextricably intertwined with that of the strange new device I had sketched.

"It does. Instead of one massive explosion, we use three stages of gentle acceleration. This keeps the organisms, or the chemical, intact. These things"—I indicated with my finger—"are horizontal rockets underneath the top, which will spin it up when they're fired. And these are flanges along the side, angled so that they push air downward when the top spins, forcing it to rise."

Kammler interrupted. "You have an ordnance background, *ja?* My devices are terrorizing London at this moment. But they required a huge labor force, a significant proportion of the wealth of the Reich, and a great deal of time to develop."

Hess muscled in, keen to collect the kudos: "But we're not into industrial production. We just need a handful of these weapons. And it doesn't have to travel three hundred kilometers to London. We only need it to rise a few hundred meters into the air, and drift for a few kilometers. Which means we can use simple technology. It also allows us to put the bulk of the weight into payload, not propulsion fuel as with your rockets." He snatched a glance at me. I gave a tiny, reassuring nod: *You got it right, Director.*

Goering's face was lined with concentration. Apart from the crackling of logs in the fire, the enormous room was as silent as death. Then: "Continue. The air pirates are still ten minutes away."

I took up the story. My mouth was dry. "Once the spinning top—I call it a flying volcano—is up, and spinning at huge speed, stage two kicks in: It shoots out hundreds of little canisters—I call them eggs—over a minute or so. These things that look like portholes are the exit points for the canisters. The spinning top glides erratically while it's doing so, and can cover several kilometers with very little further fuel expenditure."

"So you have canisters—eggs—up in the sky, covering some area?"

Hess again, anxious to appear the big man. "Correct, Excellency. Stage three happens when the eggs themselves disrupt. It's much like a big firework rocket. These eggs contain the microorganisms or the poison. They're made of thin aluminum and disrupt with a tiny quantity of detonator, which doesn't affect the gas or the pathogens. The wind does the rest. If the device is upwind from the target, in a moderate breeze, we could blanket a strip about ten kilometers long and five wide with a lethal dose of sarin gas."

Goering asked, "How do you propose to transport this bomb? In a Junker?"

I said, "It wouldn't make a practical aerial weapon. We suggest that these devices be smuggled into enemy cities. If you could smuggle one into the suburbs of London, say by way of a U-boat on a quiet coastline, you could wait until the meteorological conditions were right and then detonate it. A ten-by-five-kilometer strip would take out the whole of central London."

Heinrici said, "A devastating victory, but perhaps not the same as winning the war."

"But why stop at London?" Edith asked. Her silly hat was at her feet. Her nose and cheeks were red as if alcohol didn't agree with her.

Goering's ring-encrusted fingers were strumming on a fat thigh. "Destroying London, New York, and Washington . . . that and the threat of more to come. That would force a truce and give us time to rearm. We could then launch hundreds of these weapons. We could turn whole countries into wastelands."

Heinrici, the SA general, was looking skeptical. "But you

need to deliver and conceal the weapon, and that means clandestine activity on enemy-held territory. Suppose something went wrong? Suppose one was captured by the enemy? It could be turned against us."

Hess, a light sweat on his brow, shot the general a look of pure hatred. "Firing codes. We can arrange it so that if the wrong code is put in, the weapon self-destructs." The idea was Daniela's.

"Excellent! This is the most exciting news I have heard in a long time." Goering looked at Hess, beaming. "How many of these flying volcanoes have you built?"

Hess grew pale. "Ah, none. None just yet, Excellency. We're still at the design stage."

The silence went on for about fifteen seconds, while Goering's lips moved soundlessly, his face growing red and contorted with rage.

Hess had taken to grinning like an imbecile. "Dr. von Krafft unfortunately cost us a great deal of time. His early apparatus was faulty and exploded. Also he tells me he will have great difficulty handling sarin and anthrax. I believe . . ."

"Difficulty? Did I hear you use the word *difficulty*? Sit where I am and you'll find out what the word means, Colonel Hess." The Reichsmarschall was shouting. "We're talking about survival. Survival!"

The silence that followed was unbearable. Kammler broke it: "How long would it take you to make, say, half a dozen such weapons?"

"Twelve months."

You liar, Hess. At least two years. Bosch and I exchanged glances.

"Useless!" Goering hurled his wineglass into the fireplace, the crystal shattering into tiny shards. The sudden violence shocked us into stillness. "Are you a complete idiot? In a year the war will be over and we'll have lost."

"Not a good idea to lose the war," said Hess, with a terrified grin. Heuriger from the vineyards of Burgenland spilled on his lap, making it look as if he'd wet himself. He looked as if he might faint.

The Gestapo man stood up, approached Goering, and whispered in his ear. Goering nodded and fixed a stare on the director. Hohne asked, "How many men are working on this project?"

"Eighty-three. About ten scientists, fifty technicians, five administrative staff, and the same number of security staff. In addition, we're guarded by a detachment of Volkssturm, about thirty men, along with some flak crews and anti-aircraft guns."

"But the key people are the scientists?"

It seemed impossible, but Hess's terrified grin intensified. "The key people are the six of us here, Herr Hohne."

The Gestapo man was playing with a small unlit cigarette. "Other scientists in Germany could do the same job?"

"They would be hard to find. Take von Krafft here. How many people have expertise in both weapons engineering and ballistics?"

"But you are still replaceable," the Gestapo man insisted. His small, dark eyes were fixed keenly on Hess.

Jesus Christ. What's coming? At the other end of the semicircle from me, Bosch had grown pale.

The more Hess gave his terrified smile, the more he looked like an imbecile. "Perhaps, given time."

Hohne leaned toward Goering again, resumed the whispering. Goering kept nodding. From time to time he glanced at Hess. Those shark's eyes. A shark addicted to cocaine, its behavior impossible to predict.

I thought, *If Hess goes down, he'll take the rest of us down with him.* Bosch again, across from me, his face showing unbearable tension. Thinking the same thought.

Now Goering was saying, in a terrifyingly calm voice, "No Vienna waltzes, no runarounds. Just the truth. Are you in a position to develop at least four of these spinning tops, each capable of destroying a city and capable of fitting into a U-boat? And to have them ready for use within four months?"

"Four months!"

Don't argue, Hess. Don't plead for more time, don't make

excuses. But he'd have had to be made of stone to miss the vibrations. "Absolutely, Excellency. We can certainly do that."

Kammler, the V2 man: "What about you, von Krafft? You're the engineer. What do you think?"

A poisonous question. *Yes* was an appalling lie, *No* was the back of a truck heading for a concentration camp. Next to me I sensed Daniela freezing up. Edith was looking down at her hat in a fixed way. Bosch and Klein, terrified of being asked the question, had taken to staring into the fire, as if distancing themselves from the scene. The soldiers were watching me closely; grim, analytical, hard as nails. Not easy men to fool.

"We can do it. No Vienna waltzes." *If you're going to lie, make it big.*

Goering's ice melted. The transformation was amazing. "Splendid. Do it, and you will all live as honored citizens in the victorious Reich. Fail, and you will be shot."

"I met your father," Goering said. "He fought with distinction on the northwest sector, repulsing the Bolsheviks around the Neva. He has a good reputation as a soldier."

"He's also a very good father, Reichsmarschall."

"And which is more important, my dear? To be a good father or a good soldier?"

The bastard's toying with her, I thought. But Daniela was answering smoothly, a lighthearted smile on her face. "A National Socialist father protects both family and country, Reichsmarschall. Since the two are intertwined, your question is meaningless."

Goering slapped a fat thigh, laughing. "Would you listen to her, Heinrici!"

The drone was now overhead. They had come in huge numbers; their roar dominated everything in the room, reducing it to insignificance. Goering stood up, his face grim with the overhead passage of his Nemesis. "You cannot return to Berlin tonight. You will stay here as my guests. But before you are shown to your rooms, there's something I would like you to see. Come quickly, and bring your wine." Goering crooked his arm invitingly at Daniela and forced a smile.

Daniela took it. "You're too kind, Reichsmarschall."

"No, I'm too old." She managed a half laugh. Then Goering led her out of the room, along a corridor, and into a big elevator. The rest of us, not knowing what to expect, followed.

The room was at the top of the lodge, and it was dark, and Goering was now wheezing. Servants opened the shutters. Goering and Daniela shared a window, and I found myself momentarily squeezed up against the Gestapo man. My flesh crept.

Now the distant *whump-whump-whump* of the bombs began to reach us, almost merging into a steady thunder, overlain with the crackling of the AA guns. Searchlights were probing the sky, and light cloud was reflecting white parachute flares and crimson flames. Suddenly a number of searchlight beams congregated to a point, predators homing in on a prey. Moments later little parabolae of white light rose lazily from the ground, fireflies converging to the spot defined by the searchlights. The darkness in the room began to be broken by flashes of light as if flashbulbs were going off.

"They're going for the administrative center," Heinrici said.

"God, not the Tiergarten." I had never seen such a demonstration of raw power; it was awesome. What chance did we have against that? I wondered why Goering wanted us to see it.

"I hope they don't get the Opera House," Goering said. "I heard Bruckner's Romantic Symphony there last year. What a wonderful final movement! Do you like music, my dear?"

There was a giggle in the dark. "I used to like American jazz, Reichsmarschall, before they called it degenerate."

You're pushing your luck, Daniela! But there was only a harsh laugh, and the distant sound of war.

Orange flickering lights were beginning to play along the horizon. So far as I could make out, central Berlin was turning into a sea of smoky, red and yellow flames. I watched, hypnotized. How long the raid went on I didn't know; maybe half an hour. But then the steady *whump* of the bombs and the crackle of the flak guns stopped, and the droning died away, and there was only the red horizon, illuminating the tops of the fir trees below us, giving them a Christmasy look, and then the distant all-clear wail of the sirens.

Daniela came to me in the early hours of the morning. The big room was suffused with a dull red light; the embers of Berlin were still glowing. She didn't speak a word, and there was no sex. She just lay in my arms. Eventually her breathing became regular, and she seemed to be asleep. The perfume she had sprinkled on for the visit was still lingering faintly.

I stared at the decorative plasterwork squares in the ceiling, trying to make out the pictures inside them. I had never slept in such a big room, it was gargantuan. Everything about this place was gargantuan. The Reichsmarschall was gargantuan; likewise his grotesque palace, and the scale of the art he had looted from Russia and Europe. Even the destruction of Berlin was a huge Götterdämmerung they had brought on themselves. My Berlin, what have they done to it?

And the hidden crimes: Were they gargantuan, too? How likely was it that Natzweiler stood alone, a solitary island of depravity in a sea of civilization? And if the Gypsy boy—what was his name, Bleeker?—hadn't borne such a startling resemblance to Little Bruv, would I be thinking this way?

Gangsters? Lunatics, running the asylum. I drifted into an uneasy sleep.

"Goering knows I'm Jewish."

"Daniela . . ."

"I can't explain it. Subtleties in the voice, in the way he looked at me."

"Daniela, Oberlin knows. He asked me to spy on you."

She lay quietly for some moments, assimilating this. Then: "They'll be after my parents, I must try to warn them. Me, Max, I'm finished, just as soon as I've done the work. I won't survive the war."

London and Los Angeles

TUESDAY–WEDNESDAY

EDITH ZIMMERMAN

Pensioner's Killer "May Have Been Female"

A coroner's inquest opened in Coolidge today on the mysterious death of well-known local artist Edith Zimmerman. It emerged that one of the killers may have been a woman.

Coroner Patrick Trainer stated that much of the detail contained in his autopsy report was "unpleasant in the extreme." Eyewitnesses at the hearing described the abduction of the eighty-year-old woman in broad daylight from a supermarket parking lot. She was bundled into a red Ford Chrysler by a middle-aged man and woman. The vehicle was found two days later abandoned at a railway station in Atlanta. Dr. Edith Zimmerman's body was subsequently found in a derelict warehouse. It appeared that she had been subjected to "extreme physical abuse," the details of which the coroner wished to spare the inquiry.

One eyewitness, however, thought that both abductors may have been male. She described the "female" as having a masculine voice.

An FBI detective told the court that there was no obvious motive for the crime. Neighbors described her as a person who lived quietly and kept to herself. Dr. Zimmerman lived alone, having retired 20 years ago from an academic position at George Mason University. Born in Frankfurt, Germany, she had no close friends or known living relatives. She was a micro-biologist by profession, and was a keen artist before Parkinson's disease forced her to give up her hobby. The file on the abduction and murder is still open and any leads will be pursued vigorously.

The inquest continues.

Mr. Phoenix leans over her, putting his hands on her shoulders. His breath smells of garlic and cheese. "What's the date of this, honey?"

Neanderthal. Joanna scrolls the screen and points. "She was murdered about a year ago."

"Joanna," Caddon says patiently, "we're checking on active biochemists in the weapons programs. This old lady was eighty. How could she possibly tie in with the UFO?"

"I know it's thin." She feels a headache coming on. Part of it, she thinks, is coming from long hours peering at the screen, part of it is lack of fluid; and part of it is an oppressive sense of ridicule she feels bearing down on her. She continues stubbornly. "She was a biochemist, she was a German, and she would be the right age for being involved in a Nazi bioweapons program."

Mr. Phoenix grins. "You're new at the job, right? She's new at the job, Neal?" Joanna says nothing, feels her face flushing. *Me Tarzan, you Jane, you knuckle-grazing ape.*

Caddon is still being patient. He explains: "The Hitler lead is dead, Jo. The swastika was put there by the Phoenix militia. Either they meant it as a decoy along with the London letter or they were stupid enough to leave it as their signature. And there must be dozens of old German biochemists in the US."

"I know. But this one died such an interesting death." She passes over a printout.

Official Coroner's Report
Office of the Coroner Medical Examiner,
Clark County, Atlanta
Case no. 06-039

DECEDENT: Zimmerman, E.   **DOB:** 1920 approx
Weight: 115.0   **Hair:** White/Brown   **Eyes:** Black
Scars/tattoos and other distinguishing features:
Mole on left thigh. Appendix scar, 50-year-old approx.

Rigor mortis: None   **Livor mortis:** None
Decomposed?: No

Clothing: None
Drugs & medications: None Known
Occupation: Retired Artist. Formerly Biochemist
Agency reporting: AMC **When reported:** 07/13/08 15:15
Location of Body: AMC Trauma Unit

Type of death: Severe violence and lymphocytic peri-
carditis with eosinophils. Pinpoint burns on tongue and
stomach consistent with the passage of strong electric
current. Contributory factors diffuse alveolar damage.

Circumstances: **Date:**   **Time:**

Found dead by:
Pronounced dead by:

"The rest is just routine," Joanna declares. "Informing
relatives, except that she didn't have any, handing body over
for burial, and so on."

"So somebody didn't like her," Caddon says. "They half
drowned her, beat her, and gave her some high-voltage juice."

"They were after information."

"Which she didn't give."

"Didn't have to give. Nobody could have stood up to that."

"So what was this information?"

"Something about the poisonous UFO. Something they needed to know. Something from the Nazi past."

Me Tarzan is still grinning. "Be kind to her, Neal. She's new at the job."

Caddon's eyes are hard. "Dig a little deeper, Joanna. We can't afford a mistake."

THE SCIENTISTS

Tuesday morning, some weird hour, and the phone is ringing. Caddon's wife makes an animal noise and turns away, a gesture of annoyance refined over the years. Caddon sits up and picks up the receiver, more asleep than awake. "Caddon."

Female voice. Joanna, the new girl, her voice enthusiastic at half past two in the morning. "Neal, I think I've got something."

In the late afternoon, Sharp and Ambra disappear into the enormous kitchen, leaving Jocelyn tapping and muttering at one of the three terminals. They emerge forty minutes later after a great deal of chatter, Ambra carrying a tray with steaming Mexican rice, white fish fillets, and little plates of red and green sauce, Sharp with two uncorked bottles of red wine. Jocelyn is tapping the palms of her hands together and pacing up and down impatiently. "There's a pattern. There are factors common to the first five names on the list."

Ambra begins to spread cutlery, plates, and glasses around a low coffee table. "We're listening."

"They were all Germans, they were all old . . ." Jocelyn pours wine into glasses and takes a gulp.

"Keep going."

She rubs her eyes and joins Sharp and Ambra at the table,

hauling her ankles up to sit cross-legged. "And they all died violent deaths within the last year."

Ambra and Sharp stare at Jocelyn. She says, "Edith Zimmerman we know about. But look at the other two with crosses—Klein and von Steiner. Take this Klein. He drowned in weird circumstances. His car was found at a bridge spanning the Mississippi, keys in the ignition, headlights on, and engine turning. He'd just left a dinner. They found his body three weeks later, five hundred kilometers downriver."

"So he topped himself, or fell off the bridge drunk." Ambra, the devil's advocate.

Jocelyn shakes her head. "The inquest said he committed suicide but Klein's family deny this. They said he was in a good mental state with no problems, and his dinner companions said he was sober. How can a body float downriver for five hundred kilometers and nobody notices?"

"But was he the same Klein as the one on Petrov's list?" Sharp asks.

"I'll come to that. Now look at von Steiner," Jocelyn says. "Half a glass. Also drowned. But wait for this. Upside down in a barrel, in some farm outbuilding in Utah. An open verdict on this one. I mean, an eighty-year-old man might lean into a barrel and tip over and not be able to get out, but why would he want to lean into a barrel of rainwater in the first place?"

"It's a selection effect. You've picked out the interesting deaths from dozens of old Germans with these names."

Jocelyn shakes her head again. "No, no, no, Ambra. They were all scientists. Klein and Zimmerman were microbiologists, von Steiner was a rocket man. Now, if you wanted to build a flying bioweapon, you'd want microbiologists and rocket people."

Ambra says, "What are you saying, Jocelyn?"

"Someone's going systematically through Petrov's list. They're looking for information from these old scientists. When they don't deliver, they get an accidental death and a little cross against their name."

"What information?" Sharp wonders.

Ambra breaks the edgy silence. "Where did they live?"

"Klein in some one-horse town in Maryland, Zimmerman lived in Fairfax Virginia, von Steiner in Utah." Jocelyn stands up and jiggles about excitedly. "You see what I'm getting at, don't you? They were all Germans in their eighties, they were all scientists, and they all died violent deaths in the last few months."

Ambra asks, "What about the other Germans on Petrov's list? What about Krafft and Bauer?"

"Nothing. I don't know who or where they are."

"We know something," Ambra says. "Their names aren't scored off. Not yet."

"The intelligence services don't do burglary, Lewis. That's an urban myth."

"Tell their reporting officer to give them brownie points at ACR time, Jocelyn. Mr. Nuts and Mr. Bolts gave a terrific performance."

"For the sake of discussion, let's pretend that all this nonsense is for real. What was the giveaway?"

"The Mas-Hamilton software. Only a government department could afford it. It might as well have had CROWN PROPERTY, TECHNICAL SERVICES DEPARTMENT, written all over it." Sharp grins.

Jocelyn sips at her G&T. "You've been watching too many Bond movies."

"But they were from B4, right?" Sharp springs it on her. He thinks he sees a hint of surprise cross her face, but the moment comes and goes so quickly he can't be sure. Not many people knew about B4, which was a group of "specialist locksmiths" belonging to the Technical Services Department (TSD), part of the Communications and Information Systems Division (ISD), which came under the Foreign and Commonwealth Office (FCO), which was in essence the diplomatic service. B4 was located not in the underground dungeons of Legoland but in a secret building at Hanslope Park near Milton Keynes. It was all very confusing.

"It would take more than one government department to

carry through something like that," Jocelyn says. "Not that I'm admitting a thing."

Sharp takes that as an admission. He waves at the barman and orders another tomato juice. He waits until the man is out of earshot. They are in Andy's Bar, a pub with plush armchairs and an Irish literati theme. There are Irish rustic paintings, and Pub of the Year certificates, and glass panels etched with the faces of George Bernard Shaw, Yeats, Joyce, and other Irish writers. He's had to get out of the safe house, even for an hour; the walls were closing in on him.

She adds tonic water to her gin and watches the bubbles. "The crazy letter says London gets zapped in three days, in case you've lost track. I'm seeing Gordon first thing tomorrow. What do I report? What have you people discovered?"

"A conspiracy."

"Of course you have. You've uncovered a secret lodge of the Knights Templar."

"Nothing so harmless."

CONSPIRACY

"Ambra, You're not going to believe this."

"Try me anyway, Neal."

Caddon's face is on a flat screen in the living room of the safe house. He has bags under his eyes and a light stubble, but there's something else that Sharp can't quite place—a grimness, maybe even anger. It's midmorning in London and has to be one or two in the morning in California. "I've been into the Modern Military Branch of the National Archives and Records Service, I've been exploiting the Freedom of Information Act like hell, and I've been calling in a few favors. I've also been getting some blocking maneuvers."

"Blocking maneuvers? Who from?"

"I'm not sure, Ambra." Sharp and Jocelyn are on either side of Ambra, touching shoulders to stay in the field of view. Caddon launches into his story: "It goes back to the Allied invasion of Europe. A few thousand intelligence officers moved in behind the armies. Their job was to find Nazi scientists and bring them back to America under military custody. This operation was code-named Overcast."

"So far, so good."

"The original idea was scientific plunder, and they found

plenty. Advanced submarines, prototype jets, rocket planes, even a supersonic wind tunnel. But the most valuable loot was human, the scientists themselves. The original idea was to pull them in, suck them dry, and then spit them out, back to Germany. The trouble was that they turned out to be just too good. They were too valuable to lose. The War Department decided it wanted them kept in the States. So Overcast was replaced by a new project called Paperclip, created and signed by President Truman in 1946 to allow this."

"The Cold War was getting under way," Sharp volunteers. "You needed the new weapons and the new people."

"But what you didn't need—at least Harry Truman didn't— was war criminals in America. He ordered the War Department to conduct background investigations of the wartime activities of these scientists. And that's when the big problem began. The military wanted their skills and they didn't give a toss what these guys got into during the war."

The screen flickers slightly, then recovers. Ambra says, "Keep talking."

"The way it worked was this: The War Department's intelligence agency had to create a dossier on each scientist. The dossier went to the State Department and the Justice Department. These departments had the final say on whether a scientist was allowed to immigrate to the States."

"Which surely settled it. You're telling us the US military had a presidential directive. They couldn't go against their own president."

"They did."

"What?"

"They freaking did. The military and the CIA combined to subvert their own president. It was massive, a conspiracy to undermine the orders of the president. I'm faxing something now but it's just a sample."

Caddon's face disappears from the screen. A moment later a fax starts buzzing next to the terminal. Sharp pulls it out and they read it together as Caddon reappears.

Memorandum

To: Director of Intelligence,
    War Department General Staff
From: Director, Joint Intelligence Objectives Agency
Date: April 27, 1948
Re: Project Paperclip

(1) Security investigations conducted by the Agency have disclosed the fact that the majority of German scientists were members of either the Nazi Party or one or more of its affiliates. Our investigations disclose further that with a very few exceptions, such membership was due to exigencies which influenced the lives of every citizen of Germany at that time. It is my considered opinion that overscrupulous investigations by the Department of Justice and other agencies are damaging our efforts to recruit such personnel and are reflecting security concerns which are no longer relevant, due to the defeat of Nazi Germany (Attachment 1).

(2) The Soviet threat must override moral niceties about the nature of the people we recruit from the former Nazi Empire. In light of the situation existing in Europe today, continued delay and opposition to the immigration of these scientists could result in their eventually falling into the hands of the Russians who would then gain the valuable information and ability possessed by these men. Such an eventuality could have a most serious and adverse affect on the national security of the United States (Attachment 2).

(3) In order to systematically benefit from Operation Paperclip, this office holds that the employment of competent personnel who fit into our research program overrides all other considerations. I attach resumes

from a Paperclip prospect list. You will see that the
Nazi war machine had radiation biologists and phys-
icists, aerodynamics engineers, rocket specialists
and biochemists. We ignore this rich source of scientific talent at our peril (Attachment 3).

(4) This office believes that in the national interest and
in view of the growing Soviet threat it is not advis-
able to submit dossiers on individual scientists to
the Departments of State and Justice where there is
little possibility that these departments would approve immigration. Such reports should first be re-
viewed and suitably revised where such action is
deemed appropriate. Otherwise this may result in
the return to Germany of specialists whose skill and
knowledge should be denied other nations in the
interest of national security.

"Suitably revised, I see. What happened, Neal?"

Caddon was flicking through some offscreen sheets.
"Well, they brought in over seven hundred Nazi scientists to
the States. No matter how depraved, no matter how closely
they worked with the Nazi killing machine, engineers, scientists and doctors were rounded up. Military intelligence
sanitized their records. The scientists became American citizens, God-fearing, gum-chewing, flag-waving fucking patri-
ots. Examples. Von Braun of V2 fame and his team, all of
them Nazis, some of them unquestionably war criminals, all
of them with dossiers whitewashed by the War Department.
One of them was recalled to West Germany for a secret trial,
and do you know what happened? The army sabotaged the
trial. They witheld records that could have sent the guy to the
gallows."

The FBI man is exhausted and beginning to wander. He
seems angry. Ambra brings him back. "What about Petrov's
list?"

"Getting to it now. One of the hundreds brought in by Paperclip is a guy called Kurt Blome, now dead, hopefully with

a stake through his heart. The Nuremberg prosecutors charged him with carrying out plague experiments on Polish prisoners."

"Plague? As in bubonic?" Ambra has a thoughtful frown, sips at a white wine.

"Yeah. He got off on a close call—surprise, surprise, his army dossier doesn't even mention his Nuremberg trial. So they put him to work with the US Army Chemical Corps under Project 63—don't ask. He teams up with another charmer called von Haagen, a professor at the University of Strasbourg. He and Blome have a mighty close interest in biological weapons. Von Haagen spent the war infecting inmates with God knows what at the Natzweiler concentration camp before the military brings him over on Paperclip and puts him straight to work on germ weapons research at Camp King, just outside Washington."

Caddon has black bags under his eyes, and his whole face is sagging. Ambra says, "You said you were getting to it, Neal."

"It gets hot about now. In 1954 this Blome is interviewed by officers from Fort Detrick. He gives them a list of the bioweapons researchers who'd worked with him during the war. Their names include Zimmerman, Klein, Bauer, and Krafft."

Sharp says, "Bingo."

Jocelyn looks over at him. "They were a wartime team."

"But what were they up to?" Ambra turns to the screen again and the unblinking round eye on top of it. "Neal, what did they do?"

"I don't know, Ambra. The records have gone missing."

"Come again?"

"I don't know what's going on here, Ambra, and I don't like it. But one thing I have found out. In the 1950s the CIA built a wing of Weldon University Hospital. They paid for it secretly, channeling their money through a Dr. Carl Shaeffmann who ran the Shaeffmann Medical Research Foundation. I don't know what the CIA did there. But I do know they employed Edith Zimmerman."

"And the hospital records?" Sharp asks.

"Destroyed in 1973 on the orders of Richard Helms, the CIA director."

Ambra says, "But there have to be patients' records."

"Negative. Destroyed also. But something nasty." Caddon pauses. "We've been checking the surviving records from penitentiaries scattered around Dixieland dating from that period. A surprising number of prisoners—poor blacks mostly—took ill just before they were due for release, and were transferred to the foundation for treatment. And according to the prison records, a surprising number of them were released straight after hospitalization. The problem is, we can find no trace of what happened to them afterward. No parole records, no nothing. These were men without families, men nobody would miss."

"You mean . . . ?"

"They went into the Shaeffer Medical Research Foundation. But there's no credible record of their having come out, or of what happened to them while they were inside. And your biochemist, this Edith Zimmerman, worked there."

Caddon is talking again, as if to himself. He's looking down at the papers rather than the screen. "Operations director of Dora-Mittelbau, Arthur Rudolph, where twenty thousand people were killed by exhaustion, starvation, or hangings, becomes a US citizen and designs the Saturn V rocket used to land Americans on the moon. Kurt Blome ends up with the US Army Chemical Corps working on chemical warfare. Walter Schreiber, who organized medical experiments on concentration camp prisoners, ends up at the Air Force School of Medicine in Texas. School of medicine, for Christ's sake."

"We've got the message."

"These bastards stained my country."

"Calm down, Neal. I expect everyone was at it."

"And that, I think, is what we're seeing here."

It's against regulations to talk shop in the staff bar, but nobody is about to remind the head of MI6. Sharp looks out over the Thames and thinks again that the spooks have one of the best views in London. C looks across the table at Jocelyn. "Comments?"

"It makes sense. These people would all be in their twenties during the war. They must have been brought over to the States as part of a team for some purpose, something they were working on at the war's end. And now they're being killed off."

"But we don't have any records. We don't know what they were up to. Isn't that right? We don't know what they were up to?"

"That's right, Gordon. Whatever they were doing, it was so secret that not even the historians have dug it out. Caddon's team are combing the US National Archives right now, but the records have gone missing."

Gordon taps half a dozen buff folders piled in front of him. "We know nothing of what they did in the seventies, but after that they suddenly pop up in various parts of the States as teachers, college professors, whatever."

Sharp says, "They're geriatrics, long retired. And yet whatever it is suddenly rears its ugly head in the twenty-first century and starts to kill them."

Jocelyn says, "It has to be connected with the Arizona device."

The intelligence chief nods at Sharp. It could almost have been an acknowledgment of some sort. "I still think your theory that it really was a Third Reich weapon is a long shot. Why now? Why Arizona? But with three days to go and a credible death threat against London, it's something we must check out."

"Some names weren't scored off Petrov's list," Jocelyn points out.

Sharp stares in amazement: The intelligence chief is smiling, or at least exposing his teeth. "We have no idea about Bauer or Hosokawa. However, we've had a breakthrough on the matter of Krafft."

"He's alive?"

"We're not entirely inert in this expensive outfit, Sharp. We did follow up on your Nazi biochemist suggestion. It

turns out that military intelligence had words with this Kurt
Blome at the end of the war. It seems that Max Krafft didn't
go over to the West. For reasons we don't understand he was
taken by the Russians. And within the last hour we have
found that this Krafft is still alive and well, living in an extremely remote part of Russia. But there's a problem."

C is still exposing his teeth. "The bad news is that the
Russians wouldn't want him interviewed. He was involved in
their own bioweapons program and might talk about things
that they don't want us to know about. The good news is that
we are experienced in putting people in and out of Russia
without legitimate papers. The bad news is that time is seriously against us. The good news is that you have the special-
ized knowledge to interview him in the necessary depth. An
experienced field agent will nursemaid you."

"I want to go home."

"You can't. There's nobody else."

"I don't speak Russian."

"Miss Volpe does."

"I'm a coward."

"I could have you shot."

"We're not at war."

"You think not? But I take your point, Sharp, I can't put
you up against a wall. Just keep back from the edge of sub-
way platforms." Gordon exposes more teeth to show that he
is joking. They are all having fun.

THE DAY AFTER TOMORROW

Caddon grabs a few hours in his downtown pad and wakes up feeling haggard and guilty at the time spent asleep. The street outside is buzzing with early-morning traffic. He scurries across the road to Ingrid's Deli, scurries back with a bagel, and switches on a coffee machine. He's giving a progress report to State Department bigwigs at nine, needs to shave.

Report what?

He stares at the papers on the kitchen table with bloodshot eyes.

The slick chick has been identified, courtesy of the Chinese and Japanese secret services, of all things—globalization is surely with us, pal. She's part of Gakushi-gumi, a North Korean spy ring operating in Japan. She'd arrived in LA impersonating some opera singer whose arrest the next day led to a fine operatic performance. The airport videos tie the chick to the Macao money-laundering scam a while back wherein top-grade counterfeit dollars were filtered through Banco Delta Asia into the international money markets. She'd vanished then and she's vanished now—in and out quick, before they can blink. Caddon thinks she's maybe North Korea's answer to James Bond. And the barbecued sausages at the Globe mine shaft have been identified as Nazi-loving militiamen, one of them the Phoenix dentist. Probably Demos's Strawberry lunch mates.

He puts a sheet of paper on the kitchen table and scribbles:

The Bad Guys

Petrov (hates commies)	in cahoots with North Korean commie
Demos (hates Nazis)	in cahoots with home-grown Nazis
Petrov + Demos	in cahoots with each other
Novello (Pentagon clearance)	in cahoots with probably everyone

Enemies working together. All now vanished somewhere in Berlin, except Novello, back at his desk in Parallax Satellite Systems. Caddon scribbles more:

The Puzzles

1) UFO crashes in Apache reservation—what is this, a sixties B movie?

2) It's a Nazi wonder weapon dug up by local screwballs—pure Spielberg!

3) Crazy letter threatens London, gives 5-day warning. Two gone!!

4) Brits say crazy letter = two more devices running loose. Anthrax? Sarin?

5) If London gets one, who gets the other? And where are they??

6) The key—some elusive dame called Sophia. She'll unleash a war??

He sighs, frowns, covers his mouth with his hand in an unconscious, nervous gesture. This would give Einstein a headache. Then he prints in big letters:

WHERE ARE THE UFOS?
WHO IS SOPHIA?
WHAT WAR, AND HOW?

So far as they've been able to find out, there was only one Sophia in Petrov's life, or had been: Sophia Milankovitch, his young wife of the gulag, dead these past fifty years.

He wonders what in the name of sanity he's going to tell the State Department bigshots at nine o'clock. Wonders if he has time to shave. And he wonders about getting his wife on a plane to Mexico and telling his son to take a break from Manhattan, maybe go rafting or do a ranch holiday, someplace like Montana. Feels that it would be somehow treacherous, like insider dealing. Even so, there comes a point . . .

To: A. J. Klacka, London Resilience Forum
From: G. Byrne, British Geological Survey
Re: Query Re aftermath of major terrorist incident
Status: Top Secret

I refer to the recent visit of your team to the BGS here at Keyworth. We understand that you could cope with the disposal of up to 2,000 bodies in the event of a major terrorist attack on the London environs but that beyond that, mass burial arrangements would have to be made. We understand that in the event of such an incident access to London from outside would be denied and that all drains from the city would be blocked. We also note that in the event of an incident you would request a 24-hour standby with a 4-hour response on the suitability of specific sites for mass disposal of corpses.

For such a large area, we would carry out a Regional Appraisal using GIS and digital geology to assess the potential risk to groundwater. The chief requirement is to have a non-permeable superficial geology, with good thick clay deposits over a non-aquifer: it is vital to avoid alluvial deposits or river drainage sites that would allow the contamination of groundwater by undesirable fluids. Staff with the necessary security clearance have discussed your problem. We have used GeoSure Products and 3-D geological modeling to predict ground conditions. Fortunately the London area is rich in Paleogene clays suitable for the purpose, and we have identified a number of suitable sites in the London environs. These are shown in the appended maps for the range of scenarios requested, that is from 2,000 to 2 million bodies.

The Web sites below give some publicly available background which may be helpful (I'm sure you are familiar with the second, at least!):

www.bgs.ac.uk/products/geosure
www.londonprepared.gov.uk

We understand that the "top secret" classification is required simply to avoid any public unease over the asking of the question and that your inquiry is purely hypothetical.

Light, dark, light, dark . . .

The same godless hour. But Sharp hasn't been sleeping, he's been lying fully clothed on top of his bed, waiting for an early-morning knock. Somewhere, he knows, other people are awake in some secret room, putting together false papers, while yet others are playing logistic games that will shortly transport him from this room to the edge of civilization, somewhere in Arctic Russia.

*   *   *

Who knew where the weapons were headed? Who directed the project that created them? If he's dead, did he leave documentation buried in some mine shaft or a Swiss safe-deposit box, or handed down through his family? Someone at the present time knew where these sixty-year-old weapons were hidden. Someone who wants to bring that past alive.

Neo-Nazis?

No, they're just stupid thugs. Someone with a vision, but unhinged.

Petrov?

Petrov fought the Nazis, for goodness' sake. But for his own reasons he has made an alliance with some lunatic who wants to . . .

Why unhinged?

No one threatening a city at peace is rational.

Why now? What has triggered this?

I can only guess. But Petrov has pulled together a group of international terrorists for some purpose of his own involving America and North Korea. Maybe some secret rapprochement that the old Stalin-hater doesn't want. They still have the gulag in North Korea. His young wife died in one.

How do you know . . .

Must go . . . find what happened at the war's end. Reach for that past. Someone is trying to bring it alive.

The screen goes blank. Sharp, his nerves tingling, sits in the dark and stares at it.

Closing Vise:

THE CONVENT, 1945

SISTERS OF THE NIGHT

A shiny-faced aerodynamics expert, Felix von Steiner, turned up one morning from Kammler's rocket group. He wasn't much more than a schoolboy and he glowed with schoolboy enthusiasm everywhere he went. Within days of his arrival he transformed the design of the flying volcano. It lost its flanges: "No! No! No! Don't you see, you're just making wasteful turbulence! Just blowing air around!" Instead, he built four angled rockets into the design to give both lift and spin. He made the volcano shallower, with a big dome on top to hold the sarin or anthrax, and the lower part to hold the fuel and propulsion mechanism. In fact the machine no longer looked like a volcano; rather, it was beginning to look vaguely like a saucer holding a shallow inverted cup.

With Kammler's authority . . .

The man had a lot of authority in the Third Reich, the journalist tells me. He had fourteen million forced laborers under him, and he was in charge of nearly all the secret weapon projects. He was also a nasty piece of stuff. I don't know what to say to that, and nod.

. . . von Steiner and I took full-scale models to a huge wind tunnel south of Munich, carved out of a mountain, its entrance disguised by a row of chalets. We passed sleek two-stage rockets that looked as if they could reach New York. The wind tunnel was run by a conservative old aerodynamics engineer called Best with a double chin which waggled every time he shook his head. It did a lot of waggling as we explained what we wanted, but he quickly improvised experiments with the disks mounted on a motor-driven axle to spin them up to various rates. Foreign workers, gray-faced as if they hadn't seen sunlight for months, coated our models with a mixture of fluorescent paint and paraffin. Little flecks blew off in the slipstream and traced out the wind flow around the tilted, spinning disks.

Best grudgingly conceded that if the disk spun quickly, a gyroscope effect might make it stable, up to a point, but that without control surfaces the device would roll, bank, and sideslip away from a straight-line path. "This device is idiotic. Don't you see, the angle of attack increases as the flight progresses? The disk will first roll and bank to the right, then the pitching moment will change and it will veer to the left, and so on."

"What are you telling us, Dr. Best?" von Steiner asked, looking through the glass at the flecks of paint streaming and glittering in the spotlights.

"Without flaps and rudders your machine will never fly in a controllable manner," he warned us. "Look at those trailing vortices." His voice was quivering with professional indignation. "It's an asymmetric wake. Look at the way your disk is wobbling. It will fly like a drunken goose." And he turned to us and outlined a big S-shaped flight path with his hands—which, of course, was exactly what we needed.

We came back with an armful of numbers: sideslip, pitch, roll, lift coefficient, drag coefficient, pitching moment and rolling moment for various underside shapes, spin rates and flow velocities. Under Hess's orders, we gave these to Daniela to work out the flight dynamics, knowing it would stretch her formidable mathematical talents to the limit: Her days of underutilized talent were long past. Meantime we got on with constructing more scale models with what we'd learned.

Von Steiner seemed cheerfully indifferent to the payloads and their intended effects; the fun was in the design and building of the flying machines. He reminded me of myself eighteen months earlier. In spare moments he would chatter enthusiastically about spaceflight and the idea that one day men would walk on the moon. I got the impression that, for him, the war was just a sideline on the way to space. But his rocket experience proved invaluable: It began to look as if Goering's insane deadline could just possibly be met.

An innovation was solid fuel. The V2, von Steiner confided, was propelled by an alcohol/liquid oxygen mixture, but this was too sophisticated for our purpose. All we really wanted was a glorified skyrocket with multiple nozzles.

With the facilities of the Reich behind us we had no problem in acquiring material. Our first flying model, hastily thrown up in one of our own workshops, was about a meter across, made of aluminum and containing nothing more dangerous than water. It had four rockets, angled as von Steiner suggested to give spin as well as lift. Above a certain spin threshold, centrifugal force would open valves and water, representing sarin or anthrax, would spiral out. The "eggs" I'd envisioned were unnecessary and abandoned: The saucer would spin so fast that the spores or aerosol would be shot out for a hundred meters around; wind and drunken goose aerodynamics would do the rest.

Four of us could lift the device when it was empty. We heaved it onto the back of a truck and drove it down to the meadow, where a relay of soldiers with buckets filled it with water from an icy Alpine stream. Von Steiner lit a fuse—real schoolboy stuff, just string impregnated with saltpeter—and we scampered off to what we thought was a safe distance.

It was a spectacular disaster.

One of the four rockets didn't ignite and the machine rose on the other three, blasting out smoke and flames, roaring, and wobbling erratically while we ran for our lives. A few hundred meters up, spinning furiously, it started to spray arcs of water. Then it flipped on its back and hurtled straight at us, screaming and bellowing. We dived to the ground as the machine skimmed over our heads, touched grass, and then bounced and skipped over the meadow like a giant Catherine wheel out of control, pursued by half a dozen terrified soldiers. How it missed the cattle I don't know. It disappeared into the trees at supernatural speed, while cordite smoke and drizzle enveloped us.

Von Steiner was running up and down, arms stretched out and laughing excitedly. "It flew! It flew! First time and it flew!"

We bundled into the front of the truck with Bosch at the wheel, Daniela on von Steiner's knee, Edith and Hess squeezed in the middle. We were all caught up in von Steiner's enthusiasm. "It's much more stable than our early trials with the V2. It's the four engines. And the rotation."

"How will we get forward motion?" I asked.

"Launch it upwind and let it drift. It will stay airborne longer than a parachute, drifting along in a big lazy S while it scatters its seed. In a strong wind we might even have a transverse movement, thanks to Bernoulli's equation, like the spin on a tennis ball. I don't know how big that effect will be, though."

Hess had the look of a saint entering Paradise. "Daniela, we need your mathematics. Can we make the disks tack across the wind using this tennis ball effect? Answer within a week!"

I remember that day well. We were naughty children who had just seen their homemade rocket disappear into the clouds. In the excitement we all forgot, for a little while, what the flying disks were for.

As if her theoretical study of the flight dynamics weren't sweat enough, Hess summoned Daniela to the bishop's procuratory and ordered her to design the firing mechanism. Bosch proved remarkably adept at things mechanical and turned her abstract ideas into hardware. It was a wonderful team effort; it drove us all to exhaustion; and it made sabotage impossible. And Oberlin had now put armed guards in every corner of the convent and outside the door of every occupied room.

Daniela used the back entrance to the kitchen overnight at least once more to my knowledge; it wasn't guarded, maybe because it didn't lead to any offices, maybe because they didn't know about it. It was still a highly dangerous journey through the corridors. I followed her again, why I don't know. I was being torn apart, revolting at the treason against my country, unwilling to betray Daniela, outraged by Natzweiler. And I wanted to see what she was leaving for the spy among the forced labor.

It took me twenty minutes of silent searching in the dark kitchen, while a guard patrolled up and down outside and I sweated with fear, searching among metal pots and utensils. I eventually found the treasonable material in a massive cast-iron pot, covered by a dishcloth. It was six bars of Swiss chocolate.

Three months down the line, after countless calculations and crashed disks, we had our specifications. Krupps, despite the crumbling war effort, said they could deliver three full-sized disks. The fourth was going somewhere else. It was going somewhere else because it would be bigger, too big for our facilities and maybe too big for anything but towing behind a U-boat. It would be bigger because it was going to carry uranium oxide, which was heavy stuff. And it would carry uranium oxide because someone thought it would be a fine thing to spray the radioactive chemical over a city. There was a canteen rumor that this disk would eventually go to our Japanese allies. I don't know how that rumor started, and I don't know whether there was anything in it. But we'd escaped the firing squad. We concentrated on getting the first three disks ready for their deadly contents and Bosch, with his literary background, proposed to call them after the three Furies of Greek mythology.

"The Furies, I like the sound of that," Hess declared, nodding his drunken approval.

"Otherwise known as the Sisters of the Night." We'd raided the nuns' wine cellar and were enjoying an evening of bliss, a celebratory binge in Daniela's office. "They were gods of vengeance. They had snakes for hair, dogs' heads, and bats' wings. Their bodies were coal black and blood dripped from their eyes. They carried whips with brass studs, and their victims died in torment."

"They sound like me on a bad day," Edith said. We all laughed, and so we had names for our flying disks. Megaera, Alecto, and Tisiphone.

INCIDENT

We soon found that the wind wasn't enough. A big innovation was another two rockets, each a meter long and attached to the underside of the disk. Von Steiner touched the side of his nose late one night and told us he had contacts. This was a project classified as Geheime Reichs Sache, an SS security grading even higher than the usual Geheim Kommando Sache. He could undoubtedly have been shot for mentioning it to us. It was just that the mysterious project called for high-thrust, solid-fuel rockets to get something into the air quickly, and we could use those rockets.

It was probably the Viper project, the young man tells me. They made a machine out of wood. It was halfway between a plane and a missile. It launched vertically at over two g with the thrust from SR34 solid-fuel rockets. It went up half a mile in twelve seconds just on the boosters, then carried on up to seven miles in altitude. The pilot was supposed to glide down on the enemy bombers, but the war ended before they could use it. How does a journalist know about things like that, I ask. I wrote a piece on Nazi secret weapons some time ago, he says. I don't believe him.

Whatever their name, the rockets were ignorant and powerful brutes, banshees that screamed and roared at ear-damaging level—they must have heard our static trials in Mittelwald. The idea was to get the disk up using these roaring monsters; at a few hundred meters in height their empty casings would fall away, and the spin-up rockets would then take over, giving additional lift as well as the vital spin.

From the very first trial, they were a tremendous success. We took a trial disk up a perilous, unpaved track, skirting waterfalls and glaciated boulders as big as houses until we arrived at a plateau with a view of the Alps to die for. Bosch thought he could see the Führer's Berchtesgaden in the distance, but I wasn't so sure. It took two of us to slot the heavy banshees into place, with the disk held up by car jacks. We cleared off to the shelter of an ice-scored boulder and watched the full-scale model roar into the sky, the boosters drop off, and then the fantastic spin-up begin as the angled rockets took over. Even after these had died, the saucer glided on into the distance, weaving lazily from left to right as Best had predicted, and spraying out a blanket of yellow mist—we had dyed the water for visibility. And as the machine disappeared gracefully behind a distant hill, almost hovering and glinting in sunlight, we knew we were ready for the sarin.

Hess decided we would put anthrax in one of our saucers and sarin in the other two. Otto Klein was nervous about sarin—we all were—and asked for a colleague. Within days a man known only as Thomsen arrived from Hochwerk. He turned out to be about the same age and build as Klein, and equally devoid of humor. I thought that working with sarin maybe did that.

With the Reich collapsing about our ears, the three containment vessels finally arrived from Krupps, and Daniela finally got her wish: The Poles and Russians were allowed to sleep in the empty dormitory. I needed the laundry cleared to take the weapons, which were just too big to go into the convent. The big saucers filled the laundry room, and we had to remove some of the iron pillars supporting the roof. But it was too late to matter for the forced labor. The weather was warm, and the war would soon be over one way or another.

The babies were due for delivery and all that morning Hess had been seen everywhere at once. He had been spotted on Balthazar, riding far beyond the lake, at dawn. He had been in the library, in the refectory, in the chapel. He had walked halfway down the hairpin road and actually ran back up, puffing and red. And now at last, delivery was imminent. From the courtyard, we looked down at the army truck laboring up the mountain road, trailing black smoke. Bosch, Thomsen, and Myers were tiny figures standing next to the cable car. Hess gave a running commentary. He could hardly contain his excitement. "Here come our babies. Our beautiful babies!"

I could make out the truck halting at the cable car platform, and three soldiers jumping out. Then they were carefully unloading what looked like four milk churns and transferring them over to the waiting cable car. They seemed to be color-coded, two yellow and two blue. Then Bosch was scribbling his signature and the truck reversed and took off hastily back down the hill. I imagined that the soldiers were relieved to be shot of their perilous burden, safely delivered from Spandau. The wheelhouse whined, the cable tautened, and Hess started to pace up and down the courtyard agitatedly.

Edith was following the progress of the cable car through binoculars. It was about halfway up when she gave Hess a worried frown, then looked again. "Something's wrong."

"What?" Hess ran over and snatched the binoculars from her. We crowded together at the parapet. Someone had opened the cable car door and was on his knees at the edge of the void. It was Myers, swaying. Someone else—it looked like Thomsen—was trying to climb onto the roof. There was a thousand-meter drop below the car.

Thomsen's scrabbling increased the sway of the car. He was holding on to the roof while his legs dangled over space. The sway tipped Myers out, and we could only watch as he hurtled downward, picking up speed at a terrifying rate. One of the milk churns, a yellow one, rolled out after him, tumbling end over end. Thomsen, half on the roof, was using his elbows in a sort of lizard-like crawl, but he was sliding inexorably backward again, toward the edge. There was no sign of Bosch.

The milk churn overtook Myers on the way down, and his body fell into an exploding yellow-brown vapor before he smashed onto the rocks, making a little red splotch.

Thomsen, somehow, made it to the roof. He lay facedown, spread-eagled like a man in supplication to God. As the cable car approached, we could now see Bosch struggling to his feet. He stood upright and clutched tightly at a pole next to the open door, coughing, shaking violently, and staring up at us.

"Stop the car!" Hess screamed suddenly. Oberlin rushed toward the winch house. The car stopped, thirty meters short of its platform, swaying gently backward and forward, the taut cable creaking. Bosch, now gulping for air, stretched an arm toward us. He was sinking to his knees.

"Get your suits on!" Hess yelled, then dashed through the convent archway.

Far below, the vapor from the destroyed churn was rolling slowly over the ground, spreading and thinning. A light wind was drifting it inexorably in the direction of Mittelwald. I took off after Hess and caught up with him in the cloister. "The sarin's heading straight for Mittelwald."

"What the devil can I do about that?"

"Phone people. The church, the post office. Get the news around. Make people evacuate."

Hess stared wildly at me. "Are you mad? If people are warned, the news will get out."

"Hess, if you don't warn them, they'll die."

"The deed's done. We can't help them."

"The hell with you." I barged past Hess, heading for the director's office, one of only two with a telephone. The door was unlocked and the telephone was on the desk among a heap of papers. I would go through the operator. I lifted the receiver and was about to dial when I heard the distinct click of a gun hammer being cocked behind me. Oberlin at the door, a pistol pointing at my head, Aryan blue eyes holding no expression whatever.

Hess was behind Oberlin and his brow was damp with sweat. "If we warn Mittelwald now and people clear out, word will be around half of Bavaria by tomorrow and the Americans will be over us the day after. We'd be bombed to hell and the war would be lost. It has to be this way."

I put the receiver down carefully. Oberlin used a conciliatory tone. "Sensible fellow."

Bosch was gone by midday, shaking and gasping in the cable car, thirty meters away from us, Hess ignoring his desperate gestures to let the car into the station. Thomsen tried to climb onto the cable but slipped, fell, and slithered slowly along the the cable car roof, toward its edge. "Pull me in! Please!" he shouted frantically, staring and wild-eyed. But we just watched, mesmerized, as he kicked and scrabbled meters from us. He finally slid off the roof with a child-like wail and hurtled to his death.

Tables were set up with microscopes and agar cultures in the courtyard, the car was brought in, and Edith took swabs around the milk churns, stepping around Bosch's purple-faced corpse. In midafternoon she raised her thumbs: The surviving milk churns were still hermetically sealed. We drenched everything with formaldehyde, but still none of us dared to take off our protective suits. The fourth milk churn, we inferred, had somehow developed a leak during transfer from the truck.

A small, tough, no-nonsense Unterfeldwebel ordered a platoon of gray-faced soldiers to load the churns onto the back of a truck. They did so sullenly, while Oberlin's fingers strayed around the holster of his pistol and the sergeant adopted an aggressive, snarling tone. Hess watched nervously. Edith set off down the hill with another platoon, and an hour later drove back with the smashed bodies of Myers and Thomsen in the back of an army truck. Bosch, too, was heaved into this truck, along with ninety liters of petrol brought in relays from the garage. Edith, Hess, Oberlin with her platoon, all in protective suits, again took off down the hill. Later that evening Daniela and I stood in the minaret and watched a column of black smoke rising from the forest below. It rose higher than the convent and generated a long black trail stretching to the horizon. The vapor heading for Mittelwald had become invisible by the time it reached the brow of the hill, from where it would by now have rolled over the village like a poisonous avalanche.

The next morning brought a thin crescent moon set in a deep blue dawn, and a distant burst of gunfire. Daniela was asleep, exhausted. I jumped out of bed and crossed quickly to the window, ignoring the icy breeze on my skin. It was coming from the direction of Mittelwald and I knew the rasp, too well. MP44 machine pistol, five hundred rounds a minute, utterly reliable; the soldier's favorite for close work. I returned to the warmth of Daniela's bed and lay on my back. The bursts were coming at thirty-second intervals. I stared at the ceiling for a long time after they had stopped.

THE SHEIK OF ARABY

"It's here." She might have been a condemned prisoner opening her eyes to her last day. She was in an ankle-length white dressing gown, looking out the leaded-glass window. The sound of a powerful engine was coming up from below. "It's arrived."

I threw the blankets back and wrapped a gown around myself. It was the sort of spring morning, sharp but sunny, that made me want to take Daniela into the hills and just disappear. We looked down at a huge articulated truck, trying to negotiate the steep hairpin bend into the convent. An overweight soldier was waving his arms ineffectually at the driver, and the truck was shuddering. "We've got to get out of this, Daniela." We'd had this conversation before, too often.

"We? You're all right, Max. You're safe."

"What does that mean?"

She stroked my unshaven chin. "For you, the war's almost over. You survived. When it's finally done, you'll go back to your estate. You'll meet some nice Aryan girl, get married, have three blond kids."

"Daniela . . ."

"Hush!" Touching my lips. "Someday you'll have grandchildren. I'll become a distant memory, some wartime romance. As time goes by, you'll even forget what I looked like. You know, Max, you might even make it to the twenty-first

century? Do you think von Steiner's right? That people will
have walked on the moon? Or will they have cars that fly? I
wonder what music will be like then? You'll know. Me, I'll
be gone by next week."

I ran a hand around the back of her neck, underneath her
hair, pulled her gently toward me, kissed a damp cheek.
"There's got to be some way out of this. I'll find it while you're
gone."

"But Max, don't you see? I won't be coming back."

*She's right. As soon as she's delivered the goods in the sub-
marine pen, she's finished.* "Jump ship somewhere between
here and there. You only need to hang out a short while. The
war's nearly over. Even if they hit the big cities with the
Furies . . ."

The Prussian soldier again, doing the corridor. *Knock
knock.* "Breakfast in thirty minutes." *Knock knock.* "Breakfast in thirty minutes . . ."

"God help his family after the war," Daniela said, and
started to giggle.

Her last night in the convent, and Daniela defied the moon.

She played the forbidden music for hours. Hot music,
blues, swing, even the bebop that was sweeping through the
American radio stations that we all listened to illegally. The
atonal rhythms preached subversion in every corridor and
cloister of the convent. Around three, I could just make out
her voice, singing in English.

> *I'm the sheik of Araby*
> *Your love belongs to me*
> *At night when you're asleep*
> *Into your tent I'll creep*
> *The stars that shine above*
> *Will light our way to love*
> *You'll rule this land with me*
> *The sheik of Araby*

Against spirit like that, my own stance was derisory.

THE RED CROSS PARCEL

Hess was on a high. "This is a great day," he declared, waving bratwurst on his fork. His plate was laden with sausages, tomatoes, eggs—two fried—and landbrot, baked to perfection in the kitchen early that morning.

"So, where are our little Furies headed?" Klein asked. "And don't tell us that's forbidden knowledge."

"You can't be told." Hess smirked. "It's forbidden knowledge."

"After all we've done?"

"My guess is New York for Megaera, the Hague for Alecto, and London for Tisiphone," Edith suggested. "Am I right, Director?"

Hess smiled knowingly and said nothing. Von Steiner said, "Wherever, we know they have to make their way to U-boats. That means a trip to the far north."

"What about Berlin for all three?" I suggested.

Edith said, "Don't spoil the atmosphere, Max."

Hess sighed. "I'm tired of warning you about that kind of joke."

Joke? I stayed silent.

Nobody was taking chances. Not with the Furies. We wheeled Megaera out of the laundry at dawn, lashed down in chains like a drugged King Kong. We raised her gingerly with a heavy crane, using wooden poles to control her swaying, while Hess fussed like a fearful old spinster, his voice shrill with tension. We lowered her onto the flatbed as if she were full of nitroglycerin. Alecto and Tisiphone followed.

Welders now got busy constructing a steel box around the Furies. All we could do was watch and try to keep our nerve as they clambered around the Furies with welding equipment and big boots. A gang of grenadiers draped the box in tarpaulin and wrapped it in ropes. Then an elderly sign writer, hauled out of Munich in the early hours, made a scaffold from ladders and planks. By noon he had written HOCHWERK MEDIKAMENT on the side of the tarpaulin and painted a red cross alongside the words. It looked like a giant Red Cross parcel.

"Krafft!" Hess, in long black leather coat and boots, waved from the archway. He was slapping his thigh impatiently with leather gloves. I walked over. Walked—in the old days I marched and saluted. My stomach felt queasy; maybe it was the heavy breakfast, maybe not. "Krafft, my office, now."

We cut smartly across the quadrangle and into Hess's office, which after two years we still called the bishop's procuratory. The atmosphere was thick with hostility, and I didn't give a damn.

"Change of plan," Hess snapped. "I've just had a call from Berlin. You are to accompany the Furies in place of von Steiner."

"Why?"

"I don't question my orders and neither should you. All you need to know is that von Steiner stays, you go."

"What are you up to, Kurt?"

Hess stared at me with open hostility. "I suppose, at this late stage, there's no point in asking you to address me properly. I've put up with your unruliness, your defeatism, and your treasonable talk for long enough. You only got this far because we needed you. Well, Maximilian von Krafft, shortly I will no longer need you. It's something to bear in mind before your next bout of impertinence."

"I'm sorry, I don't know what you're getting at."

Hess put on his high-peaked cap and grew by five centimeters. "Hopefully you won't be needed. But suppose something went wrong, like a derailment. We couldn't have a lot of ignorant clodhopping railwaymen thumping and banging at the Furies. Or if something happened to Daniela."

"What could happen to Daniela?"

"Von Steiner knows aerodynamics but nothing else. No, we need somebody on hand who understands what we're dealing with. Well, come on, Krafft, grab some overnight stuff, they're waiting for us."

The convoy was waiting, a motorbike with a machine gun on its sidecar leading, followed by a black six-seater Horsch, and then the truck with the Furies, and then a lorry-load of Waffen-SS, and finally an armored car, swastika on its side. Hess settled in beside the driver of the Horsch, and I sat beside Daniela, facing Klein and Edith. Hess tapped the driver's shoulder with his gloves, the driver touched the car horn, the motorcyclist took off, and the trek got under way.

Halfway down the mountain road, I had a last backward look at the convent, my home for the last two years. It had dwindled to insignificance against the massive gray Alps.

Good-bye, Sister Lucy.

That evening, in a railway siding outside Munich, the Red Cross parcel with the HOCHWERK MEDIKAMENT sign was hoisted on a crane and swung carefully over onto open wagons while a dozen SS men with submachine guns surrounded the operation. A troop of soldiers—boys and old men—were assigned to the open wagons, squeezing between anti-aircraft guns. We climbed aboard somebody's private train, pulled by a heavy locomotive, and spread ourselves around warm carriages that would have done credit to the Orient Express. The boys and old men sat in the freezing wind outside.

The journey took three days. Hess was in a permanent state of excitement. In the evenings, in the bar, he drank to excess. And why not? We were going to snatch victory from the jaws of defeat, halt the enemy in his tracks, defeat the forces of world Jewry, and save civilization from Bolshevism. And he, Kurt Hess, had led this history-making project.

And all this time, in the dining car, in the toilets, in the private compartments, Daniela and I looked for a way out. There was none. When it was moving, the train trundled along at a steady forty kilometers an hour through flat countryside, almost featureless apart from the occasional farm. There was literally no place to run. Once, overnight, we trundled slowly through a big switching yard stuffed with endless lines of immobile freight cars. Whether the rails had been destroyed, or the trains had no fuel, I don't know. But it was becoming clear that the Third Reich was in process of collapse.

From time to time the train would stop. Always, when this happened, the old men and boys would jump on to the tracks, pointing submachine guns out over empty fields. Once it stopped in a tunnel for half an hour, to avoid the attentions of what Hess called "terror bombers."

More ominously, apart from our private compartments, we were never out of sight of black-uniformed SS men, smoking in the corridors, gazing out windows at the dull countryside, chatting. Never once looking in our direction. I began to think Daniela and I both were under surveillance. And I had a hardening suspicion that she was right, that I would be joining her in whatever fate was waiting at the end of the journey.

I went over and over the points in my head. The sudden change of plan, replacing von Steiner with me. Hess's hatred for me, now quite open. Daniela and Hess and me, the age-old triangle, except that Hess had abruptly gone cold on her after the Goering visit. Daniela the Jewess: Hess must have been told by now. *They can get me under the race laws. For the Protection of German Blood and German Honor.*

It made too much sense.

It was midnight on the second night when I answered a tap at my door. Daniela, in her white dressing gown, carrying a tray of coffee, croissants, and, incongruously, a box of matches and a menu card. She was wearing lipstick, slightly smudged, which threw the pale complexion of her face into contrast, and there were dark shadows under her eyes. She looked as if she hadn't slept since the convent.

She flopped down on the bed opposite mine. "Can we talk?"

"Are there microphones, do you mean? Of course not. Anyway, what do we have to hide?" While I was speaking, I was shaking my head. "Pour the coffee, would you?" I scribbled on the back of the menu card: *800 kms, Munich to Denmark. Probably there day after tomorrow.*

She took the card and my pen. "Two sugars, right? Real sugar." While she was speaking she wrote: *Denmark? Are we heading there?*

"It's been a long slog, but if these weapons work, it will have been worth it." *Either Denmark or the submarine pens at Bergen. Bergen is double the distance. If it's Bergen we could contact the Norwegian resistance, they might take us over the mountains to Sweden.*

"I asked the steward to heat the croissants. How's yours?" *What if it's Denmark?*

"It's fine, thanks, hot all the way through." *I don't know.*

"I hope you don't mind my calling in like this. I just needed a little company." *This is my problem. You don't have to do this.*

"I think you should get some sleep. You want to be at your best for priming the Furies." We were running out of space on the card. *Of course I have to do this, you beautiful idiot. We'll just have to grab a chance when we can get it.*

"You're right. Do you mind if I smoke? Then I'll get out."

"Smoke away. I'll join you." I scribbled *Je t'aime*. The matchbox had the eagle-and-swastika insignia and was no doubt made for some minister or high Nazi official. Daniela lit a match and held it to the corner of the card. We watched it burn to ash. She saved *Je t'aime* to the last.

Hess tapped a breakfast plate noisily with a spoon. "Ladies and gentlemen. Heil Hitler! I can now reveal our destination.

In one hour we will be approaching Hamburg. Unfortunately the bombers have destroyed much of the rail network around that fine city, not to mention the city itself. We will therefore have to detour through Lubeck. Once past Lubeck, we will have a straight run to our destination." He paused dramatically. "Denmark. Flensburg, to be exact. To be even more exact, the Flensburger Schiffau construction yard."

"When will we arrive?" Klein asked.

"Our estimated time of arrival is half past two this afternoon. There will be no leisure time. We'll have to load our little toys into three U-boats this evening, with bows specially adapted to take them. Once loaded, Daniela will prime the Furies under my supervision. And when that has been done, our work is over. Our brave Wolves, and the Führer, will take care of the rest. We can all look forward to a wonderful victory."

I asked, "Will we have time for sightseeing in Denmark?"

"Sightseeing in Denmark? Sightseeing in Denmark? We are about to win the war for the Reich, open up a new golden age, and you ask, do we have time for sightseeing in Denmark?" Hess was ham-acting, eyes wide and mouth open and raising the pitch of his voice to demonstrate his incredulity. My training sergeant again. "No, Krafft, you will not have time for sightseeing. And in case you are unaware of it, there are no mountains to climb in Denmark. The train will return us to Berlin, where it is wanted. After that we will have to use ordinary trains, like the rest of humanity."

Except for Daniela and me. We'll be in some other form of transport. I glanced at her across the table. She gave me a tense little smile. And I glanced at the clock at the head of the restaurant car.

Half past eight. Estimated time of arrival half past two. And not a chink of light in the tunnel.

KIEL CANAL

Here and there, in the distance, I saw long streams of trucks. They were heading south. I could make no strategic sense of that: No doubt our beloved Führer was directing operations. Near the Kiel canal, the railtrack cut across a road. An endless convoy of lorries, interspersed with mud-spattered panzers, field guns, and trucks, had stopped at the level crossing. Some troops, exhausted and filthy, were relieving themselves at the roadside. Daniela waved but nobody waved back. I thought, *Soldiers who don't return the wave of a pretty girl have reached the end of the rope.* We drank coffee morosely in the restaurant car. A couple of SS men were playing cards at the next table. Always ignoring us; never eye contact.

Just before noon, the rhythm of the train began to change; it was slowing down. We exchanged glances, stood up casually, and left the car. I didn't dare to look toward the SS men, not even a glance. At the end of the carriage, we pulled down the window of the door and looked out. Icy air air blew in, mixed with the sulfurous smell of the cheap *braunkohle* they were burning these days. Daniela's hair got in my eyes, and we changed places. A child waved from a back garden. We were approaching some suburban station. We looked at each other: Was this an opportunity?

Four men waiting on the platform, *Gestapo* written all over them.

"Bitte." This from behind me. One of the SS men, tall and thin, with round spectacles that made him look like a teacher or librarian. We stepped back as the train squealed to a halt. The SS man stepped off and spoke briefly to the Gestapo men. The spark of hope died. Daniela and I got back to our half-cold coffees. The Gestapo men came into the car, began to overflow the seats, got into noisy chat with the officers, lit cigarettes, ordered coffees. Daniela now got a fair share of glances. It might be the usual attention paid to a strikingly beautiful woman, except for the hardness around the eyes and the turned-down mouths. Or was it my imagination? My throat was parched.

Daniela leaned forward and whispered: "My guardian angels."

"And mine."

She gripped my hands. She was cold. "I don't have much longer, Max."

U-BOAT PEN

Hess was being important. "Dress warmly, people, it's chilly out there. Leave your things—we'll be back on board tonight if Daniela does her job properly."

In my compartment, I took out my SS major's uniform. I have no idea why I'd taken it along. I hadn't worn it for two years. I put it on and looked at the stranger in a full-length mirror, and I didn't know what to think. Maybe it was the sense that, whatever fate was waiting for me, I would meet it as a German soldier.

Then we were spilling out into the corridor. There was an air of excitement. Edith was jumping up and down on the spot, as if she were skipping. For the last hour the train had been trundling along beside the sea. It was ambling now, little more than twenty kilometers an hour. There was the occasional whiff of seaweed, or fish. There was a sprinkling of small pastel-colored houses, boating huts, and even the occasional fishing boat on a jetty. We could easily have jumped out. But the ground was flat and open, and we would have been spotted immediately by the soldiers guarding the Furies. Childhood images of holidays by the sea kept jumping into my head. I found them hard to reconcile with the knowledge that Daniela and I were perhaps reaching the end of our lives.

And now the train was almost crawling, and tall fencing topped with barbed wire was lining the track. We passed a field gun and a searchlight battery, neither of them manned. Finally, with a squeal of brakes and a *clack-clack-clack* of buffers, the train came to halt.

Someone in a railwayman's uniform opened a carriage door from outside and heaved himself up, accompanied by a fat, purple-faced soldier in his fifties. There was a lot of chatter, and then Hess was shouting, "Out! Everybody out!"

An opportunity?

Not a chance. A Gestapo man was helping Daniela off the train. Dozens of people were milling around outside: civilians, Wehrmacht soldiers, over-the-hill guards, SS men, a few female clerks with notepads.

The Flensburger yard was a different proposition from Hamburg: It was smaller, less claustrophobic, and the U-boats were apparently assembled inside what looked like huge wooden huts, hardly Lancaster-proof. The scientists were conducted along the railway track toward one of these huts. Four Gestapo men were with us. Workers—civilians, maybe forced labor—were starting to uncouple the flatbeds from the train under the eyes of soldiers with submachine guns.

Inside, it was cold and echoey, and rows of high, piercing lights provided the illumination, harsh after the gentle light of day. Here the smell of seaweed was mixed with diesel and hot oil. There were four U-boats, two on each side of a rectangle of deep black water. I had the same tingling feeling that I'd experienced at Hamburg. No question, the sight of those sleek, sinister ships brought out some atavistic feeling, some triumphalism—patriotic pride even—that I now felt uncomfortable with. A thick cable led from a massive, throbbing generator into the bowels of the nearest boat. From the dockside, the conning tower of the boat was surprisingly high; a smiling shark was painted on its side. The dockside was heaped with supplies. Sailors were throwing massive tins of food from these piles to others on the decks of the boats, and they in turn were throwing them down an open hatch. They had developed an efficient rhythm.

Someone with an air of authority—at least he had a beard and a high-peaked cap with the Reich Eagle insignia—approached the huddled scientists. "Keep together, and keep out of the way." His tone seemed unduly hostile. Keeping out of the way wasn't so easy, as small electric trucks were buzzing to and fro along the length of the dockside. For a while, fascinated by the activity, I almost forgot my situation.

"We're on!" Hess was clapping his hands. HOCHWERK MEDIKAMENT had appeared at the far end of the hut. Strips of black and dangling material, intended to keep curious eyes from the interior, were being pushed aside as the flatbeds were shunted slowly into the interior. Suddenly clouds of steam and stinking smoke were filling the hut. Somebody was shouting *"Schnell! Schnell!"* and waving. We all backed up as the flatbeds approached. And then, with a shudder, the uncoupled train disappeared back out, and sailors got busy with hoists.

"Mein Gott! Have a care!" Hess shouted as Megaera swung alarmingly under the crane.

"Excuse me." The bearded harbormaster—I could think of no other term for him—turned to Hess in high dudgeon. "I'll look after the loading, if you please."

"It mustn't be allowed to swing like that. You don't know what's inside it."

"Can it be worse than Amatol?"

"I think it would be as well if you read this." Hess produced a letter. The harbormaster scanned it, and then shrugged sourly as if to say *It's your funeral.*

The loading took two hours, about twice as long as it would have taken if the sailors had been allowed to get on with it. Hess, however, with the authority to supervise the loading and the documentation to back him up, fussed like an excited old maid. By the time three U-boats were loaded through the specially designed forward hatches, I had forgotten all about the cold. The beads of sweat on my brow and back were a mixture of physical exertion, nervous tension as the Furies swung alarmingly under Hess's incompetent directions, and a gut-wrenching apprehension about Daniela's future and my own. And all through the loading, the Gestapo men stood quietly in the shadows, watching.

PRIMING THE FURIES

It was dark outside now, and cold. The U-boats were slowly sinking against the dockside as fuel was taken onboard. At this level I could see more of the sail. It was revealing twin twenty-millimeter cannons, front and back, and an impressive array of sensors: the periscope, what looked like a sonar, a big metal DF loop, a long, thin high-frequency wire antenna, several short rod antennae. It was an imposing display of devices for radio traffic, much of it no doubt gratefully intercepted by the British.

The loading of provisions had finished. Most of the sailors were already inside the boats. At the far end of the hut, on the fourth submarine—the one without a Fury—the submariners were lined up at attention on the deck while some officer addressed them.

Now the chains were being pulled out of the "Furies hatch." The man with the beard approached. "We're ready for you." Hess nodded and waved fingers imperiously at Daniela. I watched nervously as the captain, Daniela, Hess, and a sailor carrying a toolbox crossed the narrow gangplank and disappeared through an access door at the side of the sail. I knew that, once the Furies were primed, Daniela's usefulness was gone. Anything could happen in there. She could slip and crack her skull. A gun could discharge accidentally. Anything.

It was Daniela's first time inside a submarine. Her first impression was one of warmth, after the bitter cold of the wooden hut. The captain turned. "Watch your head." Her second impression was one of congestion and narrowness. There were no concessions to human comfort here; no vases of flowers, no wallpaper, no subdued lighting. There was only a confusing mass of overhead pipes, circular handles and dials, interspersed with hanging sacks of onions, potatoes, and every sort of fruit. It smelled like a fruit shop, but this was a killing machine, pure and simple.

A killing machine manned by sex maniacs, it seemed. She ran a gauntlet of lewd grins and sotto voce comments between the crews. One or two of the older men looked less than happy; Daniela assumed she was bad luck on board, as if they needed it.

"We had to take out some bunks," the captain explained. They were in the forward torpedo room, but it was empty of torpedoes. Oilskins were hanging along either side, and they had to step over wooden chests. But there she was at the far end, a gleaming aluminium saucer taking up almost the full width of the room. Megaera, come to save the Reich.

"How long will this take?" The captain had an impatient tone.

Hess looked at Daniela expectantly. She thought, fifteen minutes. Something made her say, "Half an hour."

"Try to do it in fifteen minutes," the captain suggested.

Hess grew red-faced, began to splutter, but the captain interrupted sharply. "We should have been at sea by now. If you had left the loading to us."

"Forgive me, Captain," Daniela said, "but I'd like you to clear everyone out of the torpedo room now. Only Colonel Hess and I should be here." The captain gave her a sour look. No doubt he resented being ordered away on his own ship, by a woman at that; he surely resented heading into the Atlantic naked.

"Okay, get busy." Hess was licking his lips. He loosened his coat and pulled out a short-nosed pistol.

"What are you playing at?"

"If you make any mistakes I'll shoot you."

Now he produced a small, red hard-backed notebook. He stepped behind Daniela. She became conscious of his breathing, almost in her ear.

"You always were a bundle of fun, Kurt."

"No matter, Jewess." It was out.

"I felt like a whore with a customer, that night."

"You were."

"You coupled like a rabbit."

"Bitch."

"And you smelled."

"And you whored for nothing. Your little Dutch boy got it in the neck a month later."

The priming of Megaera was a simple operation, but it carried the potential for catastrophe. Hess handed over a key. Daniela took it over her shoulder and used it to open a small hatch at eye level. Opening this hatch swiveled the combination lock outward and exposed a space the size of a biscuit tin. The metal at the back of this space contained two coin-sized portholes, one made of thick green glass, one of red. The space was sealed off from the Fury's deadly interior; it had been flushed out repeatedly with hydrazine to remove any trace of spores, or a drop that might have evaporated into the small airspace of the hatch, waiting for Daniela to breathe.

To unleash the Fury, it was only necessary to break the red glass.

All that Daniela now had to do was turn the lock to three numbers, one at a time, clicking a toothed wheel into its correct place after each number. Hess opened his notebook and spoke the first number, clearly, repeating it to make sure there was no error. The numbers were Daniela's in the first place, and were emblazoned in her mind. It was just that, at this stage, any mistake could not be rectified and would deactivate the weapon forever. Her hand was trembling. She turned the wheel—*click click click click*—and said, "First number done." She found that she was breathing heavily.

Hess gave the second number, repeating it clearly. *Click click click click.* "Done." And the third number. Finally, she gave the external knob a few random turns.

The numbers were in. The next stage was to arm the detonator. This was a comically antiquated device, in essence a miniature crossbow. The whole apparatus was set inside a little metal box, painted red and welded to the inside of the hatch door. Hess handed over a second key and watched carefully as Daniela inserted it in the box and turned it, as if she were winding up a grandfather clock. There was a ratcheting sound, like something being wound up, and a sharp-tipped metal bolt, also red-painted, was being pulled slowly backward, sinking into a hole in the box. Inside this box, a little steel hook clicked neatly into a notch on the bolt, holding it back. She heard a distinct, double *click-clack* as it locked into place.

The bolt was now under terrific pressure from a steel strip pulled back like a bow. It was important that the steel hook stayed in the notch. If it were to lose its grip—say, if the Fury were to suffer a heavy fall—the bolt would fire, breaking the glass and unleashing Megaera. By setting the numbers, the operator who was to fire the device would pull the hook away from the notch, firing the weapon with incalculable effects for him, except for one simple device: an alarm clock timer. The agent who primed the bomb would wind the timer up with a key and set it according to his own circumstances.

It was eighteenth-century clockmaker stuff. Daniela was perversely proud of it while knowing what it would unleash. The duplicate mechanism, with everything painted green, would come into play if the wrong numbers were set. If the wrong numbers were set, a different bolt would fire, a green one, penetrating the green porthole and bursting through sacs of caustic chemicals. These would mix, creating a high-pressure foam that would neutralize the sarin or destroy the anthrax spores, depending on which of the Furies was involved. Should Megaera be captured, the enemy who experimented with the combination lock would destroy her, and so the Fury could never be turned against her creators.

The operator had to get the numbers right. First time.

The last part: booby-trap the hatch. Daniela slipped a hook at the end of a piece of fishing line into a hoop on the inside of the door. Now all she had to do was close the door. Once closed, she could never open it again. If she did, the fishing line would fire the green bolt and destroy the Fury.

The act of closing the door pointed the bolts, armed and ready to fire like crossbows, directly at the little glass portholes. She found that she was trembling. She turned to Hess, who was licking his lips. "I'm ready to close."

"Everything checked?"

"Of course."

"Do it."

The hatch door clicked shut. Megaera was ready and waiting. Hess put his pistol away, tucked the notebook into an inside pocket, and buttoned up his leather coat.

"Have you received your instructions yet, Captain?"

"In my safe. They'll be opened at sea. Why?"

"Until you read them, you must keep your crew out of the forward torpedo room. I have to insist on that."

The captain put his face within a foot of Hess's. "It may have escaped your notice, but there's not a lot of room on board a submarine. My crew need to sleep somewhere and you've already taken up half their sleeping space with your damned saucer. If they can't bunk down in the torpedo room, they'll have to sleep standing up."

"I'm so sorry, Captain, I don't wish to intrude on your domain. But I think you'll find that your instructions are clear on the matter."

"Forgive me if I seem a little resentful. But how come you know more than I do about my sailing orders?"

The tension that had lined Hess's face was replaced by a smile of glorious superiority. "Admiral Donitz and I drew them up."

ARREST

The officer emerged briskly from the U-boat, followed by Daniela, with Hess taking up the rear. She managed a glance in my direction, but I could read nothing into her expression. The trio marched quickly toward the second U-boat and disappeared into the open access door.

"Come on, come on, Daniela," Klein said, making a big thing of flapping his arms and stamping his feet. Beyond the hut, the sea was now black, and it was hard to make out where sky ended and ocean began. The breeze circulating around the big building had acquired a distinct chill.

Unaccountably, I felt the hairs prickling on the back of my neck. I looked around. The four Gestapo men were huddled together with Oberlin, making no conversation. Two of them were smoking. There were NICHTRAUCHER signs everywhere, but nobody was pointing them out. One of them glanced at me and grinned. Another smiling shark.

I wondered when they'd make the arrest. When Daniela had finished the arming? Or would they let her take the train, all unsuspecting, back to Berlin?

There was a few minutes' distraction as sailors suddenly poured out of the nearest U-boat. Commands were shouted, ropes cast off. Then the submariners stood briefly to attention. For the first time I saw their individual faces in the stark overhead lighting, saw them as farm boys, students, apprentices; but then at a sharp word of command they disappeared back into the boat as quickly as they had emerged. Within seconds the U-boat was slipping out quietly, leaving a wake that reflected back from the opposite quay: the days of brass bands and tossed bunches of flowers were long gone. Next stop some quiet coastline on Maine or Ireland. I watched the U-boat disappear into the dark. The wake was still sloshing backward and forward in the hut, making complicated patterns on the oily water.

Daniela reemerged between the officers as before, as if they were expecting her to run away. They disappeared into the third submarine.

Klein was now blowing into his hands, continuing the big Arctic Cold performance. The second U-boat, the one carrying Alecto, followed the first into the Baltic. Presumably heading for the Kiel canal, I thought, and then out into the Atlantic.

Daniela and her minders finally emerged from the last submarine. Alive, but her usefulness at an end. There was an exchange of conversation, and Hess was handing over a sheet of paper. The bearded officer signed it, using Hess's back as a prop, and then Hess was waving imperiously at us and heading toward the exit, Daniela beside him. On the track, soldiers guided us with torches. For some reason, the image of a Viking funeral jumped into my head. Ahead, I could see the orange glow from the locomotive's fire; they had turned the train around. And I could make out silhouettes about fifty meters ahead: presumably Daniela in the company of Hess and Oberlin, flanked by soldiers. Edith and Klein were together with me, and the Gestapo were somewhere behind us, taking up the rear like shepherding dogs.

"It's done, Max," Edith said excitedly. She was like a girl on her first date. "We did it."

We did it. I looked at the expanse of blackness on my left. There was nothing to be seen. But somewhere out there, the Sisters of the Night were on their way. I couldn't resolve the contradictions in my head: an immense pride in the creation of the wonderful monsters, and a guilty awareness of the horrors they would unleash.

"Yes, we did it. With what outcome, I wonder?" Klein asked.

We were speaking obliquely, aware of the soldiers and policemen around us, but aware also that our creations might change the course of history. Edith said, "Now we just wait and see."

I turned to the Gestapo man behind me. "What are you people doing here?"

"You are von Krafft, right?"

"Yes. I asked a question."

The man gave a sardonic grin. "But why do you ask the question? Maybe you have something on your conscience, von Krafft?"

I literally put my tongue between my teeth; answering *Yes, the Third Reich,* wouldn't·go down well in a People's Court.

Desperation was now building up inside me. Somewhere, I'd heard rumors that Danish fishermen smuggled spies and Jews across to Sweden. I had a brief vision of walking ahead, collecting Daniela, disappearing off the track, and vanishing unseen into the darkness. But Daniela was with Hess and I knew it was just a hopeless fantasy.

"Smell that food!" Klein was sniffing the air like a hungry dog. We walked alongside the carriages to a flight of steps and pulled ourselves aboard. It was gloriously warm, and the smell of something roasting permeated the corridor. I joined the drift toward the dining car—there was no opportunity to do anything else, and anyway Daniela would be up ahead.

An opportunity at last? I was in fear that my tension would reflect in my face, that the thumping in my heart could be heard everywhere. In the dining car the SS men were milling around haphazardly, soaking up the heat, chattering; with their duty done, they were relaxed and expansive, maybe even careless. A long table had been covered with a white lace tablecloth and set with assorted delicacies. No Daniela. She'd passed through, clever girl. Klein, holding a sausage on a cocktail stick, looked as if he wanted to say something, but

I pretended not to notice and pushed casually—casually!—toward the far end of the car.

Past the kitchens, buzzing with action, chefs sweating and swearing, sausages sizzling in a big pan, somebody basting a chicken, somebody else chop-chopping carrots at speed. Nobody noticed me. Along to the next corridor, the one with the bedrooms. Corridor empty, nobody in sight, I'm alone.

We can do this. We can clear the train, find a boat, vanish.

My whole skin is clammy. I tap at Daniela's door. It's unlocked. I turn the handle and step in. Daniela is sitting, pale and upright, on the couch. Oberlin is standing over her with a gun. There is a second man in the compartment, in civilian clothes. He's round-faced and bald, and is wearing thick-lensed spectacles. He has a beer belly and a waxy complexion; probably too old and too unhealthy for the army. He, too, has a gun. It's a standard-issue Walther, out of my reach, and he's pointing it at me almost apologetically. Too many guns. Nothing I can do. He nods toward the couch. I sit down beside Daniela. I feel gutted. Only when I'm seated do Oberlin and the fat civilian sit down, across from us.

Hess slides in and surveys the cameo at leisure. A broad smile spreads over his face. He shuts the door, turns the lock, and sits down with a happy sigh next to Oberlin. He is practically glowing with triumph.

The civilian adopts a clipped, formal tone. The big man, the important official. "Herr Maximilian von Krafft, I am arresting you under Section Two of the Law for the Protection of German Blood and German Honor of 1935."

I no longer care. *"Verpiss Dich."* His face grows purple with outrage.

Oberlin, in his smooth tone, the one he likes to use for intimidation: "We know about your background, Miss Bauer. You are the offspring of a relationship between your father and a Jewess."

Daniela laughs lightly. "My dear Oberlin, I look forward to your grovelling when this is sorted out. But it won't save you. My father will have you disemboweled."

"We have to be careful," Oberlin admits. "But you see, your father married the Jewess before September 15, 1935. That means Section One, forbidding marriages between Jews and German nationals, doesn't apply to him. Your father is in the clear. Your mother, of course, is a different matter. She has defiled the race by marrying an Aryan, as have you by coupling with Krafft here. However, I agree that if Papa finds his wife and daughter are in deep shit, he could well go on some sort of rampage, which could be embarrassing if not downright dangerous for us. Our best defense is keeping your father unaware until the deed is done."

"Max and I aren't married."

"No married couple ever performed like the pair of you." *Microphones, the bastard.* "However it doesn't save him. Section Two forbids not only marriage between Jews and Germans, but also relations outside marriage. Krafft would have to face a People's Court on that account alone."

Did they hear the pillow talk, the treason? If they did, I'll hang. They used piano wire and a butcher's hook for the July conspirators.

Hess takes a big puff. He is transported, loving the show. "You know, Max, I've dreamed of this for a very long time, and I'm loving every minute of it."

The fool is overconfident. But there are still too many guns. "You're still a failure, Kurt. What the Americans would call a Mickey Mouse. You're full of ice worlds and Atlantis and Aryans and *scheisse.*"

Hess flushes, but then the beatific smile comes back. "Maybe so, Max, maybe so. But I've got you by the balls and I'm squeezing."

The Taymyr Peninsula

TUESDAY–WEDNESDAY

INFILTRATION

Sharp has made a discovery. He has found that, until now, he never really knew what stress is.

Problem: to infiltrate two spies—Sharp and Ambra—into a village six thousand kilometers away, in a military area of Arctic Russia. To do so within the next few hours. And, their task completed, to get them out quickly. The small MI6 team assigned this problem has developed a monstrous collective headache.

A British presence in the area, they soon find, is thin to vanishing point. True, HMS *Victorious* is at that moment eight hundred kilometers to the north of the peninsula, measuring the depth of sea ice in an underwater Arctic passage, oblivious to Russian territorial claims to the region. There is a brief, far-fetched discussion about dropping the spies from a long-range Nimrod somewhere over the Arctic and collecting them in the *Victorious,* which then delivers them to Chelyuskin Point on the Poluostrov Taymyr, the northernmost peninsula on earth. But under Article Seventy-six of the Law of the Sea Convention, Russia certainly has two hundred nautical miles of offshore sea as their exclusive territory. And the Poluostrov Taymyr is on the great circle route from

Omaha, Cheyenne Peak, and the old Kansas missile silos—
stick a nose out of the water and radar stations all around the
peninsula bristle with curiosity. The team feel that if the Russians detected HMS *Victorious* in their territorial waters,
armed as it is with forty-eight nuclear warheads pre-
programmed for Russian targets, unpredictable and dangerous reactions might follow.

There is another British presence in the form of a
Liverpool-registered ship sent by Greenpeace to investigate
the dumping of nuclear waste in the Arctic, but as this has
been impounded by Russian coast guards and the crew im-
prisoned in Murmansk, the team feel that this isn't useful,
either. Murmansk, in any case, is as far from the destination
as is Aberdeen from Naples.

Runways built on drifting ice and run by commercial op-
erators are another possibility: There is an ice station at
eighty-nine degrees north with such a runway, and this is
within flying range of Khatanga. Used by polar explorers and
intrepid tourists, a switch might be arranged, with the spies
"returning" to Khatanga from their North Pole trip. However, these runways are only open in the spring; there are no
explorers to switch with.

The team learn that there is a joint Cambridge–Russian
scientific group somewhere on the drifting Arctic ice, with
an arrangement to charter Russian MIL-88 military helicopters. But they can't see how to exploit this.

Several tour ships operate in the area, and some of these
have helicopters that, at some risk, might be used for infiltration. But a quick survey shows that there are no such cruise
ships currently in operation. This is unsurprising since the
pack ice has almost closed in.

Finally, the increasingly desperate team are driven to
tackle the main problem head-on: Russian bureaucracy. The
standard Russian visa they can handle; MI6 has long experience in that line. The real headache is the rhazporezhenie, a
local permit which has to be signed by the governor of the
Taymyr Autonomous District. And there is also a military
permit to be forged, from the Frontier Directorate of the Fed-

eral Security Service of Russia for the Murmansk region. There could well be problems with the Frontier Detachment of the Murmansk military: The team quickly uncovers horror stories of visitors being arrested and held by armed guards at Khatanga airport even with all the proper permissions. But how to obtain signatures of officials, civilian and military, from this remote area of the world? For their forgeries, the document experts need them now!

The MI6 team, at last, have a much-needed breakthrough: They find an adventure trekking firm in London, with experience of expeditions taking off from Khatanga. They rouse its managing director from his Virginia Waters bed and transport him swiftly to his office in central London. Photocopies of documents signed by the authorities are removed and taken by motorcycle courier to Hanslope Park, where the technicians are standing by like emergency surgeons awaiting an accident victim. The document specialists get busy.

The flying time from London to Moscow is three hours and fifty minutes. From Moscow, there is a weekly flight to Khatanga, the last regular flight of the year taking place later that day—"regular" meaning subject to the vagaries of Arctic weather. False passports already exist for Sharp and Ambra; an improvised cover story is quickly put together. If the infiltration goes perfectly, and if Max Krafft exists and is in Khatanga, and if he isn't ga-ga, and if he's willing to talk about his wartime work, then it might—or might not—happen that he will have something useful to say.

The team leave a problem unsolved. They can get the spies into Khatanga—maybe—but they can't see how to get them out again. The last incoming flight turns and goes straight back out, fleeing the Siberian winter. The spies are going to have to find their own way home. And a polar front is moving in from the Arctic ice, and the Siberian village is about to be closed off until the following spring.

KHATANGA

Sharp's Russian is basic and he sits dumbly while Ambra does the talking. She says, "You didn't get notice we were coming?"

"Only the *Pravda* message. Nothing official." The chief of police stirs his tea with a pencil. He is a round-faced, wrinkled man who doesn't smile. Sharp remembers that Russians only smile when they have something to smile about.

The mayor isn't smiling, either. "It happens we have an American team heading for the pole. We don't meet too many Westerners out here, and two groups at once is just amazing, especially at this time of year."

Sharp is having difficulty following the conversation, but Ambra is speaking Russian like a native. They are in a big echoey hall, which seems to serve as a common room, entrance foyer to a hotel, and café all at once. Locals are crowded at the big glass window, staring in curiously, and a cleaning lady, with the leathery skin, wrinkles, and Mongoloid eyes of the Evenki, is finding a lot to do at the table next to them. And why not, Sharp thinks. Martians don't drop in every day.

The chief of police says, "I see you have a permit from the Russian Department of Tourism. That's strange." He is small, bald without the Cossack hat, and round. Sharp senses contemplation behind the man's dark eyes.

Ambra sips her lemon tea. "Really?"

"Yes. I understand there was an administrative reform in the government about six months ago. The department has been required to change its function. It no longer accepts applications for expeditions."

"We put in the application about six months ago. Perhaps we caught it at the tail end."

"Actually, now I think about it, the administrative change was nine months ago. Your permit came through three months after the department stopped issuing them. That is odd, is it not?"

Ambra laughs lightly. "I'll never understand the Russian way of doing things, sorry. It was a joint undertaking with *Pravda*. They fixed the paperwork."

The police chief shakes his head. "Moscow bureaucracy."

"What are your plans here?" the mayor wants to know.

"Just stroll around town, maybe take a few photographs, if that's all right."

"And speak to one or two people," Sharp adds in English. Ambra translates.

"Our visitors come in the spring and summer, along with our supplies. Mostly it's an influx of students doing research. We had a parachute team jumping out over the North Pole this year. I'm afraid you're catching us just as we're going into hibernation. The harbor is already closed up with several ships locked into it. We still have the airfield, but the weather could close it up anytime."

The police chief says, "If that happens, you might have a long wait before you get out." Something about the way he says it; a vague feeling of unease comes over Sharp, but he can't say why.

Ambra says, "Research students we can find anywhere. *National Geographic* wants us to speak to some of the older people with tales to tell. People who've been here a long time, who can tell us about Khatanga as it was."

The mayor says, "We're four hours ahead of Moscow time. Mind you, this close to the pole, day and night don't mean much."

The chief of police says, "But it means our bureaucrats in the Kremlin are still tucked up in bed." He doesn't bother to explain why he said that.

Sharp finishes the last of his tea. Ambra translates his comment: "We'd like to meet some of your local characters." *And get the hell out of here before Moscow wakes up.*

A cluster of young people, fur hats lightly dusted with snow, bustle in and sit down noisily at a table close to them. Their features are more Western than Mongol, and their clothes, once the fur coats have come off, could have come out of any High Street store in Kensington. One of them, a girl of about twenty with gypsy earrings, glances at Sharp, ignoring Ambra, and says something incomprehensible to the mayor.

Ambra translates: "They're having a party tonight and would like us to join them. The Americans will be there."

Sharp says, "We haven't time."

There is a rapid three-way exchange among Ambra, the girl, and the mayor, followed by nodding of heads. Sharp follows Ambra out of the doorway while the mayor and the police chief continue to chat over tea. There is a light, freezing fog and the air is bitter: Siberian bitter, a whole new meaning to the word. A husky with no visible owner is trotting along a broad, sloping street. Ice and icicles are everywhere; water has been poured over the town and froze where it hit.

Sharp flaps his arms. "What was that about?"

"I said I wanted to meet one or two of the older people with a wartime connection. They said they'd rustle up a few geriatrics. Party's in a couple of hours at the end of town. Blue-painted house. I said meantime we'd just cruise the mean streets."

"The cop was suspicious."

"Wasn't he just!"

"He'll be telephoning as soon as Moscow wakes up."

She stamps her feet on the ground. "Let's hope we can do our business and get the hell out of here before the alarm bells go off."

"They already have." Sharp looks around, both nervous

and fascinated. The roads are concrete slabs laid down on the permafrost. Every house is a foot or two above the ground. He thinks a couple of them might be shops, but it's hard to tell. Pipes encased in wooden frames crisscross between the little houses, clouds of steam in lines mapping them out. A couple of small, fat women and what look like a handful of reindeer herders are clumping along these boards, using them as walkways. A huge, four-wheeled, open truck roars past, its exhaust fumes black. A dozen locals are staring at the Martians. The Wild West is alive and well and living in Siberia.

Sharp, his face almost invisible inside a parka, says, "Think positive. They don't have the gulag to throw us in anymore. Let's paint this town red."

MAX KRAFFT

"This is Police Commissioner Gosha Pavlovski, from Khatanga. In the Taymyr District? I want to know who is in charge of all official authorizations, permits, and licenses for polar expeditions. Can you give me a number, please?"

"Commissioner, the office doesn't open for eight hours." Pavlovski visualizes a plump, stupid woman. Scolding tone; but then, she's been roused from sleep at one A.M.

"I'm aware. I want to speak to him at his home. Head of department, the Big Chief."

"I'm just the duty officer. I don't have the authority to give you his home number."

"Who would have the authority?"

A thoughtful silence, then: "That would be the secretary, Victor Dudinka."

"Ask him to call me."

"I don't have the authority for that, either."

"Just do it."

"It's one in the morning."

"This is an urgent police matter. If you want to keep out of trouble . . ."

An expressive sigh, and then: "I'll transfer you through to his house."

Pavlovski is a patient man. He is on his second cigarette,

feet up on his desk, when another disembodied female voice says, "Commissioner of Police Pavlovski?"

"Yes."

"What is the nature of your inquiry, Commissioner?"

"I need to speak to Victor Dudinka."

"My husband's with friends, I don't know where. He won't be home for some hours."

"Ask him to call me the moment he comes home."

"He's a bit . . . you know." The Beard circles a forefinger around the side of his head, in the universal gesture. His name is Stefan, he is well educated, and his magnificent black beard makes Sharp wonder if the young man is in the priesthood, or has ambitions to become a patriarch in his old age and is starting early.

"But that's what we're here for. Local color." Sharp is on his fourth vodka. He's made a determined attempt to keep the drinking down, but the hospitality is verging on the ferocious. More than once he has made his way to the little bathroom, flushed his vodka down the toilet, and refilled the glass with icy tap water. Ambra, strangely, seems neither up nor down despite sipping steadily the whole evening. She has brought along a plain black dress; suitable for any occasion, the sign of a seasoned female traveler. She looks sensational among the traditional party dresses of the local women—brightly embroidered squares on cotton—and she's flirting outrageously with whatever males happen to be nearby. Sharp isn't sure whether it comes naturally or is part of a performance. In either case, it's a side of Ambra that takes him by surprise. The Khatanga solution to life in the big Siberian freezer is simple: piping-hot radiators in every room, in the corridor, in the kitchen, in the bathroom. Wherever Sharp goes in the apartment he is immersed in heat like Jamaica. About thirty people, mostly thirtyish, are jammed into the little living room, sharing it with a sideboard, a couple of chairs, a couch, and a long table stacked with every conceivable kind of vodka and every conceivable body part of reindeer and fish. Mick Jagger, stripped to the waist and bile green, leers down from a poster on one wall, while opposite him the Beatles are scampering across a zebra crossing on the Old Kent Road.

Three Americans introduced themselves earlier. Sharp mentally calls them Tom Cruise, Judy Garland, and Marilyn Monroe, although the resemblances are worse than marginal. Judy and Marilyn are dancing unsteadily. "Chattanooga Choo-Choo" is playing on an old-fashioned tape recorder, possibly in deference to the Americans. It's on its third play.

And in the last half an hour, three old people have turned up and been introduced as Pavel Medvedev, Anna Sobolev, and Max Krafft.

The Beard shouts above the noise. "How's your German?"

"I can get by. Max speaks German?"

"And Russian with a thick German accent. Well, I warned you. Show the slightest interest and he'll talk all night. And don't expect much sense. It's mostly rubbish. I don't think the German metabolism is well suited to Russian vodka. Are you sure about this?"

"Sounds perfect for the magazine."

The Beard steers Sharp through the crowd. "Max, this is the Englishman who wants to talk to you." He grins, flicks his beard cheekily, and leaves Sharp to it.

"They think I'm mad." Krafft speaks in German. Sharp doesn't know the language well enough to place the dialect, but it certainly isn't country-boy Bavarian. The man is tall and has a big hand, still as cold as the outside air, but his handshake is firm. "Stefan told you that I'm mad, am I right?" It's an old man's face, wrinkled, but with craggy features. Sharp judges he was handsome in a film-star sort of way long ago. He still has his hair, which is white and in need of a trim. His eyes are light blue, and he is looking at Sharp intently. Sharp, under the gaze, feels uncomfortable. "He did, Mr. Krafft. But I still asked to speak to you."

"My name is Max. I like Stefan, he's a good boy, very bright, but he still lacks wisdom. Do you understand me? The difference between intelligence and wisdom?" He's having to raise his voice over Glenn Miller and the vodka-fueled party.

Sharp sips killer vodka, spots Ambra skillfully detaching herself from a cluster of young admirers and moving his way. "Not really. But then, I'm just dumb on all counts."

"He's an engineer, as I was. They're trying to build a nuclear reactor in an old naval dockyard in Kola. They've already had a dozen irradiated workers shuffled from one hospital to the next because they don't know what to do with them."

He might be a white-haired old man in his eighties, but there is no sign of dotage in his conversation. Eccentric, maybe—and who wouldn't be, living out here for half a lifetime?

"It's you I want to talk about, Max, not a nuclear reactor in Kola. How did a German end up in Khatanga?" From the corner of his eyes, Sharp sees Ambra detach herself from another group of young men and maneuver herself toward them.

"It's a long story and it would bore you to tears. Look at the pretty girls here. I'm sure they're far more interesting to you. Let me introduce you to Dora, for example." He nods toward a far corner.

Sharp doesn't follow the man's gaze. "Pretty girls I meet everywhere. But for the *National Geographic* . . ."

"Yes, they told me about that."

"Can I introduce you to my colleague?" Ambra shakes hands with Max. Sharp says, "Alice, I've found just the person. This is Max Krafft. He's a German with a long history."

"Ah, but I'm a mad German."

Something clicks with Sharp. "Forgive me, but didn't you say you were an engineer?"

"I was, during the war. I was with Hausser's panzers. I saw action in Poland and Kharkov." Spoken casually.

It doesn't fit. Max Krafft was a scientist developing a bio-weapon.

Sharp senses Ambra's alarmed sideways glance, feels a brief surge of alarm. *Two Max Kraffts and an intelligence cock-up. Max Krafft the secret weapons man, dead and buried somewhere in Obolensk. Max Krafft the tank engineer, dead and buried in Khatanga. God, no.*

"Kharkov. That would be 1943."

Krafft's eyes light up. "You know your history, young man."

"After that you were pushed back all the way to Berlin."

Krafft laughs. "No, no, no. I saw nothing of that. I was taken away, you see, pulled off the front. I spent the war in a convent in Bavaria." He laughs again—the SS soldier, hard as nuts, pulled from the Eastern Front and transferred to a convent. He's still finding it funny sixty years on. Sharp laughs, too, weak-kneed with relief.

Ambra throws back her Cruiser vodka in a single big gulp—"Real Murmansk vodka, my dear, not the Moscow shit they export to England." While the fierce liquid is still burning its way down her gullet, she says, "This is beginning to sound like the story we want to hear."

"Is that Police Commissioner Gosha Pavlovski?"

"Yes."

"Inquiring about . . . ?"

"I need to contact the head of authorizations and permits in the tourist office."

"At this hour?"

"Yes, at this hour."

"For the Taymyr District?"

"Yes, for the Taymyr District."

"One moment, please." From the intonation, Pavlovski guesses that he is in for another two-cigarette wait. But he is in no hurry.

POLAR FRONT

Sharp is surprised to find about two feet of snow already covering the path outside the house. The falling snow is heavier than anything he's seen outside of one memorable winter when he was stranded in a skiers' hut in the Alpbach for three days.

Three days. "Are we liable to be stranded here?" He is speaking to Krafft's back; his voice comes out strangely muffled in the snow. They are in single file, Krafft in the lead, Sharp and Ambra stepping in his wake.

Krafft's voice comes back equally flat. "Quite possibly."

They trudge in silence through pristine snow. Ahead of Sharp, Krafft is turning into an animated snowman. They reach the main road and trudge along tire marks left by a truck. In ten minutes the houses begin to peter out; the old man's house doesn't seem to be in the town itself. Finally he leaves the tire tracks and plows knee-deep toward an isolated bungalow.

The first thing that hits Sharp is the heat. Again. They take off gloves, hats, and coats, shedding snow on the floor, and Krafft ushers them through a narrow corridor into a brightly decorated room covered with thick-pile rugs and heaped with cardboard boxes. The old man disappears into a kitchen while Ambra and Sharp assess their new surroundings.

The boxes are filled with papers, some printed, others hand-written. There are a lot of engineering sketches around, UFO-type shapes, scribbled equations. Sharp glances at Ambra, who sticks her tongue out. Shelving all around the walls is sagging with books. Books about everything, in no order: *The Bootleggers, Comets and Dragons, Offenbahrung, Diary of a Manhattan Hooker, Im Shatten der Sensation, Fin de Siècle Vienna, Greek Myths, Fleshmarket Close, Inside the Third Reich, A Taste for Death, The Lure, Die Atomkerne, The Los Alamos Primer* . . . he can't make out the Russian titles.

A few blank spaces of wall are taken up with pictures—photographs of flying saucers for the most part, apparently torn out of magazines, the alien craft hovering over desert cacti or rooftops, crowds looking skyward, or skimming over mountains. A dining room table has an ancient, ragged toy elephant minus its tusks and a couple of black-and-white photographs.

The photographs, in cheap wooden frames. One of them shows a middle-aged Max Krafft with his arms around a thin, almost haggard woman, against a background of what looks like a chemical works. Intelligence and, Sharp thinks, a sort of despair are showing in her eyes; she looks like an archetypal Russian intellectual, possibly from the Stalin or Khrushchev era. The other photograph shows a recognizable Max Krafft—a thin, handsome man in his twenties—stretched out on a picnic rug shared with another girl, this time on what looks like an Alpine meadow. They're smiling and sharing their rug with fruit and sandwiches, a bottle of wine between them balanced precariously on a plate. Squatting behind them, cross-legged, is a bespectacled man in Lufftwaffe uniform, grinning, with a 1940s haircut. Without the uniform he could have been British or American or German or Polish or . . .

Krafft comes through carrying mugs of tea and biscuits. "I'm sure I have little to tell you of interest. Except perhaps, for my eccentric hobby." He nods toward the flying saucer photographs and smiles impishly. "Which guarantees my local reputation as a harmless lunatic."

What did you do in the war, Max? Sharp tries to think of some subtle way to steer Krafft into it. The girls in the photographs maybe; but that may be too sensitive.

Ambra solves the problem. "What did you do in the war, Max?" She flicks snow off her boots.

"Is that really something that would interest *National Geographic* readers?"

Is there a tone of suspicion in the man's voice? A sudden alertness? Sharp can't be sure. Ambra gives him a big smile, the same one he's seen her use on the males at the party. "It could be of great interest. You weren't building flying saucers, by any chance?"

Krafft pours tea, his face expressionless. Either he's not given to humor, or he doesn't see the question as funny.

Sharp says, "That's quite a pile of stuff you have here."

"Not much of it is wartime memorabilia, if that's what you're wondering. It's mostly what you might call flying saucer material. I'm an engineer, you see. The engineering aspect interests me. Propulsion, aerodynamics—that sort of thing."

A crank?

"If they exist. I understand the scientists don't take them seriously."

Krafft passes over lemon tea. "That is the consensus of opinion." He says it like a man who knows a whole lot better. "I hardly know where to start."

"Anywhere at all," Ambra says. He looks around the room thoughtfully, then nods.

"I could start with my first day in Berlin, after they pulled me off the Eastern Front. It was the start of a very strange adventure."

"That would be good."

"Yes, I loved Berlin. It was my favorite city."

End Times:

BERLIN, APRIL 1945

ESCAPE

I wasn't aware of having slept but must have done so. Sometime in the dead of night I became aware that the train was slowing. I turned in my bunk and listened, suddenly alert. A faint blue light in the ceiling now seemed bright to my dark-adapted eyes, and I saw every detail in the room. The Gestapo, I presumed, were in the corridor outside the door. I struggled up to a sitting position. A leg was still asleep, and I waggled a foot to get the circulation back. Yes, the train was definitely coming to a halt. Just a stop to replenish water? Or something more sinister? There was an indistinct exchange of voices, and the sound of footsteps hurrying along the corridor. Below the floor of my compartment, steam was escaping with a hiss.

There was a final judder and the serial *clack-clack* of buffers, and the train stopped. I stood up in my underwear, pulled on trousers, and buttoned my shirt. The door swung open and I was temporarily dazzled as someone switched on the main light. Herr Gestapo, the same idiot who had quoted the Nuremberg race laws at me some hours earlier; he was still carrying his Walther. "Out, now!"

"Where are we?"

"None of your damned business."

"Yes, definitely disemboweled," I said, covering my fear. "Are we still in Denmark?"

"Shut your mouth." He waved his gun vaguely. I could have taken it from the fat slob and stuck it down his throat, but what then?

In the corridor, sleepy-eyed scientists were being ushered toward the dining car. Black-uniformed soldiers were milling around, some still hastily buttoning up their tunics. Edith, her hair rumpled, caught my eye and gave me a puzzled, sympathetic look. The dining car was unlit apart from, bizarrely, candles on the tables, their flames threatened by extinction from the cold air drifting in from the open carriage door. SS men were disappearing through it into the dark beyond. The Gestapo man half pushed me onto a chair. I again resisted the temptation to snatch his gun and ram it down his throat.

Edith pushed her way toward me. "What's going on?"

"Don't speak to the prisoner." The Gestapo man was faking an angry tone.

"It's bloody freezing," Klein said to nobody.

"I saw trucks outside. I think we're at a level crossing." Edith said.

"I said don't speak to the prisoner."

She ignored Herr Gestapo. "I'm sorry you're in this fix, Max. And I'm sorry about Daniela."

"Sorry, nothing," Klein said, looking at me contemptuously. "He was screwing a Jewess. By the way, where is she?"

Edith shook her head, mystified. "Daniela, Jewish? That's crazy."

Hess climbed into the dining car, followed by Oberlin. There was a muttered conversation with an SS officer, and occasional glances in my direction. Then Oberlin approached our table, long-barreled gun in hand. "This is where we get off."

"And Cinderella'a carriage turns into a pumpkin." Trying for a lightness I didn't feel.

"See if you're joking tomorrow."

"I think this is good-bye, Edith."

"Never mind that," Oberlin snapped. He grabbed me by the forearm and manhandled me forward. Outside, there was a light touch of frost. A half-moon glowed down on a forested landscape, cut by a single narrow road. A long convoy of lorries was parked, and at first I thought I was destined for one of them. Then I saw wooden crates being unloaded. Of course: Goering's loot, half the art treasures of Europe taken from Karinhall and loaded, in the dead of night and safe from the Lancasters, into his train. No doubt heading for some mine shaft in Bavaria. Oberlin led the way past the lorries, his breath steaming lightly in the cold. Four soldiers were struggling to unload what looked like a tea chest, watched by an officer with a clipboard and a pencil. It seemed remarkably heavy and they were cursing profusely. I could hear the Gestapo man wheezing behind me, sense the gun pointing at my back. About twenty meters to the rear I could also hear Klein, Edith, and Hess in muted conversation.

At the end of the convoy, five cars were waiting, black Mercs, their lights dimmed by masking tape, although a few moths were fluttering, red, around the taillights.

Herr Gestapo pushed me toward the cars. I glimpsed Daniela in the back of one, squeezed between another two Gestapo types. Even in the half dark she looked pale. He pushed me toward the front car and bundled me into the backseat. I found myself squeezed between Oberlin and Herr Gestapo. Oberlin rested his gun on his lap. He said, "Any funny stuff and I'll blow your head off, simple as that."

Hess, in the passenger seat, turned to me, said nothing. Still that triumphant grin.

Oberlin said, "Get on with it." The driver, a thin-faced boy, turned on the ignition, and the car's engine gave a well-maintained purr. The convoy set off along the quiet, forested road, away from Goering's train, away from the art treasures of Europe, away from the Furies.

In a bleak dawn light, we passed over a broad river. A couple of early-morning anglers looked up as we crossed the metal bridge. A few kilometers on, we passed some horse-drawn field guns, and shortly after that the road forked. The front two cars took to the left. There was a farewell hoot from the last three cars, which took to the right, taking the scientists, I guessed, back to the convent. I wondered if I would ever see them again, my daily colleagues of the past two years.

Oberlin said, "Not long now." It was his first conversation in an hour.

I said, "What? The end of the war?"

"Funny man right to the end." The Gestapo man looked at me contemptuously with bloodshot eyes. Eyes swirling with exhaustion. He was still holding his pistol, but was resting it on his thigh; I guessed its weight was tiring. A little item of information to store away.

Now the countryside had opened up, and we were driving past barns, fields of cattle, the occasional smallholding. Daniela's car was keeping pace, a hundred meters behind. I saw a train in the distance, wondered if it was Goering's. "Where are you taking us?"

"Wouldn't you like to know?" Oberlin said. The driver was overtaking a line of mud-streaked trucks. Boys in uniform stared at us morosely from the rears. They were pale-faced, battle-weary. I knew the look. Heading away from the Western Front, toward Berlin. The Russians were less than a hundred kilometers from the Tiergarten.

"Berlin," Hess volunteered. "Me to report a successful outcome to Goering, a meeting that I am looking forward to with immense pleasure. They haven't said so, but I anticipate a meeting with the Führer himself."

"Dear Kurt, full of pride, collecting the glory earned by others. Enjoy it before the Russians come."

"But you and your Jewish whore will have to face a little questioning from the Gestapo."

"Or maybe the Americans will get here first. What do you think they'll do, Kurt? Hang you or shoot you?"

"Neither, since our work will turn the tide for us. They tell me the first floor of the Hausgefaengnis is—how can I put it?—unfriendly."

Oberlin pulled out a cigarette, opened a matchbox, struck the match, and lit the cigarette, all with his right hand. The gun stayed firmly in his left, pointing.

The Gestapo man was staring morosely out of the window. Getting careless? I looked casually at Oberlin. The security officer returned the look, half smiling, cigarette at the corner of his mouth; reading my mind. Gun resting on thigh, barrel pointing at my stomach, forefinger curled around trigger.

Hess turned to me again, grinning. "Not long now."

GESTAPO

The countryside was evolving into an unpleasant mix of dirty little towns and black slag heaps interspersed with collieries. The wheels were turning, I noted: Speer was still doing his job. There was a light orange haze in the sky and the air had a chemical smell about it, competing with the smoke from Oberlin's third cigarette. The road ran parallel to a railway track, and for a while we kept pace with a train pulling coal-laden wagons.

Something black in the sky, a crow circling. I saw it first: I had the battlefield antennae. It could have been one of ours, except that there was something business-like about the way it was curving in.

"Christ!" Hess yelled suddenly. The driver saw it and slammed on the brakes. Little puffs of dust were approaching at a terrific speed along the road, and now I could see the flashes of light from the Typhoon's machine guns.

Oberlin jumped out one door, the Gestapo man the other, leaving me in the back. I grabbed at Oberlin's gun as he exited and wrenched it out of his hand. He paid no attention and ran for the side of the road. I jumped out after him. I glimpsed the pilot, a boy, apparently looking straight at me. There was a series of loud metallic bangs and a brief, angry rasp from overhead as the aircraft, black-and-white stripes under its wings, seemed to skim the roof of the car.

The fat Gestapo man was lying facedown on the road, his hand still clutching the gun. The driver was at the wheel, his head dangling back over the seat. Blood was streaming from the back of his opened skull. So much blood! Windshield glass was everywhere, and steam was billowing up from the engine.

Behind us, Daniela's car had run into a grass shoulder and its doors were open. Someone had seized her by the hair and was trying to drag her toward a farmyard with a clutter of decrepit buildings. The others from the second car were already disappearing at speed into hay sheds and barns.

The Typhoon was going for a second pass, curving around, its engine pitch increasing. Daniela and her captor were still fighting, Daniela scratching desperately at the man's face and eyes. They were completely exposed but neither was giving in as the pilot aligned his aircraft with the road. They were about forty meters away from me and had seconds to live. I dropped on my stomach, aimed carefully at the moving, erratic target, and fired. The man dropped like a sack of potatoes. Daniela sprinted toward the car, hunched forward.

I got to my knees. Blood from a cut on my brow was blocking my vision. Oberlin and Hess were scurrying across the road about thirty meters ahead of me, trying for the rail track. They were racing the Typhoon but hadn't a hope. I dived behind the wrecked car just as the fighter's guns chattered again and clods of tar spurted up from the road. Then it had passed, buzzing angrily, and this time it was heading for the horizon.

Oberlin's head was shattered. Little white shards of bone and lumps of gray brain were everywhere. Hess had vanished.

Daniela reached the second Mercedes and I leaped in just as she raced the engine, and the rear wheels sent grass and mud arching through the air. Hess appeared ahead of us, prising the

gun from the dead Gestapo man, fumbling it, picking it up
again. His face was livid. Then the tires gripped and the car
surged, lurching heavily as Daniela took it over Oberlin's
body. Hess had time for one shot. He hunched forward, squint-
ing along the barrel of the gun; a stab of orange flame; a little
spiderweb hole in the windshield between us; and a metallic
clang from behind. And then a horrified expression came over
his face and he leaped aside. There was a huge explosion. I
glanced behind. Hess was rolling on the ground. Men were
rushing onto the road from the outbuildings, but the cameo
was dwindling rapidly and it didn't look as if they knew what
to do next. The train driver and fireman were running in and
out of a cloud of steam billowing into the sky like a genie.
Somewhere inside the cloud, presumably, was the train, the
second Typhoon's prime target. It had used its cannon; the cars,
being just a bonus, hadn't merited more than bullets.

"Papa?"

We were squeezed into the phone booth. The Berlin air
was damp and smelled of brick dust and burned wood, and a
hard-faced old crone was standing at the door, making her
impatience felt. I could just make out the general's voice.
"Daniela? Is that you?"

He hadn't heard from her in three years, Daniela had told
me. So far as Papa was concerned, she had just disappeared.
"War work."

A four-engined airplane, three of its propellers turning,
was trundling low overhead. It was just visible in the dusk,
sinking towards the Zentral-Flughafen, no doubt bringing in
senior officers from the eastern battlefront for some desperate consultation. Daniela was almost having to shout. "Papa.
I need help. Can we meet right away? At the Siegassaule? In
half an hour? Can you be alone and in civilian clothes?"

"Of course! Daniela, what's the problem? I can hardly hear
you." The big Fokke-Wulf was struggling: One of its engines
was stuttering, a heart-stopping ... *voom* ... *voom* ...
voom ... drowning out everything. The old crone was edging closer, pretending not to listen.

"I have to go . . . as soon as you can . . . please be there, Papa."

The Fokke-Wulf disappeared behind the rooftops. *Voom . . . voom . . .*

I held the door open for the old witch. She looked at us slyly. I didn't know what she'd heard and I was tempted to break her neck—I could have done it in a second, one arm wrapped round her throat from behind, the other wrenching her head. I smiled at her and thought maybe brutalization was for life after all.

It was now almost dark but Daniela gave a little shout when she saw the outline of the man on the bench. He stood up, throwing his newspaper aside. He was tall, well built, and wore a heavy black suit.

I stood back as Daniela ran toward him, let them embrace and laugh without intrusion. They spoke for a minute, and then Daniela turned and waved me forward.

He peered at me in the near dark. "Who's this?"

"Von Krafft, sir. Maximilian von Krafft."

"Max saved my life, Papa. It's a long story. Can we get out of here? We're in danger."

"We have an hour, maybe less, before the evening session. We could either get to the Zoo Bahnhof bunker or head for my apartment. The Zoo Bahnhof itself has been hit."

"Could we talk in the bunker?"

"With difficulty. Half of Berlin squeezes into it during a raid."

Daniela's father turned and led us quickly past the zoo and the blackened remains of the Hotel Eden. The Ku-damm was delineated by huge rubble heaps, dimly seen through unextinguished fires from the last raid. We turned onto the Potsdamer Strasse and found that water was gushing over the street.

We could hardly keep up. "*Mein Gott,* child, you look terrible. When did you last sleep?" Daniela was looking punch-drunk.

The long steady wail of an air raid siren, then the awful

rise and fall of pitch. People around us started to scurry. "They're early."

We joined a flood of people heading for the Zoo Bahnhof bunker. Wardens were blowing whistles and waving people in in the dark. Daniela and I held hands to keep together.

The bunker, seven floors high, was icy and cavernous and yes, half of Berlin seemed to be squeezing into it. It was lit by blue lights, giving everything an unreal appearance, like a stage set. I had the impression that some families had set up home there, with mattresses, blankets, pillows laid out on the concrete floor. It hardly seemed possible in the congested space, but people were still pouring down the stairs and we drifted with the crowd away from the huge steel door into the bunker. Somebody behind me was carrying a suitcase, and its corner kept jabbing into my back. There was a clatter of hobnailed boots as flak helpers—a class of schoolboys—ran towards the concrete stairs.

The door, presumably, closed, and the crowd settled down, jostling for space. In a few minutes anti-aircraft fire from the roof started to rattle noisily in brief, repeated bursts. From outside there was the occasional heavy thud. Some family groups settled down and produced bread and sausages, as if they were on a picnic. The cacophony of thousands of voices echoing off the concrete roof was deafening. It reminded me of the chicken huts on our estate.

"How long does this go on for?" I asked the general. In the dim lightbulbs I saw that he was old, or at least seemed to be. Or maybe the harsh blue light just exaggerated the wrinkling on his face.

"Half an hour or so. Then we have thirty or forty clear minutes before the next wave. Let's try to find someplace where we can talk."

We eased our way around blankets and bodies. The din in the huge bunker was overwhelming: children crying, young people chattering and laughing, older ones gossiping, the bursts of fire overhead, the occasional ground-shaking *thump*.

We found a space with our backs to the concrete wall. An

old woman was snoring, and a couple were hugging each other for warmth under a curtain, paying no attention to the outside world. Black bread and sausages were changing hands.

Daniela moved close to her father. "They know I'm a *Mischling*. They found out about Mama and you."

"Damn. Damn, damn." The general went silent for some moments. His mind seemed to be elsewhere. Then he looked sharply at me. "Where do you come into it?"

Daniela spoke before I had a chance to reply. "Max helped me escape. We're both finished if we're caught."

I said, "Your daughter and I were working on a project. One of the SS men on site told me Daniela's mother had been recognized in the street some time ago as Helena Rosenberg"—he drew a breath—"and they've been keeping it quiet until the project was completed because Daniela was essential to it."

"It must be some project, to let a Jew stay free."

"It could turn the Russian front," Daniela said.

"The Ivans are only seventy kilometers away, my dear. On a quiet day you can hear Zhukov's guns. Nothing will turn that."

"Maybe even win the war, Papa. Certainly force a truce."

"What, chase the Russians over the Urals and push the Americans back into the sea? The war is lost, whatever our Bohemian corporal may think. The Russians will soon attack Berlin. They'll take it in a week and God help us all when they come."

Daniela looked at her father with bright, anxious eyes. "The Gestapo arrested us the moment the project was completed, Papa."

"You got away? How?'

"Max killed a man."

The general glanced at me with something like respect. "This is bad news. There are flying tribunals in the streets. They're mad dogs. They hang people on the spot, deserters, Jews, anyone who isn't right."

"And we'll have to warn Mama right away."

"Daniela, your call was probably overheard. The Bendlerstrasse these days . . . and it won't take them long to find out about my apartment. I fear for your mother. Once the raid is over, we'll grab a suitcase and cash, and disappear."

"Would you like some bread?"

The couple under the curtain, a dumpy little woman stretching a hunk of landbrot toward us. Her fingernails were as black as the bread. Daniela smiled and shook her head. They were uncomfortably close.

Daniela's father pulled out a packet of Regie, the harsh Austrian cigarettes. I was sure it was illegal to smoke in here. I declined—the air was foul enough—and he lit one for himself. Candles on the floor were already beginning to sputter from the lack of oxygen at floor level. Children were being lifted to shoulder height. The flak guns were hammering furiously overhead and a four-year-old was bawling nearby, but still he spoke quietly. "Under Gestapo rules your mother and I are now assumed to be enemies of the state, quite apart from Mama's non-Aryan status." Having just lit the cigarette, he stubbed it out on the concrete floor and started to pace up and down a few square feet, like a caged bear. "I can't go back to the War Office."

"I should never have called you."

"If you hadn't, they'd have taken Mama without warning."

She asked again. "What'll we do, Papa?" Another thud from outside, this one close. The whole bunker shook.

General Bauer faced me. "You're not in uniform. Not in a fighting unit?"

"I was exempted. They needed me for the project."

"Which you have just deserted."

"To save your daughter's life. Unfortunately we were too closely supervised to carry out any sabotage before we cleared off."

"Sabotage. I see. And this project, you say it could turn the tide on the Russian front? Can you be serious?"

"A month ago, yes. Today I'm not so sure. I suppose it's your duty to hand us over to the Gestapo."

"Yes, yes. And to defend the Bohemian corporal to the end, which will probably be in a couple of weeks."

"So we disappear?"

Overhead, the flak guns died as if a switch had been thrown. General Bauer was looking over my shoulder. I followed his glance, as did Daniela. I felt my face going pale. A police patrol, a dozen of them checking papers, moving systematically through the bunker. Probably looking for deserters, or Jews not wearing the star. At this late stage!

There was a gust of cold air. Some people started to drift toward the exit. Others were staying put. We drifted with the crowd. The patrol wasn't coping with the sudden mass movement. We kept a mass of people between ourselves and the policemen. At the foot of the concrete spiral staircase a burning smell was flooding in from above, along with the clang of fire engines and people shouting. In the crush it was now almost impossible to talk without being overheard. Daniela's father was speaking sotto voce. "Yes, young man, we disappear. But first we must warn your mother, Daniela. She must go into hiding this instant. We'll use my staff car and join her in Salzburg. We'll find some empty chalet and stay put until Patton rolls over."

Onto the pavement. More police. But not ordinary policemen: They had the dark green uniforms and police badges of the flying tribunals. It was impossible to turn back. A hand fell on Daniela's shoulder. *"Kenkarte, bitte?"*

Siberia and Berlin

THURSDAY–FRIDAY

REBIRTH ISLAND

Sharp's head is reeling. Some of it, he thinks, is Murmansk vodka, most of it is exhaustion.

Now they know. The Nazi connection is for real. Three weapons were built. One down—the anthrax device, fired in Arizona—and two to go, each carrying sarin, according to Max. Somewhere.

Three little maids from school are we
But still you haven't found the key . . .

Two days to go and we haven't a clue and we're stuck in the Siberian Arctic. Can it get worse? Yes, we can be snowed in. He glances anxiously out the window. It's half past two in the morning. The dull gray light hasn't changed much in hours and the snow is still falling heavily, as heavy as anything he's experienced in Chamonix. He has visions of Khatanga disappearing under snow, to reappear in the spring. Can an aircraft possibly take off in this?

"What happened then?" Ambra asks. "Don't stop now!"

Max Krafft bends and stretches a leg, holding his knee. "If I sit too long, my knees go. Anyway, I'm sure you've heard enough of this old man's ramblings, and you must be worn out after your adventures."

There is a gust of icy air, and snowflakes whirl briefly into the room. A small, plump woman enters carrying a long, shiny fish by the gills. It's frozen solid and its tail almost brushes the ground. She hands it to Krafft, all the while staring curiously at the foreigners. Then she gives them a toothless smile—Sharp thinks, *Who says Russians don't smile?*—and takes off her coat and scarf to reveal a dress embroidered in colorful squares. Krafft holds the fish up admiringly. "A beauty, Anna. It'll make us a first-class kulebiaka." He turns to Ambra and Lewis. "And you will join us."

Ambra says, "We'd have loved to, but we want to get away as soon as possible."

Krafft pulls a doubtful face. "Of course. But depending on the snowstorm, you may be here for a very long time. You may yet sample my fish pie." He turns to Anna and speaks rapidly. Sharp can't follow the words, and Anna replies in some thick accent that he can barely recognize as Russian. Then she leaves in a flurry of toothless smiles and snow.

"I have asked Anna to find out if the airfield is still open."

"Is there no other way out? What about the harbor?"

Krafft shakes his head. "Pack ice closes it up at this time of year. The aircraft stop flying very soon. That's why we stock up with provisions over the summer."

"What about the military helicopters?"

"Everything stops in a blizzard. You'll know in an hour or so, when Anna gets back."

"Which gives us time to know what happened to you next," says Ambra. "Don't leave us in suspense!"

"Yes, please," says Sharp. He wants the whole story.

In the heat, the fish is beginning to give off a slight oily smell. Max disappears into the kitchen with it. When he reappears he seems older, as if the memories have aged him. He sits down and nods, as if to himself. "To have come so far! It was a flying tribunal, all right. They had a fearful reputation from the occupied territories in the east. But they had a general on their hands, and not even a police regiment could string us up, they wouldn't dare. So they took us to Prinz Albert Strasse and handed us over to the Gestapo. We were split up. I remember the interrogation cell. Some joker had put a notice over the door: BREATHE DEEPLY AND REMAIN CALM. Would you believe that even today I have nightmares about it? Would you believe that? They held me for four weeks in a cell. We listened to Zhukov's artillery getting closer every day, praying for it to come."

Max fills his pipe and starts puffing again. He looks at the rising smoke, but Sharp senses he's not really seeing it, he's easing his time machine back into the past. "They were nervous, you see. General Bauer was a senior Wehrmacht officer. I had a spot of luck. One of the guards knew my name. He'd had a cousin, Franck, in my regiment, the Second SS Panzer Corps under Papa Hausser. Anyway it seems I'd saved this Franck's life in the Kharkov fiasco. I don't even remember the incident, but he'd mentioned it in a letter. So the guard kept me informed, which was all he could do for me in that situation. He told me that army officers were sending outraged messages into the Gestapo office every day. It was a very difficult time after July 20—you know . . ."

"The assassination attempt on Hitler," Sharp says.

"The Wehrmacht legal section said that under Paragraph Eleven of the military legal code, General Bauer was entitled to a court-martial. The members of this court had to be chosen by the Führer himself. That was getting them really scared. Here is this extremely high-ranking officer, and a couple of scientists who'd just made a weapon that could turn the tide of the war, and the Gestapo had arrested them. They didn't dare go to Hitler with that."

Sharp says, "But what could the army have done?"

"A great deal, if it only had the guts. There were rumors that Wehrmacht and Gestapo were practically at war. I think the Gestapo thought the Potsdam garrison might jump into trucks and take direct action against Prinz Albert Strasse. There was a precedent for this, the Röhm business, you remember. But by that time the army had enough trouble fighting Russia and America on two fronts, thanks to the Führer's genius."

"How did you survive, a Gestapo prisoner?" Ambra asks.

"I don't know. I could hear screams and sobbing all around the floor, day and night. It was hell on earth, something out of Dante's *Inferno*. I was in constant agony wondering whether any of these screams came from Daniela. I didn't give a damn about me. What had I done? I'd had a liaison with a Jewess when I didn't even know she was Jewish. Daniela was being kept in part of the building where my guard had no access. But when the Russians closed in, the senior officers melted away, leaving us to the lower ranks. And what did these thugs care about military legal codes? One morning I was herded into a room with about a dozen others. We heard shooting. Then the clowns told us we'd been spared to prove that the Gestapo don't shoot their prisoners, would you believe that? The others were murdered."

Ambra hesitates to ask. "And Daniela? What became of her?"

"I don't know. I never saw her again." There is a long silence. Krafft is staring at his column of pipe smoke. Then: "They shot everyone but us, the twelve of us in this cell. We heard the guns getting closer to us, cell by cell. And then they stopped, and everything went quiet in the building. The Gestapo rats had scurried for shelter. Outside, Zhukov's guns got louder, and buildings were collapsing, and then, on May 2, the guns stopped firing. We waited for a day, with no food and water and not even a bucket for a toilet. We could smell smoke from the fires outside. And the next morning a key turned and there was a Russian soldier, a Mongol, I think. Never was a man hugged so eagerly."

"It meant you'd survived. You made it through the war." Sharp says.

Krafft nods silently.

Sharp has seen this on TV documentaries. Old men talking about a war that's been over for sixty years, trying to hold back tears as if it happened yesterday. And young people without the faintest idea. "And once you were released?"

"Released?" Krafft manages a smile. "They took us in a truck to Tempelhof Airport, which seemed to be a collecting point for prisoners. The devastation in the streets was terrible. Bodies everywhere. The Russians soon found out who I was and what I'd been up to. I expected to be shot—what an ending after all I'd come through! Instead they locked me up in a big warm flak tower with a few others. There was food. Fresh prisoners kept arriving. We were all mathematicians, scientists, and engineers. After a week they drove us to a provincial railway station that the bombers had missed. It was the start of a long trek, across Siberia. By that time we knew they weren't going to polish us off—we were going to be useful to them in some way.

"First they sent us to some godforsaken place called Obolensk, halfway between Moscow and the Caspian Sea. It wasn't so bad. The man in charge was a Dr. Lev Lifschitz. Lev was a scientist like ourselves. The military pumped me for information about sarin gas. Years later I learned they'd found a lot of documents that the German High Command had hidden down some mine in Silesia. It covered the whole Nazi bioweapons program and it was a much bigger business than I'd realized. But the documents said nothing about the means of delivery, which was my specialty. They said nothing about the Furies. We were a secret within a secret, you see."

"So you carried on where you left off?" Sharp asks.

"At first it was just pencil-and-paper stuff. They hadn't the facilities for anything else. After a couple of years they took me farther east, to a place in Kazakhstan. God, to think that I'd hated Obolensk! This place made Obolensk look like Paris. I spent a lot of time putting theory into practice, testing evil things on a site called Rebirth Island, in the Aral Sea. You don't want to go to Rebirth Island."

"We won't," Sharp assures him. *Actually it's been cleaned up. But the average journalist might not know that.*

"Don't."

"How long have you been here in Khatanga?"

"Fifteen years. I tried to find out what happened to Daniela after the collapse of communism, but—nothing."

Ambra says, "I hear a funny mixture of German and Russian spoken here."

"This is where they dumped Germans they no longer needed. Quite a few people here have German parents or grandparents. After Kazakhstan they took me to Novosibirsk. I worked at Vektor."

"I've heard of it," Sharp says.

Krafft raises his eyebrows in surprise. "The State Research Center of Virology and Biotechnology. Bioweapons to the ultimate degree. You wouldn't believe the things they developed there. That's where I met my Katya."

"You're married?" Ambra asks in surprise.

"Was. She was a Russian girl, a chemist. We never had children. It was a conscious decision. Novosibirsk was no place to bring up children. Too many of them died. Katya died of leukemia fifteen years ago and they sent me here. And that's my life."

"It's quite a story, Max," Sharp says quietly.

Krafft has come to the end of his pipe. He taps it into an ashtray and blows through the stem, making gurgling noises. "What's it like in Germany these days?"

The question astonishes Sharp. "Don't you know? You have television."

"When the movie comes to an end, they go back to the beginning and play it over again. We love the American videos."

Ambra says, "I think you'd like the new Berlin."

"Do they still have the Tiergarten?"

·"They have. The city's been totally rebuilt and it's a hive of construction even yet."

"But the Unter den Linden? The bombers destroyed it."

"It's been rebuilt. And there's a completely new district, Potsdamer Platz. They diverted the Spree to create a new central station for the trains . . ."

"What? They diverted the Spree? I don't believe you!"

". . . there's a restaurant two hundred meters above the ground . . ."

"Two hundred meters above the ground? Am I to believe this?"

". . . which revolves twice an hour. Hitler's bunker is buried under a car park. Speer's architecture is gone. The wartime rubble has been cleared off to the edge of the city, all overgrown. Berlin is probably the liveliest city in Europe."

"I would love to see it before I die."

There is another gust of freezing air, and Anna waddles in again. She gabbles something to Max, shaking her head. Krafft turns to Sharp and Ambra. "I'm afraid the snowstorm has closed us in. There are no planes flying in or out."

Sharp thinks, *Oh God.* "Is there really no way out? We do have urgent business."

"I thought you might have."

Ambra says, "You've no idea. We *must* get back." The "we're journalists" pretense is all but gone.

"You're stuck here at least for the duration of the storm." Krafft turns to the woman. Sharp can just follow his Russian. "Anna, this young couple are joining us for dinner. After that they will need a place to sleep."

More gabbling. Krafft translates: "Anna's son is an electrical engineer and she's very proud of him. He's in Moscow over the winter which means there's a spare room in her house. It's a squeeze, I'm afraid."

Anna is nodding happily. The young couple in love.

Sharp and Ambra exchange glances. She says, "We'll just have to make the most of it."

FLIGHT FROM KHATANGA

"This hasn't happened to me in ages," Sharp says.

"What?" Ambra, sitting on the edge of a narrow twin bed, starts to untie her bootlaces. The bed creaks. "Eating Siberian fish pie?"

"Being stuck in a snowbound cottage with a comely wench."

"Don't get any ideas, big boy." She sighs and slides her boots under the bed. "So now we know. There are two more weapons."

"If the U-boats delivered them." Sharp, on the bed opposite, is hardly a meter from her. He feels his brow, waxy from heat and alcohol.

"We daren't assume otherwise. And they're carrying a ton of sarin apiece, for dispersal at height."

"Meaning that, as people-destroying devices, they're on a par with atom bombs."

"On a par with atom bombs. Oh dear. Something puzzles me," Ambra says, slipping off heavy socks. "Max was on Petrov's *he might know* list. That means they don't have the firing codes, not yet. So how did they manage to fire the Arizona device? Maybe the bad guys have all they need to fire the other two?"

"I don't have answers, Ambra, I'm past thinking, I'm too tired."

Ambra stretches and yawns, and wriggles her ankles. "So what's next?"

"Sleep. If you're tired, you make bad decisions. I got that much out of the army." Sharp and his rucksack disappear into a small bathroom, and he emerges wearing thick, over-long pajamas with green and pink stripes. Ambra is under blankets, her head on a thick pillow, socks and black dress at the foot of the bed. She stares and puts her hand to her mouth.

"East German border guard surplus," Sharp says.

She snorts.

"They cost me fifty rubles," he complains.

She erupts.

"Is that . . . ?"

"Yes."

"I'm inquiring about a permit that your department issued to three English tourists six months ago. They have arrived in Khatanga."

"What? Did you say six months ago?"

"Yes." Pavlovski thinks, *Uh-huh.* "Yes. Six months ago."

"There must be some mistake, Commissioner. The business of issuing permits was transferred away from us nine months ago."

"I'm sorry, but I have examined these permits and they're six months old and they are carrying your signature."

"That's not possible."

Gosha Pavlovski says, "I see. In that case I think we may be dealing with illegal entry for some reason, perhaps espionage."

"My God. How can I help?"

"I'd like you to open up your office, go through your files, and check whether permits were issued on March 13 to the following people . . ."

"Commissioner Pavlovski, I can tell you now that they were not. However, I will open my office now and have my people check whether these names are anywhere on our files. I'll get back to you as soon as I can. It may take some hours."

"I'm a patient man."

Pavlovski stretches, yawns, and leans back in his chair. Being police chief out here isn't easy, it's a big territory to cover. But every now and then something comes up that makes it all worth it, compensates for the usual dreary round of drunken fights, petty thefts, and cigarette smuggling. This one smells of something serious, maybe industrial espionage involving the Norilsk copper mines, maybe something involving the security of the Motherland—like the unmapped radar station near Chelyuskin Point? He sighs again, a compound of exhaustion and satisfaction. He looks out at the thick snow drifting down outside. They aren't going anywhere. He has time for a snooze. He's looking forward to the interrogation, before the bigwigs from Murmansk turn up to steal the kudos.

Knock knock.

There's no way to tell the time from the daylight streaming under the black curtains. Sharp feels as if he's been asleep for maybe half an hour. He disengages himself from heavy blankets and sits up. His head is throbbing. Ambra's bed is empty. He can hear her in the corridor, speaking in Russian. Anna looks in, covered to the neck in a grimy dressing gown, gabbling something, and then Ambra pokes her head around the door.

"Salvation! There's a break in the weather. A couple of military transports are coming in from Murmansk and one's heading back to Moscow. We have to leave this minute."

Visibility is about a mile. The end of the runway is just visible; beyond that, ground and sky merge into a white fog. Across from them, beyond a clutter of low buildings, black, gnarled tundra is scattered over the snow and probably stretches for fifteen hundred kilometers. They stand and shiver in a breeze straight from the North Pole. Sharp keeps his earflaps down and wonders if they've missed the plane. *Come on, turn up!*

After twenty minutes, a giant four-wheel drive approaches

from the direction of Khatanga. "Pavlovski?" Ambra wonders, and Sharp feels his stomach knotting. It roars to a halt meters from them, snow chains rattling. Judy Garland, Marilyn Monroe, and Tom Cruise descend unsteadily; they're just recognizable under layers of fur. "You guys like a ride to Novaya Sibir? We can squeeze you in." The voice is Cruise's, coming from somewhere between an enormous fur hat and a turned-up fur collar.

"I'm sorry but we have no time," says Sharp. "You have the range, in that?"

"Where y'all heading, then?" Marilyn asks. Red eyes stare at them. Cruise is pulling rifles and rucksacks out of the four-wheel.

"Murmansk," Ambra lies.

"Murmansk, yeah. You got the material you wanted?"

"Uh-huh."

Judy clears her throat. "There's some real photogenic stuff where we're headed. It'll be terrific for your piece. Camp's set up and we'll be back tomorrow."

Presently a little orange propeller plane with skis emerges unsteadily from the mist. Cruise picks up rifles, tosses one to Marilyn, who catches it deftly. "Join us, it'll be a gas."

"No thanks," says Sharp.

"Come on, you'll love it." From the corner of his eye, Sharp senses something about Ambra's body language. She is edging away, casually, flapping her arms. The little plane slithers alarmingly along the snow but comes to a stop with precision, meters from the huddled group. The pilot is wearing dark glasses and a Cossack hat.

"We need to get back."

"I don't think you get it, pal. We insist." Cruise raises his rifle, pointing it at Sharp's chest. Marilyn is pointing hers at Ambra's head. "Get on board."

"What's this about?"

"Tell you what it's about. We want you on that plane."

"Will we be alive or dead when you throw us into the Sibirsk Sea?"

"Your choice. You can get it here if you like."

"You can't do a thing to us here. Bodies are evidence."

Ambra, pale-faced, says, "But as soon as we're on the plane . . ."

The propeller is revving up. And another vehicle, this one a people carrier, is emerging out of the haze from the direction of Khatanga. *Please, God, let it be Pavlovski.* It pulls to a halt next to a building yards from them. Cruise and Marilyn lower their rifles uncertainly. Judy says, *"Merde."* Half a dozen soldiers jump out, automatic weapons slung over their shoulders, earflaps down. They look incuriously at the little group. Ambra walks over to them and talks in a business-like manner, pointing to the Americans. The soldiers, riled by whatever she said, march over to the Americans. There's a lot of pushing and the Americans are hustled toward the airport terminal. Cruise looks back at Ambra and Sharp murderously, but then they vanish into the terminal.

Sharp becomes aware that his legs are trembling violently. Ambra is still pale. She says, "National intelligence, I can smell them."

"Those were Downey's killers."

"Are you serious?"

"I've just recognized the bloke. I saw him outside the safe house, on Paul's Walk. He was wearing earphones like an iPod except that he was almost certainly listening in to everything we said. And he matches the description Craig gave of one of the people he was trying to get away from."

"We all thought Craig was imagining things."

"These are our people." Sharp tries to will the trembling away, but it intensifies over the next few minutes and slowly spreads through his body. *Come on, plane, Pavloski is coming! Get us away from here, quickly!* "What did you say to the soldiers?"

"I told them the Americans didn't have proper permits to fly to the pole. I'm probably right. They should have had soldiers with them. They're supposed to notify border guards to make sure all the formalities are being observed."

"Fantastic. That should keep them held up for hours. But what about us?"

"We're going home." Ambra is flapping her arms again.

"Unless we've missed Anna's plane."

"Or Pavlovski turns up."

An agonizing forty minutes pass before glimmering headlights appear just above the horizon, followed by a heavy twin-propellered aircraft. Sharp recognizes it: an AN-26 military transport, white with red flashes, as if someone has tried to give it a trim like a sports car. It lands heavily and lumbers along the runway, throwing up clouds of snow.

And yet another people carrier, trailing smoke. God help us!

But still no police chief. Just Max Krafft, heavily wrapped against the cold and with a Cossack hat, being helped out of the people carrier by a young driver. Sharp wonders how much more cliff-hanging he can take. The transport plane is now disgorging army officers, and a truck loaded with sacks is driving up to it.

"I had to say good-bye." Already a tanker has pulled up, and someone is dragging a fuel pipe over the snow.

Ambra says, "This is unauthorized travel. I'll probably have to bribe somebody." She hurries in the direction of the pilot, who is standing next to the tanker, lighting up, while vapor from the aviation fuel shimmers the air around.

Krafft says, "There's something else." There is something in his expression: anxiety, but more than that. Sharp waits. Krafft glances at Ambra. She is talking animatedly to the pilot, who is shaking his head doubtfully. Krafft takes Sharp by the forearm and leads him a few yards away. Men are tossing sacks from the truck through the open door.

"What is it, Max?"

"Daniela." He's still gripping Sharp's forearm, and the grip has tightened.

"She defiled the Aryan race, Max, and she was Jewish. They must have killed her."

"That's it, I'm not sure. Not a hundred percent. I need to know. I need to know for certain."

The last sack is on board, and the pilot has disappeared

back into the aircraft. "If I find out, I'll get the information to you, one way or another. That's a promise."

"Lewis!" The engines are revving up and Sharp lip-reads, rather hears, his name. Ambra is waving at the door. "Lewis!"

"Lewis? Your real name is Lewis?"

"It's a long story."

"I didn't think you were journalists."

"Look, I'm not free to . . ."

"Will you be looking for Daniela? If she's still alive? Whatever you're up to."

"Max, I can't answer that."

"If you find her, tell her something. Tell her . . ."

Ambra is arm-waving frantically, hair and scarf blowing. She jumps out, ducks under the slipstream, and shouts, "They're leaving now, with or without us. I'm going, Lewis." She sprints back to the aircraft.

Sharp tries to disengage but Max's nails are digging hard into his forearm. "No, no. Tell Daniela this: Never walk backward drinking schnapps."

Sharp stares. Krafft's eyes return the stare intensely. "Tell her that. Tell nobody but Daniela."

"Never walk backward drinking schnapps?"

·   "It was a private thing. In the whole wide world, only she and I know what it means. If you tell her that, she'll know you got the message from me. She'll know that I'm still alive."

"Max. Pavlovski may be looking for us. We don't want uniforms to be waiting for us in Moscow."

"Moscow? What's this about Moscow? Didn't I hear you were waiting for the Murmansk flight? An old fool like me gets so confused. And Pavlovski's in no hurry."

Somebody is stretching for the door, looking over at Sharp.

"One last thing. Did you?"

"Did I what?"

"At Natzweiler. Did you fetch the vials from the back of the car?"

Snow is settling on Krafft's mustache. He hesitates; Sharp can't understand the expression on the old man's face. When he speaks, Lewis can hardly hear him above the whine of the engines. "Don't make judgments. It was a world you'll never know."

"Screw that. Did you?"

"It was a long time ago. I can't remember."

The fuel tanker has backed off. Ambra reappears at the aircraft door, beckoning frantically. Her scarf blows away. Sharp disengages Max's arm and sprints for the plane.

Sharp is trembling, and his brow is clammy. *Strange how the shaking starts after the danger has passed.* He glances behind. The flagon of vodka is nearly empty. A couple of men in blue overalls, unshaven, are sitting at the rear of the aircraft, no doubt with another Stoli or a Cruiser to be shared between them. At least they seem harmless. Across from him, Ambra is stretched out on a double seat, fast asleep, her coat over her like a blanket. He gazes down at the frozen taiga drifting below him. He thinks he can just make out a herd of reindeer, black spots against white.

The aircraft trundles on, over landscape that hardly changes by the hour. The distances are planetary, measured not in kilometers but in degrees of latitude and longitude. Sharp feels strangely unsettled but can't put his finger on why. It's the near miss at Khatanga, taking them to within seconds of death. No, not that. It's some time, as he slowly unwinds and the dryness in his throat eases, before he understands: He's inside a time machine. As the military transport trundles him back from the edge of the world, it's also carrying him forward in time, to plasma screens and space probes, DNA and mobile phones, Madonna and microwave ovens. Hess and Oberlin, the Führer and the Gestapo, the Death's Head and the Teutonic myths—the whole lunatic asylum of long ago—is becoming something unreal, a grainy old movie, fading into the mists of time. He glances across at Ambra and feels a twinge of admiration. The lady is not for shaking. He looks at his watch, subtracts time zones, and meditates.

THE RABBIT CONFESSES

The Grand Inquisitor pulls the tab on a can of juice and pours fizzy liquid into a tumbler. The room is bare apart from a standard civil service hat stand, a filing cabinet with combination lock, the desk and chairs. The desk, too, is bare, apart from some sheets of A4 paper in front of Jocelyn and Gordon. The view over the Thames is breathtaking but nobody is looking, not today.

Jocelyn's face is white and severe. "That American story is pure fantasy."

"No, Jocelyn, they wanted to kill us."

"Do you even begin to understand the implications of what you're saying, Lewis?"

"Of course." *Stupid question.* Sharp hasn't had a lot of sleep and can't hide his irritation.

Gordon says, "You seem to be claiming that someone is trying to wreck the investigation. Frankly I find that beyond belief."

Sharp returns the hostile stare. "How many people knew we were heading there?"

"To the Taymyr Peninsula? Jocelyn and myself. A few other senior people in this building. National intelligence colleagues such as Caddon. One or two people in the Cabinet Office and the PM's secretariat."

"Someone on that list is on the side of the bad guys."

Jocelyn puts a world of meaning into a sigh. "Let me put this in simple language."

"Please do."

"You were tired, distraught, and frightened, and your imagination did the rest. You imagined that the police commissioner spotted the forged paperwork. You imagined that a simple invitation by the Americans was an attempted abduction. The fact is, the pair of you were in a blue funk from the moment you landed in Khatanga."

From the safety of a London office, it sounds horribly plausible.

The intelligence chief starts to flick through the papers in front of him in sharp, irritated movements. He has the face of a hanging judge. "You've learned nothing. Your Siberian journey was a waste of time."

Sharp sits upright, bewildered, his exhaustion suddenly forgotten.

Jocelyn says, unpleasantly, "There have been developments in your absence."

Gordon sniffs. "This Max Krafft—he believes in flying saucers, you say?"

"He had a thick file on them, mostly old newspaper cuttings and magazine articles."

"Here's another scenario. Yes, Krafft was taken into the Soviet Union at the end of the war. The Soviets had their Paperclip, too, as had the British and the French. Maybe he was part of IG Farben and involved in the production of sarin or whatever. The Russians plundered whole factories and ended up with the biggest biochemical weapons program in history." He fidgets with the paper some more. "They abducted thousands of people from East Germany, pulling them from their beds at gunpoint even after the war."

"So what?"

"So Krafft spends the next forty or fifty years in a Siberian gulag, working on the production of biochemical weapons. Over those years he builds up a fantasy world. He believes it. He has it worked out, in his head, in every detail.

He's totally convinced when he tells you about it because, so far as he's concerned, it's the truth. But those who know him are aware that he's a crazy man and that his truth doesn't exist outside his own head. They practically told you as much at this party you mention in the report. He might with equal conviction have told you he'd been for a ride in a flying saucer. We can place no weight on his story."

"And Petrov's list?" Ambra is tight-lipped.

"Petrov was in Obolensk in the early sixties, at the same time as Max. They must have met in the gulag, probably knew each other well. Petrov probably got the same fantasy tale and wanted to check it out—bioweapons are his business. But it doesn't check out. Nothing in the documentation brought out of the Silesian mine at the war's end indicates that the Krafft weapon even existed. The fermentation vats in Spandau, yes. Twelve thousand tons of tabun gas, yes, dumped in the sea at the end of the war. But city-destroying weapons?" C shakes his head. "Not a trace, neither documentation nor evidence on the ground. What you have brought back from Khatanga are an unreliable old man's fantasies. Professor Duncan warned us about you and we should have listened."

Suddenly Sharp is fed up with the whole thing. "Let me try to help you with this. Alec Duncan is a second-rate phony. I'm the expert. You asked for my professional input and I'm giving you this: An unidentified terrorist group has somehow obtained old Nazi weapons. Expect two massive bioweapons attacks—somewhere—in a few days."

C replies brusquely. "But we can find no record in the U-boat loading lists of the cargoes Krafft describes. There's nothing in the depositions of survivors. That alone casts doubt on the whole story."

"A secret within a secret. Goering's words."

"According to Krafft. But there's a bigger problem with his story, Sharp. Krafft tells of sarin in two of the Furies. I've consulted again with Porton Down on this." C waves a CHOT printout, on the "secure" pink paper. "Sarin decays after a few weeks. It's a highly unstable chemical. The sarin in the

Furies, assuming these existed in the first place, would long since have become useless. If the terrorists have the sophistication and knowledge to locate these supposed weapons, they will also know that they contain a deactivated, harmless substance. The Krafft story cannot be true."

Sharp plays his ace. "But the Arizona bomb. That's a Nazi weapon, not an old man's fantasy."

"Krafft saw it on CNN."

"What?"

"They do have television, even in Khatanga? The news broke while you were en route there. The debris in Fossil Creek is being reassembled in Wright-Patterson AFB. We now have clear evidence that it was constructed by local militiamen. The pictures have been around the world on TV."

"And the letter? The three little maids?"

"A clever piece of work," C says. "Designed to dissipate our resources, to mislead. Why would a genuine terror group give us such a clear warning of time and place? Incidentally, we know who wrote it."

They know who wrote it.

Jocelyn says, "The swastika engraving was part of that false trail, Lewis. Krafft saw the news report, and it triggered his fairy tale. In his mind, he has transplanted some of his gulag work to his flying saucer fanaticism. The man's a complete crank, and no wonder, living out there for most of his life. His story doesn't fit. It doesn't fit the submarines, it doesn't fit the sarin. I regret ever having pulled you into this."

Gordon sips lemonade. "Nothing useful has emerged from your Siberian trip."

Sharp says, "You say the device was built by local militiamen?"

"It was, with biochemicals presumably supplied by Petrov."

"And the dead microbiologists?"

"Meaningless coincidences. You gave us a conspiracy theory built on sand."

"And your evidence for the militia?"

Gordon says, "A confession. From this Br'er Rabbit, Virgin Rabbit, whatever."

"Which you take seriously?"

"DNA places him at the launch site of the UFO. He and the fried dentist belonged to the same militia."

Jocelyn slides over a piece of paper. "You might want to take a look at this." Ambra and Sharp look at it together:

```
PHO E   ST RK (OH W T IS)
PHOENIX STORKS
```

"It's not perfect," she admits. "But according to Virgil Rabbit, the local militia call themselves the Phoenix Storks. One of the things the FBI found in their so-called log cabin was a reel of a 1917 movie called *The Black Storks,* which they tell us was a propaganda film amounting to an early precursor of the Nazi movement."

"And the other letters?"

"The FBI don't yet know, but it will no doubt emerge from interrogation of this Virgil Rabbit. He is being detained under the Patriot Act and is being questioned as we speak. Incidentally, he used to be a steelworker in Idaho, employed by Hendrix Steel."

"Hendrix Steel." Sharp briefly shuts his eyes.

"I see you're beginning to get the drift. Rabbit acquired the venturi tubes from his old workplace. They created the device and stored it down the mine shaft. Being good little modern-day Nazis, they engraved the swastika on the casing. And Rabbit wrote the letter that had us all in a panic. He confessed to that, too."

"But ..."

"But nothing, Ms. Volpe. His DNA matches that on the letter. The pair of you lost your nerve and spent precious time chasing a crank who had nothing to give but nonsense. I don't operate a blame culture," says Gordon, his voice icy, "but if I did ..."

"And the other Furies?" Sharp asks, but he knows the answer.

"What other Furies?" Sharp suddenly has a startling image of the intelligence chief as an enraged wrestler leaping at him from the ropes. "Even if they exist, there is no evidence that they constitute a threat to London."

"But they might."

"Anything is *possible*, Sharp. But where's the evidence? You should be aware that a considerable amount of time has been wasted backing up your stupid line of investigation. Senior people at the highest levels of government and the secret services have been involved in pursuing a wild goose chase. I suggest, Ms. Volpe, that you take a few days' leave and use the time to consider your future in this organization. As for you, Mr. Sharp, I suggest you go back to making pizzas or whatever you do for a living. We have no further use for you here. I am meeting the prime minister this afternoon and will be advising him to stand down Cobra. This is now an internal matter for the FBI. You're both out of the loop with immediate effect. Finished. Canceled."

Jocelyn gives Sharp a tight smile. "I never really wanted you on this team, Lewis. The Nazi connection was always a long shot."

"Not what you were saying when you found out what was happening to the old German scientists."

"And I wouldn't waste time raking around Mittelwald or the convent. These places don't exist."

MITTELWALD

"Situation analysis?" Sharp asks.

"End of a promising career." Ambra looks as if she's in shock. They emerge from the MI6 building into a light drizzle. "Uncle Dino offered me a job once, managing a café on the Royal Mile in Edinburgh . . ." The drizzle is fine, wet, and penetrating. They walk along the path at the side of the building, past the traffic barrier, conscious of watchful electronic eyes. A red London bus rumbles past. Along the street a cluster of tourists is clicking cameras, watched by the armed policewoman at the steel gate of the goods vehicle entrance. And across the road, in an archway under a railway line, the Pico Bar & Grill is stacked to capacity.

"Fancy it? Craig told me they do a terrific tapas."

Ambra shakes her head. "It's stuffed with spooks. I've had it with spooks."

Sharp says, "Okay, I know a good wine bar near the Strand. It's stuffed with yuppies."

Ambra says, "Lead me there, quick."

The Chardonnay is chilled to perfection and the bar is crowded and warm. Sharp keeps getting whiffs of garlic, and the blackboard says that today's special is *spaghetti alle vongole*. They are at a corner table. It's a good spot not to be overheard, and Sharp wonders playfully if the table is wired. "The U-boat loading lists. I want to look at them for myself."

Ambra runs a sharp-nailed finger down the condensation on her glass. "What are you getting at, Lewis?"

"Someone's trying to get in the way. Craig Downey vanishes without a trace. Petrov's safe leads us to Max Krafft in Siberia, whereupon a phony confession has everyone rushing to Arizona."

"A phony confession?"

"Designed to throw us."

"And the U-boat lists? What about them?"

"Ambra, how would I know?"

"Hello, calling Lewis, are you there? Return to Planet Earth, please."

"You think Max's story was a fantasy? Is that what you think?"

She shakes her head, takes a sip at the Chardonnay. "Something to bear in mind, Lewis. If Craig really was murdered by people on the inside, and we're the only two left chasing this line . . ."

"No worries, we're discredited. Why create ripples by bumping us off?"

"Do you know what day this is, Lewis? Thursday, Lewis, Thursday afternoon. London gets it on Saturday and we're sitting here drinking coffee."

"You're off the case, Lewis. Services no longer required."

"I know, but, Jocelyn . . ."

"You shouldn't be in the flat. You were supposed to collect your stuff and vacate it."

"This is the acid test. If Krafft's story is rubbish, this will shoot it down."

"Call you back."

Sharp has the letters arrayed on the trestle table:

```
HO      W RK
TIS PHO E
```

They wait. Jocelyn probably has the information on her desk, but it takes her seven minutes to ring back. *Bitch.*

"Okay, Lewis, here we go. I shouldn't be doing this."

"Do you have *C, H, E, I,* or *N* among the new letters?"

There's the briefest pause. Then a surprised: "Actually, yes. They've recovered *C, H,* and *N.* How did you get that?"

Ambra slides the pre-written cards into place as Sharp repeats the letters:

```
HO(C)(H)W RK
TIS PHO(N)E
```

"The letters more or less complete Hochwerk and Tisiphone."

"Tisiphone?"

"The Three Furies of Greek mythology. Three little maids by the name of Meg, Alec, and Tiffanee. The biggest secret the Nazis had, we're only now finding out about it . . ."

"If you believe this Krafft story . . ."

". . . and yet whoever wrote the letter knew about Megaera, Alecto, and Tisiphone."

This time the pause goes on so long that Sharp begins to wonder if Jocelyn is still on the line. But then she is saying, "I still go for the Phoenix Storks."

"Come on, not even *C* would buy that now. Krafft didn't see these letters on CNN?"

"They're not in the public domain. Something else. The Virgil Rabbit suspect . . ."

"The steel man . . ."

"Ah, the FBI are having problems with his testimony."

Lewis senses Jocelyn's embarrassment, doesn't feel inclined to let her off the hook. "What does that mean in plain English, Jocelyn? His story doesn't check out?"

Paper is rustling at Jocelyn's end. "The technical people have used X-ray fluorescence on the flying saucer debris. It's armaments steel all right, an alloy with carbon content less than 0.07 percent, silicon less than 0.7 percent, phosphorus less than 0.03 percent, et cetera. The thing is, Hendrix turns out dozens of steels, but not one of them has the exact composition of the Arizona tubes. And they don't do venturi tubes like the Arizona UFO. The guy's a nut."

"We're back on the case, then?"

"The first autopsies on the reservation Indians are in. Death wasn't due to anthrax, it was due to inhalation of some caustic chemical."

"Naturally. Daniela's booby trap worked. Back on the case or not?"

"But what about the sarin with its three-week life? And the U-boat lists with no mention of Krafft's machines? And the convent that doesn't exist? You're giving me an unreliable old man's dreamworld, Lewis, just as Duncan said you would."

"No, I'm giving you a choice. Either find two city-destroying machines within forty-eight hours, or someplace to bury a million people. Oh, by the way, the Plague of Thebes ha ha ha, the punishment sent by the gods in the Sophocles story?"

"What about it?"

"It was delivered by three Furies."

Jocelyn hangs up.

"The Poor Clares are the Second Order of the Friars Minor, whatever that means. They were founded in 1212 by Saint Francis of Assisi and they specialize in contemplation and penance." Ambra is lying stomach-down on the thick rug, typing on the laptop with two fingers. "The convent was built on the site of a church founded in AD 760 by Duke Odilo; it was burned by the Huns in 974 and rebuilt by Duke Frederick around 1186. Bits of it go back to then. Burned down in 1595 and rebuilt in Baroque style in 1612, whereupon it was promptly burned down yet again, this time by Swedish soldiers in the Thirty Years' War. Rebuilt, and confiscated by Emperor Joseph in 1750. Purchased by some archduke as a hunting lodge who extended it. His descendants finally returned it to the church as a gift in 1920."

Sharp says, "That explains the wine cellar that mystified Max. It was a leftover from the hunting lodge days."

"Nice one, Lewis. Occupied by the Poor Clares since then. Uneventful history until June 1942."

"And in July 1942 the scientists moved in. So what happened to the nuns? Where did they go?"

"I've got that, too." Ambra taps a little more. "I'll translate. *On June 29, 1942, the convent was raided by a brigade of SS-Oberabschnitt Danube following an informer's report that the nuns were harboring Jewish children. About thirty children were removed, along with a dozen nuns and a similar number of novitiates. Their fate is unknown.*"

"I wonder if Max ever suspected."

"The Allies flattened the convent in the closing days of the war because they thought Goering was visiting. Obviously some garbled intelligence. So Jocelyn was right in a sense. The convent doesn't exist, not anymore. But it did in Krafft's time. And look, here are the floor plans."

Sharp examines the screen. "Max got it right. His description matches. It proves he was in the convent."

Ambra is looking worried. "But in what capacity? Could he have been part of the SS-Oberabschnitt Danube?"

"What?"

"Hauling children and nuns into trucks, the Catholic SS man? Could the events of that day have haunted him for the rest of his life? Maybe over the years in the gulag he gradually replaced the whole sordid event by a heroic fantasy, like his Sister Lucy fixation? Maybe at the end, the fantasy turned into reality in his head?"

"What about Mittelwald?"

"There's no such place—I've Googled it. Lewis—my God, Lewis, could Gordon and Jocelyn be right after all?"

"If they are, I'll disembowel myself."

Ambra switches off the laptop and stands up. "Is there no central heating in this horrible place? I'm freezing."

"I have a spare pair of East Germans if you're interested."

"Down, boy. Just find the heating control."

Sharp piles the remains of the Chinese carry-out on a single plate and heads for the kitchen. Upriver, they are having yet another party. Or maybe it's the same one of a few days ago, still continuing. *Boom boom boom,* those low-frequencies penetrating the glass. He fills a kettle and puts tea bags into a couple of mugs. The clock on the microwave oven tells him it's just after two in the morning.

Ambra calls through. "Who occupied Bavaria after the war?"

"The Americans. The Bavarian redoubt, they called it. It was a big worry in the closing days of the war. There were fears that the Nazis could hold out indefinitely, and rumors that secret weapons were being developed in huge underground facilities. I guess people were getting pretty nervous as the war approached its end. Specifically, I think it was the Sixth Army."

"Could there be anything in their archives?"

"We need two months instead of two days." Sharp feels despair, tries to shrug it off, but it keeps drifting back. *Can Jocelyn and C be right after all? Is the whole thing a crazy old man's fantasy? And even if not, where are the Furies? Where are they? The whole bloody thing is hopeless.*

"We could ask Neal Caddon. Get his people to do the spadework."

"We're off the case, Ambra."

"But does Neal know it yet? We'll send an e-mail signed with Jocelyn's name, copied to us here."

"There's a devious mind behind that innocent face, Ambra."

"You don't know the half of it." She stretches. "You send the e-mail. Skip the tea, I'm for bed."

"The flat's secure. Not even the Hanslope Park locksmiths could get in."

"But for all I know you're Jack the Ripper."

Sharp, on the couch, wakens with a start. The fax machine is chattering. Ambra stumbles through from the bedroom. A strip of orange light is penetrating the curtains, and he can just make out that she is wearing his spare East German border guard pajamas after all. "It's four o'clock," she accuses him.

"Making it nine in the evening in California." He finds a table lamp switch and they blink in the sudden light.

From Microfiche New Mexico Archives 6th Army.
FWD B-Team 16 Secure.

Neal—Is this any use to your tea-drinking limey friends?
Pete.

From: I. F. Latino (Major)
        Assistant to Military Attache, Bavaria
To: see distribution list
Subject: interrogation of POW Dieter Schmidt (private)
Date: May 23, 1945
Veracity: Believed reliable
Status: SECRET

Subject surrendered to the Americans on May 14, 1945. Belonged to unit Kampfgeschwader 2. Following interrogation, he gave the deposition below.

1. Because of age and asthma I was unable to serve in the Wehrmacht and was assigned to the Home Guard. I was stationed in Munich for the duration of the war.

2. On March 3, 1944, our unit was instructed to assemble in front of the main police headquarters at 1800. We were driven in trucks about 60 kms to a village whose name was, I believe, Mittelwald.

3. About a kilometer outside the village the trucks stopped in a forested area. We were instructed to put on protective suits. Gas masks were built into those suits. We were not told what they were to protect us

against, but it was made clear that no part of our skin should be exposed to the air.

4. We then entered Mittelwald. We found that most of the hundred or so inhabitants were very ill, and had great difficulty breathing. They were all shaking uncontrollably. About thirty people, mostly the old and children, had already died. They lay curled up where they had collapsed.

5. Although the light was now fading, we were ordered to surround the village and allow nobody to enter or leave. I was stationed with three others on a narrow track leading south outside the village. I had a clear view of the church, the market square, and the buildings around it. I could see people staggering around and collapsing. Bodies were floating in the lake in front of the church.

6. Around 0300 about ten army lorries arrived and drove into the market square. We were ordered to unload coffins. These turned out to be extremely heavy. They were lined with metal which I think was zinc. By that time another 40 or so villagers had died.

7. We were ordered to dig graves in a corner of the local cemetery. We placed the corpses in these metal coffins, and then sprayed them with some substance. The coffins were then sealed and buried. There was nothing to mark the graves.

8. By dawn the following morning we had arrested nine or ten people who had turned up at Mittelwald. One of them was the local doctor who had been tending a patient in an outlying area.

9. Around 0800 an SS contingent arrived at the edge of the village and we handed over the doctor and

the others. I do not know what became of them but I heard shooting. We were told that mercy killings had taken place but I do not believe this as everyone in Mittelwald was by now dead.

10. Afterward we went from house to house, spraying some substance. Some SS men then used a flame-thrower to destroy every house in the village. The church was dynamited.

11. We were then sprayed with the substance and got out of our suits, which were soaked in gasoline and burned.

12. We were told that this lethal outbreak was caused by bad meat. We were instructed to tell no one, not even members of our families, about the incident, on pain of execution. We were then returned to Munich.

Sharp says, "I guess London's back on the menu."

"Poor Gordon—he's just told the PM to stand Cobra down and now he'll have to go back and tell him to stand it up again." Something about Ambra's look reminds Sharp of a cat that has just found a mouse.

KRYSTAL KRAMER

"Lewis. You'd better take this." Jocelyn, having the grace to look a bit sheepish, is waving a telephone receiver in the air.

The team is spread around a big oval table covered with papers, photographs, Pepsis, and carafes of water. A couple of US Army officers, groggy from a transatlantic flight, have joined them, and a studious, bespectacled FCO man of about thirty is sitting in on the proceedings.

Sharp picks up the telephone. "Hello?"

It's a policeman's voice, speaking in English with a light German accent. "My name is Superintendent Claas Fischer. I'm speaking from the federal chancellor's office in Berlin, the anti-terrorist desk. I have a young lady on the line who claims to know something about the Arizona explosion. Do you speak German?"

"Passably." He feels a sudden prickle of excitement. *Someone who knows something . . .*

"Would you like to take the call?"

Cautiously: "Of course."

"The next voice you hear will be hers. Her name is Kramer, Krystal Kramer."

"Is that her married name?"

A few muffled words in German, then a female voice,

twentyish. "I'm not married. I don't believe in it. Who am I speaking to?"

"My name is Smith," Sharp lies. "I'm part of the team investigating the device. You have some information about that?"

"I don't know. I might have. Or it might be nothing. Look, maybe this call is a mistake. It's my grandmother, you see, she's very frail, and I don't want her . . ."

"Please, Ms. Kramer, why don't you just tell me about it? It might be important."

"Of course I know it might be important, but as I say, she's very frail and I can't have her getting upset or into trouble of any sort, and my name is Krystal, Ms. Kramer is so anally retentive."

"Where are you? In Germany?"

"Yes, in Berlin." Not quite a lie. A yellow light flashing on the screen map says she is speaking from a public box in Potsdam, next to the Charlottenhof U-bahn.

"Why don't you tell me about it, Krystal? I promise your grandmother won't be upset whether or not there's anything in it." It's a promise Sharp can't possibly keep.

"She's upset already." There's a pause. Sharp half expects to hear the click of a connection being broken. Then, "She saw it on TV. She keeps active mentally, you know. She watches CNN and . . ."

"What did she see on TV, Krystal?"

"The news item on the Arizona thing. Granny got amazingly excited and upset. I was really worried about her."

"Did she say why she was excited?"

"This is so silly. This is my gran we're talking about."

Sharp waits while Ms. Kramer gets up her nerve. Then, "Granny made that device. So she says. During the war. She's very old, you know. I think maybe her memory plays tricks sometimes but she's still . . ."

"What's her full name, Krystal?"

"Granny's? It's Daniela Morrell. Grandpa Morrell died before I was born. He was a teacher in . . ."

Silently screaming. "I mean her maiden name."

"Oh, that. It's Bauer. Her maiden name is Daniela Bauer."

OLD DANIELA

The BMW drops them across from a dark building eight stories tall, and then merges into the traffic flowing like lava along the *Allee*. Fischer frowns. "Were you expecting company?"

Ambra: "Absolutely not."

It takes Sharp some seconds. But yes, there is a middle-aged man in a green windbreaker, collar turned up against the cold and hands in pockets, stamping his feet. And there is a car, a red Audi, its occupants undetectable behind tinted glass.

Fischer says, "Six up." Sharp counts up. On the sixth floor are two windows with lace curtains, and lights within. A dark shape moves behind one of the curtains, and then disappears; or he may have imagined it.

There is a gap in the traffic and it's an eighty-meter sprint across the boulevard. They make it, gasping for breath and standing at a heavy wooden door, and the man in the green windbreaker is watching them uneasily. Close up, he has the wrinkled face and watery eyes of a heavy smoker.

MORRELL, D. is hand-printed on a card next to a doorbell. Sharp presses the bell and looks back at the windbreaker man; he's having a hurried consultation with someone in the Audi. Then the man is gabbling into a mobile phone, his eyes fixed on Herr Fischer, who is watching the Audi attentively.

Sharp presses the bell again. And again. They wait a long time. Ambra says, "I know she's at home." This time Sharp keeps his thumb on it.

Male voice. *"Ja?"* None too friendly.

Sharp speaks to the intercom in German: "We want to speak to Daniela Morrell."

"What's your business with her?"

"It's private. Who am I speaking to, please?"

"She's not here. Go away." The intercom goes dead.

Herr Fischer and the man in the windbreaker are eyeing each other up, two gunfighters in a Western. Sharp curses his imagination. Guns? Of course not. This isn't the Taymyr Peninsula.

Ambra now pushes an eighth-floor button. A severe, matronly voice answers, and Ambra says a parcel needs signing for, and the door lock buzzes briefly. Fischer takes up the rear, slamming the main door behind him. The bang echoes around the stairwell. There is a worn flight of steps, dimly lit, but they take a creaky elevator to the seventh floor and descend as soon as they have left it: someone has opened the main door, down below. Voices on the other side of a heavy dark door marked MORRELL. Ambra turns the handle.

A short dark corridor leading to a spacious chintzy living room. Decor matching the period of the buildings: heavy, dull green wallpaper with big swirling patterns; high ceiling with a chandelier; a cluster of comfortable armchairs; four men and an old woman. The woman sitting, tense and upright, at a polished oak table, her hands clasped in front of her. Brown, intelligent eyes in a distressed face; white hair pulled back in a bun; a slim, elegant body draped in a black sweater and long skirt.

"Who the hell are you?" The man nearest them swivels in his chair, his face filled with surprise and hostility. He has close-shaven, black hair, a pasty complexion, and small dark eyes.

German with a Cockney accent. Ambra says in English, "What rank are you?"

"What? What do you mean?" There is a gratifying uncertainty in the man's voice.

"Unless you can beat Grade Six, I outrank you. You people look like Grades Seven and Eight. I'm taking charge here, and I'd be grateful if you would now leave."

The man hesitates. "What's your authority here?"

Ambra walks smartly toward a telephone on the sideboard. The old lady nods her assent. She seems confused. While Ambra is dialing, she says, "Will the ambassador do?"

It takes two layers, but then she is through. "Sir Richard? This is Ambra Volpe . . . I need to confirm my identity to some people here . . . We're in Daniela Bauer's flat . . . No, sir . . . With respect, Ambassador, Gordon wouldn't . . . Did he, indeed? . . . Well, all they've succeeded in doing is upsetting her . . . I'd be very grateful if you would, sir. Thank you." She waves the receiver. The man takes it, mutters into it, nodding as he speaks. He replaces the receiver gently, shoots Ambra a look, a strange mixture of venom and awe. "We're out of here."

Sharp goes through to the kitchen, explores some cupboards, and brings a plastic kettle to a boil. In the living room, Ambra is sitting next to the woman and speaking to her in a soft, conciliatory tone. He sets down a tray. The conversation is in German. He says, "I see you keep Darjeeling. I think it's the best of the teas."

The old lady says, "I have friends who prefer Ceylon."

Fischer hands an identity card to the woman. She looks at it blankly. He says, "As you see, I am Claas Fischer, madam, of the Bundesnachrichtendienst. Firstly, I must apologize for this intrusion. The people who were here came without proper authority."

"What?" Her face was lined with confusion and suspicion. "You are all strangers to me. I should call the police."

"I am the police. If you look at the card, you will see that my authority comes from the Federal Chancellor's Office. These people are English and are from the British embassy. My job is to identify them to you, and inform you that it is in the public interest that their questions be answered. Have you understood me, madam?"

She looks at the identity card again and and returns it. "Would you like to sit down? I understand very little but I have not forgotten my manners."

Fischer says, "Thank you but I cannot stay." He bows smartly—Sharp half expects him to click his heels—and a moment later the front door closes with a reassuringly heavy *clunk*.

"Why don't we sit over there? It's more comfortable." Her voice is trembling but stubborn, and has a melodious quality. It is clear and well articulated, without any accent Sharp can recognize. He feels a strange tingling thrill that the woman he knew only from Max Krafft's story has come to life, like a storybook character jumping off the page. She is here, a real, living person within arm's length! They settle into deep old armchairs and Sharp pours tea, following the old lady's instructions for adding milk.

He lets Ambra do the talking. She talks about the Arizona bomb, she talks about sarin, she talks about the fear that others have the surviving weapons. She stays silent on the London threat. She makes no mention of their Siberian adventure. She's silent on Max Krafft. The woman sits quietly. Her hands are trembling slightly and her cup shakes whenever she sips her tea; whether it's nerves, old age, or the beginning of Parkinson's, Sharp can't say. Now and then she glances in his direction, her eyes bright with curiosity.

And finally, with the tea finished and the biscuits depleted, Ambra says, "We need to find out everything we can about these flying devices."

Sharp says, "I'm a historian, specializing in Hitler's wonder weapons. I thought they were just fables."

The woman hesitates. "You must forgive me. I remember very little. But I remember enough. The machine I saw on the news was built by us during the war. It brought back many memories, some good, some terrible."

"Can you tell me how destructive one of these things would be, if it was launched over a city?"

"It would depend on many things. The direction and speed of the wind, its positioning, the temperature, the humidity." She strokes the edge of her saucer with an arthritic finger, thinking. "If everything was just right—and of course we would wait until everything was just right—then we calculated that the sarin gas would make a swath maybe ten kilometers long and five wide."

Enough to scoop out central London. Maybe a million people in the rush hour. Sharp keeps his voice level. "But sarin gas is unstable, Mrs. Morell. It degrades after three or four weeks. These weapons will now be harmless."

Daniela stays silent.

Ambra says, "That really puzzles us. The people trying to find these weapons—or who already have them—surely know this. The Arizona bomb was anthrax, not sarin. If the other two were sarin, they must now be harmless."

"How did you know that? That one was anthrax and two were sarin?"

Time to play the ace. Sharp says, "Max Krafft told us."

At first he thinks she is going to faint. The cup and saucer in her lap tremble violently. But she recovers her composure, puts the tea on the table in front of her, and says, "I think you should leave now."

Ambra says, "But why?"

"Max was killed by the Nazis sixty years ago. And whatever game you young people are playing, I want no part of it. That was cruel." And she begins to cry.

Ambra passes over a clean handkerchief. Sharp says, "Max is alive and well, living in Russia. He told us all about you."

She blows her nose. "Why are you doing this?"

"We were speaking to him two days ago."

"Lies, lies." She stands up unsteadily. "He was shot by the Gestapo a few hours before the Russians overran their prison. They found his body among all the others."

Sharp stands up, facing her. "The Russians lied. They took Max to Siberia secretly and made him work for a huge bioweapons program."

"You are a cruel young man."

"He told me he thinks of you every day."

"I want you to leave this instant."

"He asked me to give you a message should we find you. A message that in the whole wide world only you and he would understand. I can't make sense of it."

Those bright blue eyes, with tiny red veins in the white, looking into his soul. Angry eyes; but with a hint of something else? Hope? Dread? Sharp says, "Never walk backward drinking schnapps."

It takes some seconds to sink in, and Sharp has time to catch her as she falls.

GOERING'S COCKTAIL

It's going to be tricky. The old lady may clam up at any time, for any reason or none. She trembles and weeps for about fifteen minutes while Ambra tries to pacify her and Sharp paces up and down, feeling every second of the time slipping past. She wants to know about Max but for some reason Ambra firmly steers her away. ". . . He's in good health . . . He thinks of you all the time . . . We'll talk about that later . . ." He waits until Daniela has calmed down—another cup of Darjeeling tea seems to help—before he starts. "Mrs. Morrell, there are things we don't understand about the Arizona weapon. Why has it turned up now? Why Arizona? Did anyone in the team know where they would be hidden?"

"Kurt knew. That is, Dr. Hess, the director. He was visited by some high-ranking officers. One of them was a meteorologist from the Lufftwaffe, and there were naval officers. There was a lot to discuss, about the feasibility of smuggling the flying disks onto enemy territory, where they should be hidden, and so on. I believe they recommended targets to Goering for the flying disks. But we were kept out of all this."

"But there's no record?"

"I believe there is. Hess kept a diary of the project. We all knew this and used to joke about what might be in it. He kept it in a safe. I expect he kept a record of the secret meetings."

Daniela dabs at the corner of her eyes with a handkerchief, sips her tea.

Ambra says, "Some of us suspect that people may have obtained these weapons, but that doesn't make sense, not if they've been harmless for decades. Given that sarin decays so quickly."

Another sip. "Harmless? Didn't Max tell you? Of course we knew the sarin gas would decay quickly. We also knew that the weapons were so dangerous that they could not be transported, except at a snail's pace. We were scientists and engineers, we understood the monster we had created. But what about railwaymen? Can you imagine one of these bombs swinging on a crane? And as for loading them on a U-boat!" Daniela shakes her head. "We decided we could not use the stuff Spandau sent us."

"What then?" A horrible sick feeling is beginning to grip Sharp's stomach.

"We created two compartments inside the bomb, separated by a thick glass wall. Everything was lined by glass."

"No wonder transporting the Furies made you nervous," Ambra says.

"In one compartment we put DF . . ." She bows her head in thought. "How can I remember after all these years? I'm not a chemist, you know. Now, what was in the other chamber? This I remember. We called it Goering's cocktail, because it was something mixed with a type of poisonous alcohol. OPA, that was it. Whatever OPA is. A few minutes before the saucer is due to vent the sarin, the glass partition is shattered and the chemicals combine. They create fresh liquid sarin."

"Oh man," Sharp says. "Oh man."

"Am I allowed pride, to have taken part in the creation of such a monster? If these weapons still exist, they are as dangerous as the day they were made."

"The fusing mechanism. How did that work?"

"A simple time lock, set by entering six numbers on a combination lock of the kind you will find on a safe. When the disk has reached its full altitude, a spring-loaded bolt breaks the glass sheeting between the chemicals. The heat generated in the reaction, and the spin of the disk, ensures complete mixing. And then, with the sarin created, the nozzles open and the poison sprays out."

"I don't suppose you remember the numbers, after all this time."

"Actually, young man, I do."

"How is that possible?"

"I must allow myself the sin of pride once again. They are numbers of great significance. But you see, we were clever. If the weapons were ever to fall into the wrong hands—who knows how?—they might have been used against us. We therefore had what the Americans call a fail-safe mechanism. If the wrong numbers were fed in, the disks would be made harmless."

"And the numbers? The firing codes?"

"We wanted to sabotage it, you know, Max and I. But after the summons to Goering, we couldn't sneeze without attracting attention from the security people. Every corridor had an SS man and every nut and bolt was inspected. They'd found out I had a Jewish mother, you see, but they still needed me. And in the U-boat pen, when I was putting the firing code in, I had a gun at my back. They knew that was when I would feed in false numbers if I could."

"The firing codes?"

The shutters come down. "Why should I tell you?"

"I don't know. The information may be useless to us. But we need to know everything possible about these weapons. There may be others."

"There were three. Forgive me, but the information is too dangerous to give."

"Who else knows these numbers?"

"Only Hess, who is long dead, thank God, and the agents who were to fire the bombs. I expect they're long dead, too. You see, the numbers belong to me alone, and they will go with me to my grave."

Ambra says, "Max thought you were dead. How do you feel about seeing him?"

"How do I . . . ? To see Max again? Can that possibly happen?" She is having problems taking it in. Sharp begins to worry that she might faint again.

Ambra says, "We can arrange it. We know where he is. But we're the only people who know. If you want to see Max . . ."

Sharp thinks, *You heel, Ambra!* "Mrs. Morrell, if you like we can call the chancellor's office now to confirm that it's in the public interest . . ."

Daniela stands up and walks shakily across to the window, waving aside Sharp's offer of help. She is slightly stooped. She looks through the lace curtains at the traffic below. After about a minute, Sharp becomes aware that he has been holding his breath. Then she turns and beckons to him, like a child with a secret to share. She whispers in his ear. Sharp whispers back, and she nods.

"Room's clean." They are in the secure room, having passed through an inner door within a door, all accessed by codes. The room has a dead quality; it's like being in a chamber deep within a pyramid. Sharp feels a twinge of claustrophobia. Ambra waits until the Embassy man has closed the door behind him.

"Gordon Irons here. I have Professor Duncan with me as you requested. I'm putting him on."

She hands the telephone to Sharp. "Duncan? Sharp here. We found Daniela Bauer and she's told us a little about the chemicals in the weapon. It's very incomplete, I'm afraid. She did say something about mixing two chemicals in the minutes before it was to be fired."

After about fifteen seconds Sharp begins to wonder if the line has gone dead. Then, almost in a whisper, "Oh my God."

"She couldn't remember what the chemicals were. But she said something about DF."

An indecipherable mutter, maybe an obscenity.

"Sorry?"

"Difluoride. Methylphosphonyl difluoride."

"The chemical in the other compartment was something,

called OPA. She said it was mixed with alcohol. They called it Goering's cocktail."

"Isopropyl alcohol and isopropyl amine. Combine them with the DF and you have GB2, known to you as sarin." A pause, and then Duncan is speaking shakily. "It's a binary weapon. Incredible. These people developed a binary weapon."

Goering's cocktail . . . a binary weapon . . . Hubble bubble toil and trouble. Roaring drunk and seeing double. Two impossible things before breakfast. Downey had been right, there wasn't a wasted word.

And Sharp doesn't feel like taking prisoners, not after what he's been through: "You got it wrong again, then?"

"Damn you, Sharp, the West didn't develop binary weapons until the sixties."

"The Nazi weapons are still lethal? Will you confirm that?"

Duncan's voice is tortured. "I almost wish they were atom bombs."

"The Hess diary. That has to be it." Sharp and Ambra stand on the pavement with water running down their faces, ignoring the rain, ignoring rush-hour Berlin scurrying past, car tires throwing little arcs of spray up from shiny streets.

"What are you thinking, Lewis? That the bad guys have got hold of it?"

"It makes sense."

Ambra wipes water from her nose. "If Hess recorded the firing codes in his diary, they have everything and we have nothing."

"They don't have the codes, Ambra. Remember Petrov's query? *On mojet znat,* he might know? Remember what they did to Edith Zimmerman? People were trying to get something out of her, something she couldn't give."

"Maybe the Arizona device blew up because they were trying to circumvent the firing mechanism without the codes. By now they know the UFOs are booby-trapped."

"They're looking for the codes, Ambra. And Daniela has them. They could get to her at any time."

"She'll need protective custody."

Sharp shakes his head. "If the old lady's dead, the firing codes are gone forever."

"Lewis, what exactly are you saying?"

"I'm saying that half the population of London's at stake. Center of government, center of finance, center of everything. I'm saying that old ladies die every day. And I'm saying that if it occurred to me, it's occurred to someone in British intelligence. She's a trivial target for a wet job."

Ambra is unconsciously biting her lower lip. "We're talking about Her Majesty's Government here, not the Bulgarian secret police or renegade KGB."

"I wish you'd said that with more conviction, Ambra."

"That's why you wanted the firing codes, isn't it? So they'd have to get rid of you, too? So things would get harder for them? You were trying to protect the old lady from our own people." She wipes more water away from her nose. "You idiot. If you believe what you're saying, you've turned yourself into a target for both the Petrov gang and the SAS."

"Only if they know I've been given the codes."

"They probably know already. They almost certainly bugged Daniela's apartment."

"I was relying on it. But you'd have told them anyway." Sharp gives her a bleak smile.

"My loyalties lie with Six. Of course I'd have told them."

"I was relying on that, too. Daniela's a target, Ambra. Get her out of there now."

"What about you?"

"I'll book us all rooms in the Brandenburger Hof, Krafft's old hotel. I'll get hold of the loading lists, I know people. And we'll need to find out what happened to Hess after the war. We must get his diaries."

"But Lewis, you have no field experience . . ."

"Look, we're nearly out of time. Daniela needs protection now."

"Are you listening to me, you idiot? You're not trained for this."

"Excuse me, Ambra, but the London threat? The lives at stake? We can't hang about."

"Do you need reminding that Darth Vader, the Hollywood musician, and Miss North Korea are right here in Berlin?"

"They sound like villains in a Batman movie."

"Very funny, Lewis. They could be within a mile of us. Can you even imagine if they get hold of you?"

"But what do you think they're up to, playing tiddlywinks? Get Daniela to safety, Ambra, quickly."

BRANDENBURGER HOF

In the Brandenburger Hof, Sharp books rooms with a connecting door for Ambra and himself, and another room straight across the corridor for Daniela. A team of bearers brings in a laptop, reams of paper, a printer, and a fax machine, courtesy of the management, while he changes into dry clothes. Then he plugs in the laptop, looks at his watch, and gets busy.

First, he puts an urgent inquiry through to the Bundesarchiv in Freiburg. Then he makes use of an old contact in the Public Records Office in Kew. Kew fax him volumes of Ultra decodes and he plows through these, looking at messages between Berlin and the submarine pens in Denmark and Norway. Nine U-boats, it turns out, left Norway in February 1945, destined for the New York area. By that stage of the war, Sharp thinks, these were practically suicide missions, and true enough, the Americans, alerted by Bletchley, were waiting for them: a reception committee that hammered the enemy submarines, as the admiral's report put it.

Hammered the submarines. What horrors lie behind that glib phrase? Sharp wonders. But there's no time to dwell on it. The waiting massacre was called Operation Teardrop. Of course! *Sleza,* the teardrop of Petrov's list.

But the doomed submarines had been sent from Norway,

not Denmark. Were they a diversion? Could the Third Reich have deliberately sacrificed their own children, sending young men out in U-boats from Norway just to draw fire from ones sailing from Denmark, landing their cargo on dark coasts in Mexico or Ireland? Was the leadership that ruthless?

Of course. One must be hard.

True enough, there are no Furies in the loading lists, as C had said. But one entry catches Sharp's eye. In the loading list of U-864, a set of packages labeled CASPAR. He doesn't know why it's attracting his attention.

Sharp looks again at his watch. Ambra should have been here by now. Maybe the old lady's being difficult. *That's it. Daniela's being difficult.*

He goes quickly through the records of the navy meetings with Hitler. Here and there the clipped phrasing, he thinks, barely disguises some of the Führer's notorious rants. There is no mention of U-234, which surrendered at the end of the war and was found to be carrying a ton of uranium oxide to Japan. What were they doing with a ton of uranium oxide? And why was there no mention of it in the CinC records? Was it, like the Holocaust, part of a project so secret they didn't commit it to paper? In that case, what else didn't they want put on record? As he plows through the meeting reports, the silence begins to shout at him: *They're hiding something.*

Still no signs of life from the next room. He taps on the connecting door, then opens it. The room is empty. He feels a twinge of dread.

Lewis, have you thought about the mating scorpions?

Here we go. Before Sharp can type a reply, the message continues:

Think about Petrov in the gulag. And Krafft in the gulag. Can you believe that's a coincidence?

There doesn't seem much point in security; the ghostly messenger seems to know everything and anyway they're all but out of time. Sharp thinks the hell with it and takes a chance. He types: They were both in the Obolensk gulag in the fifties. Petrov could have learned about the weapons from Krafft there.

But why now? What's his trigger?

I don't know. Something to do with North Korea, if we believe . . .

Exactly. Something is coming to a head, and Petrov is being driven to stop it.

Is that a guess?

It's a deduction. Find out what's happening with North Korea, and it may lead you to the bioweapons.

How can the bioweapons possibly help both Petrov and his scorpion mate? What's in it for them?

Petrov is trying to foil the American administration in some venture. His scorpion mate is doing the same to her government. It's the only explanation.

Her government. The ghost knows about Miss North Korea. But Sharp hardly has time to assimilate the fact: The ghost is still typing. *Petrov and his scorpion mate are trying to spoil something, some secret rapprochement between their countries, and they'll use the bioweapons to do this. You must find out what's going on between the USA and North Korea!!!!!*

You're way out on a limb, chum. How can you work out so much from so little?

Trust me. It's your only chance in the time left to you.

What about London? What's in it for a man like Petrov to threaten London?

That has me baffled, Lewis. We're still missing something.

As the screen fades, Sharp thinks it odd that whenever the ghost contacts him, Ambra is away. A coincidence, no doubt. Again, he opens the adjoining door.

Nothing's wrong. They'll turn up soon.

THE HESS ESCAPE

Kurt Hess spat out a mouthful of dust and looked fearfully skyward, ready to run for his life. But the RAF fighters had vanished. The Mercedes carrying Krafft and Daniela was disappearing swiftly around a corner a few hundred meters ahead. He leaped up, furious, his heart thudding, and promptly fell down again. His left ankle was swelling like a balloon.

One of the Gestapo men from the following car rushed out at Hess from the farm building, gasping, and bawled accusingly, specks of spittle coming from his mouth.. "They've escaped!"

"I can see that, you idiot!" Hess shouted back. "Find me a car. I have to report to the Reichsmarschall."

"A car? Where do I find a car here?"

Hess brushed the man aside angrily and limped toward the farm building. Nothing but hay and carts, and a tractor that looked as if it hadn't seen petrol for years.

Something—a bicycle. He grabbed it, wobbled away. "How far to Berlin?"

"Maybe thirty kilometers to the Reichstag."

"Find a telephone. Phone your headquarters and tell them about Krafft. Give them their car's registration number, you are capable of that, are you?" Hess called back, steering clear of the dark sticky pool and flesh that were Oberlin's remains. He started to pedal furiously, trying to ignore the searing pain in his ankle.

Someone, an old farmer, passed him in the opposite direction, running toward the mayhem. Once away from the noise of the dying steam engine, he could hear birdsong and the distant *thump-thump* of artillery. *Ours or theirs?* The noise grew louder as he approached the city. Presently the road joined a main highway leading out of Berlin. Here there was a steady stream of wagons, horses, crowds of refugees heading away from the capital. Many of them looked like eastern workers, fleeing their own people. Ahead of him, ominously, a great pall of black smoke overhung the city. He weaved his way determinedly through the human stream, using the bicycle bell, and by early afternoon he was passing through suburban houses that seemed to be untouched; but many of them had windows boarded up; and the smoke was higher in the sky here; and the sun was shining balefully through a reddish haze.

He hadn't seen central Berlin for four months, and the extent of the new destruction shocked him. There was hardly a building untouched by the bombing. A convoy—half-tracks towing artillery and trucks loaded with infantry—was skirting a bomb crater in the Berliner Allee. Here dense, acrid smoke was pouring out of a huge rubble heap, mixed with brick dust that caught his throat and dried his mouth. A light aircraft was sitting on a clear strip of road outside the Brandenburg Gate.

The Air Ministry building was still standing, or at least a good bit of it. Worn out, he dropped the bicycle at the roadside, not caring whether it would be there when he reemerged, and navigated the sandbags at the entrance.

"I am Standartenführer Dr. Kurt Hess. I have to report to the Reichsmarschall personally." Exhausted or not, he couldn't help a tinge of self-importance in his voice.

But the pasty-faced little squirt facing him seemed unimpressed. "He's not here."

"But he's expecting me."

"I can't help that."

"Well, where is he then? When is he expected back? I have something of the utmost importance to tell him."

"I'm sorry, Standartenführer, but I just don't know. He drove north to Karinhall a couple of days ago."

"He's at Karinhall, then?"

"I doubt it." The little squirt leaned forward, as if to impart some confidential information. "The story is, he's had Karinhall blown up."

The news hit Hess like a slap in the face. He stepped back and took a second to assimilate the information. The Prussian Palace, the overblown opulence matching the owner's personality, the tomb of his first wife, the statues, the gardens . . . if he'd had them destroyed, it was a strong statement about the future of Germany.

But maybe it's not too late! Maybe, even now, something can be done with the Furies! London in exchange for Berlin, holding a threat over Washington or New York? Even with the Russian guns within hearing? "I must get information of a highly sensitive nature to Hermann Goering immediately. I can't overemphasize its importance."

The little squirt stared at Hess, his expression of cynicism suggesting that nothing was important anymore, not with the Russians about to encircle the city. He lifted a telephone and spoke quietly into it for a minute. And then he put down the receiver and said, "Obergruppenführer Korten is in the building. He would like to speak to you. An escort will be along."

Hess waited in a big, empty, chandeliered room, savoring his moment to come. In a minute Korten marched in. One of Goering's entourage and one of the few men in the know; he had been in on the secret meetings to decide the targets. The SS man had an elongated head and smoothed-down black hair that made him look, to Hess, like a painted Easter egg, down to the absurd little black mustache. Hess threw an arm out, announced, "Heil Hitler! The Sisters of the Night have been delivered."

"You should have delivered them two months ago." Korten's face and voice were those of a hanging judge. "They would have made a difference then. Even last month."

Hess, already weak with the unaccustomed cycle ride, felt as if he might faint. "Obergruppenführer Korten, the project was of a very advanced nature. The fact that we were able to deliver at all is a triumph of German science."

"Even two weeks. If you had come to us two weeks ago with your flying devices, we could at this moment be destroying the Hague or Washington, and threatening Moscow and Leningrad. We could have bargained—Moscow for Berlin—and forced a cease-fire, and then we could have driven a wedge between the allies."

"Even now . . ."

Korten, in a sudden rage, swiped Hess's report off the polished desktop. "It's too late now, you total fool! Haven't you noticed anything about this building? Apart from the fact that twenty-seven offices have been wrecked? It's half empty. The rats are deserting Berlin in huge numbers. Even Goering has scarpered, the second in command of the Reich, for Christ's sake! The battle for Berlin is about to start and nothing will stop it. Nothing! By the time your Furies are in place, the war will be over. If you had delivered on your promise, if your machines had come on time, you could have saved Germany this catastrophe."

Hess, suddenly knowing what was coming, found himself starting to shake. Korten, patches of red on his cheeks, observed this reaction coldly. "Which brings us to the matter of your failure, your dereliction of duty."

"With respect, Obergruppenführer Korten, not failure. I delivered the Furies."

Korten ignored the comment. "You were warned that the penalty for failure would be death, for yourself and for the senior scientists involved in this project. I expect, as is customary, the sentence shall be extended to your families."

"My orders are to report to Reichsmarschall Goering . . ."

". . . who at this moment is in Obersalzburg."

Desperation made Hess bold. "Then I should report to

him there. Report personally to the Reichsmarschall—those
are my orders."

"He will undoubtedly have you shot out of hand."

"Are you planning to overrule his orders to me, Obergruppenführer Korten? To usurp Hermann Goering?"

Korten hesitated, and Hess drove his point home. "Is Berlin open to the south?"

"At the moment, yes. But the American Sixth Army has
taken Munich."

"Can the Air Ministry supply me with a car?"

"You have had a blow to the head, perhaps?"

"A car or not?"

"Even if you got a car, where would you get the gasoline?"

"A light plane, then. I saw one at the Brandenburg Gate."

"That is Speer's, and you seem to be entering the realms
of fantasy."

"I have no time for this. I must get to Goering immediately. The outcome of the war can depend on it."

"Let me see what I can do. Stay here." Korten strode out
of the room.

Hess stood in the empty room, a light sweat on his brow
and palms, listening for footsteps. After some seconds a
ghastly thought jumped into his head: *Korten wants me arrested. He's going to have me shot.*

Korten was unarmed, and Hess had his sidearm, the Walther. An unarmed man doesn't arrest a man with a gun, not
on a capital offense.

The leadership principle, honor, duty, sacrifice, obedi-
ence, Krafft, Daniela, the Furies, the appointment with Goering, the lost war, all flew out of his head, pushed out by a
single overwhelming thought: Get out of this alive.

Give it thirty seconds.

Five, six, seven . . .

*Korten has to keep me here while he summons an SS de-
tachment. He has to pretend to go along with me.*

Ten, eleven, twelve . . .

*I can't leave the office and run down three flights of stairs,
not if Korten is in the corridor. But the Obergruppenführer*

will—maybe—disappear into someone else's office, rustling up the SS.

Eighteen, nineteen, twenty . . .

Hess's nerve gave. He slipped his journal inside his shirt, crossed quickly to the door, opened it slightly, and looked up and down the corridor. A few adjutant types walking around, two officers smoking cigarettes and chatting. He swung open the door and walked smartly past them—not too smartly!—and trotted down the broad marble stairs.

If Korten is at the front desk, I'll blow his head off and shoot my way out.

Down to the second floor, still no sign of the egg-faced Obergruppenführer.

And there was no Korten at the front desk. Workmen covered in plaster dust were carrying planks out of the entrance.

The little squirt looked up as Hess passed. "You have to sign out." Hess ignored him.

And he was out! The bicycle was still there. Hess could have wept with relief.

Lose yourself in the streets, quickly!

Into the acrid smoke and the road, and the yellow arrows pointing to air raid shelters. Around a corner. A wrecked bus was swinging on a crane. Bodies were laid out along the pavement, covered with sheets. *Korten will have discovered the office empty by now, he'll be running down the stairs crying blue murder.*

Hess stood on the pedals, ignoring the pain from his swollen ankle. He cycled swiftly past a group of children in overlarge uniforms, carrying panzerfaust grenades. They could barely carry them—no doubt some pig had fed them duty, sacrifice, and orders to throw themselves at Russian tanks before scarpering out of the city himself. Their over-large clothes gave them a circus clown look. He maneuvered through a group of prisoners with striped tunics, clearing rubble. They were gray-faced, emaciated, more dead than alive.

Emaciated prisoners. *Natzweiler!*

There would be documentation, witnesses. American and Russian judges.

And the calibration curves! ... *I now present to the court* ... *Dr. Hess, do you recognize these graphs?*

And the hangman, waiting.

Cycling desperately toward the south of the city, Hess knew that somehow he would have to get out of Germany.

DEUTSCHES JUGEND

"Daniela's gone. She's not in her apartment."

Sharp briefly closes his eyes. "If they've got Daniela, they've got the firing codes. They have everything." *They must have been minutes behind us.*

Ambra flops down on the bed, her hair and clothes dripping. "There was no sign of forced entry. No sign of a struggle in the apartment . . ."

"How did you get in?"

"Never mind that. Maybe she just went out shopping or something. I've been looking for her all over, in the nearest supermarkets, the streets around, and so on."

"We should call the cops."

She shakes her head. "No. We're British intelligence operating on German soil."

"With German approval."

"But she's a German citizen at risk. We don't need the complication of uniforms. Let's not get paranoid about this, Lewis. She'll turn up."

"Those people at the apartment when we arrived . . ."

"MI6."

"What were they up to?"

Ambra disappears under a towel.

* * *

"He got out of Germany?"

Ambra is five calls down the line and finishing the last of her coffee cake. They are in a reassuringly packed bistro, full of smoke and noise. "There were lots of ways out. The International Red Cross ran refugee camps. People with no papers were given temporary identity cards. All you needed was a good story and a false name. You then used the card to establish a new permanent identity. Also there were escape routes organized by fascist priests in Rome and Yugoslavia. And there was a sort of clearing center for fleeing Nazis in Switzerland." She licks cream from her fingers.

"So what was Hess's route?"

"Switzerland. The center operated from a hotel in Zurich, and they directed him to an illegal immigration office in downtown Berne. You should taste this. The whole thing was financed by money taken from Holocaust victims."

"The ultimate irony," Sharp says. He makes a writing motion but the waiter seems to have a bad case of tunnel vision.

"They gave Hess a forged passport and he flew to Madrid, then got on a ship for Buenos Aires. After that he moved to Argentina, which was a safe haven for Nazi war criminals, courtesy of the Perón government."

"So what did he do in Argentina?"

"That bit's murky. But whatever, he attracted the attention of the CIA. They were employing former Nazis big-time in intelligence and covert operations, and they brought him back to Germany in 1957 under his own name. He joined an outfit called the Bund Deutsches Jugend." An elderly foursome at the next table are going through a ritual of protestations, grabbing the bill from one another.

"Can't say I've heard of them."

"I'm not surprised. It's taken the CIA sixty years to release the archives, and that was under congressional pressure. It was a CIA-financed spy group based in West Germany and stuffed with nasties. It was also thoroughly penetrated—it turned out later that a lot of them were double agents. It seems that Hess joined Farben as a manager. This involved a lot of Eastern European travel, especially to

Czechoslovakia, which was big in pharmaceuticals. But his real remit was espionage, industrial and military. He worked under the code name Clarion. He also advised the CIA on 'special assignments,' whatever that means."

"The mind boggles." Sharp tries again with the waiter.

"Anyway, it seems he died in his bed a decade ago."

"What are you saying? That the trail has dried up?"

"No, Lewis, it just got hot. He has one living adult descendant, a granddaughter."

"You mean . . . ?"

"Maybe she's the link with the past. Maybe she has her grandfather's diary."

Sharp feels a surge of excitement. "If you weren't so ugly I'd kiss you. Where is she?"

"She's right here in Berlin. In fact she lives just four blocks away from Daniela, and I'll bet each of them doesn't know the other even exists. They probably shop in the same Lidl. Two small children, lives alone on social security, no known extremist connections."

Sharp looks at his watch for the third time in an hour. He thinks the waiter can go to hell and puts a bundle of euros in an ashtray and stands up. "What does the name *CASPAR* mean to you?"

"Caspar? One of the three wise men bearing gifts?"

"Three wise men bearing gifts. It just keeps getting better. Give me this granddaughter's address."

Ambra scribbles in a diary and tears out a page, then stands up. "I'll try Daniela's apartment again. If she's not there, I'll contact our embassy and advise them to bring in the local plods." She puts her face close to Lewis and whispers. "Lewis, I know we're nearly out of time, but please be very, very careful. We don't know what's out there, you have no field experience, and as a target you are just so juicy."

GRANDPA'S PEOPLE

Sharp navigates his way to the back of the old Karl Marx Allee and soon finds himself surrounded by brutalist architecture, all potholed streets and high-rise concrete flats. Big hunks of cladding have crashed into the streets and never been replaced. He tries out the address on a couple of street urchins without success and begins to wander randomly, lost in a maze of concrete. It's growing dark.

HESS, H. is taped on a paint-splattered door on the seventh floor. He taps, then tries the handle; the door is unlocked. "Frau Schwarz?" He knocks again and steps inside. Something is cooking; maybe cabbage and sausages.

He steps into the dark corridor. A door to the right is open, leading to a tiny bedroom and a baby asleep in a cot. Again, this time more quietly: "Frau Schwarz?"

"Through here."

Along to the kitchen at the far end. Sharp can't quite associate the squalor in the cramped little kitchen with the glamor of the Ramirez Garden Center party, but the woman, her hair now black and held in a ponytail by an elastic band, has the long face and shape of the German actress of Ambra's movie, glimpsed in silhouette. She is stirring a pot. "At last you found me, Mr. Sharp," she says. "Do sit down."

Sharp pulls out a kitchen chair and sits down, dumbfounded. "You are Hilda Schwarz?"

"I'd like you to speak in English, it's good practice for me. I prefer Hilda Hess. Call me Hilda."

"I'm Lewis but you already know that. That was you at the movie premiere party?"

"Yes, that was me."

"What's this about, Hilda?"

She turns down a knob on the cooker. "Come through here."

A living room scattered with toys. She pulls back a big velvet curtain, exposing a large alcove. A couple of steps up to a table draped with a Nazi flag, and on the table two silver candlesticks. Adolf Hitler faces Sharp, arms folded, visionary gaze, Charlie Chaplin mustache; safely framed on the wall. Next to Hitler are an SS dagger, a sword in its scabbard, and a Sam Browne belt with a PPK in the holster. There are other photographs. Men with rifles, parading with white belts and sashes over their long black coats. Himmler, surrounded by acolytes, giving the Nazi salute; underneath the picture is a faded scribble that Sharp can barely make out: HEINRICH AT THE TOMB OF KING HEINRICH I. QUEDLINGBURG 1943. Another photograph shows a wooded scene and a children's choir, surrounded by flags and placards with the SS symbol. One of the children's faces is circled in pencil. The caption says, HEIDI AT THE PEOPLE'S GROUP RITUAL FESTIVAL, BAD HARZBURG 1939. Hilda Hess points to the photograph. "That's my Gran. She married Grandpa Hess after the war."

"After he came back from Argentina?"

She nods. "They thought Hitler was still alive, you know."

"They?"

"Grandpa Hess told me all about it, many times. The air was full of rumors near the end, so Grandpa used to say. Especially there were rumors that Hitler had survived the war. Grandpa's people thought he'd fooled the Russians into thinking he was dead. They thought all this talk of suicide and cremation was made-up stories, and things were arranged in the bunker to let the Führer get clear. Especially when Grandpa's people learned later that Speer had landed at the Brandenburg gate in a Stork, and Jodl told Speer that the next day was the Führer's last chance to fly to Berchtesgaden. Some of them thought maybe he flew to Obersalzsburg and crossed the Pyrenees into Spain, where a U-boat picked him up and took him to Argentina, with plenty of gold. Others thought it was more likely the Führer got out by way of the submarine pens at Bergen."

"Your grandpa went to Argentina, too, after the war," Sharp says.

"Schnapps?"

"No thanks. So your people—Hess's people—thought Hitler was still alive."

"They thought he would reemerge at the right time. East and West were almost at war, just as he'd predicted. They thought he was waiting to trigger that war by unleashing the Furies at a critical moment. A sort of border incident. Then he, or a successor, would revive the National Socialist movement when East and West had destroyed each other."

"So, Grandpa Hess knew where the weapons were hidden."

"Of course he knew. Some brave people had reconnoitered in enemy territory while the war was still on. There was a mine shaft in Arizona, another one near a place called Galway in Ireland, and a third one, I can't remember where."

"The Furies were to be the trigger for a war."

"Yes. Exactly. At a critical moment."

"But it never happened," Sharp says. *Keep talking, lady.*

"It never happened. They gradually came to realize— they had to admit—that the Führer really was dead. And there was no leader in waiting to take his place."

"On the other hand, if you have a gin and tonic . . ."

Hilda moves to the sideboard and opens a door. Bottles clink. "I hardly understood any of this when Grandpa was alive. It was just a lot of stories he told me when I was a little girl. But then there was his journal, and over the years I pieced things together from that. I have London gin here, and there's Bombay. Ice?"

"Bombay, no ice, and don't bother with lime or stuff like that. In the Gulf we drank it neat out of enamel mugs. So no Führer, but you still had the Furies. What's triggered their resuscitation, Hilda?"

"A critical moment." She hands over a glass and settles back in an armchair with a sigh, holding a big tumbler of vodka martini. She kicks her shoes off and raises her glass in a mock toast. "And a Messiah."

"In the form of Vladimir Petrov?"

She sits up attentively. "So, you were the burglar? At his London house?"

"I was."

"We call him Uncle Vlad. What do you know?"

"Why should I tell you what I know?"

"Because you want to find out things from me."

"The truth is I don't know much. I suspect that Petrov is the kingpin in this business, but I'm not even sure what the business is. I think he's gathered up some nasty groups, each with their own agenda, for some operation. How much are you willing to tell me?"

"Actually, you're exactly right. We have that critical moment." She sips her drink.

"Please keep talking."

She keeps talking. "Vladimir told me his London flat had been burgled and that someone must now know about Max Krafft and Daniela Bauer. But he'd been unable to find any trace of them. Vladimir met Krafft in a gulag in Obolensk and Krafft told him all about the weapons they'd developed during the war—that's why the Russians had him there. Vladimir came too late to me about a year ago. He had guessed that my grandfather might have left me some record of his project. He had—an old journal that he gave me for safekeeping. It included the locations of the three Furies. I was glad to give him that."

"Why?"

"Thanks to Vladimir we will show the world what Germany almost achieved."

Yes, nutty as a fruitcake. "You're too young to be carrying a flag for events that took place a lifetime ago." Every nerve in Sharp's body is tingling. He actively forces himself to stay casual. "Are you trying to trigger a war, Hilda?"

She giggles. "No, no, I don't care about things like that. I'm doing this for Grandpa. It's a sort of completion. It's what he would have wanted."

"Where's the journal, Hilda?"

Another giggle. "We're mating scorpions, you and me. We each have something the other needs. You need to know where Grandpa's weapons are hidden. We need to know the firing codes. But we got there first, you see, and his flying saucers are ready to fly. My English is okay?" She smiles. "On the other hand, God has brought you here, with the codes in your head. We have Daniela, and now we have you."

It takes a moment to sink in.

TOWN HOUSE

D-DAY MINUS 2, OVERNIGHT

The man is small, muscular, about thirty, with Far Eastern features, maybe Japanese. He turns away and stamps a metal-tipped heel hard down on the top of Sharp's right foot. Sharp roars as the thin bones break. Vicious, rapid chopping blows follow to his stomach and throat and kidneys, and a knee is rammed into his testicles. A woman, also Far Eastern, grabs his hair. Hilda splashes her vodka martini in Sharp's face.

They bundle him into an open elevator with Sharp kneeling on the floor, a fireworks display of blinding lights assaulting his eyes. Outside, a big blue BMW pulls to a stop and Sharp, smelling of alcohol and hardly able to shuffle, is bundled into it. It's now dark. The cigarette and lemonade queue is still at the van. Nobody bothers about another drunk.

The car hums smoothly away, gradually picking up speed. There is a strange, animal-like whining which he can't place. Then the urge to vomit rises quickly from his stomach up through his gullet, and he spews onto the floor, retching. Somebody curses angrily in some Asiatic language. The animal whine starts again, and now he recognizes it as coming from his own mouth.

The numbers. They'll want the numbers, the firing codes that will let them detonate the remaining Furies. They'll get them in the end. And then they'll discard him. *The numbers . . . What numbers? . . . The numbers . . . The numbers . . .*

The stench of vomit fills the car. Somebody is muttering in disgust. The fact gives Sharp some small satisfaction.

After ten minutes—or is it an hour?—the car slows and gravel crunches under tires. Voices. Then a car door opens. Vomit smears his cheek as he is pulled out by the hair. He cries in pain as he puts weight onto his right foot, and they half drag him up a flight of stone steps. Sharp has a brief glimpse of a massive, Hanoverian-style house, and screening bushes and trees, and a high surrounding wall. There is traffic somewhere; late-night city stuff.

Three of them. Two Asians, one male, one female. And someone manhandling Sharp from behind. He thinks about a mule kick and a sprint into the trees, but he can hardly hop. He retches again, but this time only a thin, mucous slime dribbles out of his mouth.

The woman is fiddling with keys and then they are in, and he is being frog-marched along a carpeted corridor lined with black-and-white photographs of Bogey, Dietrich, Gable: studio poses, all cigarette smoke and harsh lighting. She leads the way to what looks like a cellar door and clicks on a light. Cold, musty air catches Sharp's throat, and he coughs. Down stone steps to a bare, concrete area from which three heavy doors lead off. Sharp hops down, in agonies, gripped from behind. Keys are hanging on a latch. She opens the center door, turns, and gives a malicious smile. Someone pats his pockets, takes his mobile phone, and sticks it in the pocket of his own jerkin.

She's in her late twenties, Japanese or Korean, and definitely in charge. Green eye makeup, delicate cheekbones accentuated with rouge, both grossly overdone, like a child's first attempt to use makeup. Short black hair, short black coat buttoned up to the neck. Smoking. Educated English, Oxbridge. Intelligent eyes. Bad news: Sharp would have preferred a no-neck thug.

The room is low-ceilinged, about six meters by six, and

stuffed with bric-a-brac. It's bric-a-brac with a difference: The walls are lined with flags of the Third Reich, interspersed with framed photographs of Hitler; there are glass cabinets of World War II pistols; and there is a jumble of heavy tables, chairs, and cabinets that wouldn't look out of place on a war movie set. And there are arrays of lamps perched on black stalks.

The Koreans exchange comments. The woman pulls out a kitchen chair, and Sharp is dumped into it. For the first time he sees that the third party, the one with his mobile phone, is European. The man is about fifty, small, and pasty-faced. He's assessing Sharp with dark, anxious eyes. Not a fighter: Sharp feels that a punch on the nose would reduce him to jelly. The Korean woman, too, possibly. But the little Korean man . . .

The men stand on either side of Sharp, and the woman sits across from him on another kitchen chair, smiling.

Breathe deeply, remain calm.

"We believe you have some numbers." Her voice is pleasant and conversational.

"Am I in for a rough night?" Sharp croaks, knowing the answer.

She smiles some more. "You have no idea. Really none."

"I could feed you any rubbish. How would you know the difference?"

"Listen to the smart man." So the European is American. The accent is hard to place; probably somewhere on the East Coast, like Boston or Philadelphia.

The woman speaks to her compatriot. He replies with a brief, angry snarl: to Sharp, his voice is more like a dog's bark than human speech. She crosses her legs. "You can call me Miki. Do you like sex?"

"Only with nice human females. You score zero on all counts."

"When was the last time?"

"I can't remember."

"You should try to. Because unless you cooperate, all you will have from now on are happy memories."

"Memories from now on? I have a future?" The effort to speak hurts his throat.

"I'd love to get to know you better, Lewis. Your dossier is fascinating, but it doesn't tell me about the inner man, you know what I mean? Sadly, there isn't time. We need those numbers tonight."

Sharp is wet with sweat. The pain, in his foot. Everywhere. He whispers, "Alecto is one two three four five. Tisiphone is five four three two one."

She sighs, stands up, and pulls the kitchen chair well back. "Oh dear."

TORTURE

The first three punches land heavily in Sharp's solar plexus and the one to his chest knocks the chair backward. His head hits the concrete floor with a *crack!* and he lies panicking, unable to breathe. The Korean man starts to use his feet, hammering at Sharp's stomach and groin. It goes on for some minutes . . . or an hour . . . or two. Somebody lifts him back onto the chair. The transition from the real world to one dominated by pain has been swift.

From time to time he hears Miki, sometimes shouting in his ear, sometimes whispering from a great distance: "The numbers, Lewis . . . the numbers . . . give me the numbers and it will stop." Pain is everywhere, filling every corner of his mind.

Sometimes he cries out, sometimes he gasps out numbers. "Nine . . . six . . . three . . ." And the Korean uses chopping motions with hands callused like horn, and Miki says, "Wrong, Lewis. Try again." Now and then the American joins in with a few haymakers, but Sharp feels that the man doesn't have his heart in it. Still, one of the unskilled punches splits his upper lip and loosens a tooth. The ceiling begins to float up and down and around. He goes into hyperventilation, faints briefly.

The little Korean is saying something, rubbing the edge of his hand. Then Miki's face is inches away. "Full Moon wants to use his skills in earnest. I said no. We need to keep your heart beating. But we're calling in a doctor. Lewis, darling, we already know the numbers."

Sharp is dribbling blood. His lower lip is almost too swollen for speech, and his voice is a whisper. "You're doing this for fun."

"Oh Lewis, I am so sorry." She sits down, facing him, and strokes his hair. "You didn't think this was the serious stuff, surely? Oh goodness no, you poor man. This is the warm-up. The real procedure starts"—she glances at her watch—"soon. Someone is on his way here with some specialist equipment. Forgive me, but I think I want to break for coffee. Ronnie, there's some parcel tape in the kitchen drawer. And put a kettle on, would you?"

An American called Ronnie. They're being careless with names, and why not? *I'm not about to leave the cellar alive.*

Ronnie is back down in two minutes, with a parcel tape and another man. Sharp is ignored in the exchange of handshakes. "The road was quiet." An Englishman, sixtyish. *Someone like me.* Sharp feels somehow comforted. "Good God, what have you been doing to him?"

Miki tee-hees, and for a startled moment Sharp has an image of three little maids from *The Mikado.* "Trying to spare him the real stuff. But he's just not reasonable."

"You've explained that you already have the numbers?" An actor, Sharp thinks. The mustache, the exaggerated army officer style, the phony Home Counties accent, the diction. The man tries out a sympathetic tone. "Look, I'm sorry about this. We have the old woman and she has given us the firing codes. But you know the score, we have to be sure they're genuine. If you give us the codes, and they match the old bat's numbers, we know we've got the real McCoy and we have no further use for either of you. We can let you go. You and the old lady. We get what we want and you get what you want, namely to stay alive."

Sharp says, "That just leaves your victims."

Oozing sympathy. "Look, I was an army man, too. I daresay you've been on an R2I course. Me too. I admire your guts, sticking it out like this. You know, things have changed since the old KUBARK manual—you know . . ."

"I've come across it." *You like the sound of your voice, chum.*

"Thought you might have. It's been updated. The British army made some very good improvements in the seventies, and of course we had Mossad and Guantanamo."

"I know." On Sharp's resistance-to-interrogation course, they'd taken him to the limit of his endurance, in one overnight session, without once touching him.

The man is droning on, making a hash of being ex-army and reinforcing Sharp's suspicion that he's probably never gone beyond bit parts in made-for-video movies. Still, it would be enough to identify him. "But basically it's the same stuff. You know we can get anything we want from you in three days. Well, in your case it might take a week. We don't have a week. On the other hand, old chap, we're not restrained by legalities. I have a couple of little gadgets with me that will make everything up to this point feel like a mild toothache. We both know you'll give me the numbers. You agree, don't you? You will eventually give me the numbers?"

"I'm sure of it."

"There. Of course you will, old chap. So why don't you save yourself the grunt and give us them now? I'm giving you a chance to avoid pain."

"Very grateful. Don't know how to thank you." Sharp nudges the loose tooth with his tongue, and thinks that there's nothing more cringeworthy than a lousy, aging actor.

"Not this caveman pain, but real scientific pain. You have my solemn promise that if you give me these numbers, and they match those from the old lady, we will let you both go. Now"—he glances at the others—"I've had a long trip and I feel like a nice cup of tea. I'll give you a little while to think about it. Don't want to rush you, but we do need to get on."

"That's enough talk," Miki says.

The Korean pins Sharp's arms to the chair, and Ronnie gets busy with the parcel tape. "Careful!" Sharp grunts as the tape wraps around a swollen shin.

"Sorry," says the American. In the circumstances the exchange is surreal. He uses the full tape.

"You should see yourself. You look like the Michelin Man." The Englishman pats Sharp on the shoulder. He pauses at the door, lights a cigarette, turns. "You know, I think I'll give you a little taster, old boy. Help you think things through." He rummages in his bag, screwing up his eyes against cigarette smoke, and pulls out a hand-sized plastic device with two metal prongs about five centimeters apart. "Open his mouth, someone."

Ronnie seizes Sharp's hair and forces his head back. The Korean puts two powerful fingers to Sharp's cheeks and squeezes, forcing Sharp's mouth open.

"A stunner, something like a taser. A few police forces have tried it out and decided that it's just too nasty to be used." The Englishman holds the prongs inches from Sharp's eyes. Sharp makes animal sounds. "It's programmed for the chest, or limbs. Not for the mouth. As for the tongue—well! Brings tears to my eyes just thinking about it. Feel this." Sharp quivers, but his head is held immobile between the Korean's hands and his chest. The Englishman drops his cigarette to the floor. He fills Sharp's vision like a dentist, lets the prongs drift in and out of his view. Then he slowly lowers them into Sharp's mouth.

All the pain, all the suffering, everything bad that has ever happened to anyone in the whole of time. It all focuses, in a single instantaneous spasm. His throat contracts and for a moment he thinks they've overdone it, they've killed him. And in the seconds before he loses consciousness, while his whole body is still writhing as much as his bonds will allow, Sharp knows that he will give them the numbers.

THE PETROV KILL

"Bring him upstairs."

Ronnie and the Korean haul Sharp to his feet. He is half dragged, half pushed up the cellar stairs. Back to soft carpeting and civilization. More stairs, a broad flight of them. A bust of someone on the first landing. Miki leads the way along a broad corridor and stops at a door. "Someone would like a word with you. If you mention any numbers, you'll both be shot." The Korean produces a black snub-nosed revolver from a back pocket and waves it in Sharp's face. Sharp doesn't care.

She's propped up with cushions on a sofa. Sharp recognizes the man standing next to her from Ambra's movie: Demos, the Hollywood musician. The man's whole face is sweaty. Daniela's head is drooping, her face is gray, and there is a sizable, multicolored bruise on her cheek. Sharp wonders that she's conscious. With an effort she raises her head and gives a faint smile. Sharp can hardly hear her words, whispered in German. "I should not have given you the numbers."

"I shouldn't have asked for them." He found he was whispering, too.

"I've given them the numbers, Lewis. I love numbers, I want to share them. They are all my beautiful little friends. Thank you, Hindus, for inventing them." She suddenly chokes, and has a fit of coughing. Then: "I love schnapps, too, but they won't let me have any."

"You heard her," Miki says. "She's given us the numbers. There's no point in holding back any longer, Lewis."

"They say they'll let us go if our numbers match, Lewis. Do you believe them? I would like to live just a little longer. There is still so much I would like to do and see."

"That's enough," Demos snaps.

But Daniela is wandering; perhaps she's been driven mad. "You know, I've seen so much that's ugly. I would like to see some beautiful things. In all my life I've never seen Halley's Comet or . . ."

"Shut up, bitch." Demos slaps Daniela. She cries out in pain. Sharp tries to break free of the grips on his forearms, but Ronnie and the fake army man hold him without even trying.

Miki turns to Sharp, gives him a sly smile. "What's this, Lewis? Do I detect a weak spot?" She indicates with her head. "Get him out of here."

The Big Man turns up, descends the cellar stairs with the musician in tow—presumably Daniela doesn't need guarding. Demos's face is still sweaty, and he has an unpleasant, tense grin fixed on it. Darth Vader stares at Sharp without blinking, speaks to the others. "What's keeping you? Why don't you have the firing code?"

The American says, "We have, from the old witch. But John Wayne's holding out."

Miki: "We have to be sure she hasn't fed us rubbish."

"I've no time for this. Sophia's almost there and the meeting starts in less than twelve hours. Get the code out of him, now."

"But we can't risk his heart giving out. We need the medic."

An irritated, sibilant hiss: "Well, where is Al-Mufty?"

Demos says, "He was at some conference. He should have been back by now. Or so his wife says."

Someone stubs a cigarette out on the back of Sharp's neck. He yelps, jerks his head back.

Petrov, his good eye staring without expression. "Do I know you?"

Yes, the Third NATO Conference on Microbiological Weapons and Countermeasures, Uppsala, three years ago. Sharp shakes his head.

"No matter. I need the code now, Mr. Sharp."

Sharp manages a whisper. "And if I give you it? I suppose you'll let me and the old lady go?"

"Is that what they promised you? Your life in exchange for the code?"

"Right." *Code, singular.* The fact registers.

"And are you foolish enough to believe them?"

"Of course not. But it seems you are."

A hint of hesitation. "What do you mean?"

"They're looking for two codes. You seem to want just one."

"Two numbers. Are they indeed?" Something in Petrov's tone. And that eye without eyelashes, unblinking. The grin is disappearing from Demos's face.

Miki says, "Why not? We have two Furies. We may as well know how to prime both of them." Her tone says, *Stupid man.*

Petrov swivels around to Miki. "No, you have one Fury. That was the arrangement."

"But you said it yourself. You wanted Megaera on standby. We can have it on site within hours."

"The seas were too rough and we couldn't risk the extra weight. We had to leave Meg behind." *The seas. The extra weight. They don't care what they're saying in front of me.* Petrov is hissing like a snake. "In any case, why should I have to explain myself to you?"

"Leave Meg behind? Where exactly?"

"Do you think I'm a fool, giving information like that to people like you? Just get Alecto out of him." Sharp thinks that Petrov would be shouting if he could.

"Oh, we'll do that." The army man sounds completely confident.

Miki asks, softly, "Where have you parked Megaera, Vladimir?"

Petrov's good eye blinks. Still that voice, stripped of emotion, a computer. Sharp has to surmise the turmoil within the man. "This isn't part of the deal."

"I know, Vladimir, I know." Miki's tone is sympathetic. "But you see, you shouldn't make deals with people like us."

Petrov and Demos don't even make it to the door.

SS DAGGER

The occasional scream, or at least that's what it might be. How can a man express pain when he doesn't have a voice to scream? The scream comes out as a buzz, a metallic monotone, long and drawn out. Is the pain worse for not having the means to express it?

Sharp is hearing the noise through a ventilator shaft close to the chair. There are snatches of conversation in German, French, English, and some Asian tongue. Words, some of them angry, on the limit of hearing. Something about the target. Nothing penetrates the cellar door. Nothing, that is, until he hears the single shot. After that the buzzing stops. Then there is a raised voice, speaking rapidly in Greek, the tone a mixture of anger and fear. And a second shot.

About ten minutes pass, and then Sharp hears them coming down the stairs.

Dreams. People talking. The clink of teacups. An English afternoon. Tee-hee.

"He'll choke on his tongue . . . do his testicles."

"The firing codes, Sharp . . . all we need are a couple of numbers . . . no time . . . nothing personal, chum . . . I'm an army man, too . . . even been on a hostage endurance course."

A flash of silver, a fish in a stream. Snowcapped mountains. A volcano. Mount Fuji? Hekla? Asiatic tongues.

What numbers? I don't know any numbers. Square root of minus one. Searing pain, this time in the groin, down through the thighs, up through the stomach. Worse than the tongue. Much much . . . square root of minus two, then.

Drink it, it's only wine. Choking, vomit, blood mixed in. My shoes, you bastard.

The American, brow sweating, suffering with me. Decent chap. For the greater good.

We're all set up. Just need John Wayne here to give us the codes. Worried about his heart, are you?

A girl, his first love. She's fourteen. Facedown, hands in stream, trying for the fish. Those legs. The bra visible through the sweater.

Talk talk talk. She loves to talk. And beautiful teeth, beautiful laugh.

More talking, people in the distance . . . where's the effing doctor? Looks played out, can't risk losing him. Wait for the quack.

The clink of teacups.

Three little maids.

Tee hee.

Parcel tape stretches.

Suffocating.

Sharp jerks awake in a panic, his tongue blocking his throat. He takes big, wheezing gulps, his ribs in agony with each breath. Eventually, with a last shuddering breath, the oxygen is restored and his windpipe cleared of vomit. His head has been lolling forward, constricting his throat. His tongue is swollen, seems to fill his mouth. The cellar is black but he feels blood and mucus soaking his trousers.

No part of his body is without pain. On a pain scale of one to ten, his left kidney is about nine, his smashed foot is ten, the area around his groin nine or ten. His ribs ache whenever he takes a breath—two or three on the scale. His arms are behind him, tied to to the chair. His legs, too, are secured with layers of parcel tape. He is alone.

Another round like the last and I'm a jellyfish.

Even as he awakens, choking, he is registering a discovery: Under prolonged pressure, parcel tape stretches. His spell of unconsciousness bent forward has given a tiny leeway to his arms. Less than a centimeter, but enough to twist them. He works at it, driven by the need to avoid more pain, to keep from shouting the firing codes, and to survive.

It's a house of noise. Background things, indistinct, but all he has to judge the enemy. An exchange of voices; footsteps coming down the cellar. Sharp cringes like a frightened child—*no more, please, no more.* But the footsteps go into an adjacent cellar room, and there is the clink of a bottle. On the limit of hearing, someone says, "Better check on the Duke." He droops his head and slouches forward, with his eyes closed.

The key turns in the cellar door and a light switches on. There is a long silence and then someone is saying, "He's not going anywhere," and the door closes again. The light clicks off and the key turns.

The hairs on his arms peel off, but in some minutes he has wriggled his right arm out, and the rest follows quickly. He gives the throbbing a minute to ease as circulation returns to his arms and feet. The cellar stinks with vomit and sour wine.

He stands up, nearly falls down, and gasps with a whole new set of pains. A glimmer of light is coming under the doorjamb, just enough to make out shapes. He limps quietly toward the door, switches on. It's an old-fashioned lock, a bolt sliding into a metal bracket screwed into the wooden doorjamb. All Sharp needs is a screwdriver. He rummages quietly, quickly, among the bric-a-brac, in terror of discovery. Sometimes the gods have to be with you.

Of course! The display of Nazi paraphernalia. The glass lid opens and he pulls out a thin dagger. An SS dagger, like Max Krafft's. From a man of the highest order? Or did he just pass an exam? Whatever, today the gods are with him.

He overbalances and clatters against a chair, which scrapes

noisily over the stone floor. All the flashing pains come back and he sits on it, gasping. A disaster. If noise filters down, it filters up.

Raised voices upstairs. ". . . John Wayne . . . Ronnie's checking." Sharp, close to panic, looks around for a weapon, realizes he has one in his hand. *Stupid!* He hobbles to the door and switches the light off.

He sees the figure in silhouette. Ronnie switches the light on and sinks to his knees with an *Oof!* as Sharp thrusts the dagger into the man's stomach. Warm blood spurts over Sharp's hand. Thrust and then cut in any direction, the manual said. Sharp can't do it, leaves Ronnie writhing on the floor, making far too much noise. Sharp bends over him, retrieves his mobile phone—he doesn't know why—whispers, "Nothing personal, chum."

There is a fuse box over the door. Sharp drags the chair, stands on it, and switches the electricity off. Upstairs, there's the sound of people complaining, running around, clicking switches on and off. Surely they can't fail to hear Ronnie?

Up the steep steps, scarcely able to climb them. Pitch black. Into the corridor. Somebody bumps into him, says *"Bitte,"* stumbles, and then runs in the direction of the cellar stairs.

Go for Daniela, upstairs? Carry an old woman out of the house while . . . ? Impossible! Faint light, shining under a door. Sharp hobbles quickly toward it, palms and brow wet with sweat, feels for a door handle. Behind him, someone is using a cigarette lighter as a candle. He pulls the door open, quietly shuts it behind him, and he is out. Door opens behind him.

Long, winding pathway, lined by shrubs and trees. He hobbles quickly along it, doubled up and gasping with pain. Dawn breaking over a well-heeled suburb; streetlights still on; dustbins being rattled toward a lorry; and a dustman, jumping with fright when a gasping, blood-soaked hunchback lurches out of a gate waving a long bloody dagger.

Berlin and London

SATURDAY, THE LAST DAY

SANCTUARY

D-DAY MINUS 1

His wallet is gone, he can't go back to his hotel, doesn't dare
to. And he can't wander the streets, not in that state. Sharp,
gasping and a mass of pain after a random dash through back
alleys, sits propped against a cold wall in somebody's back
garden, shivering, and trying to think.

A light comes on in a kitchen, flooding the garden. He
struggles up, clicks on a gate latch, and staggers again into
the streets.

Gratefully, he finds a few euros in a trouser belt pouch. It
saves him the humiliation of begging. He stands at a bus
stop, close to fainting, aware of the looks and sly comments
from the early-morning workers in the queue.

There's someone you trust who you shouldn't trust.

Watch your back.

He needs sanctuary; someplace safe, someplace to rest
and regroup. With someone he can trust. But he wonders if
she's even there anymore.

It's much as Sharp remembers it. The bus drops him off at the
road's end, and he begins to limp the kilometer toward the
house. The last time—was it really five years ago?—there
was a foot of snow, and he'd been delighted by the sight of
three deer springing across the road in front of him, mother

and children. But now every step is a spike of agony. Lightning keeps flashing inside his tongue.

The gap in the old stone dike is still there, and he takes the shortcut through it. It cuts a hundred meters off the journey but at the cost of going over rough wooded ground.

Damn. He forgot the fence. He skirts it and comes in through the big wooden gate. Smoke is streaming up from the chimney, and he catches a whiff of burning wood—she's at home. Or someone is.

In the bus it occurred to him that she may have sold the house, and that he may be met at the door by a stranger. In that case he'll pass himself off as a vagrant looking for a handout. Or maybe she's married. Probably is, handsome wench that she was. In that case he'll withdraw gracefully; an old flame looking like a man escaped from Hell might be less than welcome.

He presses the bell. The old familiar chime. A jazz quartet is playing something catchy on a radio. But now a big dog is barking, all low frequencies, and the radio clicks off. He stays vertical with a conscious effort. And then the door opens and she's standing there in a flour-stained overall, a dish towel in one hand, clutching a growling Alsatian by the collar with the other.

Five years on. Now in her late thirties.

Her hair is still red, but now it's cut short, almost boyish, giving her face a slightly rounded look. Her mouth is wider than he remembers. There are a few wrinkles around her green eyes, but they still carry the same mixture of humor and defiance, and now growing amazement. Through his exhaustion, Sharp feels a confusing jumble of old emotions. "Hello, Siggy."

"You need to get to a hospital with that foot. It needs to go into a plaster. I don't like the tongue and the testicles, but the swellings should go down quickly. No irreversible damage there, you'll be relieved to hear. The bruising around your midriff and groin is as bad as any I've seen in a long time. Somebody has been using you as a punching bag." The doctor clicks his bag shut and looks at Sharp over half-moon spectacles. "You realize it's my duty to inform the police. You've clearly been the victim of an extremely vicious attack."

"I fell down some stairs."

"It's the tongue and scrotum that puzzle me. Why the pinprick burns? You got entangled with a lightbulb on the way down?"

"Now that you mention it."

"Siggy, see that your lying friend gets to hospital soon with that foot. Otherwise he's in for a permanent limp."

Siggy gives the doctor a wide smile. That smile. She says, "Thank you so much, Leo."

The doctor glances back at Sharp as if to say, *What can a bloke do?* A minute later, from the bedroom, Sharp hears the wheels of the doctor's Jaguar popping gravel. He watches it turning up the rough track until it disappears through the trees.

THE DREAM

My goodness, you were such an easy target! And now that you're dead, I can tell you how we did it.

Three gray wolves. Three gray wolves slipping through the Kiel canal under a black sky. The first gray wolf headed for America, the second gray wolf headed for Ireland, and the third gray wolf headed for I'm-not-telling. Just like a fairy tale.

The first gray wolf landed on a quiet bit of coast in Mexico, and Tiffany came out of her tummy and was put to bed in a disused mine in Arizona.

The second gray wolf delivered Meg to a dozen men on a dark, lonely beach in Ireland. Men with long memories soaked in blood and myth. You know the type, Lewis, you fought them in the army! Out came Meg and they loaded her into the back of a truck and drove her along quiet Connemara roads toward Galway. There are hundred-year-old tin mines in Galway, where Meg, too, was laid to rest, still and cold, undead like Dracula, waiting for her day.

Sixty years later, in the dripping mine, we were kicking aside the skeletons of the Irish hard men. Look at the round holes in the skulls, Lewis; the U-boat men were harder.

The key to your death was the Hess diary, a gift from Goering, handed down through the generations. Here's Tiffany in Arizona, biding her time in X Marks the Spot; there's Meg in Connemara; and here's Alec from the third gray wolf, sleeping in I'm-not-telling. Once we had that, the rest unfolded like a Greek tragedy, tick tick tick. Tragedy for you, that is.

Wasn't the aftermath pure joy? The financial fallout, the fear that spread into Hong Kong, New York, Zurich, and even the fledgling Moscow market. Who's going to work? Who wants to join a million dead?

You think London was it, don't you? The pinnacle of our ambition, our crowning triumph against the godless West, etcetera. Wrong wrong wrong, Lewis. London was the taster. Our real target, the big scary one, is getting it now. You're too late to stop it.

And where is this big hit, the wicked witch you can't stop, the ruin of the West?

Well now, Captain Nemo. It's a fish . . . a girl from far away and long ago. She's facedown, catching a fish with her hands . . . it's not a fish, it's a god, rising from the sea . . . bellowing like a genie as it erupts out of Hekla . . . splitting the sky with bolts of lightning . . . a Norse god . . . where is she, the pretty girl catching the fish? . . . it's a place you've never even heard of. A place called . . . I'm-not-telling.

Sharp leaps out of bed, choking again, vomit in the back of his throat.

"Lewis? Are you all right?" He pushes her aside, tries to force air into his windpipe. Slowly it starts to come. And the panic subsides as the air gets into his lungs.

"Lewis?"

A voice in the dark; a whiff of perfume; a soft, feminine hand touching his brow, stroking his hair.

"Choking. Bloody tongue. I'm okay now."

"You've been muttering in your sleep. You seemed frightened of something. Really terrified."

"It's all right, Siggy. It was just a dream."

Sharp lies back, hears the click of his bedroom door, and through the plasterboard wall listens to Siggy slipping between the sheets of her bed. Moonlight is throwing shadows of swaying branches of a tree on the wall opposite. It is a formless, chaotic dance, endless and ghostly. He watches it for a long time, soothed by the sound of wind gusting through the trees.

A god . . . a Norse god.

SIGGY

0800, D-DAY

Rain. Heavy, reassuring rain, drumming on the leaves of the trees outside. And inside, a circular Jacuzzi, bubbling softly. Freshly brewed Italian coffee on the table next to it, along with guacamole dips and an early-morning buck's fizz, two-thirds freshly squeezed orange juice, one-third fizzy wine, chilled. Freshly washed and ironed clothes on the toilet seat. And a naked woman, in her thirties, red-haired, leaning back with her eyes closed, wallowing in the sensuality, breasts poking above the foam like islands in a stormy sea, or strawberry-topped blancmanges.

Strawberry. Sharp wonders again if this is the best way to save half a million lives, and thinks again, yes, it probably is. Something they said in his presence, when they assumed he was the living dead. All he has to do is remember.

Eight in the morning. Neither Alecto nor Magaera located. No clue to where they are. But rain will prevent the attack, wreck the spread of the aerosol. The morning forecast has shown a wet front sweeping up the English Channel from the Atlantic, drenching southern England until late morning. After which the rain will stop . . .

I should have rescued Daniela, gone up the stairs, carried her down in the dark. Of course it was impossible. But all the logic in the world can't quite wipe out a guilty feeling: Daniela, abandoned to her torturers. Desertion under fire . . .

He wonders if the old lady is being tormented at this moment while he wallows in luxury in the Jacuzzi; he wonders if she is still alive. A frail eighty-year-old, her heart no doubt kept beating by some degenerate medic, she couldn't have withstood the pain. They must now have the firing codes.

The genuine codes? Maybe. But they can't be sure.

Neither can Sharp be sure they're false.

He lies back, letting the bubbles and aromatherapy do their work. He shifts slightly to avoid a water jet hitting a bruise on his thigh.

A bigger target than London . . . a Norse god . . . Thor . . . Odin . . . Freya . . . ? Come on, come on, dream, where is it?

Siggy opens her eyes, stares at him curiously. "You can't be in the army anymore, not with hair that length. You look like a hobo. Did you have an argument with an express train?"

"What have you been up to these past years? Are you still an amateur actress?"

"I gave that up with the first wrinkle. And I gave up my librarian job. Now I do freelance journalism. And no, I don't have a boyfriend, I mean, would we be sharing a Jacuzzi if I had? About that express train."

"You don't want to know, Siggy."

"You're playing a rough game, darling, whatever it is. Look at you."

"I need to call someone. Do you have a mobile?"

"I have yours."

"What?" Sharp sits upright. In his dreadful state he'd forgotten about it, assumed it was lost in the course of the horrible night.

"It was flat, darling, in your back pocket, but I charged it up."

"Is it switched on?"

"I think so. Is something the matter?"

Sharp is out of the Jacuzzi before Siggy has finished talking, grabbing a pink towel from the handrail.

DEATH SQUAD

By the time they pick up the IMSI signal it's almost too weak to detect and they only just manage to triangulate the cell-phone to the bus station before the signal dies altogether.

Following a country bus by car is hard to do. On a country road you can't just stop behind it every time it lets somebody off at a farm entrance. It has taken all the man's skill to keep at a discreet distance, and yet at the same time see who's getting off where.

The bus had headed into some rural hinterland. He'd driven past it, checking that Sharp was still inside, stopped quickly at an early-morning village shop to grab a sandwich left over from yesterday. He'd emerged from the shop just in time to see the bus's brake lights about a kilometer ahead of him. Someone had stepped out at the entrance to a narrow lane. It was some kilometers on before he was able to pass the bus. Sharp was no longer inside.

Backtracking in panic, driving backward and forward along the lane, he had failed to locate the target. The area was heavily forested, and it was clear that the man had just vanished into the woods.

He'd parked the car in a layby, pulled out his suitcase of gadgets—it wouldn't do for some petty thief or policeman to open it—and trudged around the area for some hours in the morning light, frozen and panicky. He'd found a natural tunnel in the pine forest on the side of a steep hill and, not knowing what else to do, climbed up through it, cursing on occasion as branches hit his face.

The summit of the hill is clear of trees; now the man, kneeling in long wet grass, finds that he has an excellent view of the lights of houses dotting the landscape for miles around. A quick check on his laptop shows still no sign of activity from Sharp's mobile phone.

In the gray dawn light he can make out the country road down which the bus traveled. Turning off this road, and running directly below him, is the narrow lane, at its closest about three hundred meters from the summit. In the last half an hour it has seen no more than five or six cars and a couple of tractors. A kilometer to his right and well below him, the entrance to a stony track leads off this lane. This entrance is of great interest to him. It leads to the home of a Ms. Siggy Frey. The house itself might be unseen, but not the comings and goings through the entrance.

The man also has an excellent view of the surrounding countryside, and of the low, gray clouds hiding the tops of distant hills, and of yet another curtain of rain coming his way. But gratifyingly, on his laptop screen, a yellow spot winks on. The target's mobile phone is working again. Wet to the knees and shivering, he shouts *"Ja!"* and punches the air.

He reports in, tersely. Now he just has to wait for the cavalry.

The yellow spot stays firmly within the walls of the house outlined on his map. Apart from the winding track leading to the house, the map shows a small, circular lake somewhere inside the forest, and a few forest tracks winding through it. A cluster of buildings is marked SAWMILL (DISUSED); otherwise the house is on its own.

The man sighs, and waits. He glances behind again; the curtain of rain is distinctly closer. He reckons he has fifteen minutes before the drenching starts. He says out loud, "Come on, move it," to nobody in particular.

The yellow spot moves. It has left the house and is making erratically for the lakeside. He tenses up.

"Target's left the house."

"What you mean, left the house? By car?"

"Negative. He's close by. I think he's just going for a walk."

"You think. Do you see him?"

"Negative. It's hidden in a forest, real Hansel and Gretel stuff."

Now a car, a little red Alfa Romeo, appears at the entrance to Siggy Frey's forest driveway. He checks his laptop hastily. The yellow spot confirms that Sharp is still in the forest.

The two-seater sports car turns right. Quickly he rummages in a rucksack, tosses out dish towel, mug, sandwiches, finally getting to binoculars. Female driver, short blue skirt, red blouse, good looker, hand on gearstick. No question, she's alone. She joins the main road and then the little car takes off smartly, heading north.

Scheisse! The target is running, skirting the lakeside. The dot on the screen is suddenly moving at a terrific speed. Can he have known he's under surveillance? Is the woman a decoy?

He babbles urgently into the phone. "Target is making a break for it. No. No, belay that." The image has stopped: The target is standing stock-still. Catching breath, maybe.

"Don't lose him, not in any circumstances. We'll be there in two minutes."

Sharp is off again. For a man beaten half to death, he can run.

But now he's zigzagging through the trees, apparently at random. It's crazy. Occasionally he comes to an abrupt stop, and then takes off again in some other direction. "Can you do it in less? I can't make this guy out."

The dot is at last making sense: It's the track of a man fleeing for his life. Sharp is hurtling at an amazing speed through the forest once again. But suddenly he's turning . . . what the . . . ? The lunatic is rushing back the way he just came, back to the house. The man groans with relief as six cars in convoy turn off the main road and skim quickly along the lane below him.

The cars kick gravel briskly down the long curving pathway to Siggy's house. Car doors are flung open, a dozen men with guns jump out. VORSICHT HUND is printed on a notice attached to a farm gate. The HUND in question is on its hind legs, its forepaws on a spar of the gate. It's panting, tongue hanging out and tail wagging in welcome, and Sharp's mobile phone is tied to its collar with a neat pink bow.

THE DANCE OF DEATH

"Sporty suspension." A sporty suspension that causes agony to Sharp's bruises with every jarring bump on the country road. The boot of the little car is intended for a suitcase or two and he has no room to adjust his position. His ear is separated from the sporty exhaust by no more than a sheet of metal, and Siggy loves racing gear changes.

The acceleration and braking shift the pain alternately between his back and his knees. But in twenty minutes, with a final *vroom,* the car slows, turns, and stops.

A flood of daylight, Siggy laughing. "Walkies!"

Sharp, stiff and painful, eases himself out of the boot and finds himself in a crowded supermarket car park. A brother and sister, twins about ten years old, stare in astonishment and run off toward their parents. Siggy says, "You can phone your friend from here."

"Give me a second. I need to get my hearing back."

"Ambra?"

A pause. "Lewis! Is that you?" Relief and disbelief mingle in her voice. "Are you all right?"

"Well, I'm still breathing. Problem. The bad guys have the firing codes. They got them from Daniela."

A brief crackle of static on the line. Or something. "Daniela? They got Daniela? How do you know this?"

"Just listen, we're out of time. They have no way of knowing whether the numbers Daniela fed them are genuine or false."

"Lewis, where have you been?"

"Never mind that. If Daniela fed them false numbers and they put them into Alec and Meg, the Furies will freeze up and they'll be stuffed."

"Okay, Lewis, okay. But what if she gave them the real numbers?"

"They tried to get the numbers out of me, to see if they matched."

"What? They got to you? Did you give them the numbers?" Bewilderment is flooding her voice.

"It's okay, I gave them nothing and I got away. But they're looking for me now."

"Did they try to force the numbers from you? Is that why you're talking funny?"

"My tongue's a bit swollen but that's not important."

Sharp can almost feel the consternation coming down the line. "Lewis, you're telling me they have numbers from Daniela. And they could be genuine."

"They could be."

"What if they are?"

If they are, we've failed and a massive tragedy will unfold in the next few hours. Siggy, hovering just out of earshot, gives Sharp a melting smile.

"Has there been any progress in finding Alec and Meg?"

"None. None at all. Lewis, this is bad. They're threatening to fire them today and Daniela's given them the firing codes."

"Maybe."

"Where are you?"

"I don't know. It looks like some market town. I think I'm not too far from Berlin. I'm using a public phone in a Lidl supermarket."

"Can we meet, Lewis?"

"I want that. There are things I want to say face-to-face."

"What things? What more can there possibly be to know?"

"There's something rotten going on here, Ambra. Some-one's manipulating us."

A horrified silence, and then: "What?"

"I want us to meet alone. Just you and me."

"Get to Berlin and call me in an hour. I'll give you a ren-dezvous."

The Dance of Death.

Siggy maintains a stream of insults about the idiots shar-ing the wet road with her all the way to the city center. Past the Brandenburg Gate, Sharp says, "You can drop me here."

"You think I'm going to let you go just like that, do you, Lewis? After five years? You can just lift me and drop me at your pleasure, is that right?"

"Got it in one."

She pulls over to the side, double-parking, ignoring an angry toot from the car behind. "I hate you. Give me your phone number." She rummages in her handbag and passes over a small, flowery diary and a pen.

Sharp scribbles his Chamonix address. "I'll be in touch. And thanks."

She kisses him on the cheek, gives him a sly smile, and pushes him away. Then the Alfa Romeo weaves its way hap-pily through the flowing traffic, a slim hand waving out a car window.

The church, Sharp knows, is close to the Fernsehturm, the big TV tower and an easy landmark. He walks briskly, navi-gating by instinct and ignoring his throbbing foot.

It seems incredible that the bombs and cannons of seven hundred years have missed it, but there it is, a small, unas-suming medieval church in the Gothic style. And inside, the Dance of Death.

Death is a thin, sexless figure repeated, interspersing with assorted fifteenth-century characters, an official, a friar or two, a few monks, a doctor, a cardinal, a pope, a town offi-cial, a merchant . . . They are dancing to the tune of two

grotesque, deformed creatures, one of them playing a bag-
pipe, the other hunkered down on the ground. They are all
holding hands, the characters facing right, death always
looking left, into their eyes. The fresco is faded, and obviously very old, but it still has the power to chill. Ambra is
standing hypnotized at the fresco, drawn into its world.

"Interesting choice of rendezvous."

Ambra gives a little startled jump, and then hugs him
tightly. He tries not to wince with pain. "It was painted just
after an outbreak of plague in 1484. Isn't it macabre? But I
thought it was appropriate. Lewis, the prime minister's been
told about the situation. You're to give the firing codes to the
terrorists."

Lewis stares uncomprehendingly at Ambra. Her face is
grim.

She repeats, "You have to give them the numbers."

"You'd better explain that."

"They've been in touch with the embassy. They've offered
a deal."

"A deal?"

"Lewis, wake up, there's not a lot of time. They have the
Furies in place. One of the targets is London and they're going to set it off in a few hours."

"So evacuate London."

"But if we do, they'll wait until the scare is over and
people come back. We can't keep London evacuated forever,
and we can't search the whole of southeast England for one
of the Furies."

"I still don't get it. Why give them the codes? What's the
deal?"

"They'll leave London alone and hit the other target."

"And the government agreed to that?"

"They're not telling us what the second target is. But
they're giving us a solemn assurance that it's not a UK target."

"And if they don't get the numbers from me?"

"They'll take a chance with the numbers they have. If
they're wrong, they lose. If they're right, London gets it and

so does the other place. And they're throwing Daniela in as part of the deal. Alive if they get the numbers, dead if they don't. They said something about your weak spot."

Sharp repeats dully, "I'm expected to give them the firing codes?"

"That's the deal."

"And these creeps are being trusted to keep their word?"

"It's the chance HMG is taking. They have to take it. They can't gamble the safety of London on the assumption that Daniela gave them false numbers under torture. They just can't do it."

"And I just can't hand over the numbers to these people."

"You have to go to the embassy now." Ambra looks at her watch. "They're calling for the numbers in twenty minutes. The ambassador will confirm the deal."

"But someplace else will get it."

"That's the PM's decision. He's paid to make it."

"I can't do it, Ambra."

"You have to."

"Sorry."

Unexpectedly, Ambra strokes his cheek, gives a deep sigh, and steps back. "I was afraid of this. I'm sorry, too, Lewis. But you know where my loyalties lie."

Sharp senses rather than hears a presence behind him.

EMBASSY

NOON

Ahead of him, the motorcyclists pull over and straddle the pavement. Someone leans over Sharp, breathing in his ear, and unclicks his safety belt. The door is wrenched open and he is manhandled out of the car. The pavement is swarming with uniforms. Through the gates of the embassy, more men are waiting; grim, accusing faces everywhere. The transition from German to British custody takes place without a word, an exchange of paper, or a moment's relaxation of the grip on his forearm. Sharp thinks, *This is illegal.* And the rain has stopped.

Through glass doors and into the big entrance foyer. Sharp is steered firmly into an elevator, and moments later Ambra, in the company of three more minders, joins him; eight people in a lift designed for six. He is squeezed up against her, senses her trembling slightly. The air is thick with hostility. The lift descends.

Hustled along a windowless corridor, with no consideration for the pain in his foot. He can hear Ambra and her squad scurrying behind him. And then there is a heavy metal door, and another man waiting, and an inner door like the entrance to a strongroom. The man punches numbers and Sharp is pushed into the strongroom.

An enormous oval table, polished and shiny, and on the table a loudspeaker attached by a cable to a metal box, and another cable leading off from the box to a socket in the floor. Sharp recognizes his own mobile phone, the plastic cover off and its insides exposed, a corpse in a mortuary. Last seen tied to the collar of Siggy's dog.

Sharp quickly takes stock. Ambra is next to him, with an expression like a startled fawn. Two men. The ambassador, in open-necked shirt and slacks, is a man of about sixty, with gray hair and beard; he is looking at Sharp thoughtfully over steepled hands.

The other man is wearing a pin-striped suit; he has wispy white hair and a tanned skin. He has a plain green tie with a Windsor knot. Sharp has seen him around. *Where, where?* He is resting a gun with a ridiculously long barrel on his arm.

"Please."

Sharp sits down, trembling. Ambra joins him. She looks at him, pleading with her eyes: *This wasn't personal, I had to do it.*

Sharp then notices a third man, fiftyish and bald, at the back of the big room. He is carrying a mobile telephone and is spreading maps out on a table. He gives Sharp a curt nod. Plainclothes policeman, a spook, Sharp doesn't know.

The man with the tie places the pistol carefully on the table. "Ridiculous thing, like something out of a Wyatt Earp movie. Much prefer a nice Browning, it has a good feel to it. This wretched gun is called a Ruger."

The accent is Scottish, maybe polished in one of the big public schools like Fettes or Gordonstoun. Sharp's mouth is dry with fear. "So what?"

"Mark Two, to be exact. My American friend told me it's a silent gun, remarkably so. 'The weapon of professionals,' he said. He sounded like a salesman."

"What kind of professionals?" *Where have I seen you?*

"I didn't ask. Sometimes I wonder about our American cousins."

The ambassador says, "Good of you to turn up, Mr. Sharp.

We've been turning Berlin inside out looking for you. You are carrying three numbers in your head."

"And there they stay." *Chicksands, R2I. Wearing the uniform of a colonel, no less. The resistance-to-interrogation course, forty-eight hours of purgatory, psychologists standing by in case the victims went psycho. SAS.*

"I hope not."

The SAS colonel says, "Mr. Sharp, either you give us the numbers, or I will shoot you."

A sense of unreality washes over Sharp. He glances at the standing policeman, but the man's expression hasn't changed. "You can't be serious."

"I am deadly serious. Consider what's at stake."

"This is the British embassy."

The ambassador says, "Precisely. Who would believe such a thing was possible?"

"It's been arranged," the colonel explains in a calm, conversational tone that is frightening the living daylights out of Sharp. "You left late this evening. There will be reliable witnesses. And you haven't been seen since."

Ambra: "I didn't join the service for this." Her voice is shaky.

"But how else can we ensure his silence? Sometimes one must be hard, my dear." He turns back to Sharp. "By dawn tomorrow your corpse will be at the bottom of the North Sea, securely weighted down. Just off the Zuider Zee—the causeway is deserted in the early hours."

Sharp can hardly speak. "Those rumors about wet jobs . . ."

". . . they're all true."

The ambassador won't talk. The Special Branch man won't. But Ambra? She's an eyewitness to a murder. They can't let her walk away. Sharp feels a stabbing pain in his side, realizes that he has been taking big gulps of breath.

The ambassador breaks into the silence. "It won't come to this. Mr. Sharp will see sense. In fact, he will see sense within three minutes, which is all the time remaining before his psychotic friends call."

"I know these psychos better than you, Ambassador. A promise from them is worthless. If I give them the numbers, they'll use them, plain and simple."

"You may be right, but the prime minister thinks otherwise and the decision is his and not yours. Plain and simple."

"Oh, Lewis, what have I done?" Ambra's hand is over her mouth.

"Your job, Ambra. My mistake was trusting you."

The ambassador pats his trouser pockets, pulls out a small cigar, lights one. "You may feel that you are right, Sharp. You may even be right. But alas, you have no mandate. Ask the people. Would they rather put their lives in the hands of those they elect to make such decisions, or some Joe Bloggs off the streets? What's the word for it?" The ambassador manages to look bamboozled.

"Democracy?" the colonel suggests.

"Democracy! Thank you." The ambassador puffs, tries for a smoke ring, doesn't quite make it.

The colonel says, "We're in a war, Sharp. Killing you isn't nice, but the mass murder of Londoners is infinitely worse. What else can we do?"

This time the ambassador succeeds. He watches the little smoke doughnut rising up. "Give these people the numbers and you walk out of here on your solemn promise to say nothing of this meeting for as long as you live."

The colonel says, "Nobody would believe you anyway. Murder in the embassy sounds like something out of Agatha Christie."

"Daniela may have fed them rubbish. If her numbers don't match mine, how can you tell whether it was Daniela or me?"

The colonel says, "I'll go on the assumption that it was you."

The ambassador looks around for an ashtray, and then tips an inch of ash onto the carpet. He glances at his watch. "You have less than a minute to think about this."

Ambra is still taking breath in big gulps. Her speech is shaky. "Give them the numbers, Lewis. They're not bluffing."

And then a tinny, high-pitched Ride of the Valkyries comes out of the loudspeaker on the table. At the back of the room, the policeman hastily puts on headphones.

"Lewis?" She sounds a meter away.

"Miki. Sorry you got away."

"I'm sorry you got away, too, Lewis. The party had hardly warmed up. Do you have some numbers for me?" A steady, faint background whine.

The colonel picks up the pistol, resting his elbows on the table, and points it at the center of Sharp's chest. Ambra has frozen in fright; she could be a waxwork dummy.

"Of course, sweetheart. If you're ready to release Daniela."

The whine changes note, slightly.

Miki is saying, "The old lady's already released, Lewis. She's in Spandau, at the front entrance of the Wald Krankenhaus."

The policeman—or spook—is frantically scanning the map. Then he crosses quickly to the table with a scribbled note. The ambassador scans it hastily and passes it around the table:

Cell traced to 7th floor of high-rise. Ev. Wald hospital 500 m away, clear view from flat.

The colonel holds a hand out for a pencil and quickly scribbles:

Difficult even for a marksman.

Ambra reaches for the paper and adds:

Marksman maybe not in flat. Could be close by, like in boot of car.

The policeman is scribbling again:

She's in shock not speaking coherent.

Sharp says, "Miki, you could have grabbed anyone off the street. Let me speak to her."

"Am I stupid, darling? If you do, you'll get the numbers from her, and we can't have that. I need them from your head first."

"If I do that, you'll kill her for fun. Do you see her now?" Sharp asks.

"I do. You must have traced this call by now. Surely the cavalry are coming?"

Sharp glances at the Special Branch man, who holds up two fingers.

"Affirmative, Miki, they'll be on you in two minutes." *Will they hell.* "I still need proof that that's Daniela."

"I'm running out of patience, darling."

"That's mutual, ah, darling."

For a few dreadful moments Lewis thinks Miki has switched off. But then the line is live again, and Miki is saying, "Daniela has been given a mobile phone, which is switched on. We can hear what she says. When the police reach her, one of them will approach her and ask for her name. She will give her name. If the conversation goes beyond that, policeman and Daniela will both be shot dead and we'll take a chance with the numbers we have. Is that clear?"

"Perfectly." Sharp's heart is thumping in his chest.

"He'll have to be quick. And I expect your people have almost reached me, Lewis."

"I expect so."

The ambassador has jumped to his feet, mobile phone pushed against his ear, his face twisted with concentration. "Confirmed. Eighty-year-old lady, small, white-haired, stooped, says her name is Daniela Morrell, knows Max Krafft, likes schnapps."

"It's her."

Why this obsession for schnapps?

Schnapps.

Sharp looks at Ambra, stunned. *Schnapps.*

Miki: "The codes, now. You have ten seconds, then we kill her."

Sharp is taking quick, shallow breaths. "Tisiphone, the Arizona bomb."

"You know I don't need that. Five seconds."

Sharp takes a deep breath. The colonel could be a statue, sighting along the pistol. "Alecto is 828172. Megaera is 951413. Do the numbers match?" The numbers are out and Sharp finds that he is shaking all over. He can hardly hold the phone.

The ambassador says, "She's safe. She's inside the hospital."

Miki's voice is brimming with satisfaction. "Perfectly, Lewis. Thank you so much, darling."

The Special Branch man again:

Flat empty, calls being relayed from somewhere else.

Sharp scribbles quickly. He can hardly hold the pencil. *Background whine is aircraft. She's probably in Petrov's 747.*

The ambassador cuts in sharply, leaning toward the loudspeaker, his hands splayed on the table. "We've kept our part of the bargain, whoever-you-are. Now give us the London weapon. Where is it?"

A long silence, then, "Who is this?"

"Richard Adams, Her Majesty's Ambassador. The London device. Where is it?"

"Can you evacuate London in the next five minutes?"

The colonel drops the pistol on the table with a clatter, snatches at a red telephone. At the back of the room, the policeman has raised his hands to his head and is staring openmouthed. Ambra is whispering, "We should have listened to you, Lewis. We should have listened."

A fleck of saliva dribbles down from the corner of the ambassador's mouth. "Look, there's no need to do anything precipitate. We can come to some arrangement. If it's money . . ."

A giggle. "There's a light westerly breeze over London, ten knots gusting to fifteen, humidity fifteen percent. It's perfect for dispersal. You'll find Alecto in the West End, in a lockup just off Cromwell Road. No, it was Bayswater Road. Or was it Greek Street? Anyway, you want to catch it before it gets skyborne."

"We had a deal, damn you!" The ambassador is now shouting, all his urbanity gone.

"More fool you. Why don't you switch on the TV and enjoy the show? After all, you're the producer." The line goes dead.

The ambassador slumps back in his chair. The colonel is still gabbling into the telephone. The man's eyes are bulging.

And Sharp is grinning.

The grin widens, and despite the stabbing pains he laughs, and the laughter becomes manic, a mixture of hysteria and relief, and he lifts his shoe and starts to bang it on the table, Russian-style.

HALLEY'S COMET

The police escort is shifting and the chauffeur is having problems keeping up; one car in front, one behind, flanked by motorcycles; blue lights flashing everywhere, the siren penetrating even the thick glass of the ambassador's Rolls-Royce.

Sharp explains. "She asked for schnapps. *Never walk backward drinking schnapps.* It was a private joke between her and Max. She was telling me she'd given the numbers backward."

"But can you be sure, Sharp? Can you be sure the terrorists didn't twig?"

"How could they? Only Daniela, Max, and I knew the joke."

The ambassador glances out of the window. The streets are shiny with light reflecting from shops, and the pavements are crowded with umbrellas. It could be a Lowry painting. "Anything else?"

Sharp thinks. "Yes, lots of things, but she was unhinged, her mind was wandering."

"Lewis, what other things?" Ambra asks.

"She said something about Halley's Comet. 'I want to see it before I die.' And she said she loved numbers, she was grateful to the Hindus for giving us numbers. And she likes schnapps."

"You got the schnapps. But what about the other stuff? Halley and the Hindus?"

"I don't see anything in it. She was probably just wandering."

Sir Richard says, "If the first weapon doesn't fire, they'll suspect her little asides held a message in code. But they have a backup, the second weapon. If they crack the code, they'll fire it."

The car takes a hard left swerve. The ambassador leans against Sharp, who squeezes Ambra against the door. The telephone rings. The ambassador picks it up, listens and puts it back down. "A Tornado from Northolt's circling, ready to shoot down anything that rises above the rooftops. Just in case . . ."

"Not a chance. The machine would disgorge its poison before the RAF got there."

"You were saying. Hindus."

"I can't see any hidden messages in Hindus or Halley's Comet. How can you get firing codes out of that?"

"Ask her," Ambra suggests.

The ambassador lifts his telephone again, speaks briefly. The silence drags on for minutes. Outside, the rain is heavy and the houses are beginning to thin out. Then: "She's comatose. The bloody doctors have put her under heavy sedation. It'll be hours before she can talk." There is a sudden squall of rain, and the chauffeur puts the wipers on at double speed. "I'll force this Miki woman's plane to land, have it shot down if necessary. They have no place to run."

"No, Ambassador. She's leading us to the last Fury."

"Why? What's the point? They know by now the codes were false."

"But maybe Daniela fed me the numbers in code. They'll be trying to crack it."

"How can they? You had the schnapps, they didn't."

Ambra says, "Maybe there's something in Halley and Hindus. They'll be trying desperately."

The ambassador says, "If there is, we're in trouble. It's up to you, Sharp. We must beat them to the last Fury before they crack this bloody woman's coded message. You have to give us the target."

"A village more important than London. That's what they said. London was a sideshow."

"In the name of God, what village can possibly outweigh London?"

"It was something with a Norse name, like a god."

"A Norse god. Of course. Extremely useful." The road straightens out, and the convoy is racing a low-flying aircraft on a parallel course. The ambassador's phone rings again, but this time he presses a button, presumably to scramble the exchange. Adams speaks sotto voce into the phone. "The bloody woman's well out of German airspace. She's cleared the Frisian Islands, heading out over the North Sea."

"The North Sea?" Ambra says. "What gives with the North Sea?"

Radar dishes are beginning to appear, and big warehouses protected by barbed wire perimeters; the tails of big aircraft are scattered around, like brightly decorated sharks' fins.

The convoy is slowing. The escort falls back and somebody is waving at the Roller. Rain is bouncing off the tarmac. "Where is this Norse god of yours?"

"I'm trying. It's in the back of my head somewhere."

"Bring it to the front, for Christ's sake."

"Look, I was almost comatose when they talked about it and I've had one or two distractions since then, like being threatened with murder by the Queen's ambassador."

"They were rash. Mentioning the second target in your presence."

"They knew I wasn't going anywhere."

A 737 is waiting, steps down, British Airways cabin girl with smile and umbrella at the ready; an instant charter, Sharp supposes. Black clouds are streaming low overhead and curtains of rain are sweeping across the runway. The chauffeur, also with umbrella, jumps out, into a puddle. A dazzling fork of lightning is followed an instant later by a bone-shaking *Bang!*

The ambassador takes his ear from the phone. "GCHQ

are waiting for Daniela's words. I'll transmit them. They're putting their best people onto it. A bright young spark will meet you at Heathrow. By the way, they've found your town house, with three corpses therein, two shot and one of them with a knife in its stomach."

"Was there nobody else in the house?"

"There was nobody else. The house is in Potsdam and it's owned by Mythos Babelsberg, a movie company, and your friend Demos had access to it, he was about to start on a music score for them."

"Demos is one of the shot corpses. Petrov is the other one. The third guy is American, the one with the knife in his belly. I stuck it there."

"You're some sort of catastrophe machine, Mr. Sharp. Whither thou goest, death will go. And where thou lodgest, destruction will lodge."

The chauffeur opens Ambra's door. Sharp turns to the ambassador. "By the way, would the colonel really have shot me?"

"What colonel?"

"I wasn't threatened with murder in the embassy?"

The ambassador's eyebrows shoot up in astonishment. "Sharp, are you feeling quite well? I haven't the faintest idea what you're rabbiting on about. Just dredge the target up from that murky subconscious."

The cabin girl taps Sharp on the shoulder. "The pilot wants a word." Ambra and Sharp follow her to the cockpit. The pilot gives him a puzzled look. "I've been asked to tell you that there's been an explosion in London."

Jesus. "Where?"

"Shepherd's Bush, not too far from Notting Hill, near the junction of the A40 and the M40. Seems there's complete chaos spreading out. London's seizing up."

Jocelyn is biting her lip. "That's six kilometers from the city center."

"What's the wind direction there?" Sharp asks.

"East-southeast, blowing ten knots."

"Twenty minutes' drift time," Sharp says.

Ambra says, "If the saucer's exploded, it hasn't launched. Daniela's booby trap worked."

"But God help people in its neighborhood."

The pilot is following this hair-raising exchange open-mouthed. "You people know about this?"

"Just a bit."

Ambra says, "Where are they taking us?"

The pilot speaks into his mouthpiece. "They won't say, but there's a helicopter waiting for you at Battersea."

The bright young spark is Craig Downey, accompanied by Jocelyn in MI6's unofficial dress code, drab; in this case a long gray coat. They hurry Sharp and Ambra quickly along the busy concourse, past WH Smith, Thorntons, The Cigar House, the Sock Shop . . . Sharp, his injured foot in agony, says, "I guess we've both been chased by bad guys, Craig. How did you lose yours?"

"I took a flying jump on a Thames Clipper as it was taking off. Then I took the first train out of London, which happened to be going to Brighton. I've been staying in a guesthouse there, and I've been doing a lot of research. I've found things."

Jocelyn says, "But he hasn't told me what, not yet."

Downey says, "There's still a missing ingredient. Right, Lewis?"

"Right, Craig. You think you know why the scorpions are mating. And I think I know where."

Jocelyn looks baffled. Downey, puffing slightly, says, "Sorry about the cryptic stuff. I could only use short bursts in Internet cafés, jumping from one café to the next, and I didn't know who might be eavesdropping."

They're approaching the terminal exit. A couple of armed policemen show languid interest in the hurrying group. A bottle-green Daimler is waiting on double yellow lines. A chauffeur whose uniform matches the Daimler's color takes their luggage and puts it in the boot. The car takes off while they're still settling in. A thick glass partition separates them from the driver.

At the first roundabout, a car slips in front of them, another behind, so discreetly that Sharp scarcely notices. "Let's start with the codes. Did you get anywhere?"

"The first number was 314159, right?"

"Bloody hell. And the second?"

"271828?"

"How long did that take you?"

"Three seconds. I was having a bad hair day."

Three seconds, on a bad hair day.

"But I don't get the schnapps bit."

"You couldn't have, it was a private joke. But you got the firing codes right away." Sharp feels gutted.

"Dammit, nearly all my time went on the schnapps."

"Better tell us about it."

"Well, the old lady fairly piled on the clues. They said she's a mathematician. As soon as I was given your numbers, 951413 and 828172, I recognized them as *pi* and *e*, written backward. Well, nearly as soon as. Three seconds."

"*Pi* and *e*?"

"The two best-known mathematical constants. The first six digits are 3.14159 for *pi* and 2.71828 for the exponential *e*. So she was telling you in coded form that she'd given the numbers backward."

Jocelyn taps on the partition and makes a *hurry up* gesture to the driver.

Sharp says, "What clues? Are they penetrable?"

"A dawdle, Lewis. She mentioned the Hindus. They introduced our number system around AD 600. But they wrote their numbers backward compared with us—345 in our notation would be written 543 by them. I had to look Halley's Comet up on the Internet, I don't know anything about comets."

"And?"

The Doughnut is sounding apologetic. "All the planets move in one direction around the sun, but Halley's Comet goes the opposite way. Its orbit is retrograde. It's backward.

Backward comet orbit, backward Hindu numbers. If the bad guys solve that, they'll know all they need do is enter your numbers in reverse order."

"How long did Hindu and Halley take you?"

"A minute, but most of that was firing up the search engine. Of course I knew the answer the moment I saw the numbers. Lewis, it was all pretty obvious."

Jocelyn, next to him, is looking stunned. "The bastards may have cracked it. All they have to do is Google Hindu numbers and Halley. Petrov's plane . . ."

Ambra breaks a long silence. ". . . has Internet. What's this about scorpions mating?"

THE NORSE GOD

The chauffeur is taking them briskly along congested streets with a skill that, to Sharp, suggests a police advanced driving course. Police cars and motorbikes hem them in front and back, and Sharp thinks that for the rest of his life he'll sit in convoys with blue flashing lights. Here and there traffic is beginning to seize up, and twice the police cars nudge their way along pavements. A traffic policeman stops them briefly at a junction, and a string of fire brigades and ambulances scream past.

The Doughnut says, "The key has to be the alliance between the North Korean woman and Vladimir Petrov. One from the last Stalinist country, the other with a poisonous hatred of anything communist. There has to be something forcing them together like mating scorpions. Lewis?"

"TP-3?" Sharp sees signs for the Shell Wharf and Battersea Heliport. The car turns sharply into Lombard Road.

The Doughnut nods his agreement. "That's what I think."

Jocelyn says, "If the pair of you would stop talking in riddles."

"Six weeks ago North Korea test-fired a missile we call Taep'o Dong Three. It has an estimated range of ten thousand kilometers. It puts the whole western seaboard of the United States within the range of North Korea—Los Angeles,

San Francisco, the lot. Not to mention the Alaskan oil fields."
Sharp pauses; his throat is still raw.

"I'm listening," Jocelyn says tautly.

"It's a new chip on the table. If North Korea invades the
South, all they have to do to neutralize any threat of American intervention is issue a counter-threat: Keep out of it or
we'll launch TP-3 against you." Sharp feels a light sweat on
his brow as he listens to his own words. "At the Onjong-Ri
test facility they have anthrax, sarin, Marburg, you name it.
There's evidence they kept back two or three entry-level
nukes even after they signed the non-nuclear treaty and
closed Yongbyon."

The Doughnut says, "It'll take a dozen or more test firings
before they have a fully deployable system. But they can get
by with what they have. With TP-3 they could ruin Japan in
a day. Ninety percent of the population is squeezed into
half a dozen cities—Tokyo, Kyoto, Osaka, and so on. A hundred and twenty-four million people are squeezed into ten
percent of the land area of Japan. And have you seen an LA
smog? The city's a perfect aerosol trap. Japan and California
will soon be at the mercy of a nut with a button."

"It's just a bargaining tool," Jocelyn suggests. "If they
used it, they'd be obliterated."

Downey says, "Enter the second chip. Mutual deterrence
works only if both parties are rational. But the North Korean
leadership paint themselves as irrational. Nobody's sure
about them. California's not an acceptable loss. The Americans would have to throw South Korea to the wolves."

"Craig, you're a cryptographer, not a political analyst.
Where do the Furies come into this story?"

Downey says, "That's the next stage of the analysis. If
TP-3 is a big new chip, it makes sense if some secret negotiation is going on somewhere and that there are factions within
both the American and North Korean administrations that
want those negotiations to be spoiled. It all clicks beautifully
if these factions combine to use Alecto to kill their delegates.
Everybody knows North Korea has a huge bioweapons program, they'd get the blame. Except that if the North Korean

delegation gets it, the Americans will be blamed. Each accusing the other, it's a perfect border incident."

The convoy turns into Lombard Road and comes to a dead halt. The traffic has seized up. Ahead of them, the patrol car puts on its siren.

Ambra has to speak loudly over the noise. "That's your mating scorpions. The Petrov group wants America to go to war now, before their missile gets into big production and threatens the States. The North Korean faction wants an excuse to invade South Korea now, before their government strikes some bargain with the Americans."

Jocelyn says, "Petrov is dead."

Sharp says, "His group isn't. Miki isn't."

Jocelyn says, "I'm getting a headache trying to follow this. Where does the London attack come into it?" The patrol car is slowly muscling a passage.

Sharp feels his temples throbbing. "The London letter was Petrov's decoy, to put us off after the Arizona saucer exploded. Then Miki and her pals got Megaera and made the threat real. And now they have the correct firing sequence and there's no percentage in a delay. The longer they hold off, the greater the chance of discovery."

"So where is this hypothetical meeting?"

Downey says, "The FCO will know."

Sharp says, "Thorlakshofn. That's what Miki said."

"At last! That's a test for all this mad theorizing. But are you sure?"

"Positive."

"How come?" Jocelyn asks harshly.

"We passed Thorntons in the Heathrow terminal. Thorntons, Thor. Thor, the Norse god. Thorlakshofn."

Jocelyn taps at a BlackBerry with slightly arthritic hands. She looks at it, puzzled, turns to stare at Sharp. "Thorlakshofn?"

"Absolutely."

". . . is a fishing village in the southeast corner of Iceland. They have a fish-processing factory."

"Thorlakshofn. I remember the name clearly."

"All they do is make fish fingers, Lewis. Try again."

A twin-turbine machine is sitting on a flight platform, blades whipping through the air. They jump out of the Jaguar and run across the apron. They settle into the helicopter and Jocelyn turns to Lewis, shaking her head.

"Thorlakshofn. Miki's headed for Thorlakshofn."

The big machine soars into the air, heading north over central London. A thousand feet high, far to the left, they see a tall, drifting column of smoke.

"Megaera," says Jocelyn grimly.

Downey says, "Tiffany down, Meg down. They still have Alec."

They fly past the awesome black pillar, out of words. Some kilometers away, a fighter aircraft is circling uselessly around London.

PJHQ

1600

Sharp recognizes the building as they descend, and the recognition makes his skin crawl. PJHQ is for major military operations. It's a place for conducting war.

There are two ways into the Permanent Joint Headquarters of the British armed forces at Northwood: with the proper documentation, or with a major armed assault. They do it the easy way, hastily signing authorization forms in the guardhouse and getting passes with the help of a young lieutenant in an agony of impatience. Three years ago, Sharp thought he'd seen it for the last time. The wire, the dogs, the armed Royal Marines; the low concrete structure with blast doors half a meter thick; the interior, forever hidden from the public, starting with the Royal Marines ensconced behind armored glass and looking like tough bank tellers.

Sharp slips the pass, with its attached chain, around his neck. The lieutenant uses a swipe card to take them through an air-lock-type glass capsule like the MI6 ones; they hurry down stairs into the underground complex. It comes back to him—magnolia with everything.

And the steps. Thirty-six of them, in three lots of twelve between each floor. His foot is giving him hell and he half hops. *Please, not the third floor!*

Down to the first underground level: logistics, transport,

and support. A five-centimeter yellow colored stripe runs along the outer, circular corridor in case anyone forgets which level they're on. He'd forgotten about the submarine emergency breathing kits. They're all over the place, on rows of hooks. In a complex where you can't allow firefighters to enter, fire is an obsession.

Damn. Down again. The lieutenant leads the way, half running, to the Middle World, the one with the red-colored stripe running around the outer ring. Steel doors feed into a central partitioned area where crisis teams control operations, usually keeping the peace between factions in some backward hole full of excitable young men egged on by theocratic bigots of this or that persuasion.

The lieutenant doesn't stop and Sharp, hobbling badly, realizes they are heading for the Underworld, with the blue stripe. God's territory. There are clocks everywhere but still the lieutenant looks at his watch. "Sitrep's about to start." Spoken with a tinge of panic.

Jocelyn gives Sharp a look. "Is this as fast as you can go?" Her concern stops short of offering help.

"No, it's only pain."

"Well, hurry it up."

Into the bottom level, deep inside London's Paleogene clay. The lieutenant swipes a card on a white-painted steel door and ushers them them in, into the magic center, staying out himself. It's Sharp's first time in the main Ops Room. Again, clocks everywhere, showing different time zones. There are large plasma displays on the main wall. One is showing a cricket match: Sharp thinks he recognizes the pitch at Kingston, Jamaica. Another is showing aerial views of the black pillar of smoke. Sharp, familiar with three or four such secret places, wonders: *Why is it always CNN news?* The floor is divided into two rows of desks with consoles. At the back is the "balcony." A few anonymous civilians are viewing everything from behind glass.

The minister of defense, in an opened-necked white shirt, is tapping a pencil at the end of a long, oval table. Three others are spread around the table. A man, fiftyish, with a tanned face and white hair, wearing the uniform of an air commodore, sits on the minister's left. *That'll be the CJO,* Sharp thinks. The man on the minister's right is about forty, with dark, Brylcreemed hair and square-rimmed spectacles. He's almost a caricature of the classic Whitehall bureaucrat, with a striped blue shirt, a blue tie, and a pin-striped suit. Possibly a permanent undersecretary at the MoD or maybe FCO. And sitting on his own is an inconspicuous, gray, near-bald little man, sipping at a tumbler of water. There is no mistaking his provenance: He has *spook* written all over him. Ambra and he exchange distant nods of recognition.

The minister looks at Jocelyn. "Meg and Tiffany down, Alec to go."

"Correct, Minister."

The minister looks at Sharp. "Thorlakshofn, Mr. Sharp."

That was quick! Jocelyn used the Daimler's phone only twenty minutes ago; the fiber-optic connection from Vauxhall Cross did the rest. Sharp, Downey, Ambra, and Jocelyn take the empty chairs. Sharp says, "Correct again."

"An Icelandic fishing village that you say is a bigger objective than London."

"It's what my abductors say. They thought I was unconscious." Sharp's foot is a foreign land, a place where pain throbs and flesh swells. He pushes his shoe off.

"Just wanted to make sure, laddie. There's a war riding on it."

THE DOGS OF WAR

The cricket pitch is replaced by a map of the Pacific. Green concentric rings radiate out from a point in North Korea. They are labeled 3000 km, 9000 km, 15000 km.

The minister of defense says, "You claimed that a secret meeting must be taking place between America and North Korea in this Thorlakshofn. You are correct. You further claimed that renegade groups from America and North Korea have combined to assassinate the delegates with this bioweapon. It's a plausible conjecture. We may be seeing part of a power struggle in North Korea following the death of Kim Jong-il, their Dear Leader. Who knows what's really going on? Some faction may tout the incident as American aggression and use it to liberate the South, with the few TP-3s they have as protection against the threat of American intervention."

The civil servant says, "Whatever the scenarios, the whole region is dangerously unstable. Using this weapon to assassinate these negotiation teams will be like lighting a match in a gunpowder factory."

"The Japanese ambassador is with us"—the minister beckons toward the glassed-off viewing area—"and the proceedings in this Ops Room are being relayed directly to their cabinet office, to ours, and to the White House. The American delegation is approaching Iceland now. If we fail, if these delegations are wiped out, I cannot predict what decisions will be taken, including preemptive ones."

"Minister, why aren't the White House pulling back their delegates?" Jocelyn asks.

"They're sacrificing their own people. They have to. Suppose the bioweapon fires and kills the North Koreans while the Americans are pulled away? How would that look?"

Sharp says, "A man called Novello works for Parallax Satellite Systems in Pennsylvania. The Pentagon satellites use their civilian ones as relays. They'll lose surveillance over the Far East for fifteen minutes at a crucial moment."

A man in the uniform of an army major swiftly picks up a telephone, a civilian in the "balcony" likewise.

The civil servant says, "Twenty kilometers inland from Thorlakshofn there's a spiritual retreat in the mountains. It's run by a charity as a haven for people traumatized by conflict, and it's about as isolated from the world as you can get. There is nothing there, no telephones, no TV, nothing. At this moment, in this retreat, a North Korean delegation is awaiting the arrival of an American one. The American team includes George Merrifield, their secretary of defense. Officially, Merrifield is visiting the USAF base at Thule, in Greenland. That was smart deduction, people."

Jocelyn glances over at Downey, who looks embarrassed.

Sharp says, "So get them out, fast."

The air commodore tries for an icy tone. "Thank you, but please keep out of operational matters. We only got your word about this place a few minutes ago." He manages to make it sound like an accusation. A third screen shows a cyclonic mass of white, with just a few patches of blue sea showing. "Reykjavik can't fly their helicopters."

"They must have transport on site."

"Thank you again, Sharp, that has occurred to us. But the blizzard seems to have blocked the only road out from this Shangri-la, and I recall asking you to keep out of operational matters."

The minister says, "Where are the Americans now?"

The air commodore looks at a laptop in front of him.
"Seventy north, thirty-five west. She's over Greenland, just
clearing King Christian IX Land. Ten thousand meters but
beginning to lose height. They're starting their descent toward Reykjavik."

Someone at a console, a young woman in air force uniform,
calls over. "We're patching in to the American flight, sir."

A heavy-jawed face appears in close-up on the screen.
Sharp thinks he recognizes it, one of the up-and-coming un-
dersecretaries in the Department of Defense. What's his
name, Cheeseburger, Hamburger, something stupid like
that? But the picture is dissolving.

"Sir." The major. "The White House have lost communication with *Joker*. Someone's blocking it."

The air commodore says, "They land in less than four
minutes." He makes it sound like a complaint.

NIMROD

"Petrov's 747 landed at Reykjavik Airport about two hours ago," the spook reports.

"What about the passengers?" the minister asks.

"Four people of Asian appearance, all with the proper documentation."

"Where are they now?"

"Nobody can say. The Icelandic authorities had no reason to pay them any particular attention."

Downey says, "We're missing something. Sophia." The minister raises his eyebrows, and Downey explains: "American intelligence reported that someone called Sophia was essential to triggering a war. But they couldn't find any Sophia connected to Vladimir Petrov, except for his wife. And she's been dead for half a century."

Sharp says, "Petrov had a yacht. I broke into his safe and there was a bill of sale for a fifteen-meter yacht. I didn't see the name. Maybe Sophia isn't a person, maybe it's a yacht named after his late wife."

"Are you saying the third Fury, this Alecto, might be aboard a yacht?"

Jocelyn shakes her head skeptically. "Alecto must weigh over a ton. Could a yacht carry that?"

The Doughnut says, "They couldn't launch the Fury from a yacht. We're looking for two seagoing vessels, one with the primed Fury, the other to get Miki and her bunch out of it."

"Another theory, Craig."

"Sir." An air force lieutenant. Sharp thought that handle-bar mustaches had gone out with Biggles, but there it is, like something bought from a joke shop and stuck on his young, round face. "It's on its final approach."

"What is?"

"*Joker,* sir."

"Can you tell us nothing about this yacht, Mr Sharp?"

Sharp puts his hands on his head, screws up his face. "I believe it was registered in Portsmouth."

The minister stands up and splays his fingers on the table. "Air Commodore, find Petrov's yacht and destroy it."

"Right, sir." The air commodore looks around the table. "Ideas, anyone?"

"*Sophia.* Originally registered two years ago to Membranes Inc." The spook looks up from the console, a trace of satisfaction in his voice. "Membranes is a registered company in the Seychelles, owned by Petrov. A Carving and Markings note was issued by the Registrar of Shipping six months ago."

The air commodore says, "Keep talking, make it fast."

"It has a berth at the Royal Western Yacht Club in Plymouth. Something else." The spook is staring at a screen. "You said something about two ships? Petrov's company owns a research vessel by the name of *Sea Creature.*"

Sharp says, "She's blocking the communications with *Joker.* And a research vessel is heavy enough to carry the last Fury."

"Where are these ships?" the air commodore wants to know.

"The harbormaster says *Sophia* took off just over a week ago with a temporary crew. The crew were Korean and Japanese, something like that. He doesn't know where it was headed."

Sharp says, "*Sophia*'s their escape vessel. She'll be maybe five to twenty kilometers off the west coast of Iceland."

"Landsat, sir." The Landsat image is showing a scattering of icebergs, like little white dots, then wisps of cloud, and then, as the satellite drifts toward Iceland, there is just a white-out. *Useless.*

Sharp suggests, "Get a Nimrod up."

The RAF air commodore says, "Will you keep out of this." He taps Biggles on the shoulder and speaks quickly to him. Biggles lifts a telephone receiver and hands it to him.

The minister turns to Sharp. "What's going on?"

"He's speaking to Strike Command in High Wycombe. I expect they'll contact Number Three Group in Kinloss. There are three squadrons of Nimrod MR2s there. Ancient things but perfect for the job. It's a maritime patrol aircraft."

Biggles isn't about to be outdone. "And designed to operate in bad weather, Minister. It has a brilliant radar for pinpointing ships, it can hang around, and it can carry Harpoons on underwing pylons. It's a seriously mean rocket, Minister. Two hundred kilograms of Destex explosive."

"Thank you, but I do know something about the armaments under my jurisdiction."

"But I'd worry about its use against the yacht, Minister." Biggles is punching well above his weight. "The Harpoon is designed to take out substantial warships. It might just punch through a yacht without noticing."

The air commodore comes off the phone, gives Biggles a look that would set fire to a tree, speaks to the minister. "They're tinkering with the fuses now. The Harpoons will vaporize the yacht."

"But you still have to find it," the minister reminds them. "Can you really not find it by satellite? And where the hell are SIGINT?"

"Low earth satellites can't provide continuous cover, Minister. They move too fast. Anyway, look at the screen. There's nothing to be seen."

Sharp: "Minister, if there's really an American faction behind this, I expect Alecto to be fired anytime between now and *Joker* landing. We have practically no time left to seek, find, and destroy Petrov's yacht."

"I asked for SIGINT."

The spook, who has been sitting quietly to this point, says, "We don't have to wait for them."

The minister, calm like Stromboli before it erupts. "Well?"

"Chances are the *Sea Creature* has an Inmarsat phone. All we have to do is call its number. Our telephone sends a signal to the yacht, which sends a hook signal back to ours. Ours then sends another signal, which triggers the ring tone in the yacht."

The minister turns to Jocelyn. "You're Six. Can you tell me what this idiot is prattling on about?"

The MI6 man is unmoved by the minister's tone. "Ring the yacht's number, wait for the hook signal, and hang up straightaway, before the ring tone is activated. That gives us a GPS fix on the yacht's phone. If we can feed the GPS fix into the Harpoons, they'll home in on the *Sea Creature*."

"Will you stop talking and *do it*!" The minister's cool is beginning to crack.

The air commodore, at a console, calls over. "SIGINT have her. The *Sea Creature*'s about fifteen kilometers off the west coast."

"At last."

"Sir, it's in Icelandic territorial waters."

"Bloody hell."

"Two Nimrods aloft from 206 Squadron, Minister. They're clearing the Shetlands. We should get a radar picture in a couple of minutes."

"Do we *have* a couple of minutes?"

"*Joker*'s about twenty nautical miles out from Reykjavik. She'll be passing over the yacht in two minutes fifteen seconds."

The plasma screens are changing. Suddenly, with great clarity, a screen reveals dozens of small craft scattered from the ragged western shore of Iceland to the edge of the screen. And now another screen is showing what looks like the inside of a London Underground carriage, except that most of the space is taken up by half a dozen desks, sideways on, occupied by air force men concentrating on screens in front of them. Inside the Nimrod, the ride is bumpy.

"I want that yacht destroyed."

The air commodore turns to face a golf ball, with a single eye, atop a console. "Have you acquired the target?"

Another sudden change of scene. The pilot's face appears, almost dwarfed by what look like big furry earmuffs. A faint background whine from the aircraft comes over the loudspeakers. "We have, Commodore, I'll mark it now." One of the little dots starts to flash yellow. "Signal strength suggests most of the vessels are fishing boats, coming home ahead of the storm. One large signal, maybe a whaler, but it's well away from the action."

The spook, now wearing headphones, says, "SIGINT confirms radio chatter belongs to fishing vessels. And *Joker* has clearance to land."

The air commodore reminds the minister, "Minister, I remind you that the yacht's in Icelandic territorial waters."

"I want it sunk."

The RAF man hesitates. "Forgive me, but is that a legal order?"

"I don't give a toss. Sink it."

The third plasma screen is now showing a mass of technical data, essentially the control panel of the aircraft. Sharp assumes it is being piped in via a Skynet satellite. He can almost feel he is in the Nimrod.

The minister asks, "Pilot, this is the Minister of Defense. Is there any sign of Icelandic customs vessels? Have they spotted the yacht?"

"There's nothing's approaching the target, sir."

The spook, pushing a telephone against his ear. "GCHQ say Iceland has ordered a couple of naval vessels out."

There is a muffled conversation in the Nimrod, then: "It looks like two ships together. Repeat, there's a second vessel alongside the target. If we fire now, we could destroy it, too."

Sharp says, "Their escape boat. If they're transferring Alecto over, they've already primed it. Hit *Sophia* now or forget it."

The minister speaks to the image on the screen. "Blooter it."

"We're not in range, sir. We need to get within fifty or sixty nautical miles. And *Joker* is getting a bit close to the yacht."

"Any danger of hitting *Joker*?"

"Very little, sir, unless the Harpoon actually malfunctions. It has homing radar for its terminal phase."

Jocelyn says, "What's visibility like? Will the explosion be seen?"

"Lots of whitecaps down there. Six-meter waves. Sea spray is limiting visibility to five or six kilometers, I think. One or two fishing vessels might see a flash."

Jocelyn says, "We're walking into an international incident here."

Sharp says, "No, we're trying to prevent a war."

"Is this a debating society or what?"

The air commodore says, "Minister, Nimrod will be in range of Reykjavik's airport radar along with any Harpoons we fire. They'll get a grandstand view."

The pilot: "Sir, the sea vessels are separating."

The spook says, "More from GCHQ." They wait impatiently while the spook frowns in concentration. Then: "Reykjavik have spotted the Nimrods."

Jocelyn leans over the air force man, her fingers digging into his shoulders. He says, "They're coming into range. Seventy NM out."

"Roger. Sixty nautical, we've now entered firing range."

The minister: "All yours, Air Commodore."

"Fire."

Suddenly numbers are tumbling on the screen. The interior of the Nimrod vanishes and there is an image of rapidly approaching sea, glimpsed through clouds streaming past.

"What's wrong?" The air commodore's voice is edged with urgency. Sharp freezes; he can't see that anything is wrong. "Do you have FL?"

"Bugger it. Not failed at launch. But we do have IFF, repeat in-flight failure. Jesus, where's it going?"

"Fire again," the minister orders.

Radar map and altimeter are being processed into something like a video game, a three-dimensional map showing a little toy missile skimming over the sea, a little cone like torchlight coming out of its nose. The missile in the video game is corkscrewing out of control, the torchlight is everywhere. Four and a half meters long, moving at nine hundred kilometers an hour, and with a 225-kilo warhead of penetration explosives, its radar probing for a target, the Harpoon is heading toward *Joker,* which at that moment is passing six hundred meters over the *Sea Creature.* But then the torch beam finds a target, and the corkscrewing stops, and the Harpoon is moving straight, low, and fast above the big waves.

MIKI

"Jump ship, Miki. Do it now."

"Lewis, is that you? What a persistent man! I never saw an explosion like it. We're sinking, and I'm bleeding all over."

"Miki, listen. There's another one on the way in. They can't abort it. Get into a dinghy—you must have one on board. Get clear fast."

"Sharp." The minister is red-faced. "I want that bitch alive."

"Miki, get off the ship now. You only have seconds."

"Full Moon lost his head."

"Jump over the side. You'll be picked up."

"It rolled right off the deck."

"Sharp, get her off now!"

"Jump, Miki, get out of it."

"Jump? I can't even crawl. I seem to have lost a foot." Then: "Lewis."

"What?"

"It's so *fast*. It's just skimming the waves." She is beginning to gabble now, getting the words out quickly. Her voice is weakening. "You think you've won, don't you, Lewis? But you haven't. There's a big surprise coming. Will I see you in . . . ?"

The spot disappears from the screen. "Second warhead event, sir. Target gone." There is an outburst of cheering and clapping. Against all logic and reason, Sharp feels gutted.

Nemesis

ARRIVAL

The granddaughter can't get time off so it's down to Ambra and me. The ambassador offers to get us the VIP lounge but Daniela dismisses such frippery with an "Ach!" and a wave of the arm. And so here we are at the arrivals gate surrounded by all the paraphernalia of a busy airport—Starbucks, Pizza Huts, Real Irish pubs—hemmed in by boisterous children, chauffeurs carrying placards, and a fat, noisy German family. You understand she's a small, frail woman, especially against the obese creatures bellowing around us like primeval dinosaurs. Anyway, there's something in her spirit, some vivacity; I can feel it like body heat. Ambra has given up trying to look cool and sophisticated and is acting like a child waiting for Santa.

I go hunting for an arrivals screen and come back with the news that the Aeroflot will be half an hour late. Daniela pats me on the arm, tells me to calm down and it wouldn't be Max if he wasn't late and what's an extra half an hour after sixty years?

And all the time I'm wondering if this is a big mistake. They haven't seen each other for sixty years. Will two such strong characters hit it off all over again? Will they even recognize each other?

A hundred years pass and I'm at the nail-biting stage, but

at last AF 101 lands and ten minutes later the first passengers trickle through the departure gate: a smattering of heavily built Russian businessmen; a family running to the arms of Grandma; holidaymakers in T-shirts declaring that they are KGB, that they've been to the Winter Palace; a few young couples drooping with tiredness and a phalanx of elderly tourists bursting with energy. And after ten minutes the flow begins to ebb.

We wait another five minutes as the flow declines to a trickle and I feel myself sliding into a depression. Ambra is being determinedly cheerful. The wrinkles around Daniela's mouth seem to deepen as the minutes pass.

Then she sees him. She sees him before Ambra and me. She gives a little gasp.

He's had his hair cut, and he's wearing a gray suit, neatly pressed. He has a brown shoulder bag, probably made of brand-new deerskin. If I know Max, it will be stuffed with UFO reports. He has seen Daniela: The recognition is instant.

Instant recognition, after sixty years.

He's beginning to cry now, as they approach each other. It sets Daniela off, too.

And it's a trick of the light, but Max's hair is no longer white, it's blond. And his wrinkles have somehow disappeared, and the burdens of sixty years have fallen away like a sack of rocks, and he's a young man again, and by some weird illusion of space and time the airport and the crowds have dissolved into the ether.

And now Ambra's eyes are wet as she taps my arm, and we tiptoe away, leaving Max and Daniela alone on their Alpine meadow.

NEMESIS

The mobile phone. At three in the morning. Siggy buries her head under a blanket. Sharp stumbles to a wardrobe and wriggles hastily into a dressing gown. His mother, maybe? Or Robert, with that overlarge motorbike of his? No, Robert's on holiday—damn, he's climbing somewhere . . .

Fool's mate, the White Queen flashing red. Oh God.

"Hello, Lewis." Icy air when he opens the outer door. Across the valley, the Glacier du Geant, its jagged blocks throwing harsh shadows in the moonlight. A line of lights up the Aiguille du Midi. A car in his driveway, with two dark figures inside. And on his doorstep, a ghost. "Still wearing your hair long, I see. I've been watching your TV series. Loved the Genghis Khan episode. You're really very good, a natural. I guess you made it after all."

"Hello, Jocelyn. It's been a struggle but I'm getting there. And the answer is no."

"It's been over a year. Can I come in?"

"Look what happened the last time I let you in."

"Remember you had a problem with the U-boat loading lists, and some embarked from Norway, not Denmark? Please let me in. This cold's killing me."

"You should try Khatanga. No small talk, Jocelyn? No

juicy scandals in Six? How's Ambra getting on?"

"You know I can't talk about things like that. Please, or I'll drop dead in front of you."

Sharp waits.

"The last I heard Ambra was in Tajikistan. There, I've broken the Official Secrets Act just for you."

"Tajikistan. Is she doing something dangerous?"

"Yes, dodging trucks on the Tamyr Highway. Please!"

Siggy appears at the top of the stairs, wrapped in a short white dressing gown. Sharp calls up, "It's an old friend, darling."

"Would you like a coffee, old friend?"

"Thanks, but I'm not staying," Jocelyn replies, shivering.

Sharp leads her into a warm, carpeted, book-lined study. Red leather armchairs and wood carvings are scattered around, and a table is sprinkled with maps, Alpine crystals, agates, and amethysts. There's a light smell of pinewood. She shakes snow off her coat. He looks at her black briefcase and feels himself tensing up. He turns a knob on a woodstove and the fire bursts into life.

"And U-234, which surrendered, was found to be carrying a ton of uranium oxide to Japan? And to this day we don't know why? And the navy CinC meetings with Hitler nowhere mention its mission, which probably means it was so secret they didn't record it?"

"Jocelyn, I don't think you heard me. I've discovered freedom. I've had it with that stuff."

"You're right, Lewis, I didn't hear you. You remember Miki's last words? *There's a big surprise coming*?"

"Look around you. For the first time in my life things are going well. I have a contract for another series that'll clear the mortgage, I'm about to become a father, and . . ."

"That's wonderful, I'm so glad for you. And the name Hosokawa? It was on Petrov's list. Turns out he captained a Japanese submarine that sank off Papua New Guinea."

"On your broomstick, lady."

"Lewis, we need you in LA right away." She pulls out a laptop with trembling hands.

THE BACKGROUND TO *THE FURIES*

The attitudes and atmosphere existing in the Mittelwald convent reflect those that prevailed in many scientific institutes in Nazi Germany. The purging of Jewish scientists from German institutes began almost as soon as the Nazis came to power, as did the moral compromises of many who remained. Dr. Klein's drunken ravings in the convent's wine cellar are based on ideas taken seriously at the time. These weren't harmless: racial hygiene was a core belief of Nazi philosophy. This crank science had an uneasy coexistence with real, high-quality work.

The secret weapons program likewise was a chaotic mixture of crackpot notions and concepts that, had they been turned into hardware, could have altered the direction of the war. It ultimately failed because effort was dissipated among too many projects.

The medical experiments at Natzweiler are a matter of record. The camp doctor, Wernher Rohde, was hanged by the British at the end of the war. Dr. Hirt, he of the fine skull collection, committed suicide.

Operation Paperclip, the postwar plunder and looting of German scientists, was a reality, as was the conspiracy to undermine President Truman's order to keep Nazi war criminals out of America. When the Red Army overran Silesia (now part of Poland), where Hochwerk was producing hundreds of tons of nerve gas every month, they dismantled the entire factory, which then disappeared into the depths of Soviet Russia. It emerged a generation later as the Soviet Biopreparat program, a child grown into a monster. All the Allied powers were involved in the game, sometimes even kidnapping captured German scientists from each other as tensions grew between East and West.

A few tens of kilograms of anthrax, efficiently dispersed over a major city, could cause a million deaths if people were caught outdoors, say at lunchtime on a dry, sunny day. However, the problems of mass generation of anthrax and its efficient dispersal are, hopefully, beyond the resources of terrorist groups. Although there is evidence that at least two circular winged aircraft were experimented with in Nazi Germany, the "Nazi flying saucers" project is in all probability a myth, and the Furies, both the machines and their Greek namesakes, belong to the realms of imagination.

ACKNOWLEDGMENTS

I have been helped by a good many people in the preparation of this book and I'm grateful to them all. My particular thanks go to Jay Tate, formerly of the British Army, for information about UK military matters; to a UK intelligence services professional—who prefers to remain anonymous—on matters pertaining to the UK intelligence services (thank you, X!); to Holger Kessler for assistance with German; and to Mike Bartle for providing me with information about aspects of life in the extreme north of Russia. I am also indebted to Jim Harvey and my wife Nancy for their critiques of the manuscript in an earlier version.